For Ernie (1932-2005) whose encouragement and support kept me going, particularly during the times when I doubted my abilities as a writer. His belief in me, and pride in even the smallest of my successes, contributed to this, my greatest success.

1

Last night, when the dark was at its blackest, something had nipped at her fingers. She'd wiggled them and it had moved away, slithering into the unknown, no doubt waiting for another opportunity.

It was day now. She could tell because the dark had lightened to a greyish gloom.

Her head felt woozy, like it did when she'd had too much vodka. Her eyes were playing tricks on her. She fixed her gaze on the leafy canopy overhead. The branches swayed and rustled, bending towards her, clutching and reaching to pull her into their embrace.

At first she'd thought he would come back, that this was just some kinky game he was playing. But this was no game.

Left alone, tied to the tree, it hadn't been long before the glacial cold air had bitten into the core of her. Violent shivers consumed her body but there was nothing she could do to stop them. She closed her eyes, hoping for release from the icy pain. Then, during the night, she thought she'd been back in City Square celebrating the New Year. The bells had been ringing, the crowds singing and bottles shared. Now it was day and she was feeling warmer.

She desperately needed to sleep but fought against it. She struggled, pulling and pushing her wrists in a vain attempt to break free. But it was hopeless. Each time she moved her arms the bonds seared into her flesh, and pain jolted up her arms. Her shoulders, savagely pulled into a backwards embrace of the tree, throbbed. Her mouth itched under the sticky tape. Her feet were free, but it made no difference to her predicament. She could stand up, sliding her arms up the back of the tree, and sit down again – if she could bear the agony of the bark scraping the length of her arms and the wrenching pain in her shoulders – but there was no way she could free herself.

As the day lengthened and dusk gathered round the trees, her body sagged and her chin drooped. She no longer felt the cold and sleep claimed her. It was a restless sleep, disturbed by the strange rustlings in the undergrowth and the sensation of being watched.

The dark hid her companions, her sisters of the forest, silent, sleeping, decomposing slowly under a fine blanket of snowflakes.

The scurrying creatures of the forest were not the only ones who watched. He had returned. It was important for him to be there at the final moment, for he had one last task before she died or her soul would not be purified and saved. Now that the screaming was past it was time to remove the tape from her mouth, so that her soul would soar free with her last breath.

2

The pressure increased when Kara's feet left the ground. She clawed desperately at the hand tightening round her neck. But her strength was going now and she was losing the struggle. Flashing lights popped behind her eyes, and the fizzing in her ears exploded through her head. Her last thought as the darkness swallowed her was, I'm not ready to die yet.

'You should've got the money, you stupid bitch.' His voice, floating to her ears from a great distance, was silky soft in contrast to the large, rough hand gripping her throat.

Far away she could hear Charlene and Billy laughing. Thank goodness they were in the living room watching the telly. She didn't want them to see this.

'Well,' he said, shaking her until her feet swung backwards and forwards like a pendulum, 'what you going to do about the money?'

She opened her mouth to speak, to plead. But the pressure on her neck was too great. His cologne wafted round her, making her head swim, leaving the taste of perfume on her tongue. The whole world was spinning now, faster and faster. A terrible croak rasped out of her throat. Her limbs slackened, and she felt sure she was going to die.

'Leave off, Phil,' the other man said. 'You don't want to kill her yet.'

The hand loosened. Kara collapsed, gasping. She clutched wildly at the edge of the door frame and tried to stand, but her knees gave way. Her throat throbbed. She rubbed it with her hand, wincing as she touched the part where his fingers had been.

'You didn't have to do that,' she rasped. 'You've always got your money before. Anyway, it isn't me who owes you, it's Kev.'

'Go get Kev, then.'

'You know he's not here. I told you already.' Kara's knees quivered.

'Somebody's got to pay, love. You know that as well as I do.' His voice was soft, his words almost apologetic. If she hadn't known better, she would have thought he felt sorry for her.

'Yeah, but I don't see why I should have to pay Kev's dues. What he does is nothing to do with me.' Kara wrapped her arms round her middle. Her whole body was quaking now. Why couldn't she hold her tongue? This wasn't Kev she was being smart with.

Phil pushed his face so close to hers she could smell peppermint under the aftershave. 'That's where you're wrong, love,' he hissed. 'We deliver here. We get paid here. If Kev's not available, you'll do.'

'That's not fair,' Kara moaned, realising immediately that fairness was not something Phil understood. 'Anyway, I haven't got any money. I told you already, Kev cleaned out my purse before he left.'

Phil flexed his hand. 'Sorry, love, but we're not interested in your personal problems. Far as we're concerned the stuff was delivered and we need paid.'

'But the wanker's done a runner with all my money.'

'That's your problem, love. We're owed five hundred big ones.'

'Why can't you chase Kev for it?'

'We would, love, if we knew where to find him. But we don't and you're here. So, you've got a choice. Find Kev, or pay up.'

Kara knew Phil meant it and she backed away from him. 'OK. Give's another day then. I'll get the money tomorrow.'

'What d'you think, Gus?' Phil turned to look at his partner 'Will we give her another day to come up with the readies?'

Gus shrugged his shoulders. 'Tony's not going to be pleased. If she don't deliver that means we'll have to do her.'

'Aw, c'mon, guys. What's one more day? Tony won't mind. What's £500 to him?'

4

'It's the principle, love. Tony lets you off and then everyone thinks they can do it. Not good for business that.'

Kara shivered at the thought of Tony. Everyone on the estate knew he was a real bastard. He wouldn't think twice about topping her. He'd probably do the kids as well if the rumours had any truth in them.

'OK, then.' Phil gently moved a strand of hair from her forehead, carefully placing it with one of the magenta streaks that gleamed brightly in her brown hair. Then he stroked her cheek with his finger, tracing the line of her face and jaw before gripping her neck again. 'Just remember,' his voice was low and melodic. 'Be here. Don't even think of doing a runner.' He twisted his lips into a smile although his eyes were bleak and menacing. 'The only place you'd be out of Tony's reach would be six feet under.' He released his hand and she slumped back onto the wall.

Kara gripped her arms tightly in an attempt to stop the shaking. She shouldn't have opened the door to them but they'd looked like Mormons or Jehovah Witnesses with their suits, white shirts and ties. It hadn't taken her long to realise her mistake. Now she just wanted them to leave.

She shivered some more as she watched Phil adjust his tie and smooth his blond hair before sauntering along the landing closely followed by Gus. They murmured to each other, and Phil turned and waved to her, calling, 'See you tomorrow, love.'

The soft click of a door closing further along the landing broke the silence and Kara knew her neighbours had been nosing. It didn't make any difference though, Tony and his thugs were well known on the estate and no one would dare to interfere. I could have been killed and they wouldn't have done a thing about it, Kara thought, as she turned to go back into the flat.

The turn was too quick. Her head felt like mush and she staggered, clutching at the wall for support. Stinging bile hit her already aching throat. She gulped air into her lungs. She was lucky to be breathing.

She could hear the sound of the TV before she opened the

living room door. 'It's too loud,' she rasped at Charlene and Billy who were watching a cartoon. She reached for the remote control and lowered the volume. 'Anyway, I thought you were reading Billy a story.' She stared pointedly at the book lying on the floor.

Charlene turned serious eyes on her mother. 'There was lots of noise outside and I didn't want to hear.'

For a child of six she understood too much, Kara thought. But then, that was probably Kara's own fault for expecting too much of her. She'd been one week past her sixteenth birthday, still only a child herself, when she'd had Charlene and hadn't really understood what a child needed. All she knew was that she loved her daughter with a ferocity that was terrifying. No one, not even Tony Palmer, was going to threaten her kids.

Kara picked the book up and handed it to Charlene. 'It's your favourite,' she whispered.

'Billy doesn't like stories. He likes telly better.' Charlene tucked the book behind a cushion.

Billy nodded and pointed. 'Want telly.' He turned his gaze to the screen, chuckling at the trick Jerry played on Tom – the cat leaping into the air with a howl after the mousetrap snapped shut on his tail.

She leaned over and stroked his mop of dark brown hair, as if by this gesture she could compensate for the lower level of her feeling for him. Poor kid, he couldn't help having a prat for a father. If it hadn't been for Billy she would have dumped Kev long ago, but it wasn't fair to blame Billy for that.

In any case, Kev couldn't help being what he was. There were times when he tried hard to be what she wanted, and that was when she loved him most. But he couldn't look after himself, never mind a family, and he had a habit of leaving when he got tired of playing daddy. He always came back though, sometimes within a day, sometimes a week, sometimes months. Bloody Kev, she thought. If he hadn't nicked all her money she wouldn't be in this fix now. Only it was more than a fix, it was serious.

Kara knelt in front of the children, pulling them both into her arms in a bear hug.

'Mum!' Charlene wriggled, trying to see the TV.

Billy slung his little arms round her neck and kissed her wetly on the bruise made by Phil's fingers. Kara winced, but still held him close.

'Listen up, you horrors,' she said. 'Mum has to find the money to pay the men who came to the door or they'll come back. That means I have to go out to find Daddy.' She knew there was little chance of getting any money back from Kev, but she had to tell them something.

Charlene nodded, eyes older than her years. 'How long?' She didn't have to say any more, Kara knew exactly what she meant.

'A while,' she said. 'After you're sleeping.'

'Breakfast time?' Charlene moved her eyes back to the TV.

'I'll be back before then. But not till late.'

'OK.'

'You can keep the telly on, and I'll get you pillows and blankets so you can sleep on the sofa.' Kara didn't have to say this because they slept on the sofa more often than they did in their beds. They liked to cuddle down in the living room which was always warm compared to the ice boxes the Council called bedrooms. And, of course, they could watch the telly. Kara cuddled them again before she went through to the bedroom to get ready for her foray into the town.

She changed quickly, shivering with cold, her fingers almost too numb to fasten the zip on her skirt then fold the waistband over a couple of times to make it shorter. She didn't have to bend over too far before the creamy flesh of her thighs was exposed. She smoothed her fingers over black fishnet hold-ups – a present from Kev – and thrust her feet into a pair of black high-heeled shoes. Then, removing the eighth and lowest studs in each ear, she replaced them with long, gilt earrings that dangled to her bare shoulders. Finally she pulled the neck of the black blouse lower to expose more of her breasts. She was ready for business.

She hooked her finger into the loop at the back of her red mac and returned to the living room to say goodbye to the kids. She didn't like leaving them on their own. But what other choice did she have? Her neighbours were all scum. She might have trusted some of the women, but not the men. She'd seen too many black eyes and bruises, on the kids as well as the women, not to know what went on behind closed doors. She wouldn't trust any of them with a dog never mind her precious children. But they'd be all right. Charlene was a sensible child even if she was only six.

Kara cuddled them one last time. 'Look after Billy,' she instructed. 'And be good. If anyone knocks, don't answer. I'll be back before you know it.'

Charlene nodded, although her eyes never left the TV.

Kara held her breath and tiptoed along the concrete landing. She didn't want anyone to see her leaving the flat because they'd know fine she'd left the kids on their own, and she wouldn't put it past any of them to grass her up to the welfare. She reached the stairs, letting her breath out in a burst of air that hurt her throat, and clattered down the two flights to the street below.

A bus drew up at the stop a few yards away but she didn't bother to run for it because she had no money. Damn, she couldn't walk all the way into town and she didn't have transport. Never one to give up easily, she sauntered along the pavement until she was two blocks away from her own building, quickly looked round, and slipped into the car park at the rear.

It was littered with rubbish and overshadowed on three sides by the tall concrete blocks that housed many of the unemployed of Dundee. Most of the lights had been vandalised and the area was gloomy, with shadows that seemed to flicker and move. Kara's foot struck a can and it clattered away into the darkness. Keeping close to the scrubby bushes that ran along the car park wall, she slunk between the cars, trying door handles as she went, until she reached the furthest corner where the deepest shadows would cloak her movements. She moved silently, examining each car for open side windows or hidden keys.

Her lips formed a silent whistle when she found an old banger with its key in the ignition. The owner probably wanted to claim on the insurance, so she'd be doing him a favour by taking it.

It was the first piece of luck she'd had all night.

She was still now. Relaxed. A tree spirit, free and pure. The body an empty shell.

It had been eight nights since he had brought her here. Eight nights in which to embrace her new life. And now she was at peace. Her soul joined with that of her tree.

Rain pattered onto the branches above him. He raised his face, rejoicing in the drips, anointing him with their juices. It was their way of thanking him for bringing a new soul.

The whispers started again. At first they made no sense, but gradually they intensified and became clearer. The rough bark of the trunk he was leaning on undulated. The boughs bent towards him. The wind rose and the boughs whipped angrily above him, their whispering becoming louder and more insistent.

It was a sign the trees were becoming restless again. Their voices were becoming impatient, more demanding.

3

Detective Sergeant Bill Murphy sucked the end of his pencil. Even after two years he missed the fags. His teeth crunched into the wood at the thought of drawing the cool, soothing smoke into his lungs, but instead of the much longed for taste he got the flavour of wood and graphite on his tongue. Rolling down the car window, he spat into the gutter.

He could feel Sue watching him from the corner of her eyes as he slid the window up and waited for her to comment. When she didn't, he said, 'I know what you're thinking, but I don't care. I'm pissed off.'

'You're not the only one,' she muttered. 'I can think of better ways of wasting an evening than sitting waiting to see if Tommy Fraser's going to get off the London bus with a bag of smack. Should the drug squad not be doing this stakeout? Why bring us in?'

'Yeah.' Bill could just see the bonnet of Blair and Iain's car parked round the corner. He didn't doubt they'd been just as pissed off as he was, when they were asked to do a stakeout on their night off. But they were good lads, and hadn't grumbled when he'd screwed up their plans for the evening.

'Want a Polo?' He held out the packet he'd just retrieved from the glove compartment.

'You didn't answer me. Why not the drug squad? It's their territory, not ours.'

Bill shook a sweet from the packet into her hand. 'Andy says there's too much going down right now and half the squad have been hit with a flu bug.'

It was Detective Inspector Andy Michaels, their immediate boss, who'd sent them on the stakeout. 'We need to show willing,' he'd said to Bill. 'Don't know when we might need their help.' It was OK for him. He was probably sitting in his armchair watching his favourite programme – lucky sod.

'Bully for them,' Sue grumbled. 'We've been hit by the same bug, but we're not asking them to do our work.' Detective Sergeant Sue Rogers was usually cheery by nature, but tonight she seemed to have become as depressed as some of her other colleagues. Her green-flecked eyes had lost their sparkle and there was a definite droop to her mouth that Bill had never seen before.

'Yeah, I suppose so,' Bill stuck his tongue through the hole of the Polo and wiggled it. 'But they're hitting Kirkton tonight. They'd already arranged synchronised raids on the main dealers and they didn't have enough bodies for that, so they've had to draft in extra from Forfar. I suppose it's just our luck the tip off came in about Tommy at the same time.' He brooded for a moment. 'Just thank your lucky stars you're not battering down doors in Kirkton.'

'I joined the CID to do detective work, not the drug squad's work.' She eased her seat into a reclining position and propped her knees on the dashboard.

Sue was a striking woman – just under six feet, short, auburn hair and fine features. She wore black designer denim and a padded ski jacket. Bill in his faded supermarket jeans and anorak made the perfect foil for her classic good looks. He was even taller than she was. His longish, untidy hair, like his eyes, was a nondescript brown, and his features, although attractive were unconventional, marred by a misshapen nose. He'd never really suited the clipped short hair of the uniformed branches and had been determined he wasn't going to conform to any sartorial expectations when he moved to plain clothes, first in the drugs squad and then in CID.

Bill rubbed the bump on his nose. It was a reminder of his own experiences in the drug squad before he'd moved to CID, the aftermath of a raid gone wrong when a twelve-year-old kid had smashed a whisky bottle in his face, with his nose taking the brunt of the blow.

'When's that bus due in?' Sue rubbed the knee of her jeans, not quite reaching the itch underneath.

Bill squinted at his watch. 'Anytime now. You ready?'

'As ready as I'll ever be. Think he'll cause any trouble?' Sue peered through the windscreen at a bus that was just making a turn into the stance.

'Probably. He's got a rep' to keep up so he's not going to hold his hands out and say, "It's a fair cop, guv".' Bill rolled down his window and spat the remains of his Polo onto the pavement. 'I think it's time to welcome him back to Dundee.'

Kara drove into the car park in front of Tayside House and pulled into a parking place underneath the Tay Bridge approach road. The car wouldn't be seen there for some time and she might be able to use it to get home again. Although, on second thoughts, maybe that wasn't wise. She left the key in the ignition and the door unlocked. Maybe someone else would pinch it and she'd be off the hook.

Pulling her skirt down, she walked over to Dock Street. She'd only been here a few times when Kev needed money for a fix and she'd never liked what he forced her to do. But his withdrawals were scary and she hated to see him suffering. 'If you love me, you'll do it,' he'd said, and so she did. Now, even in his absence, he was still forcing her into a life she despised. Bloody Kev, she thought, as she turned into one of the side streets.

The tip of a cigarette glowed in a doorway. Kara slowed, ready to run if the need arose. It could be a punter or one of the girls. If it was one of the girls she needed to know which one, because they weren't all friendly. A few were known to be violent towards anyone they thought might be encroaching on their pitch, and Kara had no wish to have her face slashed.

The pavement glistened from an early evening shower, reflecting the glow of the streetlights from the puddles. The red tip of the cigarette wavered and danced in the dark. Kara hoped the smoker was more interested in her fag than she was in Kara.

'It's fucking cold the night.' The voice sounded vaguely familiar and not at all threatening.

'Too true,' Kara said as she joined the girl in the doorway.

Her heart was beating faster than usual. 'How's business then?'

'Slow. January's never good. If I hadn't needed the money I'd have stayed home.'

Kara knew the girl was the same age as herself, but she looked older, a shapeless sack of a female, carrying too much weight and wearing a denim jacket so tight it didn't meet in the front. She looked grubby, with her dark hair straggling in greasy strings onto her shoulders. But Kara had heard talk that Jean usually did a good trade with men who liked a bit of rough.

'It's Jean, isn't it?' Kara scrutinised her. 'We were in the same gang for a while.'

'Yeah, I remember you. Used to think you were a snotty-nosed cow. But we all come to it in the end, eh?' She dragged smoke into her lungs before throwing the fag-end into the gutter. 'Haven't seen you down here for a while. Things not so good just now?'

'They weren't bad until tonight. Then Tony's guys showed up.' She sighed. 'Couldn't pay them though. Kev's fucked off with the money and the score they want paying for.'

'You don't want to cross Tony.' Jean's voice was flat.

'Don't I know it. That's why I've got to do a bit of business.'

'You're not going to find much just now. Thursdays are quiet, and it's early yet. Fancy going to the chippie? Sit in?'

'No money. Kev took the lot.'

'Aw, come on. You can pay me back.'

The fish and chip shop in Castle Street was quiet and the two girls chose a table at the back. The vinegary smell rising from her plate of chips reminded Kara that she hadn't eaten since breakfast time. 'This is really good of you,' she told Jean.

'Aw, it's nice to have the company.' Jean pushed her chips to one side, sliced the battered fish in half and popped one piece onto Kara's plate. 'Better eat it before I change my mind.'

A slight drizzle was falling by the time they'd finished

eating and returned to the street.

'This'll keep the punters away,' Jean grumbled. 'It'll have to be in the cars tonight. Scarier though.' She turned into a doorway in Exchange Street. 'I'll stay here. You might do better along the Seagate. Better class there.'

Kara realised that Jean didn't want her on the same beat, but maybe business would be better in the Seagate, so she nodded and pulling her collar up turned away.

'Be careful,' Jean called after her. 'Some of the girls say there's a serious weirdo about.'

Kara shrugged. It didn't worry her. Running into Phil and Gus was the only thing she feared. Nothing could be worse than that. 'See you later,' she shouted over her shoulder, 'and thanks for the fish supper.' Jean was entitled to her own beat and Kara didn't grudge her.

She'd paraded up and down the Seagate, circumnavigated all the side streets, and was heading up Trades Lane when she spotted the black Mercedes-Benz, tucked into an alley. Mercs were common enough in Dundee, but there weren't many black ones, so she slid into the shadows to check it out. She hadn't been mistaken. The tinted glass window was open and she could see, quite clearly, Phil's profile as he flicked a chewing gum wrapper out of the window. She shuddered. She didn't want to run into those two again tonight. They'd scared her enough the first time.

Kara turned, intending to retrace her steps, but was afraid they'd see her, so she pulled into the shadows, waiting for them to go away. She wasn't sure how long she stood there but it seemed to be forever. A chill crept through her. Her feet were cold and her fingers tingled. This was stupid, she'd have to chance it and make a move before she froze to death. It was at that moment a bus drew up in front of the alley, waiting until the road was clear to make the turn into the bus station. A double-decker drew in behind it, revving its engine and belching fumes. Kara didn't hesitate, she darted round the back and along the side of the double-decker, keeping her fingers crossed that Gus and Phil's view was blocked. Once she was clear she ran across the road and into the bus station.

It would be easier to hide herself among the throngs of people waiting.

'Did you just see what I saw?' Phil shifted his gum to the other cheek. 'Wasn't that our little Kara who just scuttled into the bus station?'

Gus peered across to where Phil was pointing. 'I don't see anything.'

'It was her, all right. All tarted up. Quite a little cracker she is.' Phil blew a chewing gum bubble and cracked it.

'D'you have to do that?'

Phil ignored him. 'I was thinking. After we've done the business with Tommy, we might have ourselves a little fun with that one.'

'You're disgusting, you are. Just concentrate on Tommy. If anything goes wrong with the pick-up, Tony'll have our guts for garters.'

4

Kara was hardly five feet tall and, although curvy, she was quite slim. Once hidden amidst the crowd she was sure neither Gus nor Phil would be able to see her. The only problem was how she would get out of the bus station if they remained parked in the alley for any length of time. If she found a punter she could use him to get away, but she knew the chances of finding one here were slight. If a man needed to take a bus he certainly didn't have enough money to pay for her services and she wasn't going to oblige for the kind of money Jean would likely settle for.

Wind whistled along the pavement, whipping the coat edges of the people queuing. Her mac didn't give her much protection and she looked longingly into the warm café and waiting room. It would, however, be more exposed with nowhere to hide if Phil or Gus decided to cross the road. So she huddled at the back of the queues and waited while buses pulled in and out of the stance.

Every now and then she glanced across the road, but the Merc was still there. She cursed under her breath as her fingers and toes lost their feeling, numbed by the bitterness of the cold wind. What she needed was something hot to drink. She'd give anything to wrap her hands round a warm cup of coffee. She edged closer to the café wondering whether she dared go in. A waft of warm air blew round her legs as the door swung open. It was unbearable.

What can they do to me here, anyway? Kara thought as the irresistible smell of coffee drifted towards her.

It was boring sitting in the car and Phil idled the time watching Kara trying to hide among the passengers. He ran his finger along his lips. He was quite looking forward to a bit of free time after they'd done the business and who better to have a bit of fun with than little Kara. He closed his eyes, imagining what he would do to her, and tasting her fear.

'Give over,' Gus complained when Phil outlined, for the sixth time, what he was going to do to Kara. 'Tony won't like it. You know he only allows the rough stuff he sanctions himself.'

'Yeah, but who's going to complain? Not little Kara. She'd like a bit of rough, just you wait and see. After I'm done I'll put the frighteners on her so Tony won't hear about it.' The stirring in his loins increased as he thought of the pain he was going to inflict and his eyes glimmered in the dark.

'Will you concentrate? Here's the London bus. That Tommy guy better be on it or Tony's not going to like it.'

Phil stepped out of the car. 'You see him yet?'

'He's just getting off now.'

Reaching into his pocket, Phil fingered the wad of notes. The arrangement was that Tommy would dump the stuff in the waste bin at the back of the bus station. Gus would pick it up while Phil slipped the money to Tommy as he crossed the road. Once they had possession they would deliver to Tony. It was just the way Phil liked it, minimum fuss and minimum risk to them.

'Let's go, then.' Gus slammed the car door and headed for the bus station.

Bill waited until he was sure the bus was pulling into the long-distance stance. 'That's the London bus all right. We'd better go and check our man's on it.' He flashed his lights in the prearranged signal. Blair and Iain flashed back.

Sue was already out of the car before Bill had his door open. 'You're keen all of a sudden. Maybe I should leave it all to you.' He opened the car door but made no move to join her on the pavement.

'Oh, stop arsing about, the sooner we get it over with, the sooner we get home.' She pulled the zip of her jacket up until it rested just below her chin. 'Damn, it's cold out here.'

Bill pulled himself up to his full height and grinned down at her. 'Just kidding,' he mumbled. He slung an arm round Sue's shoulder. Apart from a slight wriggle to position the arm more comfortably, she didn't respond. They'd worked undercover before and they'd both learned to act naturally no matter what the other one did. Bill's eyes scanned the waiting crowd while Sue watched the bus draw up at the stance. By this time Iain and Blair had repositioned their car behind the stance buildings. It didn't matter which direction Tommy tried to go, they would get him.

A young girl, dressed in a short mac and fishnets, stood a short distance away and Bill felt his eyes drawn to her. She barely looked at him, which wasn't surprising because he still had his arm round Sue's shoulder. For a fleeting moment he wished he'd been here on his own, although that would have done little good because he wouldn't have had the gumption to do anything. Besides, the girl was too young for him. And why on earth would she want an old man pushing forty?

A whiff of diesel fumes floated on the wind. There was the hissing sound of air brakes, and the bus stopped. The door clattered open and the first of the passengers alighted. Their mark was in the middle of the group. He bounded down the steps and pulled the strap of his rucksack further onto his shoulder, before elbowing his way through the waiting crowd.

Kara was on the point of going into the café and taking her chances when she spotted Tommy Fraser. She jumped up and pushed through the crowd of people. 'Tommy,' she said. 'Fancy seeing you here. Got time for a coffee?'

Tommy was a big lad. He did boxing and weightlifting in his spare time, so if anyone could protect her from Tony's thugs it would be him. If she stayed beside him she could leave the bus station.

Tommy grinned down at her. 'This isn't a good time, Kara. I've got to meet someone.' He hesitated. 'Maybe later?'

There was a note of longing in his voice and she

deliberately leaned against him. She knew Tommy fancied her. He wouldn't let anyone harm her. 'Just a quick one, Tommy? For old times' sake.'

He slipped an arm round her. 'I'd love to,' he said. 'Give me ten minutes and I'll be back. Don't go away.' He squeezed her shoulder and strode off in the direction of the Trades Lane exit.

Kara watched him go. She was afraid to follow because he was heading in the direction of the Merc.

Bill tensed his muscles and could feel Sue doing the same. They were on the point of confronting Tommy when the girl in the mac accosted him. Bill restrained Sue. 'Might be a contact,' he whispered, his mouth close to her ear in what would appear to anyone watching as an affectionate gesture. Sue's nod was barely perceptible.

They moved closer, but the girl was only asking him to go for a coffee. Bill raised an eyebrow as he looked at Sue. 'What d'you think?' he whispered.

Tommy strode off in the direction of the road.

'False alarm,' Sue whispered. 'Will we take him now?'

'OK. Let's go!' Bill ran after Tommy, Sue close at his heels.

'Police!' Bill grabbed the strap of Tommy's rucksack with one hand and his arm with the other.

Tommy wriggled out of the rucksack, aimed a punch at Bill, then ran into the road. Bill doubled over, gasping for air. Sue barrelled round him. Tyres screeched as the back-up car, rounding the corner to head Tommy off, had to do an emergency stop to avoid a collision with Sue.

'Gotcha,' she said, felling Tommy with a rugby tackle that was the envy of both policemen and would be the talk of the station for the next week.

Gus had been almost out of sight before Phil sauntered across the road, but when Kara had put her hand on Tommy's arm and smiled up at him, his eyes had narrowed. What was she up to? But then Tommy said a few words and shook his head and he'd thought it was OK.

A few minutes later when the police converged on Tommy, Phil changed direction. His eyes were fixed on Kara and, coming up behind her, he muttered in her ear, 'Fucking slag. Why'd you shop him?'

She jumped, her head swung round and she looked at him with wide frightened eyes. 'What do you mean?' she spluttered.

His fingers itched. He wanted to grab her and shake her. Nothing would have pleased him more than to squeeze the life out of her, and he would've done it if there hadn't been so many punters around.

'Later,' he hissed. 'I'll see you later.'

He strolled back to the car. Gus already had the engine started and hardly waited for Phil to get in before accelerating out of the alley.

'What was all that about?'

'Fucking little bitch fingered him. That's what.' Phil breathed heavily.'

5

Kara hadn't seen Phil creep up behind her, so when his voice hissed in her ear she almost collapsed with fright. Luckily for her he'd left as quickly and silently as he'd arrived, but her heart continued to thump and she couldn't rid herself of the taste of bile scalding her throat.

Shaking, and wishing she were anywhere else but here, she slid back to hide in the crowd until she could slip off when no one was looking. But the crowd surged forward as people tried to see what was happening and she was caught in the crush. She could hardly breathe. Panic thumped in her chest. She had to get away. She kept her head down, not lifting it until she broke free from the mass of bodies that threatened to carry her forward again. Whatever Phil and Gus were involved in, and whatever Tommy had done she wanted no part of it.

She knew she should run while she had the chance but couldn't resist one final look back, just in time to see Tommy being manhandled into the police car and the black Merc driving off at speed. Tommy lifted his head at the sound of the revving engine and a smile twisted his mouth. He turned and shrugged his shoulders and, as he did so, his eyes met hers over the crowd. 'Why?' He mouthed in her direction.

She shook her head slightly, turned her back on him, and ran. Round the back of the bus station, across the road, and up the Seagate, not stopping for breath until she'd reached the back door of Marks & Spencer.

It took several moments before she caught her breath and stopped panting.

Cars were parked, nose to tail, in the driveway in front of Tony Palmer's large villa in Dundee's west end. Phil slowed as he drove past. 'Just our luck,' he muttered under his breath. 'He's got folk in.'

Phil got out, stretched his legs and looked up and down the deserted street. 'Come on, mate,' he said, turning to Gus. 'We'd better go and tell the boss what's happened.'

Gus hoisted himself out of the passenger seat. 'He's not going to be pleased,' he said mournfully.

'That's for sure,' Phil said. He ran a hand through his bottle-blond hair, although as usual it was immaculate. He liked to look good and – despite his well-muscled body – his Armani suits, designer shirts and shoes gave no indication that he was one of Tony's strong-arm boys. His appearance was an asset when he was making new contacts and by the time the shop or club owner realised what he was selling was protection, it was too late.

'Come on, then,' he said. 'We'd better get it over with.'

Gus was a slightly smaller version of Phil, but on him the blond hair and muscles were less appealing. Gus looked what he was, an overdressed thug on the make. But he had his uses and, as long as his loyalty didn't waver, Phil would look after him.

The villa was large, almost a mansion, with a semi-circular driveway leading to a short flight of curving stone steps. Two Grecian-style pillars stood in front of the ornate, polished oak door. Old-fashioned lamp standards bathed everything in a soft glow and a similar welcoming light shone from the windows. Tony never closed his curtains at the front of the house, giving the impression he didn't have anything to hide. He was the local boy made good and he liked to impress. It certainly never failed to impress Phil who had been brought up in a council flat. He aspired to something like this, and he vowed that one day he'd have it, with or without Tony's help.

The security surrounding Tony's place was unobtrusive. No guards were on duty and there were no electrically operated iron gates, nor blinding lights to mark this house out as any different from its neighbours. It was only those in the know who were aware of the steel doors that looked and felt like polished oak, the staff who were, in reality, bodyguards, and the hidden cameras that recorded every visitor to the house and triggered alarms inside.

They skirted the parked cars in the drive and, ignoring the front door, carried on round to the side entrance. Phil knew they would not be welcome at the front door and he had no intention of annoying Tony before he told him about tonight's events.

The lights illuminating the front of the house didn't extend round the corner to this entrance, and Phil could hear Gus cursing softly as he stumbled behind him.

'Why doesn't he light this bit then?' Gus grumbled.

'Because he doesn't want nosy parkers to see the likes of you and me coming and going. That's why.' Phil felt for the doorstep with the toe of his shoe to avoid tripping over it. 'You get used to the dark,' he said, as he rang the bell.

Gus bumped into his back. 'If you say so.'

'There's lots of things you get used to in this job.' He turned and stroked Gus's cheek, feeling a thrill of pleasure when the younger man flinched away from him. 'You're doing OK,' he said softly.

The door opened a crack and a hoarse voice muttered, 'Hello?'

'Phil. Gus. Come on, Brian, let us in. It's freezing out here.'

'Tony's busy tonight.' The door opened wider to reveal a large man, incongruously dressed in a pristine dinner suit. Brian was one of Tony's bodyguards, an ex-boxer who rarely left his side.

'Why aren't you with him then?' Phil brushed past him into the corridor.

''Cause he's giving a dinner party, that's why. There's city councillors and all sorts here.'

'Like the threads,' Phil said, fingering the lapel of Brian's jacket.

'Yeah. Makes me blend in, like.'

Phil smiled. Anyone less likely than Brian to blend in would be difficult to find. He had the physique of a gorilla and features that had taken one punch too many. The word punch-drunk came to mind.

'What do you guys want anyway? I told you the boss is busy. He doesn't want to see anyone.'

'Just tell him there's been a problem and he needs to know about it tonight. Don't want him surprised by a police raid now, do we?' Phil assumed a confident tone to hide the queasy sensation that was tearing at his gut.

Brian opened a door at the end of the corridor and ushered them into the study. 'I'll get Morag to tell him you're in the study . . . A wee cracker she is and all.' A wistful note crept into Brian's voice and Phil could swear the bodyguard's bullet-hard, black eyes had softened.

'Got a thing going with wee Morag, have you?' Phil's eyes scanned the large room that Brian had called a study. He strolled over to a bookcase and fingered the books. 'Very nice,' he said.

'Morag's no time for the likes of me,' Brian frowned. 'But I'd be good to her, if she gave me a chance.'

Phil slid a book off the bookcase and leafed through it. It stopped his stomach from doing flip-flops. 'Are you going to get Tony for us or are you going to moon there all night over Morag?'

'Yeah, OK. He's not going to like it though.' Brian glowered at Phil. 'And another thing he doesn't like – folk going through his stuff. I'd put that back before he gets here.'

Phil replaced the book. 'Yeah, yeah.'

Brian closed the study door behind him leaving the two men alone.

'What d'you reckon, Phil?' Gus spoke in a whisper. 'D'you think he'll be pissed off?'

'He'll be a lot more pissed off if we don't let him know. And for fuck's sake stop chewing your fingernails. It's a disgusting habit.'

'Sorry, Phil. I can't help it.' Gus imitated Phil and shoved his hands in his trouser pockets.

'Look, Gus, you don't want Tony to see how nervous you are. He'll start to wonder if you're up to the job.'

'I'm up for the job. You know I am, Phil. When've I ever

let you down?'

'Yeah, I know that, but Tony doesn't. You have to prove yourself first.'

'Oh, and what is it you have to prove to me?'

Phil hadn't heard the door open and wondered how long Tony had stood there listening.

'I was just saying to Gus that you don't know him that well yet, and he'd have to prove himself. The same way I did.'

'Is that a fact?' Tony said, walking over to the massive oak desk that dominated the room. 'And *have* you proved yourself to me, Phil?' He sat down and swivelled from side to side in the leather chair. 'Brian mentioned something about a problem. What's happened?'

Phil walked over to the desk and placed his hands on the polished top. Tony winced, and Phil, remembering Brian's warning about Tony not liking his things being touched, quickly straightened up and rammed them in his pockets. 'I came immediately,' he said. 'If I've disturbed your evening I'm sorry but I thought you'd want to know straight away.'

'Yes, yes,' Tony muttered, waving his hand. 'Just get on with it.'

Phil sketched out the evening's events in as few words as possible. He deliberately didn't watch Tony's reaction because to do so would have transmitted his fear. And he couldn't allow Tony to see that.

'Tommy won't blab,' Tony said, 'but what about this girl who fingered him? Where does she come into it? What does she know?'

The knots in Phil's stomach tightened. 'That's what we don't know. But we intend to find out.' He told Tony the little he knew about Kara.

'So, her man's been dealing, has he? That means she knows something about the system. But how much?'

'I don't think she knows much more than where he gets his stuff from and maybe one or two of the dealers. She wouldn't know about you, Tony,' Phil said.

Tony stood up and loomed over the desk so that he was almost nose to nose with Phil. 'Find out,' he barked. 'I want to know everything she knows, even if you have to beat it out of her. And then,' he straightened up, smoothed his tie, and smiled, 'if it's necessary, get rid of her.'

He cruised the streets looking for her. It could not be just anyone. It had to be someone the trees chose.

When the church bells chime eleven you will see her, the whisperers had said. They did not lie.

When the bells chimed she was there. Just as they had foretold.

But she was smaller than the others, with red striped hair. He would not have thought she was the one. But the trees had chosen. They were never wrong.

6

Kara spat in the gutter. The taste of the last one still lingered in her mouth and it had taken her all her willpower not to gag when she was doing him. He'd been generous, though. Now that it was over she wanted to sink into a bath and scrub herself until her skin came off. But she needed to pull one more punter, maybe two, to make up the money she needed.

She rubbed her tongue over her teeth. What she wouldn't do for a drink to wash the taste out of her mouth, but she didn't want to attract attention. The bitterly cold wind that had turned to drizzle an hour ago increased to persistent rain until the street glistened and the gutter ran with water. Kara was damp, cold and wanted to go home. Her hair clung to her neck, sending icy drips trickling inside her collar and down her back. She shivered, and longed for the scant comfort of her flat.

She pushed the collar of her jacket up, stepped off the pavement and looked up and down the road. Deserted. No girls, no punters, not even a drunk. She was daft to stay, there'd be no more trade tonight, and besides she had to get home to the kids. Thoughts of them sitting on their own in front of the telly crowded into her mind. She shouldn't have left them. She shook the drips from her hair and turned in the direction of the car park. Maybe the old banger would still be there.

At that moment the black Merc cruised round the corner.

Late at night the upper levels of Police Headquarters were quiet. Only the lower levels were busy with night shift officers. Regular night shift was one of the things Bill hadn't missed when he transferred in to plain clothes. Now – apart

CHRIS LONGMUIR

from call outs, the pressures of investigations, and surveillance work – the need to work outwith normal hours had diminished. Bill, however, revelled in unpredictability.

He'd enjoyed the surveillance tonight and, apart from the tedious waiting around, the job had been everything he'd anticipated. Now the excitement was over he was quite content to step back and leave the fiddly booking in bits to Blair and Iain.

'Thought you'd have gone home by this time,' Sue said as she joined him at the lift. She looked tired and a bit bedraggled. Her normally sleek hair stuck up in spikes where she'd pulled her fingers through it.

'Had some things to do.' Bill willed the lift doors to open. He didn't want to get into discussions about why he was always reluctant to go home. 'What about you? You look all in.'

'Just felt I was falling behind on the paperwork, you know, and wanted to clear some of it.'

Bill made a face. 'Bloody paperwork'll be the death of us.'

The lift doors slid open. Moments later they emerged on the ground floor into an exact replica of the corridor they'd just left.

'Ever get the feeling you're going round in circles?' Sue pushed open the security door into the vestibule.

'Yeah, I know what you mean,' said Bill, raising his hand in a farewell gesture to the officers on duty. 'Bloody boring that is, sitting there all night. I'm glad I don't have to do it anymore.'

'Me too,' said Sue.

Bill watched Sue get in her car, and then, swinging his keys, strolled to the end of the parking area. Sue always seemed to get parked near the entrance while he usually had to scrabble for a place at the rear. Still, he wasn't in a hurry and he enjoyed being able to stretch his legs. Even the rain, spattering onto his face and dampening his hair, didn't bother him. The cold prick of the raindrops refreshed him, reminding him he was still alive.

The thought of going home to his empty flat depressed him

so much he drove aimlessly round the streets of Dundee city centre. He wasn't looking for anything in particular but when he passed the bus station for the second time, the image of a girl – small and slim, with the most startling magenta colour in her hair – rose into his mind. The image was clear and fresh, but although he saw plenty of girls she was not among them.

He wasn't sure what time he got home although he knew it was late. Apart from driving he didn't know what he'd been doing or where he'd been. Time had a habit of doing that with him lately; he'd lose great chunks of it, and sometimes he'd wake not knowing where he was or how he'd got there.

The large ground floor flat was part of what had originally been a Victorian townhouse and might have been attractive if more care had been taken before it had deteriorated. It was also cold. Bill switched on an electric fire but it made little impact on the large rooms with their high ceilings.

Bill couldn't make up his mind whether it would be warmer to keep his damp jacket on or take it off and so took the line of least resistance. He wandered through to the kitchen, which was as vast as the lounge, and put the kettle on. The fridge yielded very little; a carton of sour milk, two slices of hard bacon and one solitary egg. He held the egg in his hand for a moment and, deciding he wasn't hungry, put it back in the fridge. He left the kettle to switch itself off when it boiled, and staggered through to his bed.

Sue clattered up the stairs to her shared flat. 'Damn it, I'm tired tonight,' she said, throwing herself into an armchair in front of the fire.

Louise removed her reading glasses, laid her book on the arm of the chair, eased her feet from underneath her, stretched her pyjama clad arms and legs as far as they would go, and yawned. 'I'm not surprised,' she said, 'it's late.' She stood up and pushed her bare feet into slippers. 'I kept some supper for you. It'll just need a few minutes in the microwave.' She was a tall woman, a year younger than Sue, but looked older. Her long brown hair, which she normally scraped into a bun or a coil at the base of her neck, hung loose on her shoulders softening the strong lines of her face.

In contrast to Sue's bubbly personality, Louise was a calm and placid woman, well suited to her job as a constable with the Child and Family Support Unit. The two young women had joined the force at the same time and formed a friendship that had never wavered – even though Sue continually pushed herself upwards in her career while Louise was content to stay where she was.

'I'm not really hungry.' Sue smiled apologetically, knowing how likely it was that Louise would take it personally. That was the trouble with Louise, far too sensitive. Sue often wondered if she was misplaced in the police force; she'd probably have made a better social worker. 'Did you have a good day?' she said, attempting to divert Louise from her need to nurture.

Louise shrugged. 'Pretty quiet,' she said. 'Maggie McKenzie was beaten up again by her boyfriend. Why she keeps on picking these charmers defeats me. But she refused to press charges. As usual. That guy'll go too far one day and we'll be left with a body. It'll be over to your team then.' Her brows pulled together in a frown and something seemed to flash behind her eyes.

'Why'd you stay in that team if it's so painful for you? Transfer out. I could talk to the DI, and I'm sure Bill would put in a word as well. He's quite pally with him.' As an afterthought, Sue said, 'Andy Michaels is one of the best DIs on the force. You'd like him.'

Louise twisted the ends of her hair round her fingers. 'I'm not sure. I kind of like it where I am.'

'I couldn't work with all those battered women . . . abused kids . . . rape victims,' Sue shuddered.

'Bodies are better?' Louise's eyes flickered and a smile tugged at the corner of her mouth.

Sue shrugged. A recollection of Bill's expression when she left him forced itself into her consciousness, and she realised he hadn't been his usual bolshie self for a few weeks now. It was as if he had no energy left to buck the system and the bureaucracy that he hated so much. It just wasn't like him.

'What's wrong?' Louise flashed a look of concern. 'You looked troubled for a moment.'

Sue leaned her head on the back of the armchair as a wave of tiredness threatened to engulf her. 'I was just thinking of Bill,' she sighed.

He'd looked so tired when he left her, but that hadn't been all, there'd been a droop to his body that spoke of more than just fatigue.

'I think he's heading for meltdown.' It was the first time she'd put her fear into words but as she said them she knew she was right.

Thinking back to how he'd been a couple of months ago. Laughing, joking, game for anything. He didn't seem the same person. Had it started when Julie left at the beginning of December? Or was it more deep-rooted than that? He'd been shattered when his marriage broke up, and Evie had cleared out with another guy, but then he'd met Julie, and Sue had thought he was recovering. But was he? She didn't really know. All she knew was that he was sliding deeper and deeper into a black pit of his own making. And there didn't seem to be anything she could do to help him.

7

'There she is!' Phil shouted, making Gus jump. 'The bitch isn't going to get away this time.'

Until he spotted Kara, Phil hadn't been in the best of moods. He'd spent the last two hours looking for her but either she'd been too smart for him, something he found hard to accept, or she'd been otherwise occupied.

He'd cruised the streets, screeching to a standstill in each one before ordering Gus out to help him explore shop doorways and alleys while he stamped angrily up and down the pavement. The vicious kicks he aimed at empty cans, rubbish lying on the pavement and even his own car tyres did little to relieve his anger at being unable to find the girl. And, on top of that, his back ached from the amount of times and the force with which he'd thrown himself back into the driving seat.

His increasing frustration had stretched his nerves to an excruciating pitch and worsened his temper, until he'd thumped the dashboard and steering wheel to gain some relief. If Gus had interfered or spoken he'd probably have thumped him as well. But, luckily for Gus, he knew when to do as he was told and when to remain silent.

But as soon as Phil saw Kara his mood changed and he grinned and patted his partner's knee. 'It's pay-off time, Gus. We'll have her and the cash she's made tonight. The bitch won't know what's hit her.'

Kara tried to run but her ankles wobbled in the ridiculous heels. How was she going to pacify Phil and Gus? She didn't have anywhere near enough money to pay them off. And now they thought she'd shopped Tommy.

She stumbled as a red estate car drew up beside her. The passenger door swung open. Another one of Tony's thugs?

'Well, are you going to get in or not?' His face was in shadow but the voice was pleasant and non-threatening. She was on the point of refusing when the black Merc increased its speed.

Kara jumped into the passenger seat.

The driver didn't look like a thug. He wore an anorak and jeans and, although a baseball cap shadowed his eyes, she could see enough of his face to be reassured. He was the kind of guy who'd sit in a corner at a party and never be noticed. She let out a sigh. It was all right, he was a punter. 'Let's go then,' she said, willing him to drive off before the Merc drew level with them.

She shook the drips out of her hair and slid low in the passenger seat, trying to make herself as small as possible, in the faint hope Phil and Gus wouldn't spot her.

The punter didn't even wait for her to buckle her seatbelt before he headed, at a fair speed, for the Dock Street dual carriageway. With a bit of luck they'd be out of sight before Phil and Gus realised what was happening.

Kara wriggled into as comfortable a position as her tight, damp clothes would allow and studied the driver, wondering how much she could take him for. The amount would depend on what he wanted of course, but if he paid up maybe she could go home. She'd have to face Phil and Gus sooner or later, but if she explained she'd nothing to do with Tommy being arrested and had the money waiting for them, maybe they would agree to leave her alone.

The punter hadn't said anything or even glanced at her, which was odd, but she supposed he must be embarrassed. It affected some of them that way. Better that than the ones who were all over you and expected you to enjoy a walloping into the bargain. That was the kind of rough trade Jean attracted and, as far as Kara was concerned, she was welcome to it.

'You're a quiet one,' Kara said, trying to ease things for him.

He smiled but still didn't look at her.

She placed a hand on his leg, sliding it up his thigh until it almost reached his crotch.

He reached down and removed her hand, saying, 'Later.'

She wriggled some more, staring out of the window at the passing traffic. She wanted it over so she could go home. Charlene was a good kid, she'd see no harm came to Billy, and they'd probably be sleeping by this time.

'The bitch. She's getting into that car. D'you see her?' Phil didn't wait for Gus's response but swung the car round into a desperate three-point turn. He averted an imminent collision with a lamp post by a savage twist of the steering wheel and pressed his foot on the accelerator.

They'd almost had her. 'Fuck,' Phil shouted when he turned the corner, 'where the hell's it gone?'

'Only one place it could go from here.' Gus flicked a glance at him before staring straight ahead. 'Dock Street and the dual carriageway.'

They reached Dock Street just in time to see the estate car driving up the opposite lane. 'Fuck, he was nippy,' Phil said as he shot a red light and sped round the roundabout. 'Keep your eyes peeled, don't lose sight of him,' he instructed Gus who was bracing himself with his hand pressed against the dashboard.

Phil sped through the next set of lights just as they were changing, and he'd caught up with the red car before they reached the Marketgait roundabout.

'I told you we wouldn't lose them. I'm too good for that.' A wolfish grin spread across his face. 'Our wee Kara's soon going to be taught a lesson she won't forget in a hurry.'

The car was travelling past Dudhope Park when Kara became certain Phil and Gus were following. The black Merc was unmistakable. And they were close behind.

Kara bit her lip. Tony must have sent them after her. If they'd just leave her alone she might be able to screw enough money out of this one to pay them off. She looked at the driver. He'd hardly spoken since she got in the car and it was making her nervous.

'Where we going then?'

He switched off the windscreen wipers. 'Someplace special.'

'Why do we have to go someplace special? The rain's stopped. And we've just passed Dudhope Park. It's quiet there.'

'Be patient,' he said. 'When we get there it'll be worth it.'

'Who for? You or me?' Kara decided she'd had enough. 'Look, just drop me off at Lochee High Street and we'll call it quits.' Lochee was always busy and she'd stand a chance there. Maybe if she screamed loud enough Phil and Gus wouldn't be able to put the strong arm on her but, if they kept on driving, the streets would get quieter and she would run out of luck.

He laughed, but it wasn't a pleasant laugh. It unsettled her. 'I won't let you change your mind,' he said. 'After all, a bargain's a bargain. And I'm looking forward to our little party.' He swung round the roundabout, on to the Coupar Angus road, leaving the lights of Lochee behind them. Already the streets were getting quieter although they were in a built up area.

Kara looked over her shoulder. The black Merc was still there. 'I don't like going so far from the town centre. I might have problems getting back again.' She bit her lip until she tasted blood.

'Oh, is that all,' he said. 'Don't worry about getting back.'

No, thought Kara, with those two behind me I'll have more to worry about than getting back, and maybe you will as well. Serve you right.

They travelled in silence. Kara brooded, trying to think of a way out and not coming up with any answers. She spent her time looking behind her to check on the black Merc, and studying the punter's face. It was dark in the car and she couldn't really see his expression except when the streetlights flickered briefly over his features. He wasn't bad-looking but there'd been something about him, when he looked at her, which set her nerves jangling. And she didn't know where he was taking her, only that he'd said it was special. Well, she hoped it was special with plenty of folk about.

'Where's he taking her?' Gus offered Phil a piece of chewing gum from the packet he'd found in his pocket.

Phil shook his head, 'Fucked if I know but it looks like he's heading for the ring road.'

'Strange place for a quick blowjob,' he said, popping a sliver of gum into his mouth.

Kara's eyes widened in fear and she cringed into her seat as soon as she realised the car wasn't going to give way to the lorry thundering up on them from the right. She was conscious of a smile flickering on the mouth of the man when they skiffed past the nose of the lorry heading to the ring road. They'd been so close to being rammed she'd seen the astonished look on the lorry driver's face and heard the blast of his horn vibrate within the car as he just missed their rear end. The only good thing about it was that the black Merc got stuck at the Give Way sign and was unable to follow them on to the overpass.

'What the bloody hell did you do that for?' She was still shaking at the near miss. 'You got a death wish or something?'

His expression didn't change and he didn't answer. It was as if she didn't exist. Stretching her legs as far as they would go into the footwell of the car, she tensed and then eased her muscles until she felt more relaxed. 'We nearly there yet?' The silence was bugging her.

'Won't be long,' he murmured, taking a sidelong look at her. Kara became even more uneasy.

They pulled off the overpass. There were high walls on one side of the road and trees on the other, then nothing but darkness. Kara was a city girl and had rarely ventured into the countryside. Open spaces made her nervous.

'You haven't said where we're going.' Kara leaned forward trying to see if there were any lights other than those made by the car, but all she could see was the grass verge and the overhanging trees. 'I don't like the dark much,' she said when he didn't answer her. She shifted in her seat, pulling at her damp skirt where it stuck to her legs. The car slowed and the beam of another car far behind them winked at her from the driver's rear mirror. She hoped it wasn't the Merc.

The punter braked hard, throwing Kara forward until her seatbelt clicked and held her, and then turned off the road into a small clearing between the trees. The sound of the engine died and he switched off the headlights.

'We're here,' he said, leaning back, stretching his arms and clasping his hands behind his head.

'You're joking!' Kara looked out of the car window into a darkness more solid than anything she'd ever seen.

She had come with him willingly. That was important. And now the woods stretched out in front of him. Dark, inviting, waiting. The trees bent towards him, rustling their branches, whispering their approval.

Soon she would be joined with them. Her soul would become a tree spirit. Soon she would be purified.

8

'Fuck!' Phil stamped on the brake. The estate car in front had shot on to the overpass just missing an approaching lorry. 'That was close,' he said, wiping his hands on his trouser legs.

Gus opened the sunroof and stuck his head out to watch the red estate speeding away. 'He's left the overpass at the Coupar Angus junction,' he said, sliding back into his seat.

Phil drummed his fingers on the steering wheel as he waited for an opening. Sweat gathered under his collar as he suddenly bulldozed his way on to the overpass, ignoring the screech of brakes and the horns that accompanied his progress.

'The Coupar Angus exit you said? You'd better be right.'

The road darkened. Camperdown Park lay on their left and the woods on their right. It wasn't their usual territory and Phil couldn't shake off a feeling of unease. He rolled down his window but even the hum of traffic had receded, getting fainter the further they drove.

'Where the hell's the red car gone?' he asked Gus. 'It can't have disappeared that quickly. Could it?' The road was clear. 'They must have turned off. That's it.'

Gus nodded. 'We've just passed the entrance to the park, but I didn't see any car lights there.' He rolled down his window as well. 'Don't hear anything,' he said. 'What about the woods? Might be a place a punter would take a girl. Mind you, if I was a girl I wouldn't want to be taken there. Wasn't that the place they found those two girls all those years ago? I remember my ma talking about it, she knew one of them.'

'Cut the chat and keep your eyes peeled.'

'Come on, then,' he said, opening the car door and getting out.

'I'm not getting out here.' Kara slumped back in her seat.

'I don't do country and I don't do lonely and dark. Take me back to Dundee.'

He walked round the car and opened her door. 'Out, or I'll drag you out.'

Kara didn't like his tone but neither did she want to get out of the car. It was safer inside. There might be animals out there among the trees. Kara had never seen so many trees in one place. Maybe this was the weirdo Jean had warned her about. The place was weird enough, anyhow.

He leaned into the car, unlocked her seatbelt and pulled. She slid out and landed on her backside on the wet grass.

'What'd you do that for?' she complained, staggering to her feet. He'd looked a bit of a wimp crouched over the steering wheel and he surprised her with his strength. She could still feel his fingers where they'd gripped her arm.

'It was the quickest way,' he said. 'Come on, so I don't have to pull you.'

'No way,' she said, grabbing hold of the car door with both hands. Maybe she could get back in and lock the doors.

He grabbed her round the middle, pulling her to him. Her hands scrabbled at the door, gradually losing their grip. She could feel a fingernail splitting and breaking and she squealed with the sharp pain it caused.

He kicked the car door shut and pushed his face close up to hers. The smell of earth and foliage mixed with the sweet, pungent smell of his aftershave wafted up her nose. His stubble scraped her chin. 'You'll come with me,' he hissed, 'and you'll do everything I tell you to do, every little thing. D'you understand?'

'Yeah. Yeah, I understand,' she rasped trying to pull away, but his grip on her was too tight.

He dragged her out of the clearing into the wood. 'I told you to come on and I meant it.' It sounded as if he'd gritted his teeth to prevent himself shouting.

Trees surrounded them. Trees larger than she'd imagined possible loomed over and round her, their massive trunks dwarfing her and creating shadows so deep her eyes couldn't penetrate the gloom. Branches and shrubs plucked at her legs, tearing her fishnets and scratching her skin. She stumbled over a tree root, falling on her knees. He yanked her up, wrenching her arm almost out of her shoulder. She gasped with pain and struggled. 'I'm not going any further,' she screamed, kicking his shin.

He relaxed his hold for a second and she took the chance, scrabbling off into the darkness, stumbling and falling. She didn't know where she was going. She just knew she had to get away from this man.

Kara was in her bare feet now, fishnets in shreds and her shoes long gone. The damp earth and moss felt slimy and cold and she kept standing on things, hard things, wet things, squishy things.

At last she sank to the ground, panting and heaving for breath. She crawled under a bush. He wouldn't be able to find her now. She'd outrun him. She lay back, exhausted. Her breath started to ease and she felt pleased with herself, thinking that there weren't many men who could get the better of her. That was the moment when the hand closed round her ankle.

'That was fun,' he said. 'I like a good chase.' He dragged her out from under the bush.

Her skirt rode up past her waist, twigs and stones scraped her buttocks, her shoulder bag caught on a branch and hung there. She strained to reach it because, despite the fix she was in, she couldn't help thinking that without the money it contained she'd be unable to pay off Phil and Gus. 'Piss off,' she spat out, as her fingers missed the bag. 'Let go of me,' she screamed, grasping the branches and trying to stop sliding forward. She kicked out with her free foot.

He grabbed her other ankle and pulled harder. 'It's time,' he said. 'This is where the fun really starts.'

'I'm not going anywhere with you.' Kara released her hold on the bush so her hands would be free to punch and scratch as soon as she was clear. 'You bastard,' she squealed, grasping her buttocks to try and lessen the pain as she slid forward.

Kara wasn't sure where the knife had come from. He hadn't had it earlier, she was sure of that, and yet she hadn't seen him take it out from anywhere. But it was there. The feel of it pricking her throat was unmistakable.

Fear silenced her and she unclenched her fists. She couldn't fight against a knife and she needed to get home to the kids. The man started to walk, his arm circling her waist and his hand clamped hard round her wrist. The undergrowth and trees seemed even thicker here, the thorns piercing her skin were almost as sharp as the knife point he held to her throat. She stumbled in front of him as he forced her to walk with him to his special place.

'We've got to find her.' Phil's heart hammered in his chest as he thought about Tony and the things he did to guys who let him down. But what else could they have done. He'd driven as far as the Coupar Angus–Meigle junction where the car's tail-lights would have been visible no matter which road it had taken, but there was nothing. Then the Liff road. Nothing.

'What about this road?' Gus said as they drove back.

Phil screeched to a halt and looked up the dark, tree-lined road. 'I don't see any tail-lights but we should give it a try.'

They drove along the road until the trees petered out, then turned and drove back. When they reached the junction of the Coupar Angus Road, Phil thumped the driving wheel with his fist. 'Where the hell's he taken her?'

'We can't tell Tony we've lost her,' Gus muttered. 'Let's go back up this road again. I have a feeling about it.'

They drove back slowly, examining every turn-off into the woods. Phil's despair mounted. He wouldn't be able to face Tony if he couldn't find her. Maybe he should emigrate.

'Stop!' Gus had turned in his seat and was looking back down the road. 'Reverse slowly. I think I saw something.' Gus stuck his head out of the window. 'Yeah, stop here! This is the place.' He slapped the outside of the car door with his hand. 'I was right. Look there it is, tucked in behind those trees.'

Phil braked and got out of the car. 'Right,' he shouted. 'We've got her now.'

The two men ran into the clearing behind the trees. 'That's

it, right enough,' Phil said, 'but it's empty.' He looked at the surrounding woods. They didn't look inviting and he wasn't too confident about being able to find anything without getting lost. But anything was better than Tony's wrath. 'They must have gone in there. Come on.'

They hadn't gone very far when they realised how hopeless it was. There were no paths in this part of the wood and trees surrounded them.

'It's fucking hopeless,' Gus muttered. 'We'll never find her in here.' He broke off a branch and whacked at the undergrowth.

Phil shrugged. 'We don't have a choice. Keep going.'

Gus whacked some more at the bushes, bent down and picked something up. 'See what I've found.' He held a high-heeled shoe up for Phil's inspection. 'That's hers, isn't it?'

Phil took it from him. 'Yeah, she can't be far away.' He gestured towards the wood. 'Maybe it's time to start scaring her,' he grinned. 'And him. He's not going to hang around if he knows we're after him.'

'How do we do that then?'

'We make a noise and let him know we're after him. He'll soon scarper.' Phil paused. 'If we let him, that is.'

'You think that'll work?'

'Don't know till we try, do we?' A wolfish smile appeared on Phil's face. 'Anyway, I owe that bitch one.'

Gus frowned. 'I'm not sure. We don't know this guy she's with. What if he's some kind of nature freak? You know, like those guys who live rough.'

'You watch too much telly, pal. This is Templeton Woods, not the Australian outback.' Phil laughed. He was also feeling uneasy but he wasn't going to admit it to Gus. 'What you waiting for? Start whacking your stick around and make plenty of noise.' He shouted. 'Kara, my love. We're coming to get you.'

Kara fell to her knees. The sharp edge of the knife sliced into her earlobe. Blood oozed and she felt it trickle down her neck and under her collar. Damp earth and moss clogged her fingernails and smeared her hands with slime. Small rocks and pine-cones gouged her shins. She stared into the dark, feeling like a trapped animal, convinced there was no way out of this mess. A sob caught in the back of her throat. How could she have been so stupid as to get herself into this?

She crouched on her hands and knees, unable to see the stars or the moon because the trees had closed so firmly around her. It was like a tomb. She shivered with the premonition that it would be *her* tomb. She'd never get out of this alive. She'd vanish, never to be seen nor heard from again. Jean had maintained that her pal, Linda, would never have left her kids behind, but gone she had – disappeared completely, her kids in care. Kara believed Jean, knowing that she would never willingly desert her own kids.

He stood over her, a dark shape among all the other dark shapes. 'Get up!' His voice was harsh. She'd never before heard anything that sounded so cold. He reached down, grasping her arm in a pincer grip, and started to pull.

A ghostly voice drifted through the trees. 'Kara, my love. We're coming to get you.' It sang and floated, sometimes whispering and sometimes shouting. It was joined by a second voice until the bushes seemed alive with whispering and singing.

Kara lifted her head, like a dog sniffing the wind. The hand grasping her arm slackened slightly and he twisted round, staring into the trees. She sensed his uncertainty and maybe a little panic.

The voices, resounding eerily through the trees, chilled Kara as much as the maniac who still had his hand on her arm. She'd heard Phil and Gus use those tones before, usually as a precursor to extreme violence. The friendlier they sounded, the more dangerous they were. A moan gathered in her throat. She clamped her teeth together to prevent it escaping, instinctively knowing she couldn't allow the man who held her to sense her fear of the others.

She tried to block out their sing-song voices, took a deep breath, and said with more bravado than she felt, 'They're my pimps. They always follow me to make sure I'm all right. They know I'm here with you.'

The punter's hand loosened completely as he jerked every which way trying to work out where the voices were coming from.

He had enjoyed the chase. It was a game he had played before. But the woods were his domain and the trees his friends.

The knife was a mistake, but she had forced him. It was sharp but would not have pierced her skin if she had not struggled. That was unfortunate. It contaminated her. Made her less than perfect.

Perhaps that was why the voices had started. The other voices. They sang through the woods, interfering with the whispers. They confused him. He clamped his hands over his ears. And she was gone. As if she had never been there.

The trees rustled their rage. But the other voices drowned them out and he could no longer decipher the words.

9

Kara, still on her hands and knees, crawled away into the undergrowth. The man didn't seem to notice so she crawled a little further. He was preoccupied with the voices floating through the trees. Finally when she thought she'd crawled far enough away she took a deep breath and rose to her feet. But when she tried to run, her legs would hardly hold her up, and she lurched and stumbled through the trees. Her body ached all over and the effort to keep moving seemed too much to bear. But she knew that if she gave up she wouldn't survive. So each time she fell, although she wanted to curl up and close her eyes, she forced herself back on to her feet to run and stagger some more. She didn't look back for quite some time and when she did, he was no longer there.

The voices continued to float through the trees and, although Kara had no idea where she was, she kept on running until the voices became fainter and then died away completely.

Branches tore her skin and pulled at her hair in her headlong flight, but still she ran. Her breath rasped noisily from her open mouth and her lungs felt as if they were on fire as each gasp she took sliced into them with an edge as sharp as the knife he'd held at her throat.

The memory of his hand round her ankle the last time she'd thought she was safe was enough to keep her going. He was in the wood somewhere and she daren't stop. So on she stumbled until exhaustion overcame her. Kara lay face down on mossy earth in a small clearing. She had no strength left. It took an effort to lift her face from the ground and turn it sideways so she could breathe. Great bursts of air whistled noisily from her throat, expelled from lungs that were almost exploding with the exertion.

Tears rolled down her cheeks and she hugged herself to make the pain go away. If he came now she wouldn't be able to fight back.

A rustle in the undergrowth sent her pulse racing. She clamped her teeth into her lip until she knew she'd drawn blood. He would like her to moan or scream, she was sure of it, and she refused to give him that pleasure.

The rustling stopped, although she sensed she was being watched. She shivered. Her heart beat faster. Maybe she could summon a last spurt of energy. She raised herself on to her elbows and opened her mouth to yell at him as soon as he revealed himself, only to collapse back to the ground when the patter of animal feet fled through the trees.

Hysteria took hold of her and she started to giggle, clamping her hand over her mouth to stifle the sound. Sitting up, she leaned forward to disentangle her foot from the root that had tripped her up. It was spongy and unpleasant, and there was a foul odour that intensified when she touched it. Something worm-like wriggled and moved under her fingers. She hated creepie-crawlies and drew her hand back wiping it on her skirt. But her foot was still caught and, despite her revulsion, she would have to wrestle with the root to free it. At that moment a shaft of moonlight filtered past the trees into the clearing and she slid forward on her bottom so she could see what she was doing.

Bile flooded her mouth and she had to turn her head to spit it out. She didn't want to look again. But she had to. Slowly she turned back to it. She wanted to scream, but daren't. He might be near. Now she was sure she was in his special place.

Her hand shook. She let it hover for a moment over the decomposing leg under which her foot was lodged; the leg that was covered with mounds of glistening white maggots, wriggling and gorging on the flesh below. Then, closing her eyes, she grabbed her foot and wrested it free.

Opening them again she tried to avert her eyes but couldn't stop herself from looking. The naked body, the putrefying flesh, the maggots clustered over wounds that small forest animals must have made in skin that had once been alive, horrified her. But it was the face she knew she would never forget; the bloated, discoloured face with the lips drawn back in a cadaverous grin, and the eyes which had slipped from their sockets to rest lopsidedly on the cheeks.

Kara shuffled backwards on her bottom until she collided with a tree. She turned to grasp it and pulled herself up. It was only when she had regained her feet that she realised that the branch she had used for balance was a fleshless arm. She staggered backwards. A skull with empty eye sockets and grinning teeth confronted her.

A scream gathered in her throat but she choked it back. If he heard her she was convinced she would soon be joining the dead. She turned, desperate to find a way out.

That was when Kara saw the girl tied to the tree. She could have been alive, but when Kara stumbled over to her she knew that the girl was as dead as the others. However, this body was even more horrific because Kara recognised her. The unmistakeable long blonde hair and the beauty that Kara had often envied. Dizziness and the urge to be sick overwhelmed her, but although she retched until her ribs ached, nothing came up.

Kara put a hand over her nose and mouth in a fruitless effort to blot out the foul odour of putrefaction that surrounded her, but even her fingers smelled of death. Hysteria claimed her and she imagined whispers drifting to her on the wind and fleshless hands reaching out to her, beseeching her to join them.

Trees swayed in the rising breeze. Drips pattered off the leaves, and the smell of rot and decaying wood turned Phil's stomach. A familiar burning pain rose in his chest, rising until he thought he would choke. He staggered. The tree he leaned on for support was wet and slimy but he was impervious to anything other than the pain.

Gus stopped whacking the undergrowth with his stick. 'What's up?' He shoved his face close to Phil's. His eyes glowed in the dark.

'Think I'm getting a bloody ulcer, that's what!' Phil drew a long breath. 'Fuck, the things I do for Tony,' he muttered as the pain started to subside. 'I'll be glad when we find that little bitch and I can get back to civilisation.'

Gus backed away from Phil and peered into the gloom of the woods. 'Doesn't look like we're going to find her though, does it?' He shuddered. 'This place is fucking horrible.' He whacked the side of a tree with his stick. 'What the hell's she doing in here anyway? I wouldn't come within a mile of this place.'

'Shut the fuck up! I thought I heard something rustling. Like someone creeping about.'

The two men set off through the woods following the sounds of someone moving rapidly away from them. Gus ran on in front, muttering and swearing as branches tore his clothes and skin. Phil's breathing grew more ragged as the pain flared again. He tried to ignore it, running with one hand clamped to his chest and the other pushing shrubbery away. His legs trembled with the effort and it was only willpower that kept him going.

A car door slammed. Both men looked at each other. 'Fuck!' Phil said. 'Get after them.'

The car engine roared, sounding louder than normal in the stillness of the woods. The two men started to run and were just in time to see the tail-lights of the red estate vanishing down the road in the direction of Dundee.

'No! We've lost them,' Phil shouted.

'What d'you think Tony will say?'

'Fucked if I know.'

10

Kara backed away from the body, pulling her knees up to her chest and swinging round so she could crawl. She desperately wanted to stand up and run, but didn't think she had enough strength. A rustling sound in the bushes bordering the small clearing made her heart race. Despite her fear, she peered into the undergrowth. Yellow unblinking slits stared back at her. She closed her eyes, held her breath, and prayed silently. When she opened them again, nothing was there.

She knew she had to get out of this awful wood, away from the bodies in the clearing, and as far away as possible from whatever had watched her from the undergrowth.

She grabbed an overhanging branch and, holding it so tightly it made her hands numb, hauled herself upright. Limping and stumbling, she started to push her way slowly through the trees. The woods seemed never ending and she walked for what felt like hours before they started to thin. She was in some kind of park, a wide, open grassy expanse with a tree here and there. But best of all, there were lights in the distance. Street lights and house lights.

Tears pricked her eyes and her body shook uncontrollably. She had no idea where she was but she didn't care as long as she was near ordinary people. She would be safe among the houses. Her spirits lifted and she stumbled on until she felt the bite of stones and gravel on her feet. She was on a path, maybe a bicycle track, so she followed it until it led her out onto the street.

The pavement was hard on her feet after the softness of the grass and she looked down at herself in dismay. She was a mess. Her fishnets now hung in tatters around her ankles. She had no idea where her shoes were. Her mac was still in one piece but was covered in mud and grass stains. She'd lost an earring and its partner dangled forlornly from one ear, snagging wisps of the hair hanging dankly on her neck. Kara didn't dare think what her face must look like.

Spotting a phone box she hurried towards it and once inside peeled off her fishnets, dropping them in a heap on the floor. She inspected her face in the cracked and dirty mirror, wetting her finger and scrubbing at the worst of the mud. She combed her fingers through her hair. At last she felt she'd done the best she could to tidy herself up but she knew she'd still attract attention if anyone was around.

Kara pushed the door open but let it swing back again as she remembered the bodies in the wood. Those poor girls didn't deserve to lie there and rot until the maggots and wildlife ate them up. Kara shuddered and placed her hand on the phone. She let it rest there for a moment, reluctant to pick the receiver up and dial. But she knew she'd never forgive herself if the girls weren't found and returned to their families.

'Which service please?' The voice sounded far off and metallic. It might have been coming from another planet.

Why the hell was she doing this? She didn't need the hassle.

The voice repeated its request.

'Police,' Kara said, biting her lip to suppress her panic. She was going to regret this, she just knew it.

As soon as she was connected, Kara blurted the words out before she could change her mind. 'Bodies. Dead girls. In the woods,' she gulped. 'I saw Denise Palmer.' She started to cry, the tears trickling down her face. 'And there's others.'

'What's your location, madam.'

'How the hell do I know?' Kara shouted. 'I was taken there. I'm bloody lucky I'm not one of them.' She banged the phone onto its cradle and ran out of the phone box. She knew she should have given them more information but they'd be tracing the call and she needed to get away.

'Fucking stench,' Phil said, sniffing the odour of tom cat, gents' toilet and rotting food. It brought back memories of his childhood, spent on an estate just like this one. 'How the hell can anyone live like this?'

'Fuck knows,' Gus said, avoiding a puddle of vomit as he climbed upwards. 'Folk that live here don't deserve any better, shit and puke everywhere.'

A door clicking shut sounded as loud as a shot in the silence of the night. Phil halted for a moment on the top step and glared along the landing. Then he smiled. He was well known here. No one would dare challenge him. 'Nosy bastards,' he muttered to Gus. 'Come on, let's get this over and done with.'

Wind whistled between the railings that bordered one side of the walkway, sending empty crisp bags and assorted stray papers whirling into the door recesses. Kara's flat was the last one on the landing. Gus raised his hand to bang on the door but Phil knocked it away, took aim with his foot and kicked the door. The shock of the blow travelled up his shin to his knee and he swore softly beneath his breath.

Gus grinned. 'Nice one,' he said. He placed his hand on the door and pushed. The last remaining nails holding the lock gave way with a screech.

The hall was dark and uninviting. Phil flicked the switch on the wall. The light fizzed on, revealing bare floorboards and grubby walls with the paper peeling off at the seams, before the bulb exploded with a bang. He stood for a moment, waiting for his eyes to adjust to the gloom. The smell of stale food, chip fat and sour milk was overwhelming.

Gus followed him inside, his footsteps clattering on the wooden floors. 'Sounds empty,' he said.

Phil peered into the bathroom first and then the bedroom, wrinkling his nose in disgust at the clothes scattered around.

He pushed the living room door open. Small whimpering noises came from the sofa in the middle of the room. He strode towards it and, grabbing the mound of blankets, heaved them onto the floor. 'Hey, what's this?' He beckoned to Gus.

Gus reached out and picked up the older child, holding her by the collar of her dress. 'Where's your mum then?' He shook her until she started to cry. 'Come on, where is she?'

The child screamed and the younger child joined in.

Gus shouted, 'Tell us where your mum is, or I'll start on your wee brother.'

Phil's stomach churned and a tightness spread across his chest. He didn't care how much pain he inflicted on adults, but he drew the line with kids. Gus was different though. Men, women, kids, it was all the same to him.

'Oh, for fuck's sake, leave them alone.' Phil had had enough. 'It's obvious they don't know. We'll keep an eye on the house and wait till she gets back.'

'You're too fucking sensitive, so you are,' Gus said, but he let go of the child and she sank back on the sofa, sobbing and staring at him with huge eyes.

The two men left the flat and jogged down the stone stairs. They could still hear the children wailing as they reached the car.

The voices followed him out of the wood. They were angry voices. They frightened him. They were not like the whispers of the trees.

The trees were his friends. At first he only heard their whispers when he was in the woods, but more recently he had heard them at other times. As if they were getting stronger, reaching out to him. They kept him company in the dark times, when he was alone.

He drove off, left the angry voices behind, listened for the whispers. But they had left him. He was alone again. Alone again in his other life.

11

Kara's bare feet slapped the wet pavement as she ran from the phone box. She had to find somewhere to hide before the police came.

The houses opposite the park were in darkness but, although the doorways and entrance halls attracted her, she turned away from them. The police might do a house to house search and if they did she'd be trapped. Most of the houses had gardens but she wanted something more substantial than a hedge to hide behind. The sheds and garages she'd tried were locked, and she began to think she would never find anything. Her footsteps slowed and her shoulders slumped. It was hopeless. Maybe she *should* just wait for them. At least she'd be safe from the man who'd taken her into the woods and Phil and Gus. But the police would ask awkward questions. They'd want to know what she'd been doing in the woods, and then there were the kids. If they found out she'd left them alone in an empty house, they'd call social services and that would be that.

A police siren screamed not too far away, breaking the night-time silence and making her heart pound with alarm. The sound drew nearer. Where could she go?

She reached the street corner, crouching quickly behind a hedge when she saw the police car speeding towards her. It sped past, siren blaring and blue light flashing. Relieved, a great weight descended on her body, feeling like a giant hand pushing her into the damp, soggy earth. She wanted to close her eyes and sleep but, knowing she couldn't stay here much longer, she forced herself to get up. She'd have to find somewhere better.

Bending low, she crept round the corner and there it was, the answer to her prayers, a burned out car left behind by joyriders. She scuttled to the rear door of the car, opened it and slid inside.

The stench of burnt metal and upholstery stung her nostrils and made her gag. She forced herself to lie on the floor. The night was no longer silent. Car engines roared, sirens sounded, fists hammered on doors, voices came and went but no one thought to look into the car wreck.

It was a long time before Kara felt safe enough to leave. Lights glimmered from a few houses and a faint smell of frying bacon permeated the air as she stretched her cramped legs and arms, and crawled out of the car. Her hands were black, there was ash in her hair and she reeked of burnt plastic. She tried not to think what the rest of her looked like but she knew that if anyone saw her they would remember her.

She stood on the pavement looking around. She needed to get home now and as inconspicuously as possible. A car, that's what she needed. She limped down the road. She'd take the first one she could get into.

Bella twitched her kitchen curtains to the side. Ever since she'd been burgled the first time she'd been sensitive to noise and movement during the night. She let go of the curtains and moved away from the window after she saw the two men emerge from the staircase onto the landing. They looked like sales reps, but sales reps didn't call in the middle of the night. She pressed her body into the corner of the kitchen furthest away from the window and prayed they hadn't seen her.

She let go her breath when she saw their shadows pass her window. At least they weren't coming for her. A massive thud reverberated through the thin walls of the building and her favourite vase – the one her daughter won at the fair – jiggled on her windowsill. Another massive thump convinced her they were trying to batter the door down. Her double chins quivered and the fat on her arms grew goose pimples because, despite her size, Bella was a coward. There were no more thuds but Bella heard the door wrench off the wall.

She scuttled through to the bedroom. Darren, her eldest

son, lay on top of the bed fully clothed and with his shoes on. 'Wake up, and get your feet off that bed!' Bella grabbed his shoulders and shook him.

'Aw, Ma. I was too tired to take them off,' Darren mumbled. 'Leave me be.'

Bella shook harder. 'For fuck's sake, will you wake up,' she roared.

He blinked at her.

'I'm not kidding. I need you to wake up.' She drew a breath and bellowed, 'Now!'

'What's up?' Darren pulled himself up and swung his feet out of the bed. He looked with alarm at the sight of his mother, quivering and shaking.

Bella grabbed his arm. 'Next door's just been kicked in and we're not going to be next.' She caught her breath in a sob. 'For fuck's sake, will you run and phone the polis. There's no credit left on my phone and I'm not leaving the house.'

'You sure you're not imagining it?' Darren stood up and stretched his arms above his head.

Bella pushed him angrily in the direction of the hall.

As they reached the front door the sound of children screaming echoed through the wall. 'Aw, no! They've started on the kids now. Will you just go and get help.' She opened the door, shoved him through it, then closed and bolted it behind him.

Bella watched Darren until he vanished out of sight on the stairs, then she crept back to the bedroom, locked herself in, and prayed.

Phil stopped with his hand on the car door. He looked back up the stairs. 'Screaming kids,' he muttered. 'Maybe we should have done them.' A knot of pain pushed its way up his gullet. He wasn't sure whether he could, but he knew Tony would expect it, if it became necessary.

'Want to go back up and finish the job?' Gus raised his eyebrows and gave him a sly look from the corner of his eyes.

He knows I don't have the guts, Phil thought. 'Too risky.

With all the racket they're making it won't be long before the cops are here.' He got in the car and started the engine. 'Better move it in case anyone's watching. We don't want the girl seeing us before we're ready for her.'

Phil tucked the Merc out of sight in the car park and, peering through the windscreen, satisfied himself he could see the stairs leading to Kara's flat. Only minutes later the first police car arrived.

'Oh, for Pete's sake can't the beat boys handle it?' Louise shook her head trying to clear the sleep out of her brain. 'What time is it anyway?' She reached out and lifted the alarm clock, squinting at the dial. 'Ten past six!' Her voice rose a notch. 'I'm not due to start until nine.' She listened for a moment. 'Ha, ha,' she said. 'I know. I've got a cushy number. You never stop reminding me. OK, give me the address.' She scribbled on a paper tissue. 'I'll get there as soon as I can. By the way, you wouldn't happen to know whether they've phoned social work? . . . Right . . . Can you? It'll save me time when I get there.' Idiots, she thought, as she hung up. What did they think social work had an out of hours service for?

Louise swung her feet out of the bed and without thinking too much about it pulled on her clothes. She dragged a brush through her long brown hair which she twisted back into a ponytail.

Her bedroom door creaked when she opened it but there was no sound from Sue's room so she crept out, stopping briefly in the kitchen to butter a slice of bread which she then rammed into her mouth. Louise knew that lots of police officers suffered from stomach ulcers through not eating properly and she was determined not to make the same mistake. She unhooked the padded ski anorak hanging by the door and thrust her arms into it.

The street was quiet and damp from the night's rain, but at least there was no frost on the roads. Her Fiesta was unpredictable at the best of times.

It didn't take her long to reach the Greenfield estate – a

massive sprawl of three-storey, flat-roofed buildings with walkways connecting each block. When it was built it had won awards for being innovative and forward-looking and the town officials had proceeded to empty the inner city tenement dwellers into these model flats. Now it huddled in an area that had seen better days. Broken windows and rubbish proliferated and graffiti was the local art form of choice.

Louise parked her car in front of the access stairs in preference to the shadowy car park. The usual grotty, smelly concrete stairs were open at the sides but roofed over to provide some shelter from the elements. She climbed upwards, careful not to touch the rail, having learned early in her career that stair railings were often encrusted with more than the grime from hundreds of sweaty hands.

The flat was easy to identify. The door hung lopsidedly from its hinges and the sounds of crying children mingled with the gruff tones of the investigating beat officers.

The entrance was not inviting. Bare floorboards, peeling wallpaper and an odd musty smell that Louise had come to associate with many of these flats. The living room, by contrast, although untidy was relatively clean and someone had painted the walls and door not too long ago. Two policemen stood in the middle of the room, the older one behind the sofa, the younger in front of it. Louise didn't know either of them.

The younger policeman was bent over the sofa trying to soothe the children. They were now screaming at the top of their voices. He looked over at Louise, giving her a crooked smile and the relief on his face was obvious.

'Maybe if you sat down you'd have more success. You look enormous to them like that,' Louise said. She crossed the room and sat on the edge of the sofa, gathering the younger child into her arms. He pulled away from her, sobbing and reaching for his sister. 'Hush now,' Louise said, 'I'm not going to hurt you. We just want to find your mummy.'

The girl pummelled her with punches. 'Let Billy go,' she hissed. 'He doesn't want you touching him.'

Louise released the squirming child and he snuggled closer

to his sister. Both children stared at her. At least their fear had been replaced by anger.

'Right. If you've got the situation under control, we'll leave you to it.' The older policeman edged towards the door. The younger one followed.

'Stay where you are.' Louise's voice was authoritative. 'You know as well as I do that where there are children there must be at least two people present.'

'Social work said they'd send somebody,' the younger officer volunteered. 'Should be here soon.'

'Until the social worker arrives, you'll stay.' Louise knew she didn't have any more authority than they did, but she wasn't going to let them off the hook. Anyway they wouldn't know she was only a constable unless she told them, and she didn't plan to do that.

She turned back to the children, addressing herself to the girl who was obviously acting as the parent child. 'Where's your mummy? Is she coming back soon? I think Billy needs her, he's upset.'

'She'll be home soon.' The child's voice was sullen and more adult than it should have been.

'That's fine. Will we wait for her then?' Louise leaned back on the sofa. 'What's your name, love. I know this is Billy but I don't know what to call you.'

The girl didn't answer.

'Charlene.' Billy patted his sister's arm and then sidled along the sofa until he was leaning against Louise. 'Mummy's coming,' he said. 'Bad men gone now.'

'Tell me about the bad men?' Louise rested her arm lightly on his shoulders.

Billy stuck his thumb into his mouth.

'It must have been scary,' Louise said, looking at Charlene.

The girl scowled and shrugged.

'You know, if your mummy doesn't come soon it might be better if we found you somewhere to sleep where the door's not broken.'

'Can't,' Charlene said. 'Mum won't know where we are.'

'I could leave a note, or come back and wait for her.'

Charlene scowled. 'Staying here.'

Footsteps sounded in the hall and Louise looked up as the door swung open. 'Sorry I took so long,' the man said. He entered the room, a nondescript-looking man with mousy brown hair and the beginnings of a beard, either that or he hadn't shaved lately. Louise was pretty certain she'd met him before but couldn't remember his name. He was that type.

'Right, lads,' she said to the two policemen. 'Now that the social worker's here, I need you to interview the neighbours and find out what we can about the mother and where she might be. While you're doing that we'll try to work out what to do with the kids.'

12

The explosive sound of the glass shattering was louder than Kara anticipated. After all she'd been through, to be caught trying to steal a car and be handed over to the police like a stupid kid, would be more than she could cope with. She crouched between the car and the hedge, holding her breath, ready to run if anyone came out of the house.

Something small and furtive rustled in the hedge leaves. Kara blanked the sound out of her mind, waiting for other sounds: slamming doors, shouts, curses, running feet, accusing voices. The rustling stopped and silence folded round her again.

Getting the car started wasn't as difficult as she'd thought, but the streets were unfamiliar. Wincing with pain, she pressed her foot on the accelerator and drove in what she hoped was the right direction.

Fatigue clouded her mind but as she drove, wind whistled through the broken window ruffling her hair and helping her to stay awake. Every so often she stabbed her foot on the accelerator, hoping the pain would keep her conscious. When, finally, she saw a bus she knew she was going to be all right.

She slowed, keeping far enough behind that it wouldn't be obvious she was stopping and starting when the bus did. She travelled for miles, through areas where the houses were large and well looked after, on to more dilapidated areas and unfamiliar housing estates. At last the bus crossed the Kingsway and Kara knew it was heading for the city centre. She continued to follow it until she knew where she was, until she was almost home.

The streets were busier now. Dundee was waking up and getting ready for another day's work. Early workers waited at bus stops, bikes and cars were on the move. Lorries trundled on their way with goods for factories and supermarkets.

She turned into the road in front of her flat and almost drew up at the kerb, when she saw the police car. What the hell was it doing parked there? She circled the block until she found a secluded parking spot with a view of her block. Hunching down in the seat, she peered through the broken window. What was going on?

A policeman came out of Bella's flat. She couldn't distinguish his features at this distance but Bella was unmistakable. Kara relaxed. Darren must have been up to his usual. He fancied himself as a housebreaker but seemed to spend more time inside Perth prison than he did at home.

Kara settled back into the seat of the car and closed her eyes. She'd doze for a while until the coast was clear.

'You can't make me.' Charlene scowled.

Louise sighed. 'It's only until we find your mum.' She wanted to reach out and cuddle the girl, but Charlene's body was rigid with defiance. She couldn't blame the child though. She would've felt the same. She knelt on the floor so that their eyes were level. 'It's for the best,' she murmured. 'It's quite cold in here, and you could be nice and warm while you wait for your mum. You'd get some breakfast too.' Louise had already looked in the cupboards and noted how little food they held.

'But she won't know where we are,' Charlene's voice wavered, 'and I promised I'd look after Billy.'

Louise stretched her hand out to the child but Charlene shrank away from her.

Louise sat back on her heels and turned to look at Billy who was curled into a tight ball at the end of the sofa, his knees tucked under his chin. He returned her gaze but pulled the blanket closer and rammed a thumb into his mouth. 'You know it makes sense, really,' she murmured.

Charlene glanced at Billy and looked away again. 'How will Mum know where we are?' The slump of her shoulders and the tiredness in her voice signalled her defeat.

'I'll leave her a note.' Louise tore a page out of her notebook. 'Look, I'll write out an address so she'll know where you are, and she'll be able to come and see that you're all right.' Louise was careful not to say that her mum could take her home again, because it wasn't going to be that easy. Charlene's mum was going to have a lot of explaining to do before that could happen. She finished scribbling and looked around. 'Now,' she said. 'Where d'you think the best place is to leave it?'

Charlene nodded towards the table and, rising to her feet, Louise placed the note face upwards so it could be seen. It wafted onto the floor as one of the policemen opened the door. Louise grabbed it and anchored it with a dirty mug.

She turned to Charlene. 'Will that do?' The child hesitated a moment and then nodded. 'That's settled then, but you're both going to need some clothes. Just enough to do you until your mum comes. D'you want to take Jerry,' she'd just remembered the social worker's name, 'through to the bedroom and show him where things are?'

Louise waited until they left the room before turning to the constable. 'Well, what did you find out?'

'Mum's name is Kara Ferguson. She has a boyfriend, his name's Kevin, no one seems to know his last name. He hasn't been seen for the last few days, but apparently that's not unusual. He comes and goes.' The constable turned a page in his notebook. 'Mrs Stewart says she thinks the two men were looking for Kara Ferguson and that they were here earlier, too, about eight o'clock or thereabouts last night. She thought they'd threatened Miss Ferguson. She said: "They grabbed Kara by the throat and swung her like a cat until she squeaked".' He closed the notebook. 'That's about all Mrs Stewart will tell us. She doesn't know when Miss Ferguson went out, but she wasn't very forthcoming and I suspect she knows more than she's saying.'

'Is it OK if we go now? The boss is getting fidgety.' There was a mute plea in the young constable's eyes. It was obvious he followed his older colleague's lead and both of them had made it plain they thought they would be better employed elsewhere.

Louise had a moment's pity for the young man. He probably hadn't been in the force very long and was unsure whose orders he should follow. 'Not yet,' she said, smiling at him. 'I'll need one of you to drive my car when we take the kids to the foster home.'

The PC shuffled his feet. 'I'd better let the boss know.' His tone of voice indicated that 'the boss' wouldn't be pleased.

'Yes, you do that.' Louise was already walking to the bedroom door. Pushing it open, she said, 'Are we ready?'

Jerry was on his knees while Charlene stood beside him, watching. He lifted a pair of small denim jeans, folded them and laid them on top of the clothes in the black bag. 'Charlene's made sure I haven't forgotten anything. Isn't that right, princess?' He ruffled her hair and grinned at her. She didn't move away. 'So, providing Charlene's happy, that's us ready.' He tied a loose knot in the polythene bag and, pushing himself up, held his hand out to Charlene. She considered for a moment and then slotted her hand into his.

Louise hid a smile as she turned away. Jerry seemed to have carved a chink out of Charlene's armour and Louise knew better than to try to interfere. 'I'll just get Billy then, and we'll go.'

Billy hadn't moved from his huddled position at the end of the sofa. His eyes were closed and his thumb stuck firmly in his mouth. Louise bent over and scooped him into her arms. 'It'll be easier if I carry him,' she said, looking over her shoulder to Charlene. 'He's almost sleeping.'

Billy threw his arms round Louise's neck. His thumb and sleeve, still wet from constant sucking, pressed damply on her skin, but she didn't mind. There was something comforting in holding a child in her arms, his head and chin tucked into her neck and his breath blowing warmly under her chin.

As Jerry drove out of the street they passed an abandoned car with broken side windows. Louise glanced at it briefly and was glad she wasn't going to have to leave her own car here to take its chances.

13

'They've taken the kids.' Phil glanced at Gus, not sure if he was sleeping or just had his eyes closed.

'Pity,' Gus said.

'You're a real bastard.'

'Yeah? Well, I learned it from you, mate. Anyway, that's what Tony pays us for.'

Phil tore the paper off a stick of chewing gum. 'Want some?'

'Yeah, go on. It'll help keep me awake.'

Phil blew a gum bubble. 'Wonder how long she'll be?' He peered round the side of the van.

'You sure she'll come home? I wouldn't if it was me.'

'She'll come for the kids.'

'I wouldn't risk it for those snotty kids.'

'I know *you* wouldn't, but you're not a mum, are you? Now shut up, and keep your eyes peeled.'

'This is it,' Jerry said. The car shuddered to a stop in front of the third house in a row of identical council houses each one with a small patch of garden behind an iron fence and a path leading to the front door. It was a tidy council estate, not like the one they'd just left. The gardens looked well cared for, the curtains clean and the doors and windows gave the impression they'd been freshly painted.

He looked at Louise who was bent forward trying to free herself from Billy's stranglehold on her neck. The child whimpered, digging his face into her shoulder and she had to struggle out of the car still holding him.

Jerry smiled sympathetically. He'd had no trouble with Charlene although she now stood sullenly with her hand in his.

It was small and warm, and he squeezed it to reassure her she'd be all right.

The black, wrought-iron gate creaked slightly as he pushed it open. 'You'll like Annie,' he said, nodding his head and smiling at Charlene. 'She'll probably have some tea brewing and I wouldn't be surprised if she had rolls ready to eat with lovely crispy bacon straight out of the frying pan.' He rambled on as he led the child to the door of the house. 'How d'you fancy a bacon roll for breakfast then? I bet that'd be a treat.' He grinned at Charlene but the child just shrugged her shoulders and looked at her feet.

Louise followed him with Billy clinging tightly round her neck. Poor wee thing, Jerry thought, he was probably terrified. But he'd be all right here. Louise looked as if she was handling him well though. She was the kind of woman any child would want to be his mother. Calm and capable, and, if he was any judge of character, loving.

The house door opened before they reached it. 'I've been looking out for you.' The woman who spoke was small and round with ample breasts that seemed overlarge for her body. Her face was creased with laughter lines and her eyes had a kindly gleam. 'This'll be the bairns then. Just bring them away in and I'll soon get them settled.'

Louise lowered herself onto the sofa in the too tidy lounge and tried to detach Billy's arms from her neck. Jerry moved forward to help her but Annie got there before him.

'Here, let me help you.' Annie gently prised Billy's fingers apart and peeled him off Louise's shoulder. 'Come and see your Auntie Annie,' she murmured to the child, rocking him in her arms.

Charlene came out from behind Jerry's legs. 'Leave Billy alone,' she shouted.

'Hush,' Jerry laid his hand on Charlene's shoulder. The child was shaking, and he wanted to pick her up and reassure her that everything would be all right and she was better off here than back home. But you weren't supposed to touch kids more than absolutely necessary these days, so he held back. 'Annie's only going to look after you and Billy until we can find your mum. That's right, isn't it, Annie?'

'That's right, and I've got breakfast ready for you. Aren't you hungry?'

'No. Don't want your breakfast. And you're not our auntie.'

'No, I'm not your auntie, but I can look after you for your mum.' Annie smiled down at the angry child. 'And, even if you're not hungry, what about Billy? I'm sure he'd like a bit of something.'

Louise rubbed her neck. Her face was flushed from the exertion of holding Billy. She was the gentlest policewoman Jerry had come across so far and, although he had never known his mother, he was sure she would have been just like Louise.

'It's best you don't stay too long,' Annie said, ushering them through the hall towards the front door. 'The kids'll be all right once you've gone.'

'You sure?' Louise glanced at Charlene. 'She doesn't look too happy.'

'I've looked after worse,' Annie said. 'Believe me, I know what I'm doing.'

The door closed and Jerry could sense that Louise was feeling she was deserting the children.

Jerry glanced at her, wanting to comfort her. 'Don't feel bad about it,' he said, concentrating on unlocking the car. 'They'll be better off here. I mean, what kind of life would they have with a mother who left them on their own all night?'

Louise nodded, but she didn't seem convinced.

The sound of kids squabbling forced its way through the curtain of sleep that held Kara in its folds. She fought her way back to consciousness, but she couldn't think where she was. It was several moments before memories began to flood back. The man in the woods. Phil and Gus. She shuddered. She knew she'd have to move but it was an effort. Only the thought of Charlene and Billy, alone in the flat, prompted her to leave the car.

She clung to the car door until the feeling started to creep back into her feet and the world stopped swaying. She tried a few tentative steps. They hurt. She tried a few more. They hurt even worse. A youth clattered down the stairs on the opposite side of the road. She turned away before he recognised her. She would be just as visible to anyone watching as Darren Stewart had been to her and, because her flat was the last one on the landing, she risked being cornered. She turned her back on her own stairwell and walked round the corner of the block to the next set of stairs.

The stairs were the worst bit but she hauled herself up by the railing, hand over hand, until she reached the top. She scuttled the remaining few yards and threw herself into the safety of her hallway. She lay on the floor panting, unable to understand why the door was open. Pulling herself up she tried to close it. That was when she noticed the burst lock, and that it was hanging by one hinge.

Kara hadn't been aware she was holding her breath until she let it out in a sharp burst, 'Charlene! Billy!' She ran into the living room. The bedroom. The kitchen. The bathroom. No one.

She sank to her knees and sobbed. Where were they? She scrubbed her eyes with the back of her hand. The bare floorboards dug into her knees and she collapsed back, resting her weight on her heels. Suddenly everything was too much. She wanted to lie down. She wanted to sleep. But the only thing she could think of was that Phil and Gus must have taken Billy and Charlene.

14

Bill woke early, panting, sweating, and unable to recall the nightmare that had disturbed his sleep. He wriggled his head on the damp pillow and plucked, with slippery fingers, at the sheet which had wound itself round his body in a stranglehold. His brain felt fuzzy, the after-effects of a night on the booze; except he hadn't been boozing last night. He'd been working, although he was struggling to remember much after the collar at the bus station. He must have been tired though, too tired to take his clothes off at any rate.

He kicked the sheet onto the floor. The street light must have gone out for there wasn't even a glimmer showing through the glass. No moon, no stars, just darkness. There was something about the depth of the blackness, something oppressive and solid that was unlike the early morning dark. Something that had the smell of fear attached to it. But what did he have to be afraid of?

Blind men didn't need to see to know where everything was, nor did he. The crack in the ceiling rosette was just up there, over the bottom of the bed; someday the crack would separate and the whole structure would fall, crash onto the floor into tiny pieces. If he turned his head to the left he'd see the spider's web dangling in the corner like lace curtains, daily growing larger, snaring the unwary fly in its depths. Sometimes he felt like the spider, sometimes the fly, but always that his life was spinning out of control. There was neglect everywhere. The wallpaper was growing a black mould and damp patches bubbled outwards where the water from a leaking pipe had soaked it. Even the untidy heaps of discarded clothing on the floor illustrated the lethargy that had overtaken him.

It seemed as if he'd always been like this and he no longer

knew when his habit of waking up in the early hours started. Tossing and turning until his alarm clock rang, forcing him to roll out of bed because he knew if he sat up to switch it off he would lie down again and sleep forever. He closed his eyes, but he knew he wouldn't sleep. And even if he did sleep there would be dreams – nightmares from which he sometimes woke up screaming, although he had no memory of what had terrified him.

Maybe if Julie hadn't gone back to Edinburgh he would have been happier. He could still see her standing on the station platform, saying, 'It's too soon, Bill. I'm not ready. We have to give it time.' But then there was nothing. No phone calls or letters. Nothing. And Bill hadn't been able to summon up enough courage to phone her. Before Evie left him he'd been able to relate to women. But not now.

It had been stupid to become attached to Julie in such a short time, particularly so soon after his marriage broke down. Evie. So beautiful it'd made him catch his breath the first time he'd seen her. He hadn't believed his luck when she married him. He'd thought he'd stolen an angel but instead he got a world-class bitch. What a fool she'd taken him for. She'd cheated him and lied to him. Treated him like the idiot he was. And even then he'd cried when she left. He had been foolish enough to think Julie was interested in him after that. After all, what woman would want to tie herself to a burnt-out cop with no ambition? A has-been, past his sell-by date. No wonder she'd run off.

And now, he felt nothing. No love, no lust, no affection for anyone, especially not himself. He was a shell, barely functioning. How long would it be before he screwed up on the job?

'C'mon, I'll take you back to your office.' Jerry's hand collided with Louise's as he reached out to open the car door for her. He felt heat rise into his cheeks and knew he was blushing. He snatched his hand back. 'Sorry,' he said, 'but one's social training will out.' He bit his lip and, turning his back on her, walked round the car to the driver's side.

'I should be the one to say sorry,' Louise murmured. 'It's been a long time since someone opened a car door for me, and there comes a time when you don't expect it anymore.'

He sneaked a glance at her as he turned the key in the ignition. She was staring out of the side window at the closed door of the Phillips' home. 'They'll be all right,' he said. 'I've known Annie for a long time and she knows how to look after kids when they're hurting.'

'I suppose,' she said, settling back into the seat. Her brown ponytail swung as her head turned and Jerry wondered what her hair would look like if she untied it.

The heat was building in his cheeks again and, not wanting to draw attention to it, Jerry pushed the car into first gear and drove off.

At first the silence between them was a relief, but then Jerry started to worry. He wanted to chat, but didn't know what to say. Strange really, he always knew what to say to kids, but was tongue-tied when he wanted to make small talk with the opposite sex. It was even worse when he was attracted to one of them, and he'd been attracted to Louise as soon as he'd seen her.

He concentrated on his driving but could sense she was looking at him. It was as if she knew what he was thinking, making him even more self-conscious. Finally she said, 'So, how long have you been in social work?' He knew the remark meant nothing. It was simply something to break the silence.

'Almost sixteen years. It seems like a lifetime.' The sweat gathered beneath his collar. He wanted to tell her what it was really like in social work. The terrible things he'd seen. The awful people he had to work with. How all of it had made him lose his faith in most human beings. 'I wanted to help people, you see. I wanted to change the world.' He knew it sounded trite and silly, but it was the truth. He'd been such an idealist when he was twenty-three, and even now he wasn't sure when he'd started to become cynical.

'I suppose that's what we all want.' Her voice was thoughtful and her eyes crinkled at the corners when she turned to smile at him. 'You shouldn't be ashamed of it.'

He steered into the car park beside the police station and wished the journey hadn't ended.

She slid out of the car and, pausing for a moment with her hand on the door, said, 'I'll probably see you at the case conference.'

The urge to follow her was strong but he'd been away from his office too long, and Jerry knew his controller would be waiting for him. Geordie Hamilton was the night duty controller and he liked to get finished before nine o'clock, so any worker returning after that could be sure of a bollocking. Jerry swung the car out of the car park, already thinking about what he would put in his report.

Charlene wormed her body further into the corner of the sofa and buried her chin in the cushion she'd pulled in front of her. Her hair flopped over her face so that the woman called Annie couldn't see the tears sliding down her cheeks. Billy was gone. Eating cornflakes in the kitchen, Annie had said, but Charlene didn't believe her. Anyway she'd no right to take Billy away. He was Charlene's brother and he needed her to look after him.

Charlene looked at Annie through the strands of her hair. The woman was fatter than anyone Charlene had ever seen, even Bella from next door, and she puffed as she bent down to pick newspapers off the floor.

Without looking up, Annie said, 'There's cornflakes in the kitchen, and I can make you a bacon roll.'

Heavy footsteps sounded on the stairs. 'More kids, Annie?' The voice sounded gravelly, like Kev's after he'd been smoking.

Charlene's eyes widened and she shivered. She'd never been so frightened in her life. She peeked through her fringe at the man standing in the door. He was the biggest man she'd ever seen. A giant, with his head touching the top of the doorframe and his arms touching its sides. He had a big belly that hung over the top of his trousers, red, bleary eyes and a stubbly chin.

'You haven't slept long,' Annie said. 'You look exhausted.'

The man grunted. 'Who can sleep with the rumpus that was going on down here? I'll catch up later.'

'You need to give up the night work.'

'Make more money on nights. I'd be daft to give it up. Besides there's too many taxis on the go during the day.' He scratched his belly and yawned. 'What's up with madam on the sofa? Does she not want any breakfast?'

'Give her time. She'll come round.' Annie placed the pile of newspapers on the rack under the coffee table. 'Won't you, pet?' She sat down beside Charlene on the sofa.

Charlene tried to squeeze herself further into the corner but her back was already hard against the fabric and there was nowhere else to go. She pushed her head deeper into the cushion. She wanted her mum but her mum wouldn't know how to find her. They'd said they would leave her mum a note but they were cops and she didn't believe them. Cops never did anything nice. A sob trembled on Charlene's lips.

The whispers had deserted him. He had heard nothing since last night. Maybe the trees were angry. They had never been angry with him before. They had been his friends for most of his life. The only friends he had.

Last summer they asked him to bring them a spirit to join them. He had seen the girl in a nightclub. She was dancing, like the leaves on the trees danced. And he knew she was the one. She was the first.

She went with him willingly. Entered the woods willingly. He had watched her soul leave her body.

The trees had been pleased.

15

Mark Gordon's spirits sank as he drove through the streets of the Greenfield estate. The gaunt, flat-roofed tenement buildings that looked like barracks, with their endless concrete walkways and ugly graffiti, depressed him. It was enough to get anyone down. Maybe he'd try for one of the hospital jobs that the grapevine said were coming up. It must be nice to work in surroundings where there was little danger of being spat at or getting your car vandalised, where the clients would be grateful for your intervention. Not like the neds on the estate who'd probably stick a knife in your ribs if you looked at them sideways. There were some people you just couldn't help.

He guided the car into the steel-fenced compound. Even this early the car park was full. To tell the truth he couldn't remember a time when it had been empty. Sighing, he considered whether to park on the street or block someone in. It didn't take too much thought before he parked behind an elderly Volvo.

His foot crunched on a beer can, flattening it and spurting its last dregs on his trouser hems. Snorting with annoyance he kicked it under the Volvo before striding towards the two-storey box that was the area social work office. He clattered through the door, shouted a greeting to the girls in reception, keyed in the access code to the inner door and galloped up the stairs before they could waylay him with any messages.

Striding along the corridor to the tiny office, which he shared with two other workers, he threw his briefcase onto the already cluttered desk, grabbed his Superman mug, still brown with the dregs of yesterday's tea, and headed for the little kitchen at the end of the corridor. He swilled the cup under the tap, running his fingers round the inside to rid it of the worst stains, bunged a teabag in and filled it with hot water from the geyser. Mark would have preferred to boil a kettle but they weren't allowed to do that anymore. A safety hazard, management said, quoting Health and Safety guidelines, but nothing could convince Mark that the water from the geyser was boiling. Too many bloody guidelines nowadays, he thought. Guidelines for this, guidelines for that. You couldn't do anything without breaching some guideline or other. Why couldn't they just let them get on with the job like they used to?

He slurped a mouthful of tea. If he hurried he could get some phoning done before the morning's allocation meeting.

Several heads turned and looked at him as he slipped into the meeting room half an hour later. He smiled, nodded a greeting and headed for a chair in the corner.

'Glad you could join us, Mark.'

For a moment he thought there was a note of sarcasm in Irene's voice but put it down to his own guilt complex at ducking referrals. Irene was too new, too young and too inexperienced as a senior social worker to risk getting on his wrong side. After all, he was the longest serving social worker in this office. She wouldn't want to offend him.

He forced another smile. 'I'm not too late, am I?' Someone in the room sniggered but he ignored it.

'Almost, but not quite,' Irene said. She smiled at him. 'We all know you wouldn't want to miss out so we've saved one for you.' She picked up several sheets of pink paper. 'Out of hours were busy last night and I've allocated everything but this one. It's just the kind of case you like. Two children left alone in a dilapidated flat – signs of violence from an external source – missing mum – children placed with foster carers in Charleston. It needs to be followed up right away.' She handed the papers to Nicky Shanks who was sitting next to her. 'Pass these along to Mark.' She smiled in his direction. 'Let me know as soon as you've arranged the case conference. Remember it has to be within three days.' She picked up her diary. 'Meeting's closed,' she said, and left the room.

Back in his office, Mark threw the referral sheets onto his

desk. 'Damn,' he said. 'I had stuff arranged for today.'

Nicky Shanks, who shared the office with him, raised her head from the case paper she was reading. 'I know, but that's why we're here. You'd hate a nine-to-five job, doing the same things day in and day out.'

'There's a limit, though. I've got all these child protection cases, and you know what it's like, one slip up and you're plastered all over the *Sun* and the *News of the World*. If there's one thing I don't need, it's more kids.' He started to read the referral. 'It's all very well for out of hours. They just sort out the immediate crisis and make sure the kids are safe. They don't have to follow it through to the bitter end.'

'Oh, stop moaning,' Nicky snapped. 'We've all got a full case load. You don't have the monopoly on the difficult stuff, you know.'

Mark looked up in surprise. Nicky was usually even-tempered. 'Sorry,' he mumbled.

'Yeah, OK,' Nicky said. 'I'll leave you to it then. I've got visits to do.'

Mark opened his diary, crossed off several entries and moved them on a couple of days. If he had to follow up this referral there wouldn't be time for anything else today. There'd be a conference to arrange. He'd have to see the kids, interview neighbours, talk to the police and all the multitude of things that needed to be done when kids come into care.

First things first, he thought, as he reached for the phone. Knowing what the police had found out would save time. Anyway, it had been a long time since he'd talked to Louise; he hadn't seen hide nor hair of her since she'd dumped him. Maybe he could persuade her to visit the estate with him so he could try to suss out where to find the kids' mum. It was worth a try.

He smiled as he dialled. Maybe following up this referral wasn't going to be so bad after all. 'Louise. How nice to hear your voice again.' Mark balanced the phone between his shoulder and ear while he pushed the door shut with his foot. With a bit of luck he'd be able to sweet talk her into a drink or two and he didn't want the whole office listening in.

There was an instance of silence followed by a sharp intake of breath. 'What d'you want, Mark?'

'I thought you'd be pleased to hear from me.'

'After all this time? What is it now, three months? You must be joking. We've said all we have to say to each other, so just piss off, Mark.'

'Wait! Don't hang up. This is a professional call.'

'Could have fooled me.'

The phone slipped from Mark's shoulder and he grabbed it before it fell. 'It's about those kids you picked up last night.'

'What kids would that be?'

Mark sighed. Louise's tone had stiffened into her policewoman's official voice. Oh, well. It was just going to take a little bit longer to soften her up.

'Don't be daft, Louise. You know the kids I mean, Charlene and Billy Ferguson.'

'Of course I know the kids you mean, but if you want professional information then ask for it in the proper manner.'

'Just tell me the details, will you? I've got to follow it up.'

'Lucky you,' Louise said.

Mark scribbled on a piece of paper as Louise talked. 'That's fine,' he said, when she finished. 'I don't suppose you'd consider coming to the flat with me to see if the mum's returned.'

Louise guffawed into the phone. 'Since when has that been official procedure,' she said, slamming the phone down.

'Well, thanks anyway,' Mark said, staring unseeingly at the receiver. He could tell it was going to be one of those days.

16

Wind rustled into the room, wafting its way under the sofa, puffing cold air and dust motes over her legs. Kara squeezed her eyelids shut, knowing the door must be open now. Tears trickled between her fingers. She knew what she had to do, but it wasn't easy.

'Don't hurt them,' she whispered, afraid to lift her face from her hands.

Footsteps shuffled over the floor. 'For why would I?' Although the voice was deep it was undeniably female.

Kara raised her face from the safe haven of her hands. 'Bella? Oh shit, Bella! I thought Phil and Gus had come back.'

Bella shuffled her slipper-clad feet on the wooden floor. 'Aye, well, I know you don't like me to interfere, but I thought you should know, those two tough guys who were here last night, well, my Darren's just seen them in the car park. Watching for you I should imagine.' She shuffled her feet again. 'I don't want a stooshie like last night, so I thought maybe you'd like to come next door with me for a spell. I'll no' tell them you're here.'

Kara struggled to stand up. 'That's awful good of you, Bella, but I can't. They've got my kids, so I'll have to go and see them even if it means they kill me.'

Bella humphed. 'They don't have your kids. The welfare took them early this morning, so there's nothing stopping you coming with me. And if I were you, I'd put a step in it before those bastards come back.'

Relief poured through Kara's body flooding her veins with warmth. Phil and Gus didn't have Billy and Charlene, but then something else hit her like a slap on the face. The welfare had them. Something she'd always dreaded. When the welfare took your kids you were lucky to get them back again, ever.

Her body sagged against the sofa as the warm feeling seeped out of her to be replaced by icy dread.

'Hurry up, lass,' Bella hissed, 'you can't stay here much longer.'

'OK, Bella,' she said, 'but if you don't mind, I'll grab some clean clothes first.' She sidled round the side of the sofa and walked across the room. 'I'll just get them from the bedroom.'

'You look a mess, Kara. Good job my electric meter's not run out of money. There'll be enough hot water to get you cleaned up. Darren'll get me more electricity cards when he's out. I can let you have some anytime. He knows where to get a supply. Don't cost him anything.' Bella placed a finger on the side of her nose and winked.

Kara stopped in the doorway, fighting back the tears that threatened to overwhelm her. She'd never even passed the time of day with her neighbour before, afraid to encourage her because the police were never off her doorstep. She'd always considered herself better than Bella and her family of wild sons and her creepy husband. And here she was, offering to help Kara, when she needed it most. 'Thanks, Bella. I won't forget it,' she choked, and turned into the bedroom.

Bella followed her. 'Better hurry,' she said. 'Those two in the car park could take it into their heads to come up here, and I don't want them turning on me. Not when my James is in Perth Prison and not here to protect me.'

Kara grabbed a hooded jacket, a pair of denim jeans and her favourite sweatshirt from the heap of clothes on the chair. 'Here, hold these,' she thrust them into Bella's arms. 'I think my trainers are under the bed.' She fished one shoe out. 'Oh, where's the other one?' She dropped onto her stomach and crawled further under the bed, extending her arms as far as possible. There was something right at the back, against the wall, just out of reach. Her fingers slid over the surface of the toe. The sagging spring gouged her back as she pushed further underneath the old-fashioned bed. She prodded the toe of the shoe, edging it nearer, until she was able to grasp it with two fingers. Wriggling backwards she emerged, coughing and sneezing the dust from her throat and nose. She flapped at the shoe with an old sock to remove the dust.

'Hurry,' Bella said, shuffling her feet in her agitation and looking back at the landing.

'Shit, they're not coming, are they?' Kara shoved the shoes at Bella. Panicking she grabbed a duffle bag and stuffed some underwear into it. 'Come on, let's get out of here.' She pushed Bella out of the room and down the hall.

'Hot cup of tea, that's what you need. Then into the shower with you and get some of that muck off.' Bella led the way into the cluttered kitchen.

'Nice place you've got here,' said Kara, looking round. She'd already noticed the thick carpet in the hallway. But the kitchen astonished her. It contained every gadget she could think of: fitted cupboards all round, like the fancy show houses on private estates; de luxe electric cooker with spaceship-type controls; the latest model microwave oven; blender; mixer; liquidiser; electronic scales and much more besides.

'Yeah,' Bella said, 'my James and Darren see I don't go short. If I fancy anything they go out and get it for me. They're good to me so they are.' She poured hot water from the kettle into the teapot, stirred it with a spoon, and then filled a china mug with the brew. 'Get that down your throat, lass. Then you can tell me what's happened and why those guys are looking for you.'

The tea scalded Kara's tongue and throat. Her stomach growled a protest, reminding her she hadn't eaten for a long time. Looking longingly at the shiny toaster she wondered whether or not to ask Bella for something to eat. However, empty cupboards were commonplace on the Greenfield estate and she didn't want to embarrass her neighbour in case she had no bread in the house.

Bella watched her as she drank the tea. 'You don't really belong on this estate, do you, lass?' She scratched her cheek with fingernails that had been bitten to the quick. 'I can tell by the way you talk and the way you hold yourself. You don't have that downtrodden look most of the lassies round here have.'

'I'm just as hard up as any of them,' Kara said, staring into her cup. 'I need somewhere to live and where else can you go except where the housing department send you.'

'Sure, but I can tell it's not what you've been used to.' Bella looked at her. 'Not that I hold it against you, like.'

Kara sighed, thinking of the Spanish hacienda that had been her home before her mother had brought her back to Dundee when she was fourteen. Some mother she was, Kara thought bitterly, couldn't get her head out of a bottle long enough to remember she had a daughter. 'I'm no different from you, Bella, and I'm not sure I have as big a heart as you have.'

'Aye, well, if a body can't help their neighbour it's a bad day, and what someone is or isn't doesn't matter in the long run,' Bella said.

Kara gulped the last of her tea. 'I won't forget this, Bella.'

'Aye, well, you'd better get cleaned up now. You can have a bath or a shower, please yourself, and I'll get you a clean towel. That Darren of mine's a mucky pup, always leaving his dirt on the towel instead of the sink.'

Phil woke with a start. He was so cold he couldn't feel his feet or hands, and he had a crick in his neck. Beside him, Gus snored, the air puffing out of his mouth in short, misty bursts.

'Hey!' he said, poking his finger into his partner's ribs. 'You're supposed to be on lookout, not snoring your head off.' He scowled as he flapped his hands on his legs and stamped his feet, trying to bring the circulation back.

'What!' Gus sat up. 'I wasn't sleeping.'

'Like hell you weren't.' He checked his watch. 'Fuck, she could have come back while you were out for the count.' He pushed himself out of the car, stamping his feet on the wet ground.

'I'm not the only one here,' Gus grumbled, coming to stand

beside him.

'I know! I know! But you were the one on watch.'

'Can't see a fucking thing anyway, it's too dark. You wouldn't think it was the middle of the morning.'

'Fucking light's gone out at that end of the landing. It was on last night.'

'Could be a coincidence.'

'No way. She's probably come back.' Phil spat out his wad of chewing gum. 'Come on, we'd better check.'

The flat was silent and dark. The two men checked every room but it was also quite, quite empty.

'Fuck it,' Phil said, aiming a kick at a chair. 'She's either not been here, or we've missed her.' He kicked the chair again, grinning as it splintered and broke. He felt the familiar high surging through him. He'd felt like this as a kid when he spraypainted graffiti and kicked windows in. Grabbing ornaments and pictures, he smashed them on the floor, put his foot through the television screen and overturned the sofa.

Gus leaned against the doorframe. 'Having fun?'

Phil kicked the sofa once more for the sheer hell of it, and said, 'That's better. Now we need to find out about Kara. I think we go next door and ask if they've seen her. We might get lucky.'

Kara turned her face up under the shower-head letting the hot water stream through her filthy hair and down her body. It was sheer bliss.

The bathroom door opened and Darren was shoved inside. At the same time a towel was lobbed into the shower cubicle. Kara grabbed it and, turning off the water, wrapped it round her body. Thankfully it was a big bath sheet. Bella hovered outside the cubicle for a moment. 'Don't worry Kara, lass,' she said. 'I've warned him that if he touches you I'll cut off his goolies.' The door slammed shut.

'What the hell,' Kara gasped, heading for the door.

Darren grabbed her wrist. 'Stay here,' he hissed, 'and keep quiet. Phil and Gus are at the door. Ma says I have to be in here so they can't get in to look for you.'

'Oh, shit!' Kara said, not knowing whether to be more alarmed about Phil and Gus, or Darren who had a hard grip on her wrist.

The whispering buzzed in his brain like angry bees in a hive. He could sense the agitation but could not decipher the words. They swirled round and round making no sense.

The trees were angry. He would have to pacify them. Find them another soul. But it had to be of their choosing. And how could he choose if he could not hear?

He had found them three souls since last summer. The first was the dancer, the second a girl from the streets, and the third from the Hogmanay party in City Square. The times between them were becoming shorter. It was only nine days since the last one.

The trees were becoming impatient, their whispers more insistent.

17

The detectives' room was usually quiet when Bill arrived, but today he was late and too tired to care. There was a headache building behind his eyes and a tightness gripping his forehead. He paused with his hand on the doorknob while the sudden assault of voices and ringing phones beat a tattoo in his head. He closed his eyes to blot out the glare of the fluorescent lights. Coming in had been a mistake.

'You look like shit.'

Another second and he'd have succumbed to the temptation to slink off, but already it was too late.

'I *feel* like shit.' Bill didn't need Sue to remind him he hadn't shaved and was wearing yesterday's shirt – the one he'd slept in. He adjusted the knot in his tie, pulling his collar closer to his neck so the grubby line wouldn't be so noticeable. Avoiding Sue's eyes, he shuffled over to his desk, threw his jacket onto the back of the chair, and slumped into the seat.

Sue followed him. She hovered for a moment as if undecided whether to say anything, before perching her bottom on the edge of his desk. 'Anything I can do to help?' The worried tone of her voice reached out to him, wrapping him in its tentacles, making him squirm.

'Not unless you want to wash a few shirts.' He tried to inject the old light-hearted note into his voice, but didn't quite succeed. 'I'm all right, Sue. Just tired. I didn't sleep too well last night. I'll be OK after a cup of coffee.'

'You sure? You don't look OK.'

'Yeah, I'm sure. What's going on anyway? The place is like a madhouse.'

'Hmm, it's no more of a madhouse than it usually is. I'd better get you that coffee.' Sue slid off the desk. 'How d'you want it?'

'Better make it black, with an aspirin or three on the side.'

Sue returned and placed a paper cup on the desk. 'Get that down you,' she said, 'and I'll update you on what's happening, so you don't look gormless when Andy comes looking. By the way, he thinks you've been downstairs following up on the anonymous call.'

Hot coffee splashed over Bill's fingers as he plonked the cup on the desk. 'What anonymous call?'

'Some woman phoned in at half past four this morning. Said she'd found some bodies in Templeton Woods.'

'And?'

'Said one of them was Denise Palmer.'

'And?'

'That's it. That's all she said, but the boss says we've got to follow it up.'

'It's probably just some nutter.'

'Yeah, but the phone box was checked. They found ripped fishnets, bloody footprints and smears of blood on the handset.'

Sue's voice faded in and out. Bill found it difficult to concentrate on what she was saying. A wave of nausea rose in his throat. He swallowed hard and wiped his fingers on his trouser leg. He felt he was in danger of losing it, but also knew he couldn't allow that to happen or he'd be as well just giving in now and signing on. 'So, what was I doing when I was downstairs?'

'You were organising the search party.' Sue grinned at him.

'I was?'

'Yeah, but don't worry. The search party's already started. I've seen to it all.'

'Searching those woods won't be easy. D'you know how big they are?'

'Thought we'd concentrate on the area nearest the phone box. A mile to each side of it to begin with. I've arranged searchers for the Camperdown side as well and hopefully they'll meet in the middle.'

'The middle of next month if you're lucky,' Bill grunted. Lifting his cup he swirled the remains of the coffee around before gulping it down. 'Why not take the credit for it yourself instead of helping me out?'

Sue shrugged. 'Maybe it's your bonnie, brown eyes that remind me of a collie dog I used to have, or maybe it's your sense of humour, although that's sadly lacking today, or maybe I just feel sorry for you because you're such a sad git. Whatever it is I wouldn't question it if I were you in case I change my mind.'

Bill's spirits lightened and he smiled. 'Don't know what I'd do without you, Sue. Mind telling me what we're going to do now?'

'Well, for a start you're going to get up off your arse and we're going to see how the search party's doing. At least that'll get you out in the fresh air instead of moping around here.'

Bill reached for his jacket and shrugged his arms into the sleeves. 'Templeton Woods . . . That was where they found the bodies of those other girls back in the seventies. They thought it was the Yorkshire Ripper, but it wasn't.'

'Before my time, I'm afraid.' Sue pulled his arm. 'What're you waiting for?'

It started to rain as Mark left the office and, swearing under his breath, he made a dash for the car. He hadn't wanted to take this case and it was only the thought of working with Louise that had made it more attractive. But she hadn't exactly been very forthcoming with information or chit chat.

Not wanting to walk too far in the pouring rain, he parked at the bottom of the stairs leading to Kara's flat. Sitting for a moment, with his hands resting on the steering wheel, he watched the rain stream down his windscreen. It wasn't a day for a dog to be out, he thought, resisting the temptation to drive off again. He'd better get it over with. At least it wouldn't take too long. Not unless Ms Ferguson had turned up, of course, in which case maybe he'd manage to close the case.

His feet clattered on the stone steps as he climbed up the dark tunnel of the stairwell. The smell of urine and cats and other unidentified odours hit him and he drew in his breath, holding it for as long as he could. There were no numbers on the doors at the top of the stairs and he hovered uncertainly for a moment before turning to his right. Two well-dressed men stood at the door of one flat talking to the householder and, as he approached them, they turned to stare at him. Mormons or insurance men, he thought, although once he was closer the dyed blond hair looked a bit out of place. 'Which flat's number fifty-eight?' He avoided looking at the men and concentrated on the large woman in the doorway.

'What d'you want there, then?' Her voice was belligerent.

'I'm looking for Kara Ferguson.'

'Everyone's looking for Kara.' Her eyes flickered towards the two men.

'Sorry.' He rummaged in his pocket. 'I should have shown some identification. I'm from social work and I really need to find her.'

'Look all you want, pal. That's her flat next door. She's not there.'

'Can I come and talk to you after I've checked? If you're not too busy with your friends, that is.'

'Friends!' The woman guffawed. 'They haven't found what they're looking for either, and they're just leaving. Isn't that right, boys?'

There was something in the men's eyes that made Mark uneasy, but it was none of his business what they wanted with the woman, so he turned away and strode along the landing.

The door to the flat hung lopsidedly from one hinge. Rain slanted in through the railings, lying in puddles on the landing and soaking the wooden hall floor. Mark hesitated at the doorway, debating whether he should go in or just leave. He knew if he went in he might be laying himself open to all sorts of allegations, but on the other hand there could be signs as to where he might find Kara Ferguson.

He went in.

The flat was a mess. Furniture upended. Upholstery ripped. Ornaments, pictures and toys broken and scattered over the floor. Mark supposed it was remotely possible Kara Ferguson lived like that, but he doubted it given the state of the front door.

He picked up a picture and, plucking the broken glass out of the frame, looked at it. It was a photo of a smiling girl with her arms round two kids. He slipped the picture into his pocket. The rest of the flat didn't hold any hints as to where he might find its tenant and he left, disappointed.

The two men had gone when he walked back along the landing, so he tapped at the door.

'Bella Stewart?'

The big woman folded her arms and glared at him. 'How come you know my name?' Her bulk took up most of the door, obstructing his view of the hall although he could hear water running in what he supposed must be the bathroom.

'I got your name from the police,' he said. 'I need to ask you some questions about your neighbour.'

'I've already had the police here, so you can ask them.' She moved back into the hall. Mark followed her so she couldn't shut the door.

'Yes, I know. But I thought maybe you might have remembered something else.' He smiled his most winsome smile. 'I really need to find her so she can get her children back home.'

Bella frowned. 'That's a likely tale. I never yet heard of social work giving the kids back just like that. Anyway, I don't know where she is. She went out last night and she didn't come back, and that's it. Now will you get off my bloody doorstep, there's a draught blowing in here like nothing on earth.'

'You sure that's all you know? Neighbours on this estate usually stick together. You sure she's not in there?' He nodded towards the bathroom door.

'Look,' Bella said, 'I don't even know my neighbours and particularly not Miss Snotty Nose next door. If you want to know who's in there, it's my Darren.' She thumped on the door. 'You going to be in there all day? Other folk might need in, you know.' A male grunt issued from within.

Kara shivered. The towel only just covered her and Darren Stewart stood between her and her clothes. A stupid smile touched the corner of his mouth as he leaned close to her, running his finger down her neck to the edge of the towel. Her muscles tensed but she was unable to do anything to stop him.

Without removing his finger, he shouted, 'Can't a man have a crap nowadays without somebody interfering?'

His mother shouted back, 'That'll be the day! When you're a man, sonny boy. So get your arse out of there.'

'Eff off,' he shouted. 'I'll come out when I'm ready and not before.'

His finger prodded the towel's edge and he turned to Kara, pulling her body close until she could feel the heat radiating from him. She bit her lip. As long as the social worker was at the door she daren't complain.

18

'We'll take my car,' Sue said, as the lift dropped to the ground floor.

'What's the matter, mine too messy for you?' Bill grumbled. The drilling sensation in his brain had eased a notch, but his temper hadn't improved.

The lift doors clanked open. Sue stepped out and strode along the empty corridor. Bill was in the mood for an argument but she hadn't taken the bait.

'What's the hurry? You afraid the search party's going to find something before you get there?'

'Oh, shut up, Bill.' There was a sparkle in her eyes that made Bill think she was laughing at him.

'What's so funny then?'

'Nothing. Only you can be a bit of a pain, you know.'

Bill grunted and followed her through the security door into the outer reception area. 'I'm not the only one who can be a pain.' He stopped at the entrance doors. 'You seen the weather out there? It's pissing down.'

'Just be thankful you're only co-ordinating the search party then, and don't have to go rummaging through the woods.'

Bill slumped in the passenger seat of Sue's smart, almost new Ford Fiesta and didn't mutter another word until they arrived at the marshalling point for the search.

'Bloody weather,' he muttered, pulling the hood of his waterproof jacket over his head and stepped out of the car into a puddle. He dug his hands into his pockets and shifted his feet out of the water. 'Hey, you!' he shouted to one of the uniforms. 'Who's in charge and what's happening?'

The PC looked at him. 'You joining the search or have you just come to ogle?'

'Careful, lad.' Sue emerged from the car. 'You're

addressing Detective Sergeant Murphy.'

'Oh, sorry, sir.' A red stain crept up the young constable's neck. 'Sergeant Johnstone is in charge. That's him over there.' He pointed in the direction of one of the police Land-Rovers.

Bill's shoes squelched as he walked over the grass. 'Hi, Jim, been a while since we talked.'

Sergeant Johnstone had aged since Bill last saw him and it was common knowledge he was marking time until his retirement. He leaned back in the driver's seat and looked past Bill into the woods. 'Shitty job this. The times I've been out here and nothing's there to be found.' He frowned, fingers drumming on the steering wheel. 'Damn it, I could do with a smoke.' He puckered his lips in a sucking motion as if tasting the stem of his pipe. 'You know what they call these woods now? The screaming woods, that's what. They say the ghosts of those two girls found in '79 and '80 are still here. Even the locals get the heebie-jeebies about Templeton Woods every now and then.'

'You think it's a wild goose chase?'

'I don't know, maybe there's something in it this time. The lads have found signs of a struggle and a woman's shoe at the other side of the woods. The Camperdown side. I've told them to bag it and set it aside for forensics.' He turned the key in the dashboard and revved the engine. 'I'm off there now. Want to come?'

'I suppose I'd better, seeing I'm supposed to be managing this circus.'

Bill watched Jim drive off then trudged back to the car expecting Sue to be waiting for him, but she wasn't. He spotted her at the edge of the woods talking to the young constable who'd put his foot in it when they'd arrived. A smile twitched at the corner of Bill's mouth as he remembered the poor guy's blush. Stupid bastard would think twice before he opened his mouth again.

Leaning over he pressed the car horn; he wasn't going to walk through the sodden grass again.

Sue looked round and waved but made no move to return. He leaned on the horn again. She laughed, waved, and then started to walk to the car.

'Took your time,' Bill grumbled.

'Just getting an update on where they're at. I'm glad I'm not part of that search party though, those woods are creepy.' She settled in the driver's seat. 'Are we going round the other side of the woods then?'

'I suppose your new conquest has told you they've found something.'

She started the engine, pulled the steering wheel hard to the right and without looking at him, said, 'You reckon a toyboy would do me good?' The car wheels spun on the mud. 'Maybe he'll give us a push.' She slid the car into second gear and the tyres gripped. 'Didn't need him after all.'

Several cars and vans lined Templeton Road. Sue pulled in behind the sergeant's Land-Rover, opened the door and got out.

Bill remained slumped in his seat.

'You coming?'

'I'm wet enough, I'll stay here for a while. Tell Jim to let me know if he finds anything.'

'OK,' she said, striding off into the clearing that led to the wilder part of the woods.

Bill watched her go. The skin on his forehead tightened and he closed his eyes hoping to dull the ache behind them. This was the exact spot he'd watched the search from when they'd found the first body back in 1979. He'd been ten, almost eleven, and he'd thrown his bike down on the grass verge before trying to sneak into the woods but he'd been spotted and told to stay on the road. He remembered the buzz of activity, the sounds of the searchers – he'd have given anything to be one of them then – and the mounting feeling of excitement.

'I'm not too young,' he'd protested to the policemen guarding the entrance to the woods, but they'd sent him packing with a 'Go home to your mammy, son'.

He hadn't gone home though. He'd stayed until they brought the body out. And then, the following year, he'd gone out to the woods with a gang of others and they'd found the second body before the police got wind of it. He'd never forgotten what he saw and the subsequent bad dreams had haunted him for most of his childhood.

He was on the verge of sleep when the tap on the window came. He prised his eyelids open and rolled the window down. 'What is it?'

'Sergeant Rogers said I should bring this to you, sir.'

Damn, all these young guys are starting to look the same, Bill thought.

'Lady's handbag, sir, lodged in a bush.' The man held up the evidence bag.

'Give it over, then.' Bill held out his hand.

The constable hesitated before saying, apologetically, 'It's evidence, sir.'

Bill tried to catch his eye but the constable was looking at his hand.

'Of course,' he muttered. He opened Sue's glove compartment and rummaged inside. She always had latex gloves. He fished a pair out and pulled them on. 'That better?'

'I didn't mean anything, sir,' the constable said, handing him the bag.

'That'll be all, constable. You can return to your duties now. I'll see forensics get this.'

'Yes, sir.'

Bill waited until the young PC was a few yards away before he opened the bag.

'Find anything interesting?' Sue said as she slid into the driver's seat.

Bill investigated in silence for a moment. Eventually he said, 'Comb, lipstick, paper hankies, mobile phone with no credit left, purse with £400 in it, ID inside says it belongs to Kara Ferguson, an address on the Greenfield estate.'

'Why would she abandon a handbag with that much money in it?' Sue mused.

'Maybe she didn't have much choice,' Bill said. 'Maybe she wasn't meant to come back out of the woods.'

'Do you think she's the one who phoned? Or d'you reckon she's still in there?' Sue shivered as she looked at the woods.

'Don't know,' Bill muttered. 'But one thing's for sure, I think we're going to find something this time.'

The front door slammed and then there was silence. Kara didn't know whether it meant the social worker had gone, or if Bella had let him in.

Her shoulders pressed hard into the tiled wall and her knee was jammed against the toilet bowl. Darren had her boxed in. The steam from the shower cooled and ran down the wall, trickling between her shoulder blades. His fingers probed at the top of the towel she'd wound tightly round her body. His breath was hot and sour.

Someone paused outside the bathroom door. Kara could hear breathing. She froze. Darren looked over his shoulder and both watched as the door handle turned.

'He's gone,' Bella shouted.

Kara breathed a sigh of relief and, letting go of her grasp on the towel, shoved Darren to the floor. 'Don't ever touch me again,' she hissed.

'What the hell's going on in there?' Bella thumped on the door. 'I'll have your guts for garters if you don't unlock this door right now, Darren.'

Bella scowled at him when he opened it and attempted to push past her. 'What'd I tell you about leaving Kara alone?' She slapped him round the head.

'I didn't do nothing.' Darren held his hands up to protect himself. 'Leave off, Ma.'

'Get out of my sight.'

Darren slunk off to his bedroom.

'Out you come, Kara, it's safe for now.' Bella entered the bathroom and picked up the wet towels. 'Best get some clothes on and then find somewhere safe to stay.'

'Thanks again, Bella, for everything you've done. Sorry I shoved Darren but I didn't know how else to get him off me.' Kara wasn't sorry at all but she owed Bella.

'Don't worry about that. He deserved it.' Bella put her arms round Kara and hugged her. 'You'd best get going.'

Kara dressed quickly and left the flat. Keeping her head down she headed downstairs, then strode purposefully away from the scheme towards the town centre, although she hadn't a clue where she was going.

19

Mark sat in his car watching the stairs.

He hadn't been convinced when Bella told him Kara Ferguson hadn't returned home. He still had his suspicions about who'd been in the shower. But what could he do? He wasn't the police. He didn't have the right to demand entry. Maybe if Louise had been with him it would have been different.

But if it had been Kara hiding in the shower she would want to leave soon so she wouldn't be caught, probably within the next half hour. She wouldn't want to hang around.

Half an hour later he turned the key in the ignition, blasted hot air on his windscreen to clear the mist, and drove off. By the time he reached the Phillips' house on the Charleston estate the rain had stopped and little patches of blue sky peeked through the dark clouds.

Annie smiled a welcome to him when she opened her door. 'I'm really glad it's you, Mark,' she said. 'There's so many new social workers nowadays you never know who's coming next.'

Grinning, Mark stepped inside.

'Right,' Annie said. 'You'll want to see Charlene and Billy, I suppose. But they're both in bed sleeping the excitement off.'

'I'll have a peek before I go. How've they settled in?'

Annie frowned. 'Billy's OK, he's a wee lamb. Put a stranglehold on my neck when he arrived and didn't want to let go. Charlene though, she's more independent and just wants her mum. Seems convinced we're baddies and had a screaming fit in the kitchen this morning when Stan tried to talk to her.'

'Poor kid's probably just scared. Give her time, she'll soon settle in.'

'I hope so,' Annie said.

It was afternoon before the search party found anything. The sandwich Bill had gulped for lunch sat in a lump somewhere between his stomach and his throat. Sitting hunched up wasn't helping the lump go away so it was a relief to get out of the car and stretch his legs.

'We've sent for the SOCOs,' the constable explained, 'but Sergeant Johnstone thought you might like to have a look before they arrive.'

Bill grimaced. Looking at dead bodies wasn't a part of the job he relished. Besides, this area of woodland was particularly wild and overgrown and he didn't fancy tramping through it. But the need to see the scene for himself overrode his reluctance, just as it had done all those years ago, and he followed the constable. It was just as he expected, gloomy and wet under the trees even though the day had brightened. His shoes were already sodden and drips fell from leaves and branches, finding their way under his collar and down his neck. He couldn't remember when he'd last felt so cold.

'Is that where the handbag was found?' Bill skirted a bush circled with blue and white tape.

'Yes, sir.' The constable continued on through the trees.

Bill was having difficulty pushing through the shrubbery and keeping up with the younger man. 'Where are we going?' he panted. 'Are we never going to get there?'

'Not far now, sir.'

The constable didn't seem to be having any bother with his breathing. He probably works out, Bill thought, not like us poor CID sods who never have enough time.

Bill almost careered into the constable's back when he stopped suddenly, in front of more blue tape. 'Here we are, sir. I won't go any further. Don't want to get a bollocking from the SOCOs.'

Bill looked at the bushes behind the tape. 'This it?'

'Yes, sir. You have to get down on your knees and crawl

through the bushes.'

Bill crawled through a leafy tunnel. The churned-up mud caked his hands and knees, and he was glad when he reached a circular clearing and was able to stand up again. Sue was already there.

He stood in silence for a moment. It was a bit like the last time he'd been in these woods, only this time there was more than one body. He felt the horror of it wash over him and for a moment he was eleven again. Struggling to regain his composure, he said, 'What do you make of it, Sue?'

'There are three bodies and they've been left at different times. Different degrees of decomposition. See that one over there, you can still see her features. I don't think she's been here very long.'

Bill pointed to the body. 'Anyone we know?'

He wasn't going to admit to Sue that he found the scene more disturbing than usual. She'd only start to wonder what was different about this one, considering some of the other horrific murder cases he'd been involved with.

'One of the constables thinks it's Tony Palmer's daughter. Says he'd seen her at one of her father's clubs, so maybe the caller wasn't joking after all.'

'Bloody hell. Palmer will go ballistic. If he gets his hands on the psycho who's done this, we can say goodbye to any chance of prosecution.'

'Look at her hands, Bill. She must have put up a struggle. The ropes have cut through to the bone.'

'Sick bastard. He left her here to die.' He clamped his lips shut against the bile rising from his stomach.

'Animals have had a field day as well. There are a lot of bite marks.'

Bill turned his back on the body, stepped over the tape and walked out of the clearing. 'I've seen enough,' he shouted to Sue. 'Let's leave it to the SOCOs now.'

'How long we going to sit here then?' Gus drummed his fingers.

It was almost midday. The early morning gloom had lifted and weak sunshine was brightening the day. The two men were tired, cold and fed up.

'As long as it takes, I suppose.' Phil's temper had deteriorated during the morning watch. 'We can't go back empty handed.'

Gus sighed, 'Yeah, I suppose, but she'd have been here by now if she was coming.'

Phil watched a stocky young man approach their car. Just a kid, he thought, when the youth drew nearer. Still, he looked as if he'd be able to handle himself.

'Looking for something?' Gus asked when the kid stopped at the open window.

'Depends,' the kid said, 'on what you want.'

'You trying to be funny? Because if you are, you've come to the wrong place.'

The youth bristled. 'I heard you were looking for Kara Ferguson and I live next door to her. But, if you don't want to know what I know . . .'

'Hang on.' Phil opened his car door and got out. 'Ignore him.' He walked round the car and laid a friendly hand on his arm. 'Is there something you wanted to help us with?'

'What's it worth?'

Phil pulled his wallet from his jacket pocket. 'A tenner do you?'

'Make it fifty and you're on.' His eyes were fixed on the wallet.

Phil riffled through the wad of paper money and watched the youth's eyes widen. 'It's a tenner or nothing,' he said softly. 'But there could be more if we find her. Or if you find her for us.'

'OK.' He grabbed at the ten-pound note but Phil pulled his hand back.

'Information first.'

'She was here just after nine o'clock, but she's gone now. Said she was going to look for her kids and she wouldn't be back.'

'That's not a lot of information for the money,' Phil said,

but he held out the ten-pound note.

The youth grabbed it and stuffed it into his pocket. 'I have the note the welfare left when they took the kids.' He handed it to Phil.

'That's no fucking help,' Phil said after reading it. 'It only says to get in touch with social work.' He replaced the wallet in his pocket.

'I can ask around and try to find her for you.'

'You do that, sonny. Here's my mobile number.' He handed over a card. 'Call me when you've got anything.'

'Will do,' he said, 'and if you've got any jobs going, Darren Stewart's the name.' He swaggered off, turning to wave as he left the car park.

Gus grinned when Phil got back in the car. 'Well, that wasn't worth a tenner.'

Phil laughed. 'Yeah, thinks he's quite the man, that one.' He started the car. 'At least we know she's been and gone. Tony's not going to like it though.'

20

Kara leaned on a pillar outside the courthouse. From where she stood she could see everyone who went in and, more importantly, everyone who came out.

The Custody Court was running late and she'd been here too long already, but Tommy thought she'd shopped him and after a night in the police cells he'd be furious. She had to talk to him.

She fidgeted, biting her lip and jiggling from foot to foot, fighting the panic bubbling inside her. What the hell was she doing here? It was risky, but she didn't have much choice if she wanted to talk to Tommy, make it all right with him. If she could convince him about last night, maybe he'd be able to sort it out with Phil and Gus so that all she'd have to worry about was finding their money.

Usually the steps leading to the courthouse were swarming with people. Today, because of the cold, most of them had pushed their way into the entry hall. Sharp-suited lawyers rubbed shoulders with petty criminals, and do-gooders served paper cups of tea to all and sundry.

A group of local lads clattered up the steps but they didn't look at her. Recognising three of them she turned away, hunching her shoulders and tucking her chin into the neck of the jacket. The woollen hat she wore pulled down over her ears covered her magenta-streaked hair, the jeans and trainers and the padded jacket disguised her shape. She hoped she looked like a boy.

She walked a few steps away from the pillar. How much longer would it be before Tommy came out? If indeed he did come out. She breathed deeply, praying that the sheriff wouldn't remand him to Perth Prison to await trial. He had to be bailed, he just had to be. He wasn't a bad man. OK, maybe he did do a bit of wheeling and dealing, and a drugs run every now and then, but that didn't make him a danger to society.

One of the court officers sidled out of the main door. He rummaged in his pocket and, after a quick glance over his shoulder, withdrew a packet of cigarettes. He was so focused on tapping one out he almost collided with Kara.

'Sorry, kid. Didn't see you there.' He leaned against the stone pillar, lit up and inhaled deeply. 'Ah, bliss.'

Kara considered moving away, but she didn't know the court officer and he didn't know her, so she stayed. 'How's the Custody Court doing?'

'Almost finished. Just one more case to go.' He blew a cloud of smoke into the air. 'It's freezing out here. You could wait inside, you know.'

'Nah, I'll stay here. I can't be doing with crowds.'

He threw the stub of the cigarette onto the ground and crushed it under his heel. 'I'd better get back before I'm missed.'

It was half an hour before Tommy sauntered through the doors and down the steps. Kara waited until she was sure he was alone before she followed. She caught up with him after he crossed the road and turned into North Lindsay Street.

'Wait a minute, Tommy.' She grasped the sleeve of his jacket.

'Shit, Kara. What're you doing here?' He shook her hand off his sleeve. 'Haven't you done enough damage?'

'I didn't shop you, Tommy.'

'Like fuck you didn't. If it hadn't been for you I wouldn't have landed up in there.' He nodded in the direction of the courthouse. 'I'm bound to get time,' he said angrily, 'the amount of stuff I was carrying.'

'But I didn't know. Honest, Tommy. You've got to make it all right with Phil and Gus.' Tears gathered in Kara's eyes.

'Why the hell should I? After what you did. I won't be forgetting that in a hurry.'

'But I didn't do anything. I really didn't. All I wanted was to talk to you, get a cup of tea.'

'You expect me to believe that?'

'Please, Tommy. It's really bad with Phil and Gus. You've got to help me.'

'Tough, Kara. I don't forget grasses.' He clenched his hand into a fist and raised it.

Kara flinched but didn't step back.

'Oh, fuck off, Kara.' Tommy lowered his fist and stomped off down the street.

'But I didn't do anything,' Kara screamed after him. She leaned against the wall, watching Tommy. It was hopeless.

'Any ideas?' Sue said after they left the clearing.

'Not one,' Bill muttered through clenched lips. 'Let's get out of this damnable place.' He hunched his shoulders, rammed his fists in his pockets, and pushed through the trees.

It seemed to take forever before they reached the road. Bill was not in the best of tempers when he spotted the reporter arguing with a police constable.

'What's up, constable?' Bill eyed the reporter.

'Says he's from the *Courier*, sir. He wants to go into the woods and photograph the crime scene.'

'So there is a crime scene.' The reporter's eyes glittered with triumph.

'No comment,' Bill said, 'and you know as well as I do that you can't interfere with a search party.'

'Is it true you've found bodies?'

'You'll have to wait for the press conference.'

The reporter smiled as if Bill had just told him something important. 'Is it true,' he continued 'that one of the bodies is Tony Palmer's daughter?'

'No comment,' Bill said. He wasn't any use at this PR stuff and just wished the reporter would go away. 'Take my advice, sonny. Don't interfere with an investigation or I'll have you for trying to pervert the course of justice.'

The reporter took a step backwards. 'Can I quote you?'

'No, you bloody well can't.' Bill turned away from the man before the temptation to punch him became too great.

'That went well,' Sue said as she followed him to the car.

'Sarcasm doesn't suit you,' Bill said. 'I can't stand these interfering bastards. Time after time they screw up investigations by jumping the gun. Anyway, how did he know about Tony Palmer's daughter?'

'Search me,' Sue said, looking thoughtful. 'But it looks as if Tony's going to know about his daughter before we're ready to approach him.'

'It's the proverbial stone and hard place,' Bill said. 'We don't know for sure it's her and I doubt we'll get the bodies into the morgue, ready for identification, before tomorrow. If we approach Tony Palmer before then he's going to want to come out and see for himself.'

'Yeah, but guaranteed the press will approach him today, given what that guy just told us. And heavens knows how he'll react.'

'I know,' Bill said with a sigh. He slumped against the car.

'It might be better if you phoned the DI and got his go-ahead to visit Palmer. Either way, whether he says yes or no, we're in the clear.'

'I suppose.' Bill's eyes focused on a white van driving towards them. 'Although I've never been good at watching my back.' The van swerved round the car and stopped in front of it.

'About time too.' Bill slapped the side of the van and grinned at the driver. He'd known Colin Watson for several years and they occasionally went for a pint together. 'If you'd been any later the whole of Dundee would've been out here trying their best to trample over the site. It's starting to become the latest tourist attraction.' He nodded in the direction of the reporter.

'Still the same old Bill,' Colin said, 'wanting everything yesterday.' He swung his legs out of the driver's seat. 'Right, lads,' he shouted over his shoulder to his two passengers, 'we've work to do.'

Bill followed him to the side door of the van and watched them put on the white boiler suits and bootees. 'That lot's not going to stay white very long,' he commented. 'Anyway you'll be lucky if you find anything that'll be of any value to the prosecution. There's been too many feet already and the site's well and truly contaminated.'

'Never know your luck though. The killer might have left some sort of trace.' Colin rummaged in the van for his equipment.

'Don't suppose you could get me a head shot of the girl who's still identifiable. We think we know who she is and want to get to her father before that eejit over there.' Bill nodded in the direction of the reporter who was hovering just out of earshot.

'I think we could manage that. Follow us in and I'll get a Polaroid shot for you.'

'Thanks,' Bill said, thinking gloomily that his shoes and trousers would only be fit for the rubbish bin by the time they'd finished here. 'You coming?' he shouted to Sue.

'No, I'll be keeping an eye on that *Courier* guy so he doesn't sneak in after you.'

'OK.' Bill turned and plodded into the woods after Colin and his team.

The photographing of the bodies didn't take long and Bill was soon pushing his way back through the trees. He waved to Sue as soon as he emerged from the wood.

'Let's go,' he said. 'And to hell with the consequences.'

The whispers clamoured to be heard. But they still made no sense. They only increased his agitation. His communion with the trees would have to wait until his emotions were under control. It never worked when he was het up.

When the time was right the whispers would be clearer. He would be calmer. Then he would know what to do; what he had done wrong.

21

Kara sat on one of the leatherette sofas on the top level of the Overgate Shopping Mall. She'd pulled the zip of her jacket up over her chin and the edge of her woollen hat down until it almost covered her eyebrows, but her eyes were alert. People passed without giving her a second glance.

She needed time to think, but the more she thought the more her mind went round in circles and magnified her problems. She didn't know where her kids were. She didn't know how to deal with Phil and Gus. She couldn't go home because Phil and Gus would be watching for her. She couldn't go to social work or the police in case they arrested her for neglecting the kids. She knew she shouldn't have left them, but Charlene was sensible and they'd have been all right. How could she have known she'd have a run-in with a psycho? Shivering at the thought of those bodies in the wood reminded her how lucky she'd been.

Kara pushed herself out of the sofa and headed for the escalator. It was time she was out of there.

It was only when she passed Dundee University's tower block that she realised she was heading in the direction of her mother's house. Her steps faltered. It had been four years since she'd spoken to her mother. They'd both been in the wrong and the argument had been bitter, but neither of them would admit it, and make up.

Her mother hadn't wanted her to leave home, and when Kev moved in with her that had made it worse. 'He's a waster,' she'd said, 'and he'll pull you down into the gutter.'

Kara had retorted, 'And you're so bloody perfect. Can't keep your nose out of a bottle long enough to be a proper mum. I don't want Charlene to see you lying on the floor, out of your mind with drink. Better no granny than one who's never sober.'

At that point her mother had gone quiet, turned her back on Kara, and left the room. Kara hadn't spoken to her since that day.

The thing Kara found difficult to accept was that her mother had been right. Kev was a waste of space. But that didn't give her the right to tell Kara how to live her life. It was going to take a lot of guts to face up to her mother given the mess she was in, but she didn't have much choice. She quickened her pace. It was worth a try.

The phone box at the junction of Blackness Avenue was occupied. She waited until the middle-aged man was finished and, trying to look appealing, she placed a hand on his arm, saying, 'I've had my purse stolen. I don't suppose you could spare me some change to make a phone call.' She smiled up at him. 'I need to let my mum know so she'll come and pick me up, otherwise I don't know how I'll get home. Please . . .'

The man frowned at her, but dug in his pocket and handed her a few coins. 'Here,' he said. 'That should be enough.'

'Thanks a lot.' Kara didn't have to force the gratitude in her voice.

He watched for a moment as she dialled and slid the coins into the slot.

'Dundee City Council,' the voice at the other end said.

'I need to speak to somebody about my kids.'

'Which social worker?'

'I don't know. My kids were taken into care today and I don't know where they are.'

'Which social work office, then?' The voice sounded bored.

'I don't know. Probably the one that's nearest the Greenfield estate.'

'Putting you through now.'

'Social work,' the new voice said.

Kara explained the situation and demanded to know where Charlene and Billy were.

'Sorry, you'll have to speak to Mark Gordon. He's dealing with that.'

'Well, can I speak to him?'

'Sorry, he's out.'

'How the hell do I find my kids, then?'

The voice at the other end of the phone became cooler. 'I suggest you come to the child protection conference on Monday. It's here in the office at 10 a.m.'

'I don't want to come to any bloody conference. I just want to know where they are.'

'I'm afraid that's all I can tell . . .' The pips sounded and the phone went dead.

Half an hour later she stood, hesitating, outside her mother's bungalow. The house looked much the same as it had when she'd left home. The same colour of paint on the doors and windows, the same curtains, even the same doormat. And it was virtually indistinguishable from its neighbours. She took several deep breaths then opened the wooden gate. The doorbell was a silent one and Kara wasn't sure whether it was working, but after a few moments the door opened and she forced a smile.

Her mother hadn't changed; perfect make-up, black designer trousers and jacket, and an immaculate cream silk shirt. She looked the ultimate career woman, although Kara knew she hadn't worked for years. Her face was smooth and unlined, and as beautiful as ever.

Kara, overwhelmed by the usual lack of self-confidence her mother inspired, felt like an ugly little girl again. A flash of anger shivered through her and she wondered, spitefully, whether her mum was as sober as she appeared to be. With alcoholics it was often difficult to know.

'Well, I must say, you've got a nerve coming here.' A wave of whisky-scented breath enveloped Kara.

She stiffened. It was just as she'd expected. Her mother had neither forgotten nor forgiven, and she hadn't stopped drinking either.

'I still think we should consult Andy first.' Sue stepped on the brake at the junction.

The seat belt tightened over Bill's stomach, reminding him it was empty. Apart from the sandwich he'd eaten at midday he couldn't remember when he'd last had a proper meal.

'I feel sick,' he said.

'D'you want me to stop?' Sue eased her foot off the accelerator.

'No. It's not that kind of sickness. It's a horrible empty feeling I've got in my stomach that makes me feel kind of queasy.'

'It's a good meal you need, pal, or you'll end up with stomach ulcers. When did you last eat properly?'

'Can't remember,' Bill muttered. 'I suppose if we stop at the chippy I could get something, although I'm not really in the mood.'

'I bet that's what you're living on, fish suppers and carry-outs.'

Bill grunted.

'I knew it.' She swung the car round a corner. 'You,' she said, 'are going to get some decent food inside you before we see Tony bloody Palmer. He can wait.'

'If he finds out about Denise before we inform him . . .' Bill frowned. 'He's got friends in high places.'

'So?' Sue's fingers tightened on the steering wheel. 'At the end of the day he's just a crook. Why should we run to him? It's not going to bring his daughter back. Besides who's to know we've taken a detour?'

'You're the one who usually goes on about watching our backs.'

'Half an hour's not going to make much difference. You can always phone Andy and put him in the picture while I'm nuking a chicken chasseur.' She pulled the car over to the kerb. 'Out you get. No argument.'

'You'll be turning into my mother if you don't watch out,' Bill grumbled as he followed her into the building and up the stairs.

'Don't count on it.' Sue unlocked her door. 'I'm only looking out for myself. I can't have you flaking out on me at a crucial moment. It wouldn't do my career much good.' She threw her coat onto a comfortable-looking blue sofa. 'The phone's on that table and the bathroom's at the end of the hall.'

She vanished through a door that Bill guessed must lead to the kitchen. He stood for a moment, feeling awkward, before removing his jacket and placing it beside Sue's coat. The flat was compact and cosy, unlike his mausoleum of a place.

Conscious of his muddy shoes and trousers, he left the lounge in search of the bathroom. Once there he stripped off his shirt, strip washed and rubbed his teeth with a forefinger and a blob of her toothpaste, then did his best to scrape the mud off his shoes and trousers with a nailbrush. Dressed again and feeling slightly more presentable he returned to the lounge to phone the DI.

'I don't think Andy's in,' he called out to Sue.

'Try his mobile,' she shouted back. 'The number's on the pad.'

This time the phone was answered almost immediately. 'Where are you?' Bill said, wondering if Andy had gone to the murder site. 'I tried the office but there was no answer.'

Andy and Bill had joined the force at the same time and were good friends despite Andy's promotion. 'Bad luck, mate,' Andy had said. 'Next time it'll be you.' That'd be the day. Bill knew he would never make detective inspector. Too much baggage.

'I've just been with the Chief Constable,' Andy said. 'I'm on my way back to the office now.'

'What'd the Chief want?'

'Oh, nothing to concern you at the moment, just a pep talk about budgets – seems we're more overspent than usual.'

'It's not going to get any better then, not after what's been found in Templeton Woods.'

'Shit,' Andy said, after Bill had filled in the details, 'I see what you mean. I don't like it but you'll have to go ahead. But remember, nobody goes in to see Palmer on their own, and make sure you get a couple of experienced female officers to do the needful. Palmer reacts better to them. He gets too stroppy with males.'

'Sure,' Bill said, looking at his watch and wondering where he was going to find a second female officer, with the necessary experience, at this time of night.

22

'Never mind.' Kara turned away. 'It was a bad idea coming here in the first place.' She squared her shoulders and strode down the path. 'See if I care,' she shouted as she swung the gate open.

'For heaven's sake, you always did jump to conclusions.'

Kara's hand tightened on the handle of the gate. But her resentment eased a little and was replaced with a flicker of hope.

'You'd better come in.'

There was no welcoming tone in her voice and Kara knew her mother was probably prompted by what the neighbours might be thinking rather than any great desire to see her daughter. More than anything she wanted to tell her mother to stuff it, but she needed a safe haven, somewhere to hide until she could pick up her kids and get out of Dundee. So she forced a smile to her lips, and followed her mother into the house.

'You'd better have a wash. You know where the bathroom is. After you've done that, we can have tea and sandwiches in the lounge.'

Kara bit back a retort and went meekly to the bathroom. She felt much better after a shower and was suddenly ravenous.

Her mother looked up when she opened the door.

'Come right in, Kara.' Her voice was warmer now. 'You remember Madge Palmer?' She nodded in the direction of the blonde woman sitting on the white leather sofa. 'Denise's mother. I've just been commiserating. Apparently Denise is leading her parents a merry dance as well. She hasn't been home since New Year's Eve.'

'That's right, isn't it, Madge?'

Kara's first instinct had been to run but she realised how ridiculous it would appear and forced herself to walk into the lounge and sit down.

Madge laid her cup on the coffee table, turning her hand so the light sparked off the diamond rings she wore. 'She's usually a good girl, but this past year she's been staying out more often. It used to be just a night or two but now she sometimes stays away for a week at a time. I don't know what's come over her.'

The scent of leaves and mould flooded Kara's nose and she was back in the wood again. In the glade where the girls embraced the trees.

Denise's eyes. Her head swam. Madge's voice was coming from faraway. Kara knew only too well where Denise was but how on earth could she tell Madge.

'You don't look well, dear. Have some tea, it'll warm you up.'

A cup was forced into Kara's hand and she lifted it to her lips. Her teeth chattered on the edge of the china and she struggled to hold herself together. Now it was only a matter of time before Tony knew where to find her.

'Well?' Kara's mother snapped as soon as Madge had gone. 'Has he left you or are you chasing money? And where's Charlene?'

She didn't mention Billy but that didn't surprise Kara. Her mother had never accepted Kev, so she wasn't likely to acknowledge his child.

Kara bristled with anger. 'If that's what you think of me, then I'm sorry I came.'

'Hmm, still the same old Kara.' Helen gathered the china cups and saucers onto a tray. 'Well, what *have* you come for?'

'Nothing you can give me, that's obvious.' Kara slapped her hand on the underside of the tray, watching with satisfaction as the tea, milk, sugar and sandwiches exploded over Helen's beautiful white furniture and cream pile carpet. Fragments of rose-pattern china littered the floor and coffee table.

'That was my best Crown Derby tea set,' Helen screamed.

'What's got into you? Get out!'

'With pleasure,' Kara said, slamming the lounge door behind her. Blood pounded in her temples and she had difficulty focusing. Fighting back tears of anger and desperation she crept towards the front door, halting momentarily at the hall table where her mother's handbag sat, enticingly open. She dipped her hand into the bag, opened the purse and extracted two ten-pound notes.

She left without looking back and headed towards the city centre.

'I'm beat.' Louise looked at the clock. It was only a few minutes past four. She shuffled the papers on top of her desk into a drawer. 'I think I'll go home.'

'That's not like you.' Meg Peters looked up from the report she was compiling.

'I know. But I was called out early this morning and I'm still not sure why it had to be me. Surely one of the officers attached to the Child Protection Unit would have been better.'

'It's because you're more amenable. You never say no and you always pick up the phone.' Meg tapped her pen against her teeth. 'You'll probably have to follow it through now you've started. I'll bet that child protection lot are laughing up their sleeves.'

'Maybe you're right.' Louise sighed. 'But I don't really mind that much.'

'You never do, that's your trouble. Anyway it's Friday, off you go. If anything comes in I'll cover for you.'

'You're a pal.' Louise lifted her jacket off the coat hook.

'If you crack on you'll get home before five and miss the rush hour.'

As she drove, Louise reflected on Charlene and Billy. The two kids had got to her and she didn't know why. Maybe her maternal instincts, which had been dormant for so long, had surfaced. Heaven forbid!

An uneasy feeling crept through Louise. It was the same feeling she'd had when she left the kids with the Phillipses.

She hoped they'd be all right. Perhaps she should phone Jerry tonight and check out how well he knew the carers.

Just as Bill replaced the phone in its cradle the front door slammed.

'Hi there,' Louise said as she entered the lounge. 'I don't think we've had the pleasure of your company before.' She looked at him speculatively.

'Sue's in the kitchen.' Bill, guessing what Louise was thinking, felt awkward. 'She reckoned I needed feeding up.'

'Not often she acts like a mother hen. You must really be on the skids.'

Bill shrugged. 'Just self-neglect, I suppose. She felt sorry for me.'

'Never known her to take in a stray before – dog or cat – never mind a man. Usually I'm the one who's a sucker for strays.' She laughed at herself.

Bill felt himself warming to her despite her comments. 'You don't seem to be as institutionalised as the rest of us. Which bit of the force are you in?'

'I'm part of the Community Team. Domestic abuse or family liaison describes best what I do. You know, battered wives, family violence, that sort of thing.'

'You're experienced in family liaison?' It would be a bit unconventional, but the answer to his problem might be standing right in front of him.

Helen Ferguson sat on the cream pile carpet. Tears streamed down her face as she picked up broken china. What had she done to deserve this? Her daughter had been like a stranger to her ever since she'd brought her back to Scotland. Hadn't she always tried to do her best to bring her up? Although it hadn't been easy after Rafe was murdered. Kara had only been fourteen, a difficult age, and she hadn't wanted to leave Spain. But what choice did they have? It was either sell up and come home, or stay and share Rafe's fate. What good would she have been to Kara if she'd been six feet under?

Wiping the tears from her face, she slumped into an armchair, staring blankly at the mess around her. Kara hadn't said what was troubling her, and she hadn't said where Charlene was. Sighing, Helen rose and went to the kitchen. There was a bottle there. She'd feel better after a drink. She always did.

23

Bill's fork chased the last few grains of rice round his plate as he waited for Louise's answer. Sue hadn't been pleased when he'd asked, he could tell by her grim-faced exit from the room with the soup bowls. Now the distant sound of dishes clattering in the kitchen broke the silence that had gathered after he'd made his suggestion.

The only reason Bill had asked Louise to accompany Sue to the Palmer residence was because she had impressed him as a calm, professional type who would be sensitive and do a better job of handling Tony Palmer than anyone else he could think of. And because the DI had suggested getting another woman along.

'OK, I'll do it,' Louise said.

The tension building in Bill's chest subsided. 'If there's any flak I'll take it.' He smiled encouragingly at Louise and pushed his chair away from the table.

Sue barged in from the kitchen, whipping the plate from in front of him and holding out her hand for his fork. 'That's big of you.' The green flecks in her eyes burned into Bill with their intensity. 'You do realise that there will be *loads* of flak, don't you?'

She turned to Louise. 'You sure you want to do this? It's not the nicest of jobs.'

'If Bill's sure he'll be able to square it with my boss, then I don't see why I shouldn't.'

'You're too soft. It's Bill's job and he's copping out.'

Bill squirmed on his chair. He was perfectly aware he didn't like this kind of task but Sue didn't need to be so scathing. 'Andy made it plain he wanted female officers and said they shouldn't be rookies but, if you feel that way about it,' he hesitated for a moment before forcing himself to say,

'I'm happy to do it myself.' Once the words left his mouth he felt better, even though he hoped he wouldn't be taken up on his offer.

'Oh, sure you are,' Sue said as she turned back to the kitchen.

Louise glanced sympathetically at Bill, and followed Sue out of the room. 'She'll be all right,' she whispered as she passed him. 'Leave her to me.'

Bill rose from the table and walked to the window. Maybe he should tell Louise not to bother. Maybe he should just go ahead and talk to Tony instead of trying to avoid it. Sue was his partner, his best mate, and he was in danger of alienating her. But there was no getting round it; Louise would do the better job.

The two women emerged from the kitchen. 'Well, we're ready to go,' Sue said calmly. 'Will we give you a lift home or take you back to Bell Street for your car?'

Bill sighed. The prospect of going home didn't appeal to him. 'I'll come with you.'

'What's the point of that?' Sue left the room returning a moment later with his coat which she held out to him. 'Don't you think three's a bit over the top? Palmer won't take kindly to us appearing en masse.' She had apparently accepted that Louise was the one to accompany her.

'I'll wait outside in the car, just in case.'

She gave him a long, cool stare. 'OK then,' she sighed. 'I suppose it's only fair that you're not lazing about at home when Louise is doing your job for you. Let's get to it then.'

Tony Palmer wiped his palette knife on a multi-coloured rag. He liked working in oils. It was soothing and took his mind off the drug deal that had just gone sour, or who might be ripping him off.

Standing back he admired the almost completed portrait of his daughter. She smiled back at him with painted lips not yet dry, her blonde hair hanging round her shoulders. He usually had difficulty getting the eyes right, but this time it had been easy. A few brush strokes to her dress and the painting would be ready for her birthday.

The door opened behind him. He didn't look round, Madge was the only person allowed in the studio.

'What d'you think? Look like her?' He knew Madge would give him an honest answer. They'd been together since she left school and, despite his frequent dalliances with the club girls, he'd never leave her. Their attachment to each other was too strong.

'Yeah, it's spot on.' Madge walked over to the canvas. 'Don't know why you bother though, not when she doesn't even trouble herself to come home or let us know where she is.'

'She'll be home for her birthday.' He picked up the palette knife and scraped a flake of paint off the canvas. 'She's always here for her birthday.'

'You spoil her, you know.'

'Sure. The same way I spoil you.' He ran his finger over the diamond rings on the hand nearest to him.

'Give over,' she said snatching her hand away. 'You'll get paint on them.'

'I'll buy you some more.' He slung an arm round her waist and kissed the point of her nose. Stroking the blonde curls back from her face, he said, 'She looks just like you did when we first made it.'

'Is that why you stay with me?' Madge's voice was quiet.

Tony shrugged. Madge knew about his girls. She never said anything to him but sometimes he could sense her fear. Fear that she'd lose him.

'Of course not. You were my first love. You gave me yourself, then you gave me Denise. What more could a man want?' He knew he hadn't answered her question fully, but then he didn't know the answer himself.

Madge changed the subject, a sure indication that she regretted her question. 'I visited Helen Ferguson today.'

Tony studied the painting. He wanted to allow her time to recover her composure. 'I didn't think you still saw her.'

'I met her in town and she invited me for coffee. It would

118

have been rude to refuse.'

'I thought you said she had a drink problem?'

'She was OK today . . . well, maybe she'd had a few, but it wasn't obvious. Anyway, that's not what I wanted to tell you. When I was there her daughter turned up. The first time she'd come home in years apparently. Then suddenly, out of the blue there she is, looking as if she'd been pulled through a hedge backwards. Not nicely turned out like our Denise.'

Tony tightened his arm round her waist. 'You do go on, Madge.'

'Wait, I haven't finished. Kara was a pal of Denise's. Don't you remember? They went to the High School together. A wee skinny thing with straight brown hair, wouldn't say boo to a mouse. Well, anyway, I thought Kara might have seen Denise, so I asked her, and she gave me the weirdest look.'

'What did you say her name was?' Tony had only been half listening but the girl's name had struck him. Surely there couldn't be too many girls named Kara in Dundee.

'Kara, surely you haven't forgotten her? She came to Denise's fifteenth birthday party, but then she dropped out of sight. Boyfriend stuff.'

'Second name, Madge. What's her second name?'

'Ferguson, like Helen, of course. Anyway what are you getting so uptight about?'

So, he'd found her without the help of Phil or Gus. Pair of useless bastards that they were. The money was in the bank.

'You go on downstairs, my love, and switch on the news. I'll be down as soon as I've made a phone call.'

24

The beeping of the mobile cut into Phil's reverie.

'Where the hell have you been?' Tony's voice bellowed in his ear. 'And what the hell have you been up to? I haven't heard from you since last night.'

Phil looked at Gus across the café's formica table and shrugged his shoulders.

'Sorry, boss. I've been looking for that Kara bitch, just like you told us.'

'Well, have you found her?'

'Not yet, boss. But I've recruited some spies who'll let us know when she appears.'

'Been looking in the wrong places then, haven't you?' Tony's voice softened. Phil didn't like it but tried to hold on to his composure so that his junior partner wouldn't notice.

'We're doing our best, boss.' He grinned at Gus and gave him a thumbs-up sign.

'Not good enough, Phil. Not good enough.'

Phil cringed inwardly. Tony knew something, he could tell by the sound of his voice.

'I've . . . fucking . . . found . . . her . . . you idiots.'

'What do you mean, you've *found* her?' Phil couldn't keep the surprise out of his voice.

'I know where she was this afternoon, and if you get your arse up there at the double you might catch her or at least find out where she's gone.'

Phil's heart sank. 'Tell me where. We're on our way.'

Sue parked the car on the street at the end of Tony Palmer's drive.

'Is this it?' Louise looked at the large villa. 'It's not what I imagined.'

'Wait till you see inside,' Bill muttered from the back seat.

'You've been inside?'

'Yeah, but you couldn't describe my visits as social calls. I've got up his nose on more than one occasion.'

'Is that why you wanted me to take your place?' Louise smiled at him. She decided she quite liked Bill, even if he was a bit of a misery guts. Something to do with her fondness for strays, she supposed. He aroused her protective streak.

'You could say that,' Bill said, relaxing into his seat. 'I'll see you when you get back. Give us a shout if you need reinforcements.'

Sue sighed. 'I doubt that'll be necessary, given the circumstances.' She got out of the car and slammed the door.

'Come on, then. Let's get it over with.' Louise led the way up the semi-circular paved drive, mounted the curving stone steps and rang the doorbell.

It seemed to take forever before the door opened and, rubbing a hand on a prickly area at the back of her neck, Louise had the distinct feeling they were being observed, and not just by Bill.

Hunger was punching holes in Kara's stomach lining by the time she reached the university tower block. She gazed longingly at the bright lights of the restaurant opposite, but a meal there was bound to cost more than she had to spend. She'd have to find something cheaper or the money wouldn't last long. She strode on down the Nethergate, past the pub on the corner – pubs were out because she might run into Phil and Gus inside any of them – past the Queens Hotel at the other side of the road, and past the end of South Tay Street.

A faint aroma of fried fish hung in the air. She followed the smell, her mouth filling with saliva. When she reached the Deep Sea fish and chip restaurant she plunged through the narrow door and stood at the takeaway counter. 'Fish and chips, and a Coke,' she said, fingering the notes in her pocket, separating them to pull one out. It would have been nice to sit at one of the tables with a pot of tea, but she couldn't take the chance of being seen, so she watched as the fish supper was wrapped in paper. Thrusting the can of juice into her jacket pocket and picking up the food parcel, she turned to go outside.

A queue had built up behind her and a group of students blocked her exit. 'Excuse me,' she muttered politely, although the niggling in the pit of her stomach made her want to shove them. It was made worse by the vinegar seeping through the paper and intensifying the smell of the food inside. She could barely stand it. Wriggling a hot potato chip from the end of the packet she thrust it into her mouth. It only made her hunger worse.

Kara retraced her footsteps until she came to the Queens Hotel. Looking over her shoulder, she slipped down the alley to the hotel car park and its darkest corner. The ground was cold and the brick wall dug into her back but she didn't care. Half an hour later, pleasantly full but feeling distinctly greasy, she walked back up the alley to the Nethergate.

'How'd Tony find out about Kara's old lady?' Gus frowned as he drove.

The gum had lost its flavour long ago but Phil chewed savagely. He was still smarting after Tony's reprimand. 'Fucked if I know, just drive, and mind you don't run over one of those poxy students.' He scanned the groups of young folk thronging down the Nethergate. 'See them,' he said. 'They've got it easy; they don't know what life's all about. I could've gone to uni, you know. But my ma didn't have the money.' He thought for a moment. 'Not that I'd've wanted to, mind. But if we'd had the money these wee shites have, I could've gone all right.'

'What are you bothered about, if you didn't want it anyway?'

'Well, it's the principle, isn't it? Poxy students.' He watched a young lad in a hoodie clutching a fish supper duck down the alley beside the Queens Hotel. There was something furtive about the way he looked round first. 'I bet he's up to no good,' he muttered, 'or maybe he's gone to pick up the family Rolls-Royce.' He laughed at his own joke although Gus didn't seem to appreciate it.

The road quietened after they passed the university tower building. 'We're doing OK now,' Gus said, 'even if we didn't get an education. I bet a lot of them would pack it in tomorrow if they could make the amount of dosh we do.'

Phil laughed. 'Yeah, maybe.' He extracted the gum from his mouth, wound down the window, and flicked it out onto the road.

Ten minutes later Gus drew up at the kerb in front of a stone bungalow with a slightly neglected garden. 'You sure this is the right address?'

'It's the one Tony gave me and he's not often wrong.' A curtain moved at the window of a house two doors away. 'I don't like this,' Phil said. 'It's too Neighbourhood Watch. Phoning the cops'll be second nature here.'

'Yeah,' Gus said. 'But Tony's not going to like it if we don't check it out.'

Phil fingered the stick of chewing gum in his pocket, resisting the temptation to unwrap it. A gum-chewing thug on this doorstep wouldn't get very far. 'You stay in the car,' he said. 'I think this is a job for brains rather than brawn. If I need you I'll give you a shout.'

The woman who opened the door was attractive, but drunk. Fair hair straggled over her face and she kept flicking it back over her head with an unsteady hand. Her cream shirt hung over the waistband of her trousers at one side and she wobbled precariously on ridiculously high heels.

'Mrs Ferguson,' Phil said, looking her up and down and smiling. 'Kara never told me she had such an attractive mother.' He leaned closer, almost gagging on the smell of whisky fumes.

'That bitch,' Helen spluttered. 'If you see her you can tell her she's not welcome here.'

'Oh, that's a shame. It's just that I've some money to give her.' Phil pulled some notes out of his pocket. 'And I was told

I might find her here.'

Helen swayed. 'You want to come in?'

Phil hesitated, trying to give the impression he was thinking about it. 'I don't actually have much time just now. I tell you what though, after I've seen Kara and given her the money, maybe I could come back?'

Helen giggled. 'You're a right charmer.'

Phil smiled at her and, lifting his finger, pushed her hair back off her face. 'I can't wait. I don't suppose you know where I can find Kara?'

'She's been here today, but she's gone now.' Helen frowned. 'Bitch broke my best tea set.'

'How long since she went?' Phil wasn't sure how much longer he could sustain the front.

'Oh, half an hour, maybe an hour . . . I don't know. But not that long. You might catch her on the road into town.'

'She's not driving then?'

'No, Kara doesn't have a car. She's walking, or maybe she took the bus.'

Phil leaned over and aimed a kiss at her cheek. 'Thanks, love. You've been a great help.'

'Name's Helen,' she shouted after him. 'Hurry back.'

Phil lifted a hand and waved.

'Get a move on,' he said as he got back into the car. 'She's been here but left to walk back to the town.'

Gus accelerated away from the kerb.

Phil took a strip of gum from his pocket, unwrapped it, and popped it into his mouth. This time they'd get her.

25

Sue tapped her foot impatiently as the large man studied their ID, squinting at the photographs and then at them. Louise placed a hand on Sue's arm and she stopped tapping.

'Seems to be in order,' the big man said. 'Photos don't do you justice though.' He handed the cards back to them.

'We need to speak to Mr and Mrs Palmer,' Sue said, 'right away, if you don't mind.'

'What's it about?'

'Just get them and hurry up about it.'

The man stiffened. 'No need to take that tone. I'm just doing my job. Wait in there.' He pointed to a door leading off the hall. 'I'll see if they're available.'

'They'd better be,' Sue muttered as he vanished into the interior of the house.

'You were a bit short with him.'

'Yeah, well if you knew him like I do, you'd be short as well. That, my friend, is Brian Crowe. Used to be OK when he was a boxer, but now he's one of our local villains. Drug dealer, housebreaker, thug; you name it, he's done it, and gone down for it once or twice. Seems like he's Tony's minder now. I suppose they're well matched.'

Louise had stopped listening. She stood with her hand on the door handle, staring. 'Will you look at this room?' she whispered. 'Crime certainly pays.'

Sue gave her a push. 'I can't see it unless you move out of my way.'

Louise took a few steps forward. Her feet sank into the autumn gold carpet; it was like walking on soft sand. She'd never been in a room as large as this in an ordinary home. Large deep-cushioned sofas sat at right angles to each other at one end of the room, while several matching armchairs and recliners formed semicircles round polished wooden coffee tables. The colour scheme was red and gold, reflected in the fleur-de-lys curtains, and furniture covers. The wallpaper looked as if it was decorated with gold leaf.

'A bit ornate for my taste,' Sue said. 'Some fabulous paintings though.'

'D'you think that's a Renoir hanging over the fireplace? Or just a copy?'

'I wouldn't know a Renoir from a drawing by one of my nephews. Art's not my thing.'

Louise gulped. She'd just spotted what looked like a Lowry. 'There's some serious money in here,' she said. 'I hope he has it all insured.'

'I see you're admiring my art collection.'

Louise hadn't heard Palmer come in and wondered how long he'd been listening to them. 'It's amazing. Must be a temptation for thieves though. Aren't you afraid someone will break in and take them?'

Palmer smiled. 'No one would dare. Now, ladies, I understand you wish to speak to me.' He ambled into the room, pulling his shirt cuffs down so that they showed below the sleeves of his immaculately cut grey suit.

'Your wife, Mr Palmer. Is she at home?'

He studied Louise through eyes slightly too small for his heavy, jowled face. 'You want to speak to my wife as well?'

'Yes, please.'

His brow creased with puzzlement. 'Very well.' He walked over to a tasselled bell pull by the fireplace. 'Will you fetch Mrs Palmer?' he said when the maid opened the door. She scuttled away and a few minutes later a tall blonde woman entered the room.

'You wanted me, darling?'

'Yes, dear.' Taking her hand, he led her to a sofa. 'These two police officers wish to speak to us.'

'Police officers?' Her blue eyes widened in alarm. 'It's not Denise, is it? She hasn't had an accident, has she?'

'I think it might be better if we all sat down.' He pulled two chairs over to face the sofa and gestured for Sue and

Louise to sit. Then he sat on the sofa, still grasping his wife's hand.

Tony was used to dealing with the police but this was no run of the mill visit or they wouldn't have asked Madge to be present. He narrowed his eyes and studied the women perched on the edge of two of his chairs. That was out of the ordinary as well, two women, and not in uniform; the police usually came to Tony Palmer in male pairs, big dominant men to intimidate him. Only Tony wasn't easily intimidated. These two, however, were different. The auburn-haired one looked as if she could handle herself, but the brunette with the soft brown eyes oozed sympathy. Somehow Tony found that more frightening than any of the hard men he was used to confronting.

Madge's hand felt cold, her nails dug into his palm, and her arm quivered against his. It didn't help. 'So,' he said, 'what's this all about?'

'We are currently involved in an investigation that may concern you and we wanted to check something out.' Louise's voice was gentle and she looked at him with a strange expression in her eyes. 'When did you last see your daughter, Denise?'

'Why do you want to know?'

'Please answer the question, Mr Palmer.'

'New Year's Eve, but she comes and goes.'

'Something's happened to her,' Madge gasped. The fear in her voice sent a shiver through Tony like wind on water. It was a sensation he'd never experienced before.

'We'd like you to have a look at this photograph and tell us if you think it could be Denise.'

Tony took the photograph from the one who'd introduced herself as Louise, the sympathetic one. He closed his eyes, trying to obliterate the image of his daughter's face. A face that had no life in it at all. He opened them again, and nodded. 'She's dead, isn't she?'

A vision of his daughter lying in the mangled wreck of her

car flooded Tony's mind and the room closed in around him. His head spun. 'It's not true, it can't be true. Not my Denise.' His voice was anguished. 'I should never have given her that car.'

'I'm afraid it wasn't a car accident, Mr Palmer.'

'What do you mean?'

'A number of bodies have been found in Templeton Woods. One of our constables thought he may have recognised your daughter.'

Madge laid her head on Tony's shoulder. 'It's not,' she sobbed, 'it can't be Denise. It must be someone else.'

'Hush now,' he said, stroking her cheek. Tony pulled Madge's head into his chest, cradling her body with his arms. He felt helpless. He was breaking up inside. Denise couldn't be dead, he wouldn't allow it; he wanted to deny what they were telling him, make them take the photograph back. It couldn't be Denise, not his daughter. She *couldn't* be dead.

'We'll need you to officially identify the body. Perhaps tomorrow . . .'

'Tell me how it happened.' Tony struggled against the tears that threatened to overwhelm him. He had a reputation to preserve. He was tough. He never cried. He hadn't even cried when his mother died, but then she hadn't been much of a mother. Denise was different; he loved Denise more than anything else in the world. But still he couldn't cry over her, not yet.

'It appears that Denise was killed by person or persons as yet unknown, Mr Palmer. There were a number of bodies at the scene.'

Madge shuddered. She was crying silently, her face pressed into Tony's chest.

'You're telling me a serial killer murdered my daughter?' Tony's voice rose in disbelief. Who would be stupid enough to go against him? Anyone who knew him would know they were signing their own death warrant if they so much as laid a finger on Denise.

'Give me the details. All of them.' His voice hardened with anger. Someone was going to pay for this.

'We won't know how Denise died until after the post mortem. What we do know is that the victims were stripped and tied to a tree. No clothes were found at the scene.'

'I see.' Tony thought for a moment. He was having difficulty suppressing the rage gripping his guts. 'The place where she was found, I want to see it.'

'I'm afraid that won't be possible,' Sue cut in. 'The crime scene is still being processed.'

Tony turned to Louise, 'I want to know everything. Once the post mortem is completed I'll want to know the results.'

'Of course, Mr Palmer.' Louise stood up. 'There's nothing else we can add for the moment, we'll contact you with an appointment for the official identification.'

Tony nodded. His arms tightened round his wife's body. He didn't know how to comfort her.

'We'll see ourselves out.' Louise hesitated for a moment. 'Maybe your doctor could give your wife something to help.'

'Yes, yes,' Tony muttered. His world was collapsing in on him. This happened to other people, not them.

Tony was still sitting clutching Madge when Brian came into the room having shown the two policewomen out. 'Denise is dead,' he said in a flat voice. 'Murdered. Get hold of Phil and Gus.'

'Yes, boss.'

'Someone's going to pay for this.'

Bill was bored. He'd discussed the case with Andy, agreed a time tomorrow for the briefing meeting, and informed him of Louise's involvement. He tried to think of something else to do to fill in the time. He fidgeted in his seat, trying to relieve the pressure on his backside. What the hell were they doing in there? They'd been inside the house for the best part of half an hour. Tony didn't usually put up with a police visit for more than ten minutes. His legs were tingling with cramp. There wasn't enough room in the back seat of Sue's car for a hamster, never mind a bog-standard sized copper.

He felt in his pocket for cigarettes that weren't there. He

was always forgetting things lately. Maybe he should put in for his holiday entitlement and sleep for a fortnight. But he knew only too well that he wouldn't actually sleep even if he got to bed.

Leaning over the front seat, he reached into the glove compartment. Maybe Sue might have a sweet or a bar of chocolate, it'd be better than nothing. He came up empty-handed. His legs twitched. They often did that when he was tired, a nervous reaction the doc had said when he mentioned it. He was becoming more restless and fidgety every second. His mind flitted from thought to thought although he would have been hard put to it to say what he was thinking. He'd have to find something to do, it was driving him crazy just sitting here.

The two women came out of the house. It felt like hours but, looking at his watch, Bill realised it was still only just a little over half an hour. 'Thank goodness you're back. I was beginning to think you were staying the night.'

'It was your idea to come. Not ours,' said Sue.

'How'd it go?' He wasn't in the mood for an argument.

'I felt sorry for them.' Louise met Bill's eyes in the rear-view mirror. 'She went to pieces and he seemed totally gobsmacked.'

'I wouldn't feel too sorry for Tony. He's a vicious bastard.'

'Well, I got the impression he genuinely loved her . . .' Louise sighed.

'Yeah, maybe,' Bill said, 'but the nutter who's done this had better pray we find him before Tony does.'

'Where to?' Sue edged the car out into the road. 'Home or the pub?'

'Let's make it the pub, we can't do any more tonight.' Bill leaned back in his seat. Anywhere was better than home.

26

The Nethergate was quiet when Kara emerged from the alley. Most of the students had dispersed to their digs. A stream of cars, released by the traffic lights at the end of the street, pinpointed her with their headlamps.

She tugged her woollen cap further down. It had been easier to hide in the crowds, but now she had the pavement to herself she felt vulnerable.

She didn't stop running until she reached the entrance to the railway station. There was no one manning the ticket barrier so she vaulted over and darted along the platform.

A train was just pulling in.

She watched as passengers piled out. Women with carrier bags from Jenners and M&S returning from a day's shopping in Edinburgh. Men in suits, women in suits. All hurrying home. Tempted to climb aboard she took a couple of steps towards one of the open doors. But then she remembered Charlene, thought of her crying for her mum and trying to comfort Billy.

A disgruntled man pushed past her, tutting.

Confused, she turned away. What kind of a mother ran from her kids? But what use would she be to them if she was dead.

With a shudder she remembered the faces of the dead in the woods and Denise's empty staring eyes. But the maniac who had taken her there would never find *her* again. She'd make sure of that.

On the other hand, Phil and Gus would never give up looking. Her bruises were still raw, reminding her of Phil's hands on her throat and the horrible sensation of being swallowed by darkness.

She turned back to the train, hovering in front of the doors.

Blanking thoughts of Charlene from her mind she stepped into the carriage, found a seat and closed her eyes.

'Get a move on,' Phil said, 'we can't lose her this time.'

'If I drive much faster we'll fucking take off. How are you going to spot her if we're going this fast.'

Phil ignored Gus, peering out at the dark streets and inspecting every lone pedestrian. 'Council wants to do something about this street lighting. That's the second light out.' He rolled down the window and peered back at a woman they'd just passed. 'Too old. Too fat.'

Gus steered the car down the Perth Road. 'Wild goose chase, this.'

Neither of them spoke for the next ten minutes. Perth Road imperceptibly changed to the Nethergate. They passed the university tower, the Queens Hotel, and the much newer DCA centre. The road was getting busier and it wasn't long before they could see the Overgate Centre with the dual carriageway separating it from the Nethergate.

'Where would you go if you were running?' Phil said.

'I'd get out of Dundee, that's for sure.'

'The bus station it is then.'

'Keep the engine running,' Phil said as he eyed up the queues waiting for buses a few minutes later. After five minutes he returned with a shrug.

'What now?' Gus asked.

'The train station, of course. It's easier to dodge paying.'

Leaving the car outside, they hurried to the station entrance. The stair to the platforms was jammed with people coming up from the Edinburgh train.

'There's a train in and it's still sitting at the platform. Come on!' Phil started to run.

Donovan's was Bill's favourite pub, but he hadn't been inside since Julie had left Dundee. It hadn't seemed right without her. But this was where Sue had taken them and he didn't have the willpower to resist. What could he say anyway? 'I can't go there without Julie.' They'd think him a complete wanker if he admitted that. Bill gritted his teeth and followed her in through the swing doors.

It wasn't as bad as he'd thought it would be. The cheerful clatter of voices made it feel like coming home after being away for a time. Suddenly he didn't feel so sick and tired.

He ordered three pints of lager, piled the glasses on a tray and took them to the corner table Sue had managed to grab.

'I knew I should have gone for the drinks.' Sue eyed the tray. 'There's more lager in the tray than there is in the glasses.'

'If you want the tray, Louise and I'll manage your pint.' Bill grinned.

Sue hesitated, then she smiled. 'Ah, the old Bill is back. No more Mr Doom and Gloom.' She grabbed one of the pint glasses and, holding it aloft, she said, 'Welcome back, Bill. Long may you remain with us.'

Charlene, Billy, Billy, Charlene . . . the names went round and round. Was it only last night she'd left them in the house?

She opened her eyes and pushed herself upright. She had to get off the train. But in her heart she knew turning back wouldn't solve anything. Slowly she sank back in her seat. The kids are better off without me. What can I give them? Fear and poverty, that's what.

The doors of the train whined shut. She'd be safe now. The kids would be safe. A tear trickled down her cheek. She brushed it off with a finger and looked out the window. The empty platform slid past and was soon left behind. She kept thinking, I'm safe, I'm safe, but there was a pain inside her that wouldn't go away. Charlene's face replaced her own reflection in the window glass, with wee Billy behind her.

'Are you all right?' The elderly gentleman sitting opposite looked at her with concern.

'I shouldn't be on the train,' she mumbled, another tear sliding down her cheek. 'It was a mistake.'

'If you need to get off, the next stop's Leuchars. We'll be there in about five or ten minutes. You could wait there for the next train back.'

The Tay was just visible flowing beneath the bridge, running to the sea, only to be forced back again when the tide turned. There was a rhythm to it, like life, and it didn't matter what happened: you always had to come back.

Suddenly her mind was made up. Running away wasn't helping, not without her kids. She'd find them, and take them away from the welfare, with or without their permission. And then, if she couldn't sort things out, they'd all run. She'd find somewhere for them. Somewhere they'd be safe together.

Looking up, she smiled at the elderly passenger. 'Thanks for your help.'

Frowning slightly, he said, 'It's a quiet station, Leuchars. Might be a bit dark, but most of the Dundee trains stop there, so hopefully it won't be too long.'

'I'll be fine, thanks,' Kara said.

Trade was slow and Jean was rattled. She'd seen Kara get in the red car last night, and now the word on the street was that bodies had been found in Templeton Woods. There were all sorts of rumours flying around. Jean thought about Linda who'd run out on her boyfriend and kids the week before Christmas, and wondered. There were one or two other girls who hadn't been around lately, too. Maybe they were lying there in the woods, all cold and wet and horribly murdered. Jean shivered.

A car drew up at the kerb. The window slid down.

Jean hesitated. It would be daft to get in a strange car, she thought, what with all the rumours. But she needed the money.

She walked over to the car. 'Looking for business?'

'How much?'

If she was going to take a risk then it'd have to be worth her while. 'Fifty,' she said. It was more than she usually asked, because she knew she wasn't the most attractive girl on the beat, but a lot of the girls were keeping a low profile tonight and there wouldn't be much choice for a desperate punter.

'Pounds? I wouldn't give you fifty pence.'

A roar of laughter sounded from the back seat of the car. 'You tell her.'

The driver spat in her face. 'Dirty old slag,' he shouted. The car accelerated, turned the corner and was gone.

Jean wiped the spittle off her face with a paper hankie. Well, she supposed, it could have been worse. It could have been the nutter from the woods. As soon as she'd made fifty quid she'd pack it in for the night and go home.

27

By the time Phil had pushed his way down the stairs, argued with the ticket collectors and reached the platform, the train was already moving out of the station.

'Was she on it? Did you see her?' Gus yelled.

'Couldn't get a good look,' said Phil.

Phil's mobile phone vibrated against his leg.

'Oh fuck,' he said gloomily, taking it out of his pocket and holding it to his ear.

'Yeah,' he said. 'Yeah. Yeah.'

'What's Tony want?'

'It was Brian. Tony wants us back at the house. Says there's a "crisis" and we'd better get there pronto.'

'D'you think he's found her?'

'If he has, we're not going to be popular . . .'

The doctor arrived fifteen minutes after the phone call. He was a locum, young and fresh-faced. Hardly out of nappies, Tony thought.

'I could give her something to take but an injection will work faster.'

Tony nodded his permission. 'I haven't seen you before,' he said as he watched the doctor jab the needle into Madge's thigh.

She hadn't stopped crying since she'd been told about Denise. The heart wrenching screams had stopped though and she was now sobbing steadily into her pillow.

'No,' he said, 'Doctor Morrison's out on another call and thought it'd be better if I came right away.'

Tony, tears pricking the back of his eyelids, bit his lip. 'What are you giving her?'

'It's just a sedative. It'll help her sleep and hopefully she'll be calmer in the morning.'

Tony doubted it but at least if she slept it would relieve the pressure on him tonight. 'What if she's still the same when she wakes up?'

'We could always try something stronger, but I'm not too keen. Wouldn't want to start her on something she might come to depend on.'

'No, that wouldn't be good,' said Tony, thinking about all the junkies who contributed to his bank balance. It was OK for them, but he didn't want his wife to become one. 'Brian will see you out.'

He sat on the edge of the bed and stroked his wife's hand. It was cold and limp.

'You'll take care of things. Won't you, Tony?' Madge had trouble getting the words out and her eyes were glazed. 'Promise?'

'Yes, my love. I'll take care of things.'

There was nothing more certain. He'd take care of things all right, he thought savagely.

'Get some sleep now. You'll feel a lot better in the morning.'

He patted her hand but there was no response. The fluttering lids had finally closed over her eyes. Her breathing deepened. He envied her, knowing there'd be no sleep for him until this business was settled.

Tony rose from the bed and crept from the room closing the door silently behind him. Leaning over the banister, he shouted, 'Phil and Gus here yet?'

'They're on their way, boss'

'Let me know when they get here, I'll be in the studio.' He wanted somewhere quiet, somewhere he could be alone.

Tony's studio took up the whole top floor of the house. He'd converted a series of attics into one large loft space with glass skylights stretching the length of the south side of the roof.

He closed the door behind him and stood in the dark looking up at the sky, imagining his daughter under a tree, terrified, in the pitch black. She'd been afraid of the dark when she was a little girl, and he vowed revenge on her killer.

'What took you so long?' Brian said. 'He's been waiting for ages.'

Phil bristled. They'd almost broken the speed barrier getting here. 'Why does he want to see us anyway?'

'You'll find out,' Brian said grimly, and left the room.

'I don't like the sound of that.' Gus looked anxious.

'Brian's always been a doom merchant. It'll be fine.' Phil paced round the room, looking at the paintings and books.

The door crashed open, banging into Gus's elbow. He yelped and jumped out of the way.

Tony gave no indication he'd noticed. 'You got here then,' he growled. 'About bloody time.' He sat in the leather chair behind his desk and began to swivel it from side to side.

Phil choked back the excuses that rose to his lips. Tony had only one way of seeing things. His way.

'Sit down then. Don't just stand there like a pair of dickheads.'

Phil pulled a chair over to the desk, gesturing to Gus to do the same. He perched on the edge of the seat. It was unnerving to be asked to sit, Tony usually kept them standing.

'Got here as soon as we could, boss.'

'Yes, yes.' Tony swung his chair and brooded.

Phil shivered. 'We've tried to find Kara . . .'

'It's not that,' Tony cut in. 'It's something worse. Much worse.' He pulled his earlobe. 'It's Denise.'

Phil caught his breath. What Tony would do to someone who'd been screwing his daughter didn't bear thinking about. Maybe that was why Gus had been asked to come. 'Denise?' Phil forced the name through parched lips.

'She's dead.' Tony didn't look at him.

'Dead?' Phil stuttered, unable to take it in. 'How?'

'Murdered, that's how.' Tony's voice was cold. He clenched his fist and smashed the desk. 'And I want the fucker caught. I want him brought to me. I want the fucker to suffer the way he made my Denise suffer . . . Do you understand?'

'We'll get the bastard.'

Phil remembered the last time he'd seen Denise. It was on Hogmanay at the club. She'd had a little too much to drink and they'd snogged in the bin recess at the back door. 'You like me, don't you?' she'd asked. Phil had said, 'Depends on whether you tell your old man.'

'What did the bastard do to her?' Phil asked.

'I won't know until after the post mortem. But they found her naked and tied to a tree in Templeton Woods . . .' Tony hesitated. 'And she wasn't the only one.'

'Templeton Woods?' Gus spoke for the first time, swallowing quickly.

'That's what the boss just said,' Phil cut in quickly, frowning at Gus. He knew what Gus was thinking. That was where they'd followed Kara and the punter in the red estate. Maybe it was just a coincidence, maybe not. 'What d'you want us to do, boss?'

'I told you. Find the bastard who's done this and bring him to me at the club.'

'What about Kara? What d'you want us to do about her?'

'Forget her for now.'

'Right, boss. We'll sort it.' Phil decided not to tell Tony they'd still be looking for Kara. She might be able to point them in the right direction as well as refund the missing cash.

Kara watched the train vanish down the line. The few people who'd got off hadn't lingered and the platform was empty and quiet. Too quiet. The ticket office was closed although there were still lights on the platform. But beyond it was darkness. There wasn't even a street or a house. Nothing but fields. It reminded her of last night in the woods, the impenetrable darkness, the feeling of isolation. At least there were no trees.

After the last of the cars had left the car park the silence gathered round her like a blanket. She was used to people and traffic and noise. Not this unnatural hush, this lack of living things. Already she was regretting leaving the cosy warmth of the train. Looking around, she spotted a seat in the shadow of the ticket office. It was better than nothing.

She leaned her head back and tried to find a comfortable position. Pulling her knees up, she settled down to wait for the Dundee train.

28

'Why didn't you tell Tony about following Kara to Templeton Woods?'

Why hadn't he? Phil wasn't sure. 'We don't really know if it's got anything to do with what happened to Denise. Maybe it was just a coincidence.'

Gus lapsed into silence and concentrated on his driving.

'Wouldn't want to get Tony's hopes up until we've checked it out.' Phil rummaged in his pockets. 'I'm out of gum,' he said gloomily. 'If you see a shop, pull over.'

Gus grinned, slipped his hand into his pocket, and pulled out a full packet. He tossed it into Phil's lap. 'I knew you'd need this sooner or later.'

'I think we should head back to the woods, see what we can find out.' Phil thought for a moment. 'Cops will probably still be there so we're not likely to see where the bodies were found but we can look for a friendly face and see what's what.'

Gus swung the car round the roundabout on the flyover. A steady stream of lights and the rumble of traffic sounded from the Kingsway below. Taking the Coupar Angus turn-off, he sped up the road leaving the lights of Dundee far behind.

It wasn't long before they reached a line of vehicles parked nose to tail at the side of the road.

Phil and Gus got out of the car and strolled along the road until they reached a medium-sized white van which looked like the mobile incident room.

'You can't stop here, sir. You'll have to move on.'

Phil smiled. 'Sorry, officer,' he said, 'but my boss sent me. He's been informed his daughter's been found here.'

The young man reddened. 'I'm a PC, sir. I'll get Sergeant Johnstone to speak to you. If you'll just wait here I'll get him for you.'

Phil watched him approach a group of officers conferring at the edge of the wood. One of them turned and looked in his direction but made no effort to move. It didn't worry Phil, he wasn't in any hurry. It gave him more time to study what was going on. Leaning against the van he yawned to signify his boredom to anyone watching, and surreptitiously studied the woods. This was the exact spot they'd followed Kara to.

'Well, well, if it isn't Tony Palmer's two blue-eyed boys.' Sergeant Johnstone strode out of the darkness and stood in front of them.

Phil shrugged. 'I thought you'd retired,' he said gently.

'Not quite, sonny, not quite. I'm just vegetating at the Downfield Station. Biding my time, you know. Now what can I do for you?'

'Tony sent us.'

'Surprise, surprise.'

Phil sighed. Johnstone wasn't making it easy. He considered a backhander, but one look at the old bastard's face ruled that out.

'Tony's been informed by the polis that his daughter's in there. He just wants to know what's what.'

'No doubt he does, but that's what we have liaison officers for. It's not up to me to give you information.'

'What harm can it do to give me something to take back to him. Have a heart, the man's just lost his only daughter.'

Johnstone thought for a minute. 'I can tell you that the bodies will be taken out tonight. Should be ready for identification in the morning.'

'Apart from Denise, was anyone else found?' Phil tried to make his voice sound casual. He still had this vision of Kara being one of them despite Tony's announcement.

'Read the papers tomorrow, pal. They'll be able to tell you more than I can, probably half of it made up.' Johnstone frowned. 'Now I'm really going to have to move you on.' He turned and walked away.

'Why?' Phil shouted. 'You're letting that lot up there stay.' He gestured towards the men clustered round the TV van.

'Aye, but they've got permission. You haven't.'

'Tony's not going to like it,' said Phil over his shoulder as he headed back to the car.

'Then Tony's going to have to lump it.' Johnstone grinned. 'I've been dying to say that for years.'

It was just under an hour before a train trundled down the line into Leuchars Station, although to Kara it felt like a lifetime.

The train finally arrived just when she was beginning to think she would be marooned in this desolate place. Ten minutes later she got off at Dundee having avoided the ticket collector.

Kara didn't feel safe until she'd left the station. Once she'd crossed the road to Whitehall Crescent she felt better. She knew how to handle herself on the streets, how to avoid anyone she didn't want to see, where to hide.

The door of Donovan's swung open, letting out a stream of light and noise. She ducked into a doorway until the group of men cavorted across the road and passed out of sight up Whitehall Street. Kev might be inside, drinking her money, buying drugs and acting the big man. If she could get her hands on him she'd make him pay. But she daren't go into the pub to look for him.

She hurried down the street, passed under the shadow of Tayside House and started to jog when she reached Shore Terrace, which was far too exposed for her liking. She didn't stop until she reached the safety of Exchange Street, a short, dark street with plenty of nooks and crannies. This was where she'd left Jean last night. But Jean wasn't about.

Kara found a darkened doorway and squatted in the corner to wait. If Jean didn't come she hadn't a clue what she would do next.

The door swung open, letting in a welcome blast of fresh air as well as a noisy bunch of young lads, some of whom looked hardly old enough to be drinking. The noise level went up by a couple of decibels. Bill didn't care. He was halfway to being drunk. It was a pleasant feeling and he smiled benignly on his two companions.

'You're the best partner I ever had.' He grinned inanely at Sue.

'You're drunk.' She laughed. 'Still it makes you better company than you've been for ages.'

'I'm not drunk. I never get drunk.' He smiled at Louise, quietly sipping the drink it was obvious she wasn't really enjoying. She reminded him of Julie. She had that same quiet, calm air about her. He liked that in a woman. He'd had enough of spontaneity and high spirits to last him a lifetime. Evie had seen to that during their short, tumultuous marriage, which had ended when she'd taken off with a sergeant from the drug squad.

'Don't kid yourself, and stop ogling Louise. You're embarrassing her.'

'I wasn't ogling.' His voice thickened with indignation. 'I was just thinking how much she reminded me of Julie.' He stared broodily into his pint.

'You haven't heard from her, have you?' Sue leaned over the table and patted his hand. 'Why don't you phone her? She's probably waiting for your call.'

'I'm not chasing after her, Sue. I ran after one woman and made a fool of myself, I'm not running after another.'

Sue spluttered. 'You're so pigheaded. Julie's nothing like Evie, and you know it.' She gathered the empty glasses together. 'I'm off to get another round. Give us a hand, Louise.'

'Get me a whisky this time,' Bill said. 'I'm getting bloated with all the beer I've been drinking.'

29

Tony rang for Morag. 'Keep an eye on Madge,' he ordered. 'I have to go to the club.' He picked up his gold cigarette case and slid it into his pocket. The case was an affectation. He'd bid for it at an auction and it pleased him to use it. 'She'll probably sleep until morning but I'd feel happier if you looked in on her now and then.'

'Yes, sir.' Morag slid past Brian who was standing in the doorway.

'Car's ready, boss,' he said, watching Morag scuttling up the stairs.

'Fancy her, do you?' Tony buttoned his jacket and pulled his shirt cuffs down.

Brian shuffled his feet.

Tony gave him a hard look. 'As long as you remember we don't shit on our own doorstep.'

'Aye. You ready to go?'

From the outside, the club didn't look anything special. An old cinema converted, despite neighbourhood opposition, to a night club. Tony hadn't wanted it looking too fancy, preferring to attract custom through word of mouth. The steps leading up to the entrance were the original tiled marble. The cinema name, painted out so many years ago Tony couldn't remember what it was, had been replaced by the club's name – Teasers.

Two good-looking, broad-shouldered men, clad in black dinner suits and bow ties, stood guard at the door. Nodding recognition they watched Tony approach. Each had an earphone and tiny camera clasped to his head like a child's Alice band, and Tony knew the club staff were being forewarned of his arrival. He knew they all had their little scams, and he knew exactly what those scams were. It didn't bother him, so long as they didn't get too greedy.

One of the men stepped forward, opening the door. The thump of music seeped out into the night air.

'Any trouble tonight?' Tony smiled for the camera.

'Not just now, sir. It's pretty quiet for a Friday, but there's a crowd of students in and sometimes they get out of hand.'

'I've no doubt you'll handle things. Don't want the law on our back.'

'Aye, sir.'

The door swung shut behind him and Tony stood for a moment to allow his eyes to accustom themselves to the gloom. The door on his right led into the main club room where most of the young lads and lasses congregated, drinking and dancing. In the old days Tony would have called it a disco, but a disco was old hat, so it was simply called the club. He pushed the door open and stood watching. The crowd was boisterous, voices competing with the thump of the music.

He elbowed his way to the bar.

'Drink, boss?' Victor laid a glass of Laphroaig in front of him.

Tony swirled the malt whisky round in the glass. 'You're busy tonight.' He nodded towards the dance floor.

'Yeah.' Victor polished a glass and placed it on a shelf behind him. 'They're a good-natured crowd just now. Hope it stays that way.'

Tony swallowed his drink, feeling its warmth slide all the way down his gullet. It wasn't the way malt should be drunk. It should be sipped and savoured, but Tony needed the comfort, the good feeling it gave him.

'Another one?'

'No, Victor.' He eased himself away from the bar. 'See you later.'

A little further down the corridor, on the opposite side, was the door to the lounge bar. This, to the uninitiated, looked like an ordinary lounge bar. Only a select few knew about the door at the rear that led to the gaming rooms and the small private cinema area.

A second glass of Laphroaig was waiting for him. 'Many folk back there tonight?' Tony lifted the glass and held it to his lips, savouring the aroma of the malt.

'A few, but it's a wee bit early.' Kenny pushed a bowl of nuts in front of Tony. 'You want to go back and take a look?'

'Naw, I'm going upstairs.' Tony lifted his drink.

Upstairs was where Teasers came into its own. One large room with a bar stretching almost the length of one wall. Most of the floor area was taken up with tables, all facing a stage at the end of the room. Lights shone upwards from below the stage and long, silvery poles were implanted in it, reaching from the floor to the roof. Girls slithered and danced round the poles illuminated by randomly flickering spotlights and a large glitterball that hung from the ceiling. Scantily clad hostesses served drinks at the tables and sat with customers, provided they were willing to pay.

This was Tony's favourite room. He liked to watch the dancers, their oiled skin gleaming under the blinking lights. He took up a stance at the bar, leaned back, sipped his drink and watched the show.

He sensed, rather than saw Marlene standing behind him. 'Who's the new dancer?' he said pointing to one of the girls.

'Gives her name as Angel.' Marlene shrugged. 'Who knows with these girls. I suspect half of them were born with names like Tracey or Linda.'

'She's good.' Tony slipped his glass over the bar. 'Be a love and get me a refill.'

Marlene bent down and retrieved a bottle from under the bar. She poured a good measure into the glass. 'She comes from Edinburgh, says she worked the clubs there.'

'She should make a fair bit when they come out and table dance.'

'Aye, she is good. She was saying the latest thing in the city clubs is lap dancing. It takes table dancing a step further.' Marlene leaned over, the bar supporting her chest. 'I was wondering whether we might go in for lap dancing here? I could get Angel to take the girls through it.'

'Good idea,' Tony said, finishing his drink. 'I'm off to the office. Send Angel up when she's free.'

Tony picked up his drink and walked to the end of the bar.

The wall was covered by a deep red velvet hanging. He slipped behind it, swiped his card in the lock of the door it concealed and pushed it open far enough to slip through. The door swung closed behind him, effectively cutting off the noise of the club. Breathing a sigh of relief he allowed his shoulders to slump and, wearily, he climbed the three stairs to his office.

It was a large room which sat above and to the rear of the club room below. One wall was glass, mirror-glazed on the club side, transparent on the office side. Through this he could view the club and the bar without being seen. The staff all knew about it but the punters didn't.

A long leather settee was positioned in front of one wall. Two matching wing chairs sat at each side. A third wing chair was drawn up in front of the glass wall. The office was dominated by a large, antique mahogany desk behind which sat an executive leather swivel chair. It was here that Tony did most of the paperwork the club generated. Though he employed an accountant, he liked to check all the incomings and outgoings. He allowed his staff their little scams, but no one was going to get the opportunity to rip him off, accountant included.

Tonight though, he wasn't in the mood to work. The thought of pulling out the account books, which he usually enjoyed, depressed him. Slumping in the window chair, he watched the girls wind their gleaming limbs around the silvery poles in a wild, sensuous, mating ritual. His eyes blurred with tears. They were so young, so full of life, just like his Denise. But her life had been snuffed out. Reaching for the internal phone he dialled the bar. 'Marlene, I've changed my mind. Don't bother to send Angel. I'll speak to her another time.' He hung up. There were too many thoughts of Denise floating round his mind tonight, all he would see while he was with Angel would be Denise's face.

Louise toyed with her glass of lager. She wasn't much of a drinker and disliked noisy pubs, but she never refused an invitation from any of her work colleagues, because she knew how important it was to fit in. Even a policewoman needed to be one of the lads or she got the reputation of being standoffish. That was professional suicide.

They'd been in Donovan's for nearly three hours and it was a lot noisier now, making it difficult to catch what Bill and Sue were saying. So she slumped back in her corner seat and smiled now and again at comments she couldn't hear.

Sue spoke to her and she smiled back, nodding her head. Sue leaned closer and shouted in her ear, 'Someone at the bar's waving to you.'

Louise turned to look, the smile dying on her lips when she saw Mark. There had been a time when she'd thought she was in love with him, but he'd enjoyed playing the field too much and it was more than she could bear to see him ogling other women. Who did he think he was, waltzing in here? As if she'd give him a second chance . . .

Sue raised her eyebrows as Mark pushed his way through the crowd. 'He looks gorgeous,' she shouted at Louise. 'Who is he?'

'Someone I used to know,' Louise mumbled. 'He's a social worker.' She willed Mark to go away.

'Louise. I thought it was you.' Mark leaned over the table and kissed her on the cheek.

Louise shrank back, but with the wall behind her she couldn't avoid his lips. If she'd been alone she would have belted him one and it annoyed her that he'd taken advantage because she was with friends.

'D'you mind if I join you?' He looked round and grabbed a chair someone had just vacated.

Louise frowned. She tried signalling her displeasure to Bill but he just sat there with a foolish grin on his face. Sue, busy shunting her chair round the table to make space for Mark, wasn't looking so didn't see Louise's frown and shake of the head. Mark continued to edge his chair into a space at their table and refused to take the hint.

'A social worker,' Sue said, settling back in her chair, 'that must be interesting.'

Louise bit her lip, hard, and wished herself elsewhere.

Mark leaned towards her until their shoulders were touching. 'We've known each other for yonks. In fact we were a bit of an item at one time. Weren't we, Louise?'

'Actually,' Louise said, 'I was just thinking it was time we took Bill home.' She aimed a kick at Sue under the table.

Sue flinched and looked at Louise. 'It's early yet,' she said.

'You stay then.' Louise gritted her teeth. 'But I'll need the car to take Bill home.'

'Oh, don't go Louise, I've just got here.' Mark looked disappointed.

Ignoring him, she stood up. 'Come on, Bill. Time to go.'

Bill looked surprised. 'I thought we'd stay for a bit.'

Louise sighed. He'd need persuading. 'I can't go home on my own,' she pleaded. 'I need you to come with me.'

Bill lifted his glass. 'It's empty,' he said, mournfully.

'Please,' Louise said.

'OK.' Bill struggled out of his chair.

Louise slung her arm round him and, although she was fairly tall and strong, it took her all her time to hold him upright. 'You not coming, Sue?'

'I'll stay if Mark'll give me a lift home,' Sue said, smiling at the social worker.

'No problem,' he said.

'Come on then, Bill. Home we go,' said Louise.

'Your place or mine?' Bill said, as they stumbled outside.

Exchange Street was dark. The doorway Kara crouched in was sheltered from the bitter blasts that blew in from the River Tay, and few folk walked there unless they were looking for a quiet place to do business. The city noise and the rumble of traffic sounded so distant it was an effort to remember how close she was to the centre of Dundee. A few cars crawled along the street. Clive walked past a couple of times, checking up on his girls. Two young lads stopped across the street to shoot up. An old man walked his dog. But there was still no sign of Jean.

Somewhere nearby a clock struck eleven, reminding Kara she'd been there for almost an hour. Jean wasn't coming. Either she wasn't working tonight or she'd found a punter who'd paid her for a long time. Kara hoped she hadn't taken on the weirdo with the red car and shivered at the thought.

'Get your fuckin' arse out of there. That's my doorway.'

Kara turned, ready to apologise for invading another girl's territory. She didn't want any hassle.

'Jean?' Relief surged through her body. 'Is that you? I've been waiting here all night.'

Jean peered at her. 'Kara? I didn't spot you in that get up. You won't get much trade like that.'

Tears ran down Kara's cheeks. She couldn't stop them.

'Aw, Kara. What's up, love?'

Jean grabbed her, holding her in a firm grip. It only made Kara cry even more. Through her tears she told Jean everything that had happened since last night. 'I feel so daft,' she said when she'd finished. 'I've never cried like this since I was a kid.'

'Looks to me you've got a lot to cry about,' Jean said. 'If it was me I'd be topping myself. What're you going to do now?'

'I don't know. I can't go home. I've got nowhere to go.'

'I'm finished for the night,' Jean said. 'Away and come home with me.'

'You sure?'

'Aye, I'm sure. You'd do the same for me wouldn't you?'

Kara wasn't sure about that but kept her thoughts to herself. 'You're a pal,' she said.

He understood why the trees were angry. Men and flashlights pierced the darkness. Midnight, and his special place invaded. The bodies, gone. Their spirits remained though. Rustling through the trees and dancing in the wind.

He mourned with the trees. Understood their anger. Understood their pain. He felt helpless. Unable to make it right for them.

30

Louise woke early and was in the kitchen making coffee when Sue stumbled through wiping sleep from her eyes.

'You look a bit groggy this morning. Better have some coffee.' Louise slid a cup towards Sue.

'Thanks for the compliment, but we didn't all skive off home early last night.' Sue slurped a mouthful of coffee. 'Oh, that's good. You wouldn't happen to have a paracetamol as well?'

Louise reached into a cupboard and tossed a packet at her.

'Thanks.' Sue popped a capsule out of its foil container and put it in her mouth. 'What happened with you and Bill last night?'

'Why? Should anything have happened?'

'Oh, I don't know. You seemed so anxious to get him home. That's all.' Sue pulled out a chair and sat down, leaning her arms on the kitchen table.

'I just wanted to get out of the pub and it was as good a way as any.'

'Hmm.' Sue drank her coffee. 'You were OK until Mark joined us.' She gazed into her cup. 'Something going on there I should know about?'

'Mark is past history. I don't particularly want to get involved again.'

'OK if I have a go at him?' Sue didn't look up.

'Please yourself. It doesn't bother me. Though I wouldn't recommend it.'

'That's OK then. Now tell me what happened with Bill?'

'Nothing really. I drove him home. Helped him up the stairs and he just collapsed on his bed. I took his shoes off, pulled a quilt over him and left him to it.'

'That all?'

'Just about. His flat's a real mess so I tidied it up a bit and washed a mountain of dishes before I came home.'

'Next thing you'll be getting broody.'

Heat crept up Louise's neck and she knew she was blushing. 'Don't be daft. I was just trying to be helpful. Anyway it's not much different from you feeding him up yesterday. If I didn't know better I'd think you had a thing for him.' She grinned at Sue's discomfiture and topped up her coffee. 'I told him we'd collect him this morning because his car's still at Bell Street, so drink up and get dressed, it's time we weren't here.'

Last night had been a disaster. Mark wasn't used to being sidelined and Louise had gone out of her way to escape his attentions. At least her pal, Sue, had been more co-operative. He'd thought he was onto a sure thing but in the end she'd played hard to get. But it was only a matter of time before he got what he wanted. He could wait.

He bent to pick up the newspaper. Big mistake. The hammers inside his head went into overdrive. Just as well it was Saturday. He leaned on the door and gradually straightened. Staggering through to the kitchen, he threw the paper onto the table and stirred hot water into the coffee granules waiting in his mug.

Taking a sip of the coffee he unfolded the newspaper, spreading it out on the table. The headline took his breath away. *Templeton Woods Murders*. The words danced on the page and blurred, and he was back in the nightmare that had never left him.

When the other boys said they were going to Templeton Woods, nine-year-old Mark hadn't been keen. It wasn't the first time a body had been found in these woods, and he was so scared he almost wet himself. But he couldn't say anything to the others or they'd kick him out of the gang. And belonging to the gang was important because it provided him with protection from the bullies, and the name calling.

Cycling out wasn't so bad although he puffed a bit on the

hills. But when they got to the woods he pushed forward in a show of bravado, although he made sure he stayed close behind Jamie, Bill and Andy. He tried not to look too far into the trees, there were too many shadows. Over to his right something rustled. It sounded like a large body pushing through the undergrowth, but none of the boys was over there.

He shivered. Maybe it was the guy who'd killed that woman last year. Her body had been found in these woods. When the police had brought her out it had seemed as if all Dundee was there to witness it. All ten gang members had been there then. Bill had said, 'I dare you,' so they'd come out on their bikes not really knowing what they were going to see. But the police had turned them back, telling them to 'Go home to your mammies'. Bill and Andy hadn't been pleased and had sworn all the way home.

What if the guy who murdered that girl was still hanging about in the woods? What if they ran into him?

Bill was pushing further into the wood. It was even darker and more overgrown in this part and the trees towered overhead. They'd never been this far in before. Mark's imagination was working overtime. He thought he saw menacing figures behind every tree.

'Let's turn back before we get lost,' he said after a time, biting his lip to stop himself saying please.

Jamie jeered at him, 'Marky-warky wants to go home to his mammy. We should tie him up and leave him here. Maybe the trees will listen to his moans.'

Mark shuddered. They wouldn't do that, would they? But looking at Jamie he thought they might.

Bill continued to march ahead. 'Leave it,' he said to Jamie. 'Let the eejit turn back if he wants.'

'Go on then, off you go.' Jamie waved his hand at Mark in a gesture of dismissal.

Mark looked back through the trees. He didn't want to go on but he didn't want to turn back on his own either. He swallowed hard, tried not to think of bogeymen, and reluctantly followed the rest of the boys.

Bill stopped suddenly and looked at something on the

ground. He prodded it with his foot. 'What d'you think it is?'

Mark pushed forward. 'Maybe it's treasure.' *Treasure Island* was the set book at school this year.

Heat suffused his face when Andy laughed at him.

'Who'd leave treasure out here?' Andy pulled the blanket back. A gasp rippled round the group when they saw what was underneath.

Mark's breath caught in his throat, choking him, but he couldn't stop looking. His limbs froze and the world went into slow motion. Silence descended on the gang, broken only by the sound of breathing and the whispering of the wind in the trees. Eventually the horrible sick feeling rising in Mark's gullet became too much to bear and he forced himself to move. Robot-like, he turned back the way they'd come, so he didn't have to look anymore.

He almost fell over wee Jerry being sick in the bushes. 'What a wimp,' he said, glad there a was a bigger wally than him.

From behind came a shout, 'Let's get out of here.' It was the best thing he'd heard Bill say all day.

Mark said nothing about finding the body in the woods, because his ma wouldn't have wanted him to go there and he liked to please his ma.

Mark blinked and shuddered. It had all come back, every single detail. He'd had nightmares for years afterwards but never told his mother or the psychiatrist what he'd seen that day. The psychiatrist had diagnosed a food additive problem and put him on a diet. He'd lost weight, wasn't called fatty anymore, and he'd stayed away from the gang.

But now, looking at the headline, he knew it wasn't over.

Bill scraped a teaspoon over the solidified remains in the bottom of the jar, loosening just enough to make a cup of weak coffee. It did nothing to relieve the pounding in his temples.

Last night was a blank. He vaguely remembered leaving the pub with Louise but couldn't remember a thing after that.

Someone had washed his dishes and tidied the flat though and he was sure he hadn't done it. Had Louise stayed? Had they slept together?

Finishing his coffee, he dumped the cup in the sink and walked through to the lounge to look out the front window. His car wasn't in the drive. He was still frowning when Louise and Sue drove up and tooted the horn. Grabbing his jacket, he slammed out of the house before they tooted again and had the neighbours complaining. He was still pushing his arms into the sleeves when he slid into the back seat. 'You got home all right, then?'

Louise didn't look at him, but nodded her head and murmured something indistinguishable as she let the clutch out and moved away from the kerb. Sue didn't comment.

Bill looked at the back of Louise's head. Her hair was gathered into a loose ponytail, and he had a sudden urge to lean forward and loosen it, stroke it. Pushing his hands deeper into his pockets, he said, desperately, 'Have you ever been to a homicide briefing before?'

'No, not a homicide one.'

Bill checked the rear-view mirror, willing her to look into it, but Louise kept her eyes on the road.

'I don't suppose they're much different from any other kind of briefing.'

'What she's not saying is that you omitted to tell her she'd have to provide feedback to the briefing about our liaison meeting with Tony Palmer.' Sue twisted round in her seat so she could look at him. 'But it's all right, Bill. I've told her all about it.'

It didn't take long to get to headquarters and, as Louise slid into a convenient parking place in front of the modern building, Bill spotted his car. He breathed a sigh of relief. That was one problem resolved. The next one was the briefing.

The large open-plan office hummed with noise. It wasn't like her own office, which she shared with Meg, and Louise wondered how anyone could ever do any work here.

'C'mon over to my desk until we find out which room the briefing's in.'

Sue led the way, shouting greetings to several of her male colleagues. She pulled an extra chair over to her desk and motioned to Louise to sit. 'Wait there and I'll get some coffee. We can take it in with us.' She returned a moment later, plonked a paper cup of coffee in front of Louise and then wandered over to Bill who sat at an adjacent desk. 'Get this down you. You'll feel better.'

Bill mumbled his thanks and, grabbing the cup, took a long drink. He surfaced, spluttering. 'Damn, it's boiling.'

'Well, what d'you expect? Cold coffee?' Sue stalked back to her own desk.

'You're in a funny mood. What'd I do?'

Detective Inspector Andy Michaels was in charge of the briefing. Louise took one of the chairs at the conference table and watched him as he instructed a man who was moving the position of a white board. After he'd finished he turned round to inspect the room, staring straight at Louise. He hesitated a moment as if he wasn't sure who she was or why she was there, then walked over to her. She could feel her neck grow hot and hoped she wasn't blushing.

He leaned over her, placing both his hands flat on the table. 'Thanks for your help yesterday,' he said. 'I've had you seconded to the investigation for the time being so you can be the official liaison officer with the Palmer family. There's too much history between Tony Palmer and some of my officers.' He looked over at Bill pointedly.

'Yes, sir,' Louise said. 'I'll do my best.'

'You all know why you're here.' Andy looked round the room before turning to one of the white boards. 'Let's see what we've got.' He lifted a marker pen. 'Three bodies,' he scribbled on the board. 'Found in Templeton Woods yesterday,' he wrote *Friday 9 Jan.* on the board. 'In varying degrees of decomposition. Only one body was identifiable. Thought to be the body of Denise Palmer, daughter of Tony Palmer.' He pinned a photograph to a sheet of paper pinned to the wall, and turned to face the officers in the room. 'And we all know who Tony Palmer is. Constable Louise Walker has joined us,' he motioned in her direction, 'and will act as liaison with Denise Palmer's family.'

Several of the officers turned to look at Louise.

'The first task, of course, will be the formal identification. We can go ahead with that after the briefing meeting. Get it out of the way this morning. Post mortem on the Palmer girl is this afternoon, four o'clock – Bill and Sue will be the attending officers. The other two post mortems will be next week.

'We don't have much to go on at the moment but I'll expect an investigation into any reports of missing women, and of course we'll need to go ahead with DNA testing and so on.' He scribbled a task list on the board. 'We also need to trace the woman who phoned the information in.' He added this to the task list. 'And check on the owner of the handbag found in the woods. The name inside was Kara Ferguson.' He wrote – *Handbag – Kara Ferguson.* 'She may be one of the victims or she could be the woman who phoned. If that's the case then it's likely the killer took her there but somehow she managed to escape. I can't impress on you enough that we need to find her.'

Andy's voice droned on, but after Kara Ferguson's name was written on the board, Louise's mind was elsewhere.

'Well, any questions?' Andy had finished his briefing.

Louise stood up. 'I think I know who Kara Ferguson is. Unless there's two of them in town . . . I was called out to two children left on their own early on Friday morning. The mother's name was Kara Ferguson. She'd gone out on Thursday night and not returned. The children were taken into care and there's a case conference on Monday morning.'

Andy scribbled on the whiteboard. 'You'll attend the case conference, of course, and Bill, you go as well.'

The meeting ended and the room emptied. Louise hovered beside Sue's desk trying not to look as much of a spare part as she felt. Already she was regretting her willingness to help out last night. If she hadn't agreed to break the news of his daughter's death to Tony Palmer she'd have been on a day off back at her desk on Monday morning. As it was, she was in an unfamiliar office, expected to work with strangers, doing a job she wasn't equipped for, and she didn't even have a desk.

Tony sat at his desk long after the club closed. The dancers had finished their routines hours ago and the silvery poles glimmered, lifeless, under the dim security lights. A bottle of Laphroaig sat on the floor beside his chair, empty, but he wasn't drunk. It was customary for one of the dancers to join him after the performance was over, but their dancing had left him cold and he had no need of their flesh. Tonight all he could think about was his daughter – Denise, his only child – Denise whom he'd loved with every atom of his being.

Eventually he roused himself and went home. He couldn't recall the journey. It was as if he'd become a zombie, unseeing, unfeeling, not quite dead. He sat on the side of his wife's bed and watched her sleep. Then he lay down beside her.

When he woke, not having expected to sleep, it was daylight, a new day, a day without Denise. He stroked the hair back over his wife's forehead. She mumbled something and turned over.

There was a light tap on the door. 'The police are on the phone, sir.' Morag spoke quietly.

'See if Brian can handle it. I don't want to disturb Madge.' Tony eased himself off the bed and walked downstairs, his shoeless feet making no sound on the carpet.

'They're ready for the identification, boss,' Brian said. 'D'you want to speak to them?'

He shook his head. 'Just see to the arrangements. I'll have a quick shower, make myself presentable.'

Brian turned back to the phone.

Tony heard him say, 'It won't be necessary to send a car. We'll meet you there.' He climbed the stairs two at a time, anxious suddenly to wash the grime and dirt of yesterday off his body.

31

'This isn't going to be easy,' Louise said.

'I know that.' Tony's voice shook. The sick feeling in the pit of his stomach was rising, threatening to choke him. 'Let's get it over with.'

Louise led the way, holding the door open for him. He hesitated for a moment and then followed her. Apart from two chairs the room was bare, painted white, with one mirrored wall. It reminded Tony of the mirrored wall in his office and he had an insane urge to laugh.

'I'm ready,' he said, staring through the window at the trolley with the sheet-covered body. Louise nodded and the mortuary assistant lifted the sheet.

Tony's breath caught in his throat. He nodded. 'Yes, it's Denise.' He was glad Madge wasn't here to see her. 'What happens now?'

'The post mortem, this afternoon.' Louise avoided his eyes; she knew how painful this was for him.

'They're going to cut her up?' He almost felt the knife slicing into Denise's flesh. 'They can't!' It was almost a howl.

Louise put her hand on his arm. 'I'm sorry but it has to be done.'

'I won't allow it. She's been desecrated enough.'

'We need to know how and why she died. Surely you want that too?' Louise sighed. 'I'm afraid your permission isn't required.'

Tiredness swept through Tony and he slumped into one of the chairs, head in his hands. 'I have influence, you know.'

'It won't make any difference.' Louise sat in the chair beside him. 'It's murder, Mr Palmer, and we have to investigate. Part of that investigation is the post mortem, and no one has enough power or influence to prevent it taking place.' She was silent for a moment and then said, 'I'm sorry.'

The warmth in the woman's voice comforted him. He felt like leaning his head on her shoulder and crying till there were no tears left. Instead he raised his head and looked into her eyes, meeting her sympathy with a feeling akin to despair.

'Someone's going to pay for this,' he whispered.

She'd felt so sorry for him and then, all of a sudden, he'd turned into a raging animal, slamming out of the room and yelling at everyone. The kind of man she'd been warned he was, but hadn't believed until now.

Louise took a final look at the body and left.

Palmer was standing beside the car when she left the building. 'I shouldn't have shouted at you. I know none of this is your fault.'

'That's OK,' she said. 'I'd probably have done the same.'

'Will you keep in touch? Let me know what's happening?'

'Of course.' It would make her job easier if he was encouraging further contact. 'I'll need you and your wife to tell me all you can about Denise. The more we know about her friends and her movements, the better.'

His eyes became expressionless. 'It'll be difficult for Madge.'

Louise knew he included himself in that. 'The sooner the better, then. Get it over with. Maybe later today?'

He sighed. 'Yes, I suppose so. Do we have to come to the station?'

'I can come to the house, if you prefer.'

'That would probably be best.' He opened the car door and got in. 'Phone me when you're coming.'

Louise nodded. She wasn't looking forward to the interview, her first in a murder investigation and it had to be with the biggest gangster in the city.

Phil was still in bed when the call came. 'Yeah,' he said, pulling himself into a sitting position. 'Right away, boss.'

'Bugger,' Gus said, when Phil spoke to him. 'I was looking forward to a long lie.'

The roads were clogged with cars heading into the town centre, making Phil fume each time they waited in a queue at the traffic lights. 'Did you have to drive this way?' he grumbled, drumming his fingers on the dashboard.

At last they turned the corner into the Nethergate and Perth Road, and the traffic thinned. Phil sighed with relief as the car picked up speed.

Tony was in the study when they arrived. Hands clasped behind his back, he paced the room. 'Well, what have you found out?'

Phil swallowed. There wasn't anything to report. 'We went to Templeton Woods . . .'

'And?'

'We spoke to a copper but he wasn't very forthcoming.'

'What copper? Anyone we know?' Tony's expression suggested he'd like to have the policeman's balls.

'Yeah, it was that old guy Johnstone. Remember him?'

'Him! Thought he'd retired.'

'No such luck.'

'Anything else?' Tony's pacing was becoming more manic.

'Not really.'

Tony stopped pacing and glared at him.

'What d'you mean – not really?'

'It's nothing much really, but when we were chasing Kara on Thursday night she met a punter who took her to Templeton Woods.'

'And!'

Phil drew a deep breath. 'It was the exact same place the police were investigating – the part of the woods that led to where the bodies were found. That's where we lost them.'

Tony frowned and started pacing again. After a few moments he looked up. 'You're saying a punter took her there?'

'Yeah.'

'Who was this punter?'

Phil shrugged his shoulders. 'Just a punter, a guy in a red estate. We followed them into the woods and then lost them.'

'How the fuck did you manage to lose them?'

'He just gave us the slip, must have gone round us. The last we saw was his car heading back to Dundee. We thought Kara was with him, but maybe she wasn't. Maybe she was still in the woods.'

'But Kara's alive. Madge saw her yesterday.'

'Yeah, I know. That's why I'm not sure if it's connected.'

Tony turned suddenly.

Pushing his face close to Phil's, he hissed, 'Find Kara. Quick. I want her brought to the club – alive. And find out who that punter was.'

'OK, boss.'

'Fuck off out of here and get onto it then,' he yelled.

Phil felt Tony's spittle hit his cheek but didn't dare wipe it away. 'Come on, Gus,' he said, fighting the urge to run from the room. He didn't stop sweating until he was sitting in the car.

'How'd you get on with Tony Palmer?'

Bill sprinted along the pavement and caught up with Louise at the door.

'OK, I suppose.' Louise followed Bill into the lift. 'I know Tony's supposed to be a real tough guy, but I felt sorry for him seeing his daughter like that.'

'He's tougher than you could ever imagine. He'll survive.'

'I don't know, Bill. He was really broken up.'

'Did you get anything out of him?'

'Not yet, but I'm going back to see him and his wife this afternoon.'

'Be careful, Louise.' The lift doors swung open and Bill stood back to let her leave first. 'He probably wants something from you.'

'Like what?'

'Like any evidence we have about who might have been responsible. He'll have his own ideas about the punishment fitting the crime.'

'I shouldn't have any problems then,' Louise pushed the office door open, 'because as far as I can see, we haven't got a clue just now. Anyway let's get down to the important things. Where am I supposed to sit?'

'I knew you'd say that.' Bill pulled her over to a desk at the window. '*Ta da!* It's all yours. Your own private desk, chair and telephone. The computer's coming in . . .' he looked at his watch, 'approximately half an hour. What more could you want?'

'Four walls would be nice,' Louise muttered, looking round at the large room crammed with desks and jangling telephones. 'How can anyone work in this racket?'

'Oh, you'll get used to it.'

32

'She can't have vanished into thin air.' Phil patted his pockets, looking for gum. 'She has to be somewhere.'

'Aye, but where?'

Phil shrugged. 'Maybe she's gone home.' He removed the silver wrapping and popped the gum into his mouth. 'It's worth a try. And if we sit here much longer Tony's going to start wondering what we're doing.' He glanced anxiously at the front of the house.

Gus edged the car out of Tony's drive. Half an hour later they pulled into the parking area in front of the Greenfield flats. Gus leaned his arms on the steering wheel and rested his chin on them. Staring up at Kara's building, he said, 'Her door's shut.'

'So?'

'It was hanging open when we left yesterday.'

Phil eased himself out of the car. 'Come on then. We don't want her to run for it before we get there.'

A door slammed as they reached the top of the stairs but when they turned the corner onto the landing, it was deserted. Ignoring the slight twitch of the neighbour's curtains and the feeling he was being watched, Phil strode to Kara's door and pushed. It creaked open, hanging lopsidedly from its broken hinges. Phil stood, listening, then with a signal to Gus to stay where he was, he went up the hallway and kicked the lounge door open. No one. Disgustedly he kicked all the other doors open.

'OK, there's no point guarding the door,' he said. 'She's not here.' He slumped onto the sofa and closed his eyes. 'Where the fuck is she?'

'Check the mail,' Gus said. 'It was sitting behind the door.'

Phil grabbed the bunch of letters. 'Bill, another fucking

165

bill, bumph, bill.' Hardly looking at them, he flicked the open letters onto the floor. 'This one looks more interesting.' He ripped the top open. 'It's from the Council . . . We've got her!' He thumped Gus on the arm. 'D'you know what this is?' He waved the letter under Gus's nose. 'It's only an invite to a meeting about her kids, that's what. There's no way she'll miss that. All we have to do is wait for her on Monday morning outside the office.' He waggled the letter.

'But if the letter's here how's she going to know?'

'She's a mum, isn't she? She'll have checked up. Bound to.'

Gus frowned. 'Even if she does go, how are we going to grab her?'

'If we don't get her on the way in, we'll get her when she leaves.' Phil stood up, grinning. 'Come on, let's get some food. I'm starving.'

Jean scratched her head. The hair felt slightly greasy between her fingers and flakes of dandruff fell to her shoulders. Maybe she should wash it, but even if she did it would never look like Kara's. She wandered through to the living room. The old coat she'd covered Kara with was on the floor. She replaced it on the sleeping girl. Kara stirred.

'Thought you'd never wake up,' Jean said.

Kara yawned. 'It was ages before I could get to sleep. I kept thinking of those snakes.'

'They won't hurt you. They're not poisonous, but their jaws lock when they bite anything. It could break your bones but it wouldn't kill you.' Jean walked over and peered into one of the large glass tanks lining the living room walls. 'Who's a pretty boy then?' she cooed, scratching the glass. She opened the top of the glass case and ran her finger along the body of the large python.

'For fuck's sake put the lid on that tank.' Kara cowered into the corner of the sofa.

Jean smiled maliciously as she replaced it. 'You should thank your lucky stars they're here. I can't see Phil and Gus trying any funny stuff with them around.'

Kara didn't look convinced. 'What d'you want three of them for? Is one not enough?'

'Ach, Willie got them. They were just tiny, but they grew.'

'Willie? I didn't know you had a man around.'

'He's in Perth Prison, the now, so you don't have to worry.'

'D'you mean he's left you to look after his snakes?' Kara shivered. 'If it was me I'd be shot of them before he came back.'

'Naw, I couldn't do that. Besides I've got used to them, and like I said, they're great protection.' Jean reached into the cavity beneath the snake tank. Pulling out a wooden box, she edged the lid open, reached into it and removed the small furry animal inside. She dangled the mouse by the tail, in front of Kara's horrified eyes.

Jean laughed. She was getting a kick out of Kara's anxiety. 'Just lunch,' she said, dropping the mouse into the glass tank.

The mouse froze.

'Why's it not running away?'

'They always do that. Willie says the snake hypnotises them.' Her eyes glittered as she watched.

Jean pulled her dressing gown tightly round her body, tying the belt in a loose knot. She was chunkier than Kara. Her legs were shorter, her tummy flabbier, her skin greasier. She didn't have Kara's striking looks and she was sure if she tried streaks in her own hair she'd look daft. What an idiot she'd been to invite Kara back to her place. It only made her feel crappy and ugly.

'You don't have to stay if you don't want to.'

'It's not that.' Kara said. 'I'm really grateful. It's just that the snakes take a bit of getting used to.'

Jean studied her through half-closed lids. 'How long d'you think you'll need to stay?'

'I don't know, Jean. The weekend would be fine. If I can just lie low until the meeting about the kids. Then when I get them back, I'm heading out of town.'

'What if you don't get them back? What if the welfare

decide to keep them for a while?'

'I'm not leaving Dundee without Billy and Charlene.' Kara's voice was stubborn. 'I've tried it and it didn't work.'

'Yeah, I can see you wouldn't want to do that.' Jean slumped into the armchair. Kara was sitting with her knees pulled up on the couch. She was so pretty, it hurt. 'You can put up with the snakes? You won't be scared?'

'I can put up with anything apart from being without the kids,' Kara said. 'You said they were safe anyway.'

'Yeah, I did, didn't I?' Jean looked at the three massive snakes in their tanks, one on each wall, circling the sofa. She'd let Kara stay today and tomorrow. After that, well, she'd have to see. Maybe she'd leave one of the tank lids a wee bit open. See how Kara liked having a python cuddling up to her.

Tony's phone call came just after two o'clock. 'Madge's woken up,' he said, 'but if you want to talk to her, you should come now because the doctor's given her a tranquillizer.'

'I'll come right away,' Louise said, stuffing a notebook and pen in her shoulder bag.

Tony was waiting at the door when she drove up. 'Madge is in the lounge,' he said, ushering her inside. 'She's been terribly upset and her mood's all over the place.' A frown creased his forehead. 'I don't like her taking sleeping pills, but I didn't know what else to do.'

'I understand,' Louise said, although she couldn't help thinking about the drugs Tony was known to distribute.

Madge looked up as they entered the room. 'It's a mistake,' she said. 'Tell me it's all a mistake.'

'I'm afraid not, Mrs Palmer.' Louise sat on the chair facing her. 'I wish I could tell you otherwise.'

Madge's shoulders started to shake and tears trickled down her cheeks. She wore no make-up and her fair hair hung lank and uncombed. There was no remnant of the sophisticated woman Louise had seen yesterday.

'Hush, now,' Tony said, pulling her towards him until her head nestled under his chin. 'I'll take care of everything.'

Madge pulled herself away from him. 'You can't bring her back though.'

Tony looked at Louise and shrugged his shoulders. There was something boyish and helpless in the gesture and Louise couldn't help wondering who was consoling him in his grief.

'Maybe we can't bring Denise back,' she said, looking directly at Madge, 'but we can try to find whoever has done this terrible thing and make sure he doesn't do it again.'

'That's not going to help Denise.'

'No,' Louise agreed, 'but it could prevent another girl's parents from going through what you're suffering.'

Madge twisted the silk material of her skirt between her hands. 'What d'you want to know?' she whispered.

'I'd like to get to know Denise. What kind of girl she was. Who her friends were. What she liked to do. That kind of thing.'

'She was a lovely girl. Kind, considerate, never a harsh word for anyone. She had lots of friends, but no one in particular. She liked to ring the changes. She was popular.' Madge paused for breath. 'But she was a good girl, a nice girl. Never gave us any cause for worry.'

Louise nodded, wondering how realistic Madge's description was. 'Did she live at home? Or did she have her own place?'

'She wanted her independence.' Tony's hand tightened on Madge's shoulder. 'But I didn't want her to move out so I built an extension at the back of the house for her. It was like a self-contained flat with a connecting door to the main house.'

'But she always comes in for her meals,' Madge said. 'We see . . . saw her every day.'

Louise wondered whether she should mention anything about the need for police access to the flat, but decided against it just now in case it broke the mood.

'I know this is difficult for you,' Louise said, 'but I need to know when you last saw her and how she seemed to you.'

'It was about a week and a half ago. Hogmanay.' Madge twisted her skirt, winding it round her fingers until they went white. 'There was a party at the club. Just the young folks. I didn't go.' She caught her breath on a sob. 'I wish I'd gone with her.'

Tony put his arm round her shoulders. 'You never go to the club, Madge. It's not your thing. Anyway, Denise wouldn't have wanted her parents hanging around when she was with her pals.'

'*You* went to the club.' Madge spat it out like an accusation.

'I always go,' Tony said, gently, 'it's my job.'

'You saw her last, then?' Louise scribbled in her notebook.

'You could say that, I suppose. But I wasn't at the party. I spent most of my time in the office.' A wistful expression crept into Tony's eyes. 'She looked as if she was having a good time.'

'Did you see her leave?'

'No, I was in my office. But I knew a bunch of them had planned to go to City Square to hear the bells. After that I suppose they went first footing.'

'Didn't you worry when she didn't come home?'

'Not right away,' Tony said. 'We just assumed she'd stayed with one of her pals.'

'Was she in the habit of doing that?'

'Sometimes,' Tony said. 'We didn't worry because she was a sensible girl.'

'I was worried,' Madge said. 'She'd never stayed away so long before.'

'I can ask around the club – see if anyone there saw her leave.'

'That would be helpful.' Louise turned a page in her notebook. 'Now if you could give me a list of her friends, and maybe a recent photograph?'

Tony gently removed his arm from his wife, easing her head onto the cushioned back of the settee. He opened his wallet and removed a snapshot. 'Will you let me have it back when you're finished?'

'Of course,' Louise said.

'I'll have a list of the friends that were with her that night sent on to you. Now, if that's all, perhaps I'd better get Madge up to bed. She's exhausted.'

Louise rose and tucked the notebook into her bag. 'I'll be in touch.'

33

Bill wasn't sure whether it was the booze from last night, the meat pie he'd had for lunch, or the thought of what he was going to have to observe in the next half hour, that turned his stomach. But he knew if he didn't do something soon, the lump pushing its way up his gullet was in danger of erupting all over the corridor floor.

'Won't be a minute,' he muttered to Sue as he made a dash for the toilet.

Banging a stall door open he fell to his knees and, embracing the porcelain bowl, he retched until his ribs were sore. Pushing himself up, he staggered to a sink and splashed cold water over his face, then, leaning his forehead on the cold tiles, he drew several deep breaths until the spasms stopped.

'Sue gave him a sharp look when he met her in the corridor. 'You don't look too great. You sure you're up to this?'

If Sue hadn't queried whether he was up to it, he might have called off with a plea of not feeling too well, but misplaced pride wouldn't let him. 'I'm fine, just a tummy bug, probably that pie I had for lunch.'

'Yeah, yeah.' Sue grinned at him. 'Come on then, let's get it over with.'

Bill shoved his hands in his pockets and strode down the corridor with a feigned eagerness.

'I started without you.' The grey-haired woman, scraping under the fingernails of the corpse, didn't look up. 'I've almost finished with the preliminaries. I'll be opening her up in a minute or two.' Her voice sounded slightly disembodied as it filtered through the intercom system.

'Fine.' Bill swallowed hard, thankful there was a glass wall separating him from the dissection area.

The grey-haired woman was doing the cutting and speaking, a second pathologist was taking notes. Beside the body, stretched out on the steel gurney, was a small table holding dissection tools and scales for weighing organs. It reminded Bill of a butcher's shop.

'Who's your colleague? We haven't been introduced.' The first pathologist snipped a nail and placed it in a small polythene bag before replacing the scissors in a steel tray. She still didn't look up.

'Sorry,' Bill struggled to speak. 'DS Sue Rogers, it's her first post mortem. Sue, Doctor Rose Armstrong.'

The pathologist looked up for the first time and smiled. It transformed her face, smoothing out the lines and almost making her beautiful.

'Feel free to ask any questions. He,' she pointed at Bill, 'never does. Thinks he knows it all and won't admit to being squeamish. But that's men for you.'

'Thanks,' Sue said, 'but I'll be guided by Bill. It's his show.'

Bill flashed her a smile. Sue always thought about his feelings before she committed herself to anything. He'd have to remember to make it up to her afterwards.

Rose shrugged her shoulders. 'For the record, I've done the visual examination, taken photographs, and skin, hair and nail samples. Body fluids have been collected, including the usual swabs. I'm now going to make the Y incision and take a look at what's inside.'

Bill leaned against the window, fighting the nausea and wishing he was anywhere else but here. 'Any conclusions yet?' His voice sounded faraway.

'You know better than to ask that.' Rose inserted the point of the knife above the breastbone. 'It's too early to tell.'

'What about an educated guess based on what you've done so far.'

'Hmm.' She sliced down towards the sternum. 'Without knowing what's gone on inside, I'd say this girl died from hypothermia.'

'Hypothermia? Not strangulation?'

'That's what I said. As a matter of interest,' she said without looking up, 'what made you think it might be strangulation?'

'I just wanted to rule it out as the cause of death. There were two previous murders in the same vicinity way back in the late seventies.'

'You think there's a connection, Bill?' Sue said.

'There doesn't seem to be, but you never know.' He was glad of the excuse to look at Sue instead of at what Rose Armstrong was doing.

'In most cases a hypothermic death would make it natural causes.' Rose raised her head and looked at Bill. 'Makes it interesting, wouldn't you say?'

Bill closed his eyes and summoned up a mental picture of the bodies in the wood. He opened them again. 'Yes, but the hypothermia had a little help from someone. So does that make it murder, or criminal neglect?'

'Lawyers are going to have a field day.' Rose sliced down the abdomen towards the groin, completing the Y. 'Still, you won't know what else I find until I've finished.'

'Swallow this.' Tony handed Madge the small pill and a glass of water. 'You'll feel better after you've slept.'

Madge sat on the edge of the bed. 'I can't sleep forever,' she said, popping the pill in her mouth.

'I know, but it will help you to get on an even keel.'

'Will it?' Madge lay back on the pillow and closed her eyes.

Tony got up and walked across the room. Pausing a moment in the doorway he turned to say something, but her eyes were closed. She should sleep for a few hours and it would give him time to do what he had to.

The car was waiting, Brian in the driver's seat.

Fifteen minutes later they were driving slowly up Templeton Road. The woods stretched as far as the eye could see and Tony despaired of finding the spot his daughter had died. He was on the point of phoning Louise when he spotted the police Land-Rover.

'Pull up here,' he said to Brian.

A policeman got out of the Land-Rover and strolled to the car.

Tony stepped out onto the road. 'Jim Johnstone,' he said. 'It's been a long time.'

The policeman's eyes narrowed. 'What d'you want, Tony?'

Tony stared into the wood with bleak eyes. 'I want to see where they found my daughter.'

'What good's that going to do?'

'I don't know. I just want to see the place. But I need someone to show me.'

'I can't do that.'

Tony turned to look at him. 'When you were in that bit of trouble I saw you right.'

Johnstone nodded.

'You could have been kicked out of the force if it hadn't been for me.'

Johnstone shifted his feet and looked uncomfortable.

'What harm would it do to take me in there?' Tony nodded towards the woods.

'Well, I suppose it wouldn't do much harm now forensics have finished.'

Johnstone led the way to the clearing. 'You have to crawl through this shrubbery.'

The branches closed around Tony.

He didn't spook easily but thinking of Denise, that she must have come this way . . . Moments later he was brushing the dirt from his knees and standing up. The clearing seemed peaceful although there was an unusual smell lingering in the air.

'This place is pretty much hidden,' Johnstone said. 'You'd hardly know it was here.'

The policeman's voice came from a great distance as Tony struggled with his breathing. The trees danced in front of his eyes and the clearing closed in on him. This was where Denise had died. He could see impressions on the ground in front of three of the trees and wondered which one of them was made by her.

He pointed to the trees. 'Where exactly was she found?' His voice was hoarse with the effort of speaking.

'I'm afraid I don't know. All I know is there were three bodies.'

Tony shuddered. He'd had enough. 'Let's go,' he said, not trusting himself to say anything more without cracking.

When they got back to the road he turned to face Johnstone. 'Thanks,' he said. 'I won't forget how helpful you've been.'

Johnstone shrugged his shoulders. 'Just don't mention it to anyone.'

Tony got in the car. 'Take me home.'

Madge was still sleeping when Tony got back to the house. He stroked her hair and gently kissed her forehead. She turned in her sleep and mumbled something that he couldn't quite hear, but she didn't open her eyes.

Quietly, he left the room, returning to the lounge where he poured himself a large Laphroaig. He took one sip and laid the glass down. Tears gathered in his eyes. Visions of his daughter, dying alone in the dark, in those godforsaken woods rose in his mind. He blinked hard.

Upstairs, he pulled the dust sheet from the unfinished canvas. His daughter's face glowed, full of radiant life, as if he'd captured her spirit. He reached out a hand to touch the cold canvas and wept.

How long he remained there he didn't know. But dusk gradually gathered round him, touching the canvas with gentle fingers, drawing a veil over Denise until she vanished altogether in the darkness.

He wiped his eyes with the back of his hand. He'd had enough of tears. Pulling himself to his feet he flipped on the light, walked to the sink that smelled of turpentine, and splashed cold water over his face. Angrily he scattered the paintbrushes and tubes of oils. Now that Denise was gone he didn't think he'd ever have the heart to paint again. Lifting a knife from the draining board, he walked back to the painting and stood looking at it. This canvas wasn't Denise. It was a cold image that didn't live or breathe. If he couldn't have his daughter he didn't want a substitute. When he reached out to Denise's face, however, his hand stopped. He couldn't do it. Throwing the knife down, he covered her with a dust sheet, turned his back on the painting, and left the studio.

'Brian,' he shouted as he ran down the stairs. 'Get the car out. We're going to the club.'

'D'you have to go out?' Kara eyed the snakes. Admittedly they hadn't moved much during the day, but they still gave her the creeps.

Jean pulled a brush through her hair. 'I have to, I need the money.'

Kara bit her lip. Being here wasn't helping Jean. 'If I'm in the way, I'll go,' she mumbled, although she had no idea where.

'Don't be daft.' Jean pulled on her jacket. 'I'll be back as soon as I make enough for the Sunday dinner.'

'I should come with you,' Kara said. 'With two of us working we'd make a bit more.'

'Yeah, and what if Gus and Phil see you? No, you stay here. It's safer. And don't worry about the snakes, they can't get out of their tanks. Not unless you lift the lids.'

Kara gazed at the tanks, almost as hypnotised as the mouse had been.

'Cheerio, then. See you later.'

'Good luck,' Kara shouted after her, and settled back to watch the pythons for signs of movement.

The flat was dark and cold when Bill got home. He lit the gas fire in the lounge, plonked himself in an armchair, and unscrewed the cap of the whisky bottle he'd rescued from the kitchen. Tilting the bottle, he swigged a large mouthful from it and swilled it round his mouth. He needed a drink after the horrors of the post mortem.

The whisky settled his stomach, warming him and lifting his mood. He felt the heat seeping through his limbs, making them heavy. Gradually his eyelids closed and he slipped into a doze.

The harsh buzz of the doorbell jerked him awake and, setting the bottle on the carpet at the side of his chair, he rose to answer it.

'Fancy a carryout?' Louise held up a plastic bag. 'Hope you like sweet and sour chicken.'

She'd combed her hair out and it lay in loose, brown waves on her shoulders. It made her look younger and more vulnerable. No make-up covered her skin, which was rosy and glowing with the cold. He glanced down the path to see if Sue was bringing up the rear, but she was alone. After an initial moment of surprise he stood back and held the door open for her.

She looked at him anxiously for a moment. 'I nearly got pork but I thought chicken would be safer.'

Bill realised he hadn't spoken. 'Yes,' he said, struggling for something to say. 'Yes, sweet and sour's fine.'

She stepped past him, then hovered in the hall. 'We don't need plates, and I have plastic forks.'

'I'm afraid the house is a bit cold,' Bill apologised awkwardly, 'but I've got some heat going in the lounge, and I've got a bottle. You go on in and I'll join you in a minute.'

When he returned to the lounge with two glasses he'd grabbed from the kitchen, Louise had arranged two foil dishes on the coffee table beside his chair. He set the two glasses beside them and rescued the whisky bottle from the floor. Without looking at Louise he poured some whisky into each glass.

She handed him a plastic fork. 'You don't have to look so embarrassed.'

'I'm not,' he stuttered, feeling the heat seep up from his

neck.

She popped a portion of chicken into her mouth and chewed thoughtfully. 'I'm not going to eat *you*. This isn't a come-on. I just thought you needed some feeding up and there's nothing in your fridge.'

'Mmhmm.' Bill wiped a trickle of sauce from the side of his mouth. 'Sue did say you were a bit of a do-gooder and that you liked to collect strays. Am I one of your strays?'

'It's possible.' Louise grinned at him. 'What else did she say?'

'Said she thought you'd make a better social worker than a police officer.'

'Well, whatever, your virtue is safe with me.'

'But,' Bill grinned, 'is yours safe with me?'

'I'll risk it. Now just eat up and shut up.'

Tony ignored Marlene's worried looks. He'd been drinking solidly since he arrived at the club, but he didn't feel drunk. Marlene was just a fusspot. It had been years since he'd had a fling with her but she still seemed to feel responsible for him. Kind of like a mother hen.

He leaned back against the bar, narrowed his eyes and watched the new girl. Angel, Marlene had said she was called, and she certainly looked like an angel with those big blue, innocent-looking eyes and the long sweep of blonde hair. As he watched, she bent forward, letting her hair fall in front of her face and swinging it back and forth in time with the movement of her neat little, almost bare, backside. Perspiration broke out on his forehead, if she shoved it any nearer that punter his nose would vanish up the crack.

Tony lifted his glass and almost emptied it with one swallow. 'It's late,' he said. 'I'll probably sleep here tonight. Send Angel up to the office when she's finished. It's time we became acquainted.'

'She's a good kid, Tony, and she's a real asset to the club.' Marlene bent down and rearranged something underneath the bar.

Tony grinned as he studied the top of her head. Marlene didn't usually display any jealousy and he wondered what made this girl different.

'It's time she met the boss,' he said, swaying slightly as he stood up.

Marlene straightened and looked him in the eye. 'Don't mark her, Tony. It was weeks before the last one was able to work again. This girl's too good for that.'

'Don't take shit from no one,' Tony slurred. 'Should've been more obliging then nothing would've happened.'

'I don't want her marked.' Marlene's voice was serious. 'You expect me to turn a profit here and *she* makes money.'

'Don't push it, Marlene.' Tony glowered at her. 'I'll expect the girl when she's finished her act.'

He sees them. Three girls. Tall, blonde. Hair flowing in the wind. Dancing hand in hand. The trees bend forward to greet them. Rustling their leaves and branches. Whispering.

Another girl. Smaller, red striped hair. Breaks into the circle. The girls turn. Crumble into dust.

The trees shake their branches in anger and the whispering is ugly.

34

The smell of frying bacon woke Bill. He blinked his eyes open, staring unbelievingly at the morning sun forcing its way past the dirt through his windows. He couldn't remember the last time he'd slept through the night. Nor could he remember the last time he'd felt so hungry.

Pushing his feet out of the bed he padded over to a chair and rummaged for his old dressing gown, which he found nestling at the bottom of a heap of discarded clothes. His slippers had apparently stopped co-operating and he could only find one, so he pulled on a pair of socks and went to explore the source of the mouth-watering smell.

The kitchen was at the back of the house and the door at the end of the corridor hung, tantalisingly open. Louise, her hair clipped back loosely and one of his tea towels tied round her middle, looked at home standing in front of the cooker with her back to him. He watched for a moment as she flipped the bacon over in the pan. It reminded him of an earlier time: when this had been Evie's kitchen; before she started to play around with other men.

'That smells good,' he said. 'Where'd you get the bacon?'

'I went to the supermarket. You were low on groceries so I stocked up. I got you a paper as well. There's a big write up in it about the murders, thought you'd be interested. You can pay me later.'

Bill noticed for the first time his socks were different colours. How come he hadn't seen that when he pulled them on? But it was like all the other things he didn't notice, or forgot altogether, they crept up on him when he wasn't looking. And it was becoming more frequent. Last night seemed so long ago, lost in a pleasant, hazy fog. As usual, he'd drunk too much and the last thing he remembered was

Louise's shoulder under his armpit and her arm round his waist as he stumbled to bed. It looked as if she'd stayed all night and he wondered if they'd slept together. Frowning, he tried to remember but, like so many other nights, the memory of what had happened after they'd finished the bottle of whisky had dropped into a deep, dark hole.

Louise flipped the bacon out of the pan onto a plate, closely followed by a fried egg, fried bread and two halves of a tomato. 'Here,' she said, 'eat it while it's hot.'

He removed a stack of newspapers from a chair, plonked them on the top of the washing machine, and sat down. The top of the pine table looked as if it had been scrubbed, the cutlery was gleaming and the breakfast looked delicious. He cut a piece of bacon and popped it into his mouth. 'I didn't expect you to cook breakfast for me,' he mumbled.

Louise placed a china mug in front of him and poured coffee. 'I made it black, it'll clear your head.'

'Was I that drunk last night?'

'Mmm,' she made a rocking motion with her hand, 'so-so.' Her calm, brown eyes sparkled with amusement. 'You flaked out so I tucked you up and left you to sleep.'

'You didn't go home though?'

'It was late and I'd had a wee bit too much to drink so, like the good cop I am, I decided it would be unwise to drive.' She poured another cup of coffee and sat in the chair opposite.

Bill was finding it difficult to swallow the lump of bacon in his mouth. He looked up from his plate to find her studying him over the rim of her cup.

'Where?' He couldn't finish the question and he was sure she was laughing at him.

'Oh, that wasn't a problem.' She placed her cup back on the table. 'You were out cold so I just crawled in at your back. You never even knew I was there.'

Bill sighed, not knowing whether to be disappointed or relieved. 'So we're still friends?'

'Sure,' she said, 'although I did have an ulterior motive when I decided to stay over.'

The sinking feeling in his gut deepened. He pushed his

plate away, and grasped his cup of coffee. 'And what would that be?'

'I've only seen mock-ups and never had the opportunity to see a murder scene before, so I want you to take me out there. I want to see where the bodies were found. As part of my professional education.'

Bill almost choked on his coffee. 'Sue could take you.'

'Sue has other arrangements today. She's going somewhere with Mark.' Louise frowned into her cup. 'I tried to warn her he's a selfish good-for-nothing but she wouldn't listen.'

Bill leaned back in his chair. 'Looks like I'm stuck with it then,' he said gloomily, thinking of the desolate glade in the wood. He wished he could send the memory of those girls with their staring eyes, protruding bones, and maggots heaving in raw flesh, into the dark hole where other memories went. But the image was seared on his mind along with those other girls, all those years ago, who met their deaths in the same woods. Images he would never forget. Stumbling to his feet, he rushed to the bathroom.

It was early afternoon before Bill parked his car at the edge of the clearing that led into the wood. Sunlight glinted off the white car sitting at the side of the road in front of him.

He breathed a sigh of relief. If the SOCO team were still investigating the scene it would be a good excuse not to go into the wood. 'Looks like the SOCOs are still here. I'd better check before we go in.'

A chill breeze hit him as he slid out of the car. He would've preferred Louise to wait, but she followed him out.

The white car was empty.

'Where d'you think the driver's gone?'

Bill turned his gaze to the woods. Sun rays slanted onto the grass at the edge of the road and the wood looked less forbidding than it had yesterday. It lightened his mood a little and he didn't feel quite so bad about coming here after all. Maybe he'd even lay some ghosts to rest.

'Let's go have a look,' Bill said, hopping over the verge.

They'd hardly entered the wood before the snapping of branches being pushed aside alerted them to another presence. Bill held his finger to his lips and waited until someone appeared from the trees.

Bill's smile broadened as he recognised the familiar figure of Jim Johnstone. He stepped sideways, blocking his way.

'What the hell?' Sergeant Johnstone jumped back a pace. 'Oh, it's you, Bill?' He was breathing heavily. 'I wondered when you'd come back.'

Bill eyed Sergeant Johnstone. 'I hope the SOCOs are finished, the way you were charging about in there.'

'Yeah, they finished this morning. Said they'd got everything they needed and the scene didn't need to be protected any longer, then they just took off. But seeing it was Sunday I thought I'd keep an eye out for any rubberneckers.' He took a handkerchief from his pocket and wiped his forehead. 'It's heavy going in there.'

Bill eyed the sergeant. He seemed uneasy, like a small boy caught with his hand in the sweetie jar. What had he been up to in the wood? Having a sly look at the crime scene when no one was there, or maybe just taking a leak. Keeping his voice non-committal, Bill said, 'So, what are you doing in the wood instead of sitting in your car?'

'Thought there might be somebody here. There's a bike dumped in the undergrowth over there.'

'Well, was there? Somebody here, I mean?'

'Didn't see anybody. But it doesn't mean nobody's here.' He looked back into the wood. 'I remember the last time. Back in seventy-nine it was, when they found the first one. They came out on bikes and everything, even the kids.'

Bill said nothing. He'd been one of those kids, but Jim Johnstone wouldn't remember that.

'What last time?' Louise chimed in.

'Two girls, one in 1979, the other in 1980. March, I think it was. They found their bodies not very far from this clearing. We never got anybody for those murders and some people think that whoever it was has come back.'

Bill shivered. 'It's a long time to wait.'

'Not impossible.' Johnstone' eyes were thoughtful. 'Maybe he's been somewhere else, or maybe something's happened to give him the urge again.'

'Maybe,' Bill said, staring past Johnstone. The wind whispered through the branches and he felt fear wash over him, pricking the back of his neck, the same way it had when he was eleven.

'I'll keep an eye out while you're in there,' Sergeant Johnstone said, 'so you're not disturbed.'

'You sure you want to go in there?' Bill said as soon as Sergeant Johnstone left them.

'That's what I came for,' Louise said. 'Did you think I'd change my mind?'

'No.' Bill frowned, reluctant to tell her how the wood affected him. 'But seeing there's only us, I thought you might have second thoughts.'

Louise laughed. 'You mean, you thought I'd be afraid of the big bad bogeyman.'

Bill shrugged. 'It was just a thought.'

The trees and shrubbery swallowed them, growing thicker the further they went. Strange creaking noises were magnified in the stillness beneath the canopy. It was easy to imagine monsters waiting in the gloom that the sun failed to penetrate.

There'd been a crowd of them, he remembered. They'd cycled out hoping to see something. Once the fuss had died down they'd started coming to the woods a lot. Acting out the murder, taking it in turns to be the body and play dead. It was like a bizarre game of cowboys and Indians. A year later they'd stumbled on the second body.

They'd gone further in than they'd ever gone before, pushing through the shrubbery, joking and laughing, trying to outdo one another in their show of bravado. Bill hadn't felt very brave, but he'd swaggered as much as any of them. He had to act tough, even if he didn't feel it, because he knew that if his pals guessed how vulnerable he was, they wouldn't let him be. Only one of them had ever jeered, 'Your ma's run off with the tally man.' After Bill had thumped him, no one else mentioned it, and none of them knew how he'd sobbed when he was alone in his bed every night. The gang didn't show their emotions, and Bill was one of the gang.

Bill was the one who found the body, only he didn't know it was a body then. It just looked like some rubbish wrapped in a blanket. But it was Andy who'd uncovered it. The gang had crowded round, silent, shocked. It was one thing to play at dead bodies, quite another to encounter one.

One of the younger kids at the rear of the group had been sick in the bushes, but apart from that they'd all acted as if finding a body was an everyday occurrence, although Bill was never sure just how much they'd seen. Bill, however, had seen everything. It wasn't the first time he'd seen a woman with no clothes on, but it was the first time he'd seen a naked, dead woman.

They'd all sworn an oath never to talk about what they found that day in the woods, and when the body was discovered by a dog walker, two days later, they'd joined the crowds heading out to the woods for a look, just to make sure they hadn't been imagining it.

And now, here he was again, in the same wood, with the memory of not one but four naked, and very dead women to accompany him.

Someone who was less fit than Louise might have had difficulty keeping up with Bill, but she wasn't even out of breath when they came to the entrance to the clearing. He stopped so suddenly she almost bumped into him.

'This is it,' he said, 'but you'll have to crawl to get to the crime scene.'

Police tape still fluttered round the edges of the bushes, the grass had been trampled and, inside the clearing, there were several flattened areas in front of the trees.

'You saw them before they were taken away . . .'

Bill crouched down in the centre of the clearing. His eyes glazed and he seemed to go off into a world of his own.

Louise hesitated, wondering what he was seeing, reluctant to break the spell. She was still watching Bill when a man in a hoodie stepped from behind one of the trees to her left.

'It's been a long time,' the newcomer said, squatting down beside Bill, 'but I can see you're remembering.'

Louise felt like an intruder, watching some strange initiation ceremony. It was obvious Bill knew the man. But why wasn't he surprised? And what the hell was anyone else doing here? Hadn't Johnstone said he was keeping people away from the scene.

Bill turned his face towards the man. 'Hello! What made you come out here?'

'Same as you, pal. Memories.'

'But that's not why I came,' Bill said. 'I came because I'm part of the official investigation.'

Louise stepped over the tape and approached the two men. 'Is this a private party, or can anyone join in?'

They both turned their heads to look at her and it was only then she recognised the newcomer. 'Jerry!' she said. 'What are you doing out here?'

The social worker smiled at her. 'I saw you arrive and was going to come across and speak to you, but I didn't want to make you jump. So I spoke to Bill first.'

'You know each other?'

'Yeah, we were at school together. There's been a lot of water under the bridge since then.' He looked pensively at Bill. 'It's like old times though, seeing you here.'

Bill stood up. 'I suppose it might seem that way, Jerry. But you haven't answered the question. What the hell are *you* doing here?'

Jerry extended a hand to Louise. 'Give's a hand up,' he said, 'I think I've got cramp.'

Louise's hand felt warm in his and as Jerry rose, her brown eyes met his blue eyes. They were kind eyes, caring eyes. He looked away.

Turning to Bill, he said, 'Same reason we came out when

we were kids. D'you remember that, Bill? How we crouched in the undergrowth and watched them. I suppose it was the similarity of the situation that got to me and I wanted to come out and remind myself. But I'm a bit too late anyway. Not like the last time, when we saw everything there was to see.'

The rest of the gang members usually ignored Jerry – he was younger and smaller than the others – but he'd tagged along behind them so often, they'd eventually accepted him. So when the other gang members said they were going to Templeton Woods, Jerry went along as usual.

He was behind fatty Mark, who was moaning a lot. And, although he was having difficulty keeping up with the gang, he was afraid to complain because he didn't want to be jeered at the way Mark was. So he put on a fearless front to make up for his lack of size.

The trees closed round him, branches reached out and scratched his face and he stumbled over roots, but he kept going. When Bill found the woman, Jerry was right behind Mark. He pushed forward so he could see because if there was treasure, like Mark said, he wanted to be part of it. But he wasn't prepared for the sight of the body and he thought for a moment that it might be his mother, but it wasn't. He wondered if the woman had suffered. He didn't like pain and suffering. He stepped back not wanting to throw up over the body and was violently sick all down his new trousers. His gran gave him hell.

He didn't remember much about pushing out of the wood nor of cycling home, and he was off school the next day.

'You've lost me,' Louise said. 'What last time?' She looked at both men. There was something going on between them and she wasn't sure what.

Jerry glanced sideways at Bill. 'It was something when we were kids. We came out here to try and see the bodies they found. Didn't get much more than a glimpse, though.'

Louise turned to face Bill. 'You never told me that.'

'Nothing to tell. Half of Dundee came out. We were just part of the crowd.'

'I see,' she said, not convinced, but it was obvious that Bill didn't want to talk about it.

They walked back through the wood together. Bill stalked in front, lost in his own thoughts. Jerry walked beside her and every now and again looked at her as if he was going to say something.

She watched him pick up his bike and cycle off in the direction of Dundee before she turned to Bill. 'You want to tell me what really went on between you and Jerry?'

'Nothing,' Bill said. 'It's like he said, just something that happened when we were kids.'

Midnight. The end of the Sabbath. The police, gone. The flashlights, gone. The small forest animals, gone. Nothing stirred except the wind. Small sounds he made as he crept to his special place, now empty.

He tore a fluttering piece of blue police tape from a bush and trampled it into the ground. His anger erupted. What right did they have to desecrate this place. This sacred spot.

Indentations at the base of three trees, bare patches where the grass did not grow. The only sign of the previous occupants of the glade. But that had merely been their shells, their spirits lived on.

The branches above him rustled angrily, reminding him that there should have been a fourth.

35

It was dark when Kara woke on Monday morning. This was the day of the case conference. This was the day she'd see Billy and Charlene. But what if they wouldn't hand them over to her? She was their mum, they'd have to.

She could hear the snakes moving in the tank. Jean had told her they couldn't get out of their tanks, but Kara didn't quite believe her. What was to stop them breaking out? They were huge. She'd seen one of them try to stretch out to its full length. When it did, the tank, which extended the length of the room, wasn't long enough.

The slithering sound continued. Maybe it was her imagination but she thought it was coming from a different direction. It sounded as if it was on the floor in front of the sofa. She wanted to get up and put the light on, but she daren't.

She tried to think about Monday. She'd never been to the welfare before and didn't quite know what to expect. There'd be all sorts of officials there, she supposed, including the police. But the one she'd have to watch out for was the social worker, Mark somebody or other. She wondered what he would be like. Would he be young and approachable or old and grizzly? Probably old, she thought, and stern. She could see him now, frowning at her and banging the table with his fist.

Her eyes were getting used to the darkness in the room. It wasn't helpful though, there were too many shadows. She hoped daylight would come early today, like it had yesterday. She didn't want to get off the sofa in the dark.

Something moved in the shadows. Something slid across the floor.

She held her breath, straining to see what it was, but could see only darkness and shadows.

'Oh, please God, no . . .'

She could just make out the tank at the end of the sofa and the hint of movement within it. Relaxing a little, she thought, *bloody reptiles are getting to me.*

Tentatively she swung one foot off the sofa. The carpet felt scratchy on her sole. She let her breath out in a sigh and swung her other foot to the floor. It landed on something round and bulky – something that moved under her foot.

She froze. The snake slithered over her other foot. She could feel it circling her ankle. It was too late to jump back onto the sofa.

'Oh, please God, please God, I'll be good. I'll never do another bad thing again.' Her voice sounded weak and quavery but at least her vocal cords were working. 'Jean,' she croaked, and then, 'Jean.' This time it came out as a scream.

The bedroom door opened. 'For fuck's sake,' Jean said, scratching her midriff through the grubby nightgown she wore.

'It's the snake. It's got my leg.' The words exploded out of Kara.

Jean flicked on the light. 'It's only Charlie. He's just being friendly.'

'Get it off me!' Kara looked at the snake sprawled over the floor. 'Please, Jean. Just take it off me!'

Jean bent and gathered the snake up, allowing it to twine itself round her body. 'See,' she said, kissing the snake's head. 'He's just a big softie.' She carried him over to the tank behind the sofa and let him uncoil into it. 'There now,' she said, pulling the cover over the top of the tank, 'you be a good boy and I'll get you a nice, tasty, baby rabbit.'

'Damn it, Jean.' Kara couldn't stop shaking.

'Lot of fuss about nothing,' Jean mumbled. 'I'm going back to bed.'

'I've got the kids' case conference at ten o'clock, Jean. I'll need to start getting ready. If I don't see you before I go, thanks for everything.'

A smile twitched at the corner of Jean's mouth. 'Will you

be coming back after the meeting?'

Kara looked at the snakes in their tanks and shivered. 'I don't think so, Jean.' She started to pull her clothes on. 'If I get the kids, I'm away out of Dundee.'

'Good luck.' Jean's sly grin seemed to say, *Yeah, but what will you do if you don't get them?*

Kara turned away. She hadn't a clue what she'd do if she didn't get her kids back. But one thing she knew for sure, she wasn't going to spend another night with Jean's friends.

Sue passed Bill in the corridor. 'Can't stop . . . I've been checking out the rubberneckers' cars at the woods, and I've folk to see.' She pressed the lift button. 'How come I get all the rubbish jobs?'

Bill shrugged. 'The luck of the draw?' he suggested, and pushed into the incident room before she had time to reply.

Andy was rubbing his chest and studying the whiteboards and charts. 'It's a bad business.' He shook his head. 'How far on are we?'

'Not very,' Bill said. 'The first post mortem's been done, but there's nothing conclusive so far. Rose seems to think she died of hypothermia.'

'Hypothermia? Who did the post mortem?'

'Rose Armstrong. She's usually pretty reliable.'

Andy looked thoughtful. 'It's not the same as the first lot then.'

Bill immediately knew what Andy was referring to. 'No, it's not like them.' He was silent for a moment. 'You remember when a crowd of us went to Templeton Woods in 1980?'

Andy sat on the end of the conference table. 'Of course I remember,' he said quietly.

'Well, when I went out to the scene again, yesterday, one of the old gang was there.'

'Who?' Andy looked interested.

'Jerry Forbes. I haven't seen him for years – he's some kind of social worker now. Louise knows him, says he works for the out of hours service.'

'I remember him, quiet sort of lad. Wouldn't strike me as being the ghoulish type. Why d'you think he was there?'

Bill shrugged. 'He said he was just curious, because of the similarities.'

'Far as I can see there aren't any.'

'Worth looking at though.'

'I've already thought of that. Iain's looking through the old files. Only problem is, they seem to be experiencing difficulty locating them.'

'I'm not surprised,' Bill said. 'Have you seen how they store old files? Anyway if the MO isn't the same d'you think they'll be much help?'

'Maybe not, but we should still check them out.'

Mark scooped a handful of papers back into the file and slipped it into his briefcase. He wasn't ready for this conference. The brief look he'd been able to give the file this morning hadn't told him much. He'd seen the kids, but not since Friday. The boy was a bit quiet. What the hell was his name again? He pulled the file back out of his briefcase and leafed through it. There it was. Billy, that was it, and the girl was Charlene. Stroppy little kid she was.

He gulped a mouthful of tea and sent up a mental prayer that the mum would turn up. There'd been a note in his pigeonhole saying she'd phoned on Friday, so hopefully she'd be there. He didn't want to keep the kids in care too long, too much paperwork. He'd probably have to get their names put on the child protection register, but if he could just get them home it would save the Council money and save him a lot of unnecessary work.

The conference room was empty. He looked at his watch and gave it a shake.

'Not like you to be early.' Glenda, the minute taker, followed him in and started up her laptop.

'Watch must be fast,' he muttered. 'How much time do I have?'

Glenda looked at her watch. 'Ten minutes.'

'I'll just nip out for a quick fag then.'

The car park was full, so Jerry parked his car on the street. Child protection conferences were a nuisance. None of the out of hours' workers liked them because it meant they couldn't go home to their beds after being on shift all night.

He yawned and stretched. He'd had Saturday night off so he hadn't gone to his bed yesterday and he was feeling the need of it now.

Tiredness crept over him and he leaned his head back and closed his eyes. He woke with a jerk when someone tapped the side window. He hadn't meant to doze off. Blinking, he rolled down the window.

'Heavy night was it?' Stan Phillips grinned at him.

Jerry grinned sheepishly at the carer. 'Thanks, pal,' he said. 'Where's the wife?'

'I dropped her at the door and came back here to park.' He gestured at the taxi cab behind Jerry's car.

Jerry stroked his chin. 'Damn it, I could do with a shave.' He stretched and got out of the car. He was as tall as Stan but didn't carry the weight of the older man. 'Charlene and Billy settle down all right?'

'Billy's a wee lamb, but that Charlene, she's something else again. Lives in a dream world, she does. Calls Annie a witch and acts shit scared of me. It's early days yet though.'

The two men walked towards the office, passing Mark Gordon in the doorway. Jerry nodded recognition but didn't stop to chat with the social worker. He'd never got on that well with Mark. They seemed to rub each other up the wrong way.

'Maybe they'll have found the mum,' Jerry said to Stan.

'D'you think they'll send them home?'

'Depends,' Jerry said. 'But nowadays they don't like to keep kids in care too long. The psychologists say it's damaging for them.'

'What do bloody psychologists know?' Stan grumbled.

'The kids we get are always well looked after.'

'I don't doubt it,' Jerry said.

Mark's eyes narrowed as he watched Louise and Bill walk across the car park. He was still smarting from Louise's offhand treatment at Donovan's and felt a pang of jealousy. She was smiling and nodding while the copper seemed to have a lot to say for himself. Surely she couldn't be attracted to him. He looked like a walking scarecrow.

Bill nodded to Mark as they approached the door.

'You don't remember me, do you?' Mark threw his cigarette end on the ground.

'Yeah I do. You're Mark. We met you in Donovan's on Friday night.'

'Before that,' Mark said.

Bill looked puzzled. 'Sorry. No, I don't.'

'We went to school at the same time. You were older than me though, so we weren't in the same year.'

'That's probably why I don't remember.'

Louise looked troubled. 'Is there anyone in Dundee you didn't go to school with?'

Ignoring her question Bill turned to her and said, 'We'd better get inside or we'll be late.'

Mark grasped Bill's arm. 'One or two of us hung out with your gang even though we were younger.'

Bill eyed Mark's hand on his arm. He didn't like people grabbing him and he was tempted to shove the man away.

'You still don't get it, do you,' Mark said. 'Templeton Woods? Does that ring any bells?'

Bill shook his arm free. 'I remember now,' he said, coldly. 'You were the fat little eejit at the back who was scared. Anyway, why bring that up?'

'I would have thought it was obvious considering what you're dealing with just now.'

Bill ignored him and marched into the office.

'What was that all about?' Louise looked at him, curiously. 'Everyone's cracking up about Templeton Woods.'

'It's nothing,' Bill said. 'Just something we all got up to when we were kids.'

'Seems to be a lot of things you got up to when you were kids.'

Mark swore under his breath. He hadn't handled that well. All he'd wanted was some information. But nobody would tell him anything.

He'd even spent the whole of yesterday with Sue trying his best to get something out of her. But she was so hung up about confidentiality she wouldn't talk about it, and she wouldn't take him out to see where the bodies were found. Waste of a good Sunday.

He followed the police officers into the building. Another thing, he thought, it was weird that Bill was attending the case conference. Since when had he been involved with child protection?

36

Kara wiped her sweaty hands on her jeans.

They'd put her in this room to wait until she was sent for, but that was ages ago. What was keeping them? Didn't they know she was here?

She opened the door and wandered out to the reception area. It was quite large, with a box of toys in the corner and a plant in front of the window. The receptionists were boxed in behind a glass partition. She knocked on it and one of them slid it open.

'It's not time yet,' she said, smiling. 'Go back and wait, I'll let you know when they're ready for you.'

Kara nodded. How could the woman smile at her when she knew they'd taken her kids? Cheeky cow.

She returned to the little waiting room, sat down on one of the soft chairs and reached blindly for one of the magazines scattered on top of the coffee table. They were tatty and soiled, like the table and carpet underneath.

Her nerves were wound so tight she wanted to scream. Compared to the anxiety she felt now, everything else that had happened over the last couple of days was nothing. She'd rather lose her life than lose Charlene and Billy.

Sweat trickled down her back and the ends of her hair clung damply to her neck. Her jeans were stained and her trainers grubby. They'd think she was a tramp. She should have gone home and put on something decent.

She picked up a teddy bear lying forlornly on the floor. It had one eye and an ear that hung by a single thread. She hugged the poor neglected toy to her breast.

Everything was so unfriendly. Was this the kind of room her children would have to get used to?

She shuddered and, rising from the chair, gently placed the

teddy among the other toys in the red plastic basket on the windowsill. What was taking them so long?

Bill traced a pattern on the conference table with his finger. The chairperson, a senior social worker, although she seemed to be the youngest person there, droned on about the background details to the case. She was attractive in a businesslike way, he thought. He didn't like formal meetings and shifted uneasily in his seat. Louise was busy taking notes, so he allowed his mind to wander.

Mark sat next to the chairperson and Bill studiously avoided his gaze. Louise sat on his right and Jerry was next to her. On his left was the health visitor, hardly more than a girl but she seemed to know the family well. And beyond her, the foster carers. The GP sat at the end of the table and, by the look on his face, he was wishing he was somewhere else. Charlene's teacher, a middle-aged, dumpy woman with spectacles, sat next to him. The only person who was missing was Kara Ferguson.

'I think we can bring the mother in now.' The chairperson leaned back in her chair. 'Would someone like to fetch her?'

Mark started to rise, but Louise jumped up, and said, 'I'll go. After all I was the one who helped take the children into care.'

Mark sat down again and nodded.

Jerry gave a slight smile and Bill wondered if Louise realised she'd just dismissed his part in things.

The door swung shut behind her and he listened to the sound of her feet clattering down the stairs.

'I'm Louise, Child Liaison' she said. 'I bet you're fed up waiting.' Her voice was fairly deep for a woman, but she had a warm smile.

'Is it time?' Kara whispered.

'Yes, they're ready for you now.'

Kara tried to smile but felt her lips wobble.

'You look quite pale,' Louise said. 'Are you feeling all right?'

Kara nodded.

'It's nerves, isn't it?' Sympathy oozed from Louise's voice. 'You'll be wondering about Charlene and Billy.'

Kara nodded. 'I don't know where they are,' she whispered.

'They're safe.' Louise took Kara's hand. 'But I'm sure they're missing you.'

It had been a long time since someone had held Kara's hand like this, and it felt warm and safe and comfortable.

'I miss them too.' She blinked hard but couldn't prevent some tears escaping.

'Come on, then. Let's get it over with.'

Kara felt an urgent need to explain. 'I didn't want to leave them alone,' she whispered, 'and I meant to be back as quick as I could. But then . . . stuff happened . . .' Images from Thursday night flashed. She shivered. 'I had to find some money, or they were going to kill me.'

'Who was going to kill you?'

'My boyfriend Kev owed them. A lot. But it was me and my kids they came after. They said if I gave them what Kev owed they'd leave us alone. So I had to go out.' She desperately wanted Louise to tell her it was all right. That she understood. That it hadn't been her fault she had to leave Charlene and Billy on their own, that if she could have done anything else she would have done.

'Calm down, Kara. Who was threatening you? Was it the man who took you to Templeton Woods?'

'How did you know about him?'

'There's a lot we know, Kara. Was it him?'

'No,' Kara moaned. 'I got away from him.' She could smell the wood, taste the earth, feel the wriggling flesh under her hand. 'He doesn't know who I am and I want it to stay that way.'

'But if he doesn't know who you are, how will he manage to chase you for the money Kev owes?' Louise's voice sounded puzzled.

'You don't understand,' Kara's voice rose and her breathing came in short bursts. 'He wasn't the one chasing me. He just came after. He was a nightmare.' She was hyperventilating and was almost unable to speak. 'It was another two guys, drug suppliers, who were after me. And they'll kill me if I don't get them the money Kev owes.'

'Sit down.' Louise pushed her into a chair. 'Now breathe deeply. No one can hurt you here.'

Gradually Kara's breathing slowed. She looked up at Louise. 'D'you think they'll give me the kids now I'm here?'

'I don't know, Kara. But you'll have to tell them everything so they can understand why you felt forced to leave your children alone.'

Kara stood up. 'I suppose I'd better get it over with.'

Louise led her out onto the stairs. They were scrubbed stone and the echo of their footsteps beat loudly in Kara's ears. It was like a death knell. At last they reached a door. Louise pushed it open and stood aside to let her enter.

Kara took two steps into the room and looked around. All these faces but she only saw one. His eyes lit with recognition as soon as he looked at her, she could see it. Blood pounded in Kara's ears and she almost blacked out. She smelled the foul odour of the earth and the trees closed in on her. She was back in the the cold – running for her life.

'No,' she screamed, hoarsely.

She had to get out of here. She had to. She had to. She had to get as far away from here as she could. He knew who she was.

Bill was chewing the end of his pencil and half-heartedly studying the social worker's report when Louise and Kara entered the conference room.

He looked up, smiling at Louise and studying the girl she'd brought into the room. A wee lass who looked vaguely familiar. Maybe he'd come across her when he'd been in the drugs squad. But it was seven years since he'd worked drugs and she didn't look old enough. She didn't look old enough to be the mother of two kids either, he thought. Give it time though, it would come to him.

Her appearance was a bit of a surprise. He'd expected a young woman who was either worn out and old before her time, or flashy and hard. This girl seemed little more than a child herself, smaller than he'd imagined her, with a slim boyish figure that was accentuated by the blue jeans, trainers, sweat shirt and padded jacket. She wore no make-up and no jewellery, only her streaked shoulder-length hair made her stand out.

It jogged his memory. Of course, it was the girl he'd seen at the bus station when they were on the drugs stakeout. He smiled to himself. She'd been dressed in a red mac. A lot different to the way she looked today.

Kara's scream echoed round the conference room, making Bill drop his pencil and scrunch the report he'd been studying between his fingers.

Pushing Louise out of the way, Kara fled from the room.

Louise ran after her, shouting, 'What's wrong?'

'It's him. He's here. He knows who I am.' Kara shook Louise's hand off her arm, pushed her away and hurtled down the stairs.

Louise staggered, lost her balance and sat down with a thump. Pain shot up her spine, bringing tears to her eyes. Gasping, she sat until the cold from the stone step seeped through her. Her hand stung where it had hit the wall as she'd fallen, but she massaged her lower back until she felt better and eased herself downstairs. Maybe Kara would be waiting in reception. She'd seemed so anxious to get her children back she might have had second thoughts. Louise tried to convince herself but knew Kara wouldn't be there. The girl had been terrified. So terrified she was probably long gone.

'The fucker's always in a meeting. Every time I want to see him he's in a bloody meeting. I'm no shifting until I've seen him.' The scruffy woman at reception leaned over the wooden counter.

The harassed receptionist, and the woman haranguing her, looked up as Louise pushed through the security door. She raised her eyebrows and pointed to the front door. Louise nodded her thanks and stepped round the children playing on the floor in the middle of the reception area.

'What you bloody pointing at when I'm speaking to you?' The angry voice faded away when Louise stepped outside.

Louise scanned the car park and the street beyond but there was no sign of Kara. She leaned against the wall. The girl had been all right until she went into the conference room. A bit anxious and afraid, perhaps, but she'd seemed determined to get her children back.

So what caused her to run off? Who did she see? What or who had she meant by 'It's him!'

Louise turned the girl's words over and over in her mind. Kara had said, 'It's him, he's here.' Who was she talking about? It couldn't be the men chasing her for money because presumably they already knew who she was.

Kara had said, 'He knows who I am.' And earlier she'd said she was safe from the man who'd taken her into Templeton Woods because he didn't know who she was.

Louise swallowed hard. That could only mean the man from the woods was in the conference room.

She pressed her head against the stone wall of the building. That meant it must be the GP, Stan Phillips, Mark, Jerry, or, she swallowed again, Bill.

Her first instinct was to tell Bill. He'd know what to do. He'd arrange for the checks to be done, the questioning, the weeding out of the suspects until there was only one possible answer.

But what if 'he' *was* Bill?

It was her. The voices, no longer whispering, howled through his head. Loud, painful. His breath caught in his throat, choking him.

Why had the voices come now? When other people were here? They must have heard. He looked round the table but they were all staring at her.

She'd acknowledged him. She'd run. He could not follow. Not now. But later he would find her.

The voices calmed. Whispered. Worming into his brain. Interfering with his concentration.

He forced them away. No one must know.

37

Phil had intended to be outside the social work office at half past ten but a phone call from Tony had delayed him.

'D'you think she'll come?' Gus said.

'She'll come all right.' Phil burst a chewing-gum bubble.

'D'you have to do that?' Gus gave Phil a disgusted look. 'You're like a schoolkid.'

Phil smiled. 'Naw, the weans round here prefer smack and dope. Chewing gum's too tame for them.' He settled back in his seat to watch the office. 'Me, now, I don't intend to pump any of my profits into my veins. I mean to make money. And the only way to make real money is to stay off the bloody stuff.'

'Doesn't stop you supplying it, though.'

'Too bloody right it doesn't. How d'you think Tony made his millions? Same bloody way. He doesn't ram it up his nose or in his veins either. He's too smart for that.' Phil looked moodily out of the window. 'If you take my advice, pal, steer clear of the merchandise.'

Gus sniffed. 'Nothing wrong with a little bit to make a party go with a swing.'

'Take that attitude and you'll be a junkie before you know it.'

Phil grinned, viciously. 'And when that happens, Tony's not going to have any use for you.'

Kara careered down the stairs, several at a time, skidding and running, grasping the banister when she lost her balance. The door at the foot of the stairs loomed up in front of her and she almost smashed into it. Luckily, it wasn't locked on the inside. Pulling it open she shot through, colliding with a woman and almost falling over the kids trailing behind her.

'Watch it,' the woman screeched.

'Sorry,' Kara gasped, heading for the door to the car park.

Once outside she kept on running – away from the office, down the street and round the corner.

Fear prodded her on. In her mind she could feel his breath on the back of her neck.

A car engine growled behind her, sending her scurrying for the footpath behind the buildings.

Her feet slowed but, even though no car could follow her here, she knew it was too soon to give in to her fatigue. She staggered on, only stopping when she felt safe – when there was no way she could be seen from the road and the social work office.

Bright lights flickered in front of her eyes and in the midst of them she saw his face. It floated in front of her, enigmatic, hiding his thoughts. She'd never forget it. She shuddered. It was obvious he hadn't forgotten her either. The flicker of recognition when he'd caught her eye across the conference table had given him away. He'd be coming after her.

Cold sweat trickled down her forehead. Going to the meeting had been a mistake, but what choice had there been. She'd needed to find out where Charlene and Billy were, and get them back with her where they belonged. How was she to know he'd be there. Waiting for her.

In any case, why had he been there? Who was he? What business did he have with her kids?

Blinking hard, her vision cleared. At least she'd outrun him this time. She was safe for the time being.

Bending forward she covered her face with her hands. That was when she thought of the woman who'd been nice to her. What was her name? Lisa? Louise, that was it. She'd said she knew where Charlene and Billy were. She'd find Louise, that's what she'd do. Once Louise knew what had happened to her, she'd understand why she was so scared and would help her get the kids.

Kara flicked the tears off her cheeks with her fingers and opened her eyes.

'Oh, for fuck's sake,' she said, staring at the shiny, brown shoes in front of her.

The people gathered round the conference table broke off their discussion to acknowledge Louise's return.

'I take it Miss Ferguson's not coming back.'

Louise shook her head.

'Did you speak to her?' Irene Massie, the chairperson, fixed Louise with a sharp stare.

There was a rustle of interest and a leaning forward of bodies as they waited for her reply. She hesitated, wanting to say something, but knowing that someone here would be interested for the wrong reason.

'She was too fast for me,' Louise said in as crisp a tone as she could manage. 'I never caught up with her.'

Did she imagine it? Did a sigh float round the room? If it did, Louise couldn't detect where it came from.

Irene Massie flicked through some papers in front of her. 'Let's get on with it,' she said, 'or we'll be here all day.'

Louise explained her involvement with the children, detailing the events in a logical and businesslike way, then sat back and studied the others as they fed information into the meeting.

Bill didn't contribute anything, simply saying he was there in an official police capacity. Louise, surprised he didn't explain the Templeton Woods connection, raised a questioning eyebrow. He shook his head slightly and frowned when he saw her watching, then his eyes slid away from hers.

Questions whirled through Louise's brain. Surely the information was essential in order to understand Kara's actions. So why didn't he say so?

Jerry was speaking now, in a voice so soft it could hardly be heard. Suddenly he looked across the table at her, as if he'd felt her watching him. His face reddened. He was so shy she couldn't help but smile encouragingly. He smiled back and continued to speak, consulting his notes as if he needed prompting. His eyes lit up, however, when he started to talk about the children.

The GP didn't have much to contribute. He hardly knew the family, they were just one of a number of single parent families in the neighbourhood. His voice was heavy with disapproval. He was the only one in the room, Louise thought, who might be capable of murder. He'd probably think he was doing the world a favour. But just because he was grumpy didn't mean he was a killer, he was just an unpleasant man with little compassion for those less well off than himself.

Louise caught Mandy, the health visitor, throwing him an annoyed glance, and it was evident when she started to speak that the burden of supporting young families in the estate was passed over to the nursing staff. Mandy was high in her praise of Kara's care of the children in difficult circumstances; scathing about Kara's partner who was only around now and again; and bewildered why Kara would leave her children alone.

The teacher, Louise didn't catch her name, mumbled something about no problems in school and that Charlene was a bright child.

Mark, looking officious, read from his notes. He recommended the children stay where they were until their mother was traced and that they should have their names placed on the child protection register under the category of neglect.

Prick, thought Louise, studying him the same way she'd studied everyone else, but apart from being a prick he looked no more like her idea of a serial murderer than the rest of them.

'There's tea and coffee in the kitchen for those of you who want it,' Irene said as she called the meeting to a close. Then turning to Mark, she said, 'A word before you go.'

Mark looked across the table at Louise and shrugged his shoulders.

'That was a lucky escape,' Louise muttered to Bill.

'Eh?' he said, frowning. It was obvious he'd missed the interchange.

'Oh, never mind.' Louise stuffed papers into her briefcase.

'Let's get back to the office. There's something I want to ask you.'

The GP, obviously in a hurry, pushed his way out of the door.

The health visitor smiled ruefully at Louise. 'He never wants to come to these things, he's just making his point. Thinks he's the only one who's busy.'

Jerry sidled round the table. 'Louise,' he said. 'It's so nice to see you again.' A flush spread across his face.

'Yes, you too,' Louise said. She wanted to leave before Mark stopped talking to Irene. 'Was there something else, Jerry?'

He pulled his ear, 'I was just wondering . . .'

'Yes?'

'Seeing we're both here . . .' He looked at her desperately.

She had a sudden urge to pat him on the hand and reassure him, in the same way she'd pat a stray dog's head. Besides, he reminded Louise so much of her younger brother before he reached the bolshie stage that she was having difficulty seeing him as a potential suspect.

'Whether you'd like to join me for a cup of coffee . . . or something?'

'That would be lovely.' Louise wondered how she could refuse without hurting his feelings. 'The only problem is I'm here with a colleague,' she nodded in Bill's direction, 'and we came in the same car.'

'Oh.' Jerry's shoulders drooped as the tension left him. 'I see.'

'I would've joined you,' she said, trying to make it all right for him, 'but I've got to get back to the office.' His disappointment was so obvious, she added, 'Not unless you could drop me off there after.'

He looked away from her. 'I can't, sorry. I use pool cars for work, I don't have one of my own. There wasn't one available today so I came on my bike.'

'Maybe we could meet later. Have a coffee or a drink, or something.' She fished a piece of paper out of her briefcase and scribbled her phone number on it. 'Here,' she said, 'give me a call when you're free.' A meeting with Jerry might answer a lot of her questions about him, Mark and Bill, and what they'd got up to as wee boys that seemed to be having such an effect on them all.

'Thanks,' he said, stuffing the paper into his trouser pocket.

He smiled and his eyes brightened in the same way they had when he'd talked about the children. He leaned forward but then drew back, shrugged his shoulders, and said, 'I'll phone . . . probably tomorrow or the next day, if that's all right.'

Louise nodded. She couldn't make up her mind whether he interested her in some way or whether she was just sorry for him, whether he was just another of her strays.

Out of the corner of her eye she saw Mark finish his discussion with Irene. He turned and looked in her direction before starting to gather up his papers.

Avoiding Mark's eyes she turned to Bill and said, 'Let's get out of here.'

Wondering why Louise was in such a hurry, Bill clattered down the stairs in her wake and followed her to the car. He fished in his pocket for the keys and it was only when they were both seated that he asked, 'What was that all about?'

'I wanted to get out of there before Mark caught me.'

'Hmm.' Bill turned the key in the ignition. 'I suppose I can understand that, but it was you and Jerry I was referring to.' He concentrated on driving, staring hard out of the window. Louise was in a strange mood, tetchy and reserved at the same time. He wondered if there was something going on between her and Jerry.

'Oh, that,' she said, with a tone of amusement in her voice although he thought her laugh sounded forced. 'He just wanted to go for a cup of coffee. I said I was sharing a car with you and had to get back to the office.'

'You could have gone,' he said. 'I wouldn't have minded.' After all it wasn't as if anything was going on between them.

38

It wasn't an illusion. It wasn't a passer-by. The brown shoes, so shiny she could almost see her face reflected, were real and pointed in her direction. So close she could have bent down and touched them.

'Fuck,' Kara said again, slowly looking up, seeing the grey trousers with their immaculate crease down the centre, upwards again, past the matching jacket, the sparkling white shirt and silver-grey tie, to the face above. The face she expected to see – Phil's face. 'Fuck, fuck, fuck.'

She shrank back. 'I haven't got the money,' she said despairingly. 'I had it, but I lost it.'

'You're coming with us. Now,' Phil said, his face and voice expressionless.

'Please? Just give me a little bit more time – I can get the money again.'

'Time's run out, Kara.' Phil bent down and gripped her arm. 'Don't make a fuss.' He pulled her to her feet and pushed her along the path.

She knew he'd need to make an example of her to make sure no one else tried to rip Tony Palmer off. Knew he'd either mutilate or kill her. Knew she couldn't get away.

Her only hope was going along with him until she found an opportunity to escape. It was a slim hope, but maybe, when the path ended at the shopping centre, there'd be someone who might help her.

They were almost there. The rear walls of the shops, with their barred and bricked-up windows, were in sight. They'd soon be in the square. Somehow or other she'd have to attract someone's attention. And then she'd take her chance, even if she had to go to the police.

Phil veered off the path before he reached the shops,

shoving her over the broken stone edging, scrubby plants and broken glass. Taken by surprise, Kara stumbled on the rough ground, almost falling. He jerked her up. His fingers bit into her arm, twisting it, until she felt her shoulder would come out of its socket.

She moaned. Phil grinned and pulled harder. Pain shot through her shoulder but she bit her lips hard, determined to deny him the pleasure of hearing her scream or moan again.

He stopped for a moment to pull a mobile phone from his pocket. 'I've got her,' he said. 'Service area.' He clicked the phone off and rammed it back into his pocket.

Kara's shoulders slumped. He wasn't taking her through the shopping centre. He was heading for the deserted bit of ground at the other side. It was unlikely there'd be anyone there except for alkies and junkies.

Phil dragged her round the corner to the black Merc. Gus stood at the back of the car, leaning on the boot.

There was something in Gus's smile that made Kara think he might be worse than Phil if he was given his head. She tried to pull away but Phil shoved her into Gus's arms. He opened the boot, grabbed her legs, and together they swung her inside. They closed the boot, and the darkness engulfed her.

Opening her mouth she tried to shout but nothing came out.

Templeton Woods Killer Strikes Again – Tony's hands shook as he noticed the headline in Monday's *Courier*. He threw the newspaper at Brian. 'Get rid of that before Madge comes down.'

'Let me see that.'

Startled, Tony swung round. He hadn't heard her creep up on him. She held out her hand, and Brian, after a glance towards Tony, handed the paper to Madge.

She swayed slightly as she read the details and, for a moment, Tony thought she was going to faint. He tucked his arm round her waist and gently prised the newspaper from her grasp. 'Bin it,' he said to Brian.

'You shouldn't be reading that, love. It'll just distress you.'

He remembered her hysterics over the weekend and looked at her, anxiously.

'I've done all my crying, for now,' she said, leaning into his shoulder and staring into his face as if he were a stranger. 'No more pills, Tony, I'm all right now.'

Tony nodded guiltily, thinking of the tranquillizers the doctors had encouraged him to give her. He led her into the lounge.

'Sit down,' he said, 'we'll have our coffee in here for a change.'

'Phone, boss.' Brian popped his head round the door. 'It's Phil,' he muttered to Tony as he passed him the receiver.

'Find Morag and get her to bring coffee through to the lounge. And get her to find out if Madge wants anything to eat.'

'This better be good,' he said to Phil.

'We've got her, boss.'

'Got her?' Tony's mind whirled, he was still thinking of Madge.

'Kara. Kara Ferguson.'

'Where is she?'

'In the boot and we're driving down the Arbroath Road. Where d'you want her, boss?'

'The club, of course.' Surely the morons didn't think he wanted her brought to the house. 'And make sure no one sees her.'

'No problem.'

'I won't be able to come to the club until later, so keep an eye on her.'

'Yeah, yeah.'

'And don't touch her.'

Tony slammed the phone down. Those two bastards were getting above themselves.

Mark stuffed his papers into a cardboard folder, tucked it under his arm and hurried out of the conference room, hoping to catch up with Louise.

He vaulted down the stairs, barged through the reception area and hurtled out the front door, just in time to see Louise drive off with Bill.

'Shit,' he said, turning back into the office.

'Here, you,' the female standing in front of the reception desk challenged him. 'I've been trying to see you, but these fuckers say I've got to make an appointment.'

'That's right,' Mark said. 'Can't stop now. I'm in a meeting.'

'Fucker's always in a meeting,' floated after him as he let the inner door close behind him.

'You were in some hurry,' Jerry said. He was sitting on the bottom step of the stairs.

'Yeah.' Mark stood over him. 'Thought I might catch Louise, but I was too late.'

'She was in a rush to get back to headquarters,' Jerry said. 'She's working on this murder inquiry. You know, the Templeton Woods thing.'

'Is she now?' Mark supposed he had known although he hadn't thought about it. 'D'you remember when we went out there the last time?'

'That was a long time ago. We were just lads.' Jerry's voice was soft. 'But I remember tagging along. I didn't really want to, but I didn't want you lads laughing at me for being a coward.'

He was silent for a moment. 'You forced me to look and I was sick. My gran gave me hell.'

'I'd forgotten you lived with your gran,' Mark said. 'Where was your mother?'

Jerry shrugged and looked embarrassed.

'Family secret,' he muttered. 'They never told me. She just wasn't there.'

'Oh . . .' It was Mark's turn to look embarrassed. 'Anyway, fancy a cup of coffee, talk about old times?'

'Some other time,' Jerry murmured. He rose and pushed through the door to reception.

Mark watched him go. Weirdo, he thought.

He turned and climbed the stairs, mentally planning his

day. A visit to Charlene and Billy first; then he'd have to get back on the hunt for their mother.

The slam of the car doors and the rumble of the engine starting jolted Kara into consciousness.

Angrily she wiped the tears from her face and tried to turn over. There wasn't much room to manoeuvre but she wriggled her legs and arms, pushing against the solid side of the car until she lay on her back. The floor of the boot vibrated beneath her, beating its uneven rhythm into her spine as it bumped over the potholed ground. The final, spine-jarring bump threw her body against the hard framework of the car, twisting her arm and wrenching her shoulder.

'Bastards,' she shouted, wishing they'd hear her but knowing they wouldn't.

Guessing they must be on the main road by now, Kara thumped her fists on the boot lid until her knuckles were raw and sticky. Sucking her fingers and tasting the blood she realised that her banging wasn't going to be heard over the noise of the traffic. To keep her mind alert, she started to explore the boot with her fingers. She felt round the metal sides and roof and a smooth leathery surface that was probably the other side of the back seat. But there were no obvious chinks that her fingers could find. Digging up the covering beneath her, she poked and prodded until she found a recess. Her fingers were numb but she tugged and pulled at the cover until it gave way. Inside was a tool box, and inside it was a spanner. Wrapping her fingers round the cold metal, she hugged it to her.

She wasn't going to come out of the boot without a fight.

Louise sneaked a glance at Bill but his face was expressionless.

She hadn't known him long but she was as sure as she could be that this man was not a murderer. But what, if anything, *did* she know about him? He'd been Sue's partner for the past two years. Sue trusted him. He'd been a policeman for a long time, probably fifteen years, if not more. His colleagues seemed to like him and she'd thought she might be falling for him. He certainly ticked all her boxes. He wasn't particularly macho – macho men were a real turn-off – he was sensitive, a bit depressed maybe, but he obviously had his reasons. He was good-looking apart from his misshapen nose but in her eyes that only added to the attraction. And he needed to be looked after.

It wasn't a lot, she admitted to herself, staring idly at the large black car travelling in front of them. Not enough to wipe him off her list of suspects.

She slid sideways in her seat as Bill pulled out to overtake. Adjusting herself in her seat she noticed Bill glowering at the other car and turned her head in time to see the driver point his middle finger in the air in a rude gesture.

'What was that all about?' Louise turned and looked back at the black car as Bill swung into the lane in front of it.

He grinned mischievously. 'Oh, just a couple of Tony Palmer's thugs who haven't forgiven me for running them in a couple of years ago.'

'They run about in a pretty classy car.'

Bill laughed. 'That won't be theirs, it'll be Tony's. You know, that *nice* guy you've been seeing.'

'He didn't seem that bad when I interviewed him,' she said stiffly.

'Aye, well, it's difficult to tell the baddies from the goodies these days.'

'Yeah, that *is* the trouble,' said Louise, looking sidelong at Bill.

Phil shook his head in disbelief as he watched Gus give the finger to the copper.

'What the hell'd you do that for? You want to get us pulled over?'

'Aw, he had it coming.'

'Yeah, well, before you do things like that, remember

who's in the boot.'

'Oh, right enough. I'd *forgotten.*'

'Just mind what you do.'

'Sure, OK.' Gus turned the corners of his mouth down in a sulky expression.

Phil sighed. 'Look, pal, I'm only telling you for your own good.'

Gus didn't answer.

39

The wind, whipping the hem of Marlene's coat, seemed to be coming straight from the North Sea. She didn't have to be here, she thought, as she turned the corner, she could have stayed in bed where it was nice and warm. It wasn't as if she didn't need the sleep.

But she was worried.

Last night had been the second in a row Tony had asked for Angel and his temper hadn't improved since Saturday night. Angel had seemed pale and tired after the first session and Marlene had sensed the girl's reluctance when Tony sent for her again.

She didn't like to think what he might have done to her if Angel had resisted him.

Marlene fumbled the key into the lock of the rear door, with fingers that were blue with the cold. Then she hurried along the corridor and up the narrow stairs leading to Tony's office.

Angel lay sprawled on the leather sofa, her fair hair flopping in strands over her face and shoulders, her G-string adorning the door knob.

Marlene drew a sharp breath. The girl was so still she might have been dead.

Hurrying over to the sofa, she smoothed the damp hair away from Angel's face and bent her ear to the girl's mouth, heaving a sigh of relief as she detected the faint sound of breathing.

She shook the girl. 'Wake up.'

Angel's eyelids flickered momentarily.

'Wake up.' Marlene lifted her by the shoulders and shook her again, increasing the pressure.

Angel's head flopped backwards.

'Aw, what shit's he given you?' Marlene dived to the desk and lifted the phone. She'd dialled the first number before thumping the phone back onto its cradle. If she sent for an ambulance there was bound to be questions. She couldn't do that to Tony. She'd just have to try and bring the girl round herself.

She crossed the room, slid a mirrored door aside and went into the bathroom. That'll do, she thought, as she grabbed a towel and held it under the cold tap. But Angel only flinched when Marlene patted her face with it, she didn't regain consciousness.

'Don't you go dying on me,' she shouted, before turning to run down the stairs.

Gus reversed the car up to the rear door of the club, as close as he could, then Phil jumped out and unlocked the door.

'You ready?' Phil had taken the car keys from him and was preparing to open the boot.

Gus flexed his shoulders. 'Sure,' he said, 'let's get her out of there.'

Phil slowly turned the key of the boot. Kara was silent. Tony would go berserk if she'd suffocated. He flung the boot open, half expecting her to be unconscious.

With a yell, Kara leapt up, swinging the spanner.

'Aw, for fuck's sake!' It caught Gus a glancing blow on the side of his head.

Phil jumped back, raised his hand, and karate chopped Kara's wrist. The spanner twanged onto the ground and he kicked it away.

She scrabbled over the side of the boot and Phil lunged for her, grabbing her round the waist with one arm and clamping his hand over her mouth to silence her scream. He felt her teeth sink into his palm but ignoring the pain he dug his fingers into her cheeks.

Panting, she let go.

Dragging her into the corridor, he growled at Gus, 'Kick the door shut and give's a hand.'

Gus rubbed a trickle of blood off his forehead and viciously kicked the door. 'Fucking wee bitch,' he said, grabbing her legs and twisting.

'Easy,' Phil cautioned. 'She's not to be hurt.'

'Fuck Tony.' Gus twisted Kara's legs again.

Phil saw her eyes widen and felt her shudder.

'It's not worth it, mate.'

'I'm not scared of Tony.'

'Then you're more stupid than I thought.' Phil paused to tighten his grip on Kara. 'Come on. Let's get her into the cellar, then we can relax for a bit.'

The two men, shuffling crablike, carted Kara up the corridor.

'Shit,' Phil said as an open door caught his ankle. He put out a hand to balance himself and his grip on Kara loosened.

She gasped some air into her lungs to generate the energy to scream but he clamped his hand back over her mouth before she could utter a sound.

'Somebody's in there,' Gus muttered, nodding his head at the door.

Phil stuck his foot into the gap between door and wall and pushed it open.

His eyes narrowed. 'What the hell're you doing in there, Marlene.'

'Cleaning up after Tony, as usual,' she said, her eyes shifting quickly away from the girl they were carrying.

Phil glanced at her for a moment, wondering if he should do anything about her. But Marlene would keep her mouth shut.

Coming to a decision, he leaned towards her. 'You didn't see anything.'

'What's to see?' she said, turning back to the cupboard.

Marlene gripped the handle of her bucket and only emerged from the cupboard after she heard the cellar door close.

She scurried up the stairs into Tony's office, locking the door behind her. Not that it would do any good if Phil decided to come after her.

Leaning her back against the door she took several deep breaths until she stopped shaking.

It was bad luck she'd seen them carry that girl in. But she had. And she'd recognised her. That was what made it worse.

Angel hadn't stirred. She felt for a pulse in the girl's neck keeping her finger there until she was convinced it was stronger than it had been before.

She went to the bathroom and filled the bucket with cold water. Returning to the sofa she dribbled the water over Angel's body. She didn't want to make too much mess on Tony's leather sofa – though it would serve him right if she did.

Angel stirred.

Marlene dribbled more water over her.

'Whassat.' Angel's eyelids fluttered.

'That's my girl,' Marlene said. 'You ready to wake up now?'

Angel groaned.

'There's a shledgehammer in my head and the room'sh going round.'

'I'm not surprised. What'd you take to get in a state like this?'

Angel struggled to a sitting position. 'Don't know,' she said. 'Tony gave me some pills . . . said they'd make me high.'

'If you'd been any higher you might not have come down again,' Marlene said. 'Let's get you off that sofa and into the shower. It'll make you feel better.' She helped the girl off the sofa, manoeuvred her into the shower and turned the cold water on.

Angel shrieked. 'It's freezing.'

'It's meant to be,' Marlene said. 'Stay under it and I'll come back in ten minutes to get you out.'

She propped the girl against the wall and turned to leave the bathroom. Without the support Angel slid down the wall into a foetal position.

Marlene sat in one of the chairs looking out over the clubroom. It was bare and tawdry without the lights and the girls, but she hardly noticed. Her mind was full of what she'd seen downstairs.

Phil and Gus were bastards. She shivered at the thought of confronting them. But the girl they were forcing into the cellar hadn't been just any girl. It'd been Helen's girl.

How could she do nothing?

Helen had been the top girl when Marlene had first come to work at the club and she'd taken the new girl under her wing. She'd shown her the ropes, what to do, how to get on Tony's good side, how to advance herself in the business. Marlene owed a lot to Helen.

But did she owe Helen enough to save her daughter? Enough to cross Tony?

Marlene stood up and leaned her head against the two-way glass. It was cold against her forehead. She had crossed Tony once in the past and survived.

Helen had been scared when she left and Marlene hadn't told him where she vanished to. Hadn't told him about Helen's change of name. Hadn't told him about the baby Helen had been expecting when she left Dundee. He'd never found out.

This was different though. He'd be bound to find out. There was no way she could let the girl out of the cellar, even when Phil and Gus left.

Still shaking she walked to the bathroom to help Angel out of the shower. She'd think about it again once she'd got this girl sorted out.

The ropes binding Kara to the chair bit into her wrists when Phil pulled them tight. 'That should do it until Tony gets here.'

The gag in Kara's mouth tasted of chalk and something else she couldn't identify. Dust from the strip of material trickled into the back of her throat, choking her. She tried to cough but only managed to make grunting noises that she hoped would clear her throat.

'Try and get out of that,' he laughed, turning to leave. 'Cheerio.' He waved a hand and strode out of the room, slamming the door and turning the key.

The room was dark but Kara had seen enough, while the light shone through the door, to know it wasn't large and, apart from the chair she was tied to, it was bare and windowless.

She tried thumping her feet but they made little sound on the earth floor. Besides, there was another cellar in front of this one, which was filled with bottles and beer kegs and was probably only used by bar staff. There'd be no help from them because, of course, they all worked for Tony.

Clenching her fists, she pulled against the ropes but Phil had made a good job of tying her up and she couldn't shift them. She'd probably be able to topple the chair but what good would that do?

There was nothing she could do but wait for Tony Palmer.

She thought of Charlene and Billy and hoped their foster parents would be good to them. Tears blinded her eyes. She'd probably never see them again. Poor wee souls were probably better off without her, she thought, although she couldn't quite convince herself.

She wondered if her mother had ever thought about her the way she thought about Charlene and Billy, and regretted the arguments they'd had. Too late now to make amends.

Remembering a prayer her mother taught her when she was a child, she started to recite it soundlessly in her head. It couldn't do any harm.

40

There were no parking spaces left in front of the station building when Louise and Bill got back.

'I'll go on up.' Louise got out of the car, leaving Bill to head off to the multi-storey car park further along the road.

She didn't know the keypad number and had to ask a constable in reception to open the door for her.

He made her sign in, turning the book round to read her entry and commenting with a cheeky grin, 'They want to train you folks in CID a bit better. The number's not that hard to remember.'

'I'm new here, OK? Nobody told me the number,' Louise retorted. Then relenting, she smiled apologetically.

The team room was quiet when she got there with nothing but the low hum of computers and flickering screensavers to disturb her. Swirling geometric patterns, animals, cannibal fish, Winnie the Pooh, and Harry Potter proliferated. Noticing that Bill's computer screen was alive with cannibal fish, she wondered if screensavers reflected personalities and, if so, maybe her suspicion was justified.

The whiteboards and various charts had been moved into the room since she'd last been here. Now they were clustered near the large block of chipboard pinned to the wall. The out of date messages, yellowing memos and posters it usually held had all been removed and piled on an adjacent desk. Louise was glad it wasn't hers.

An enlarged photograph of Denise Palmer was pinned to the chipboard along with two sheets of paper, each with the outline of a face and a question mark in the middle. Under that was a list with the names and ages of missing girls and the dates they disappeared.

Louise frowned. It was a long list.

On the whiteboard, set up next to the display, a plan was drawn up with various headings: known prostitutes, club dancers and hostesses, young women, housewives and teenagers. The name of each girl was listed under a category.

'Interesting, isn't it?'

Louise started. She hadn't heard the DI enter the room.

She nodded.

'See this girl here, and this one, and this one. They all worked at Teasers. That's where Denise was last seen. Her dad's place.' Andy hoisted himself onto the desk sending some posters fluttering to the floor. 'Maybe it's something, or maybe it's nothing. But it needs to be checked out.'

'D'you want me to take this up with Palmer?' Louise's hands were damp and she wiped them on her trousers.

'I was thinking more along the lines of you and Bill checking out Teasers, speaking to the staff, that sort of thing.'

'Sure,' Louise said, 'but I thought Sue was Bill's partner. I wouldn't like to step on any toes.

'Don't worry about that. You're the liaison with Palmer and he's a difficult bugger. Anyway, Sue's busy checking out some other stuff at the moment so she wouldn't have time.'

'D'you think we should let Palmer know first?'

'Hmm, I suppose it wouldn't do any harm. Be careful though.'

Louise stiffened. 'I'm not afraid of him.'

'No, and I wouldn't expect you to be. But he has some serious legal muscle behind him so we have to be sure of our ground before we do anything that concerns him.'

'Then it's probably better if I prepare him. Tell him it's routine. That sort of thing.'

'Good idea.' Andy beamed. 'You're going to be an asset to the team.'

Louise bit back a retort that she was only there temporarily and he shouldn't start making assumptions. She'd be glad to get back to the Child and Family Support Unit when this case was closed.

Andy slid off the desk. 'When Bill gets in, come and see me to report back on the case conference.' He took an antacid tablet out of a packet in his top pocket, smiled at her, and ambled off in the direction of his office.

Louise stretched out a hand, ready to call him back. She didn't want to tell him about Kara's identifying her attacker when Bill was there. It would be too tricky. But then, remembering that Bill and Andy were friends, she let her hand drop.

If she did tell Andy what she knew, it would affect her friendship with Bill and he'd probably be taken off the case, which wouldn't do his career any good at all either.

It was something she'd seen happen before. Dave Peterson had been a good cop, but allegations had been made that he'd taken a backhander and he'd never recovered from it. The investigation that followed cleared him but the cloud remained. He'd found it so intolerable he'd left the force.

She couldn't do that to Bill, not when his personal life was such a mess. There was no one she could trust, so she'd just have to check it out herself.

No noise or light infiltrated the cellar. Kara felt as if she'd been buried alive. Time was meaningless. She could have been there for minutes or hours.

Phil had laughed when he slammed the door, leaving her in the dark. At first she'd thought they'd return with Tony pretty soon, but they hadn't. At one point an oblong of grey appeared in front of her, as if a door had opened, and a faint light filtered into the cellar. She strained to see and thought she could make out a figure of someone standing there, silently watching her.

She'd frozen. Was this it? Had they come to finish what they'd started.

After a time the greyish oblong merged with the dark and she knew she was alone again.

Helen Ferguson forced her eyes open and peered at the bedside clock. It showed ten past three. Her tongue clung to the roof of her mouth, her throat was sandpaper, and her head cotton wool. No chink of light showed through the heavy curtains on the window. Was it horribly early morning or mid-afternoon?

She reached for the bottle on the bedside cabinet.

It wasn't there.

'Damn,' she said, rolling to the edge of the bed and peering on the floor. Her fingers scrabbled along the carpet. It rushed up to meet her and the pressure behind her eyes increased until it felt as if the top of her head was coming off. She was just about ready to give up when her fingers brushed against the familiar feel of the glass bottle. Lunging forward to grasp it she almost fell out of bed.

Flinging herself back onto her pillows, she muttered, 'Damn it, I need a drink.' She raised the bottle to her mouth. Seconds later she flung it across the room. 'Damn, damn, and double damn,' she groaned, the sound of the bottle hitting the wardrobe ripping through her brain like an electric saw.

The bloody thing was empty.

'Kitchen,' she muttered, rolling out of bed. She always had one in the kitchen.

Clutching her head, she padded out of the bedroom. Daylight reflecting off the white tiles in the kitchen was too much for Helen's eyes. Where had the day gone, she thought, as she rummaged beneath the sink, bringing out an armful of empty bottles.

She couldn't possibly have drunk all of them.

She let them fall and sat back on her heels. Where were her other stashes?

She was still trying to remember when the phone rang.

Her tongue felt too large for her mouth but she managed to answer it without slurring her words too horrendously.

'Marlene . . .' she said, trying to remember who Marlene was. 'Oh, I remember now. Marlene French. It must be twenty years since we last saw each other.'

'That's right,' Marlene said. 'I thought it was safer not to keep in touch after you left. Not with the way things were.'

'I understand. So . . . why are you phoning now?'

'Before I tell you, you must promise not to let Tony know that I was the one to tell you.'

'What d'you mean?'

'Just promise.' Marlene's voice sounded harsh.

'OK.' Helen's mind was racing, pushing the cobwebs out of her brain.

'Something you need to know. Promise not to tell anyone?'

'Yes, yes.' It must be something important to make Marlene so nervous.

'Tony's got your girl.'

'My girl?'

'Your Kara. She's tied up in Teasers' cellar.'

Helen sagged onto the seat beside the phone. 'What's he got her there for?'

'If I knew, I'd tell you . . .' Marlene hesitated. 'But it doesn't look good. You know what Tony's like.'

Helen knew perfectly well what Tony was like. That was why she'd left the club all those years ago, and why she'd never told him about the baby she was carrying. She didn't want to get involved with Tony Palmer again, not ever.

'Can't you sneak in and let her go?'

'No, I can't.' Marlene's voice was flat and emphatic. 'It's too dangerous. He'd just go looking for her again.'

'OK.'

Marlene's voice softened. 'This is something only you can do, Helen.'

Helen's head throbbed. She leaned it against the wall. 'Yeah,' she said quietly, 'I know.'

'Remember, we haven't talked for twenty years. And we won't be talking for another twenty.'

Helen swallowed. 'You can trust me,' she said. And she meant it.

Tony's heart ached for Madge. He'd thought she'd started to pull herself together, but now she hardly seemed aware of him sitting beside her, holding her hand. Now and again a solitary tear trickled down her face.

Finally Madge's misery had become too much for him and he'd gone downstairs to wait for the policewoman who, although she didn't know it, was going to tell him what he needed to know, like it or not.

It was late afternoon by the time Louise drove up to the Palmers' villa. Tony, who'd been pacing from window to window, saw her arrive and opened the door almost before her finger left the bell.

'I came as soon as I could,' she said, following him into the lounge.

'It's been a nightmare.' Tony's lips twisted. 'It's Madge.' He looked at his hands. 'I don't know what to do to help her.' He paced to the window and looked out. 'I want to help her but I can't come to terms with it myself.' He didn't have to force a note of agony in his voice, it was there despite himself.

Louise followed him to the window. She stood behind him, almost matching him in height. 'I don't know what to say,' she murmured. 'It's such a horrendous thing to have to come to terms with.'

He could feel her breath on his neck.

'There is no way I can imagine what you're feeling,' she continued. 'It would be foolish of me to try.'

He turned, grasping her hands within his own. 'The only thing that will help now is being told everything there is to know.' Her hands quivered beneath his grasp. 'I couldn't bear it if things were kept back from me. You won't keep anything back, will you?'

'I'll tell you everything I can.' Her fingers wriggled free from his grasp but she didn't turn away from him.

'It's killing me, not knowing. I have to know.'

Suddenly he had difficulty breathing and he pulled at his collar. 'Denise is . . . was my only child.'

'Why don't you sit down?' Louise cupped his elbow in her hand and led him to a sofa. Sitting down beside him, she said, 'That's what I'm here for, to keep you up to date with the investigation.'

Tony slumped back in the seat. His elbow tingled where she'd held it and he wished she would touch him again. He contemplated reaching out to her, holding her hands, moving his leg next to hers so he could feel the heat of her body. But he resisted the impulse. He had her sympathy and it might win him the knowledge he needed, it would be stupid to ruin it now with a careless move.

'So? Where's the investigation at?' He kept his voice low.

'Still in the early stages, at the moment,' she said, shifting uncomfortably on the sofa cushion. 'We're trying to trace the other girls, hoping to get a lead from them.'

'I heard there'd been a witness.'

'We're not sure. We think there might have been one girl who got away. But we haven't traced her yet.'

Tony smiled to himself, thinking of Kara in the club cellar.

'You'll tell me when you find her?'

'Of course,' Louise said.

'Of course,' Tony repeated softly.

'We've been checking all the records of missing girls.' Louise's cheeks reddened. 'Several of them were last seen at Teasers and I've been asked to help check it out – it could be a link.'

Tony's expression hardened. 'Club girls are always moving on. They don't always leave forwarding addresses.'

'I didn't say they were club girls, but you're right, they were.'

Anger surged through him in a red-hot wave and he got to his feet. 'You don't think I had anything to do with it, do you?'

'I didn't say that.' Louise reached out a conciliatory hand. 'All I said was they'd gone missing from your club and we wanted to check them out. You know. Speak to your employees.'

'Club girls lead a fast life. They meet up with all sorts.' Tony forced himself to calm down and returned to sit beside her. 'So when's this check going to take place?'

'We thought we'd come tonight. The sooner the better. It might give us the lead we want.'

'OK,' Tony said, 'provided you keep me informed of anything useful.'

He moved to the window when Louise left and watched until she drove off. Pity she was a policewoman, she'd have made an excellent pole dancer with those legs.

41

Helen's legs quivered and her head pounded as she pulled herself up. She leaned against the wall. What good was she to anyone in this state.

Angrily she brushed the self-pitying tears away. She knew what she had to do. OK, Kara had left home, she'd made her bed and by all accounts it wasn't a very comfortable one. She'd rejected her mother and hadn't allowed her children to know their granny. But that wasn't Helen's fault. It wasn't as if she'd told Kara not to come back. Or had she? She shook her head; she couldn't remember. In any case, what did it matter? Kara was her daughter and she wasn't going to let someone like Tony Palmer threaten her.

She would have to face up to him. After all these years of keeping her secret, Helen would have to tell him something she'd kept to herself for years. But first she'd have to clear her head and make herself look respectable so Tony wouldn't get the better of her before she had her say.

Her hands and legs were numb by the time she twisted the shower's controls to warm, but her head had stopped pounding, either the result of the icy shower or the effects of the painkillers she'd swallowed half an hour ago.

She towelled herself dry, rubbing hard until a warm glow spread throughout her body. Feeling a lot better, she was now more than ready to face Tony bloody Palmer.

She flicked on the hairdryer and sat on the dressing table stool, watching her reflection in the mirror with satisfaction as her blonde hair blew round her face in the warm air. Tony had always been susceptible to blondes and, unlike Madge, Helen hadn't yet had to resort to the dye bottle.

Make-up was next. Her complexion was still good, so a smidgin of foundation and powder was enough. She swithered over three shades of lipstick, then decided on a subtle red, finishing with a little bit of eye-shadow and liner.

Good, she thought. Now for the rest.

Before deciding what to wear, she examined her body in the mirrored doors of the wardrobe. Not too bad, considering, she thought. A bit fuller than it was when she was younger maybe, but still shapely and not too flabby.

Sliding the mirrored door aside, she contemplated her clothes. After a bit of thought she pulled on a pair of smart jeans, easing them over her hips and holding her breath to get them zipped up. Then she plucked a white cotton shirt from a silk-covered hanger, pulled it over her head and buttoned it. The shirt flared over her hips masking the slight protrusion of her belly. After a moment's thought she unfastened the top three buttons. Maybe a bit too casual, she thought, tucking the shirt in and reaching for a wide black belt, which she fastened round her waist. A black fitted jacket added a touch of formality. Now for the shoes. Her hand hovered over a pair of black high-heeled shoes, but then she said, 'The hell with it,' and pushed her feet into a pair of red stilettos.

Ignoring her overcoat, even though it was cold outside, she grabbed her car keys and strode to the garage.

She was all set – she'd fight hard for her daughter despite their differences.

Tony poured a generous measure of Laphroaig into a crystal glass, holding it up and turning the glass so that light shone, translucent and glowing, through the amber liquid. He sipped it, allowing trickles of smoky fire to slide down his throat and warm his stomach. But this time it gave him no pleasure.

The door opened. He turned, frowning.

'Boss, there's a woman at the door, says she wants to see you, name's Helen Ferguson.'

Tony scowled. What the hell was she doing here? He didn't like Madge associating with her, particularly after she'd told him Helen had an alcohol problem. But Madge insisted she was an old friend who just needed a bit of support and refused to cut her off. Tony had given in with bad grace and, luckily, Madge had the sense not to bring her to the house.

'Tell her Madge is indisposed and get rid of her,' he barked.

'Too late. I'm in.'

Tony watched in disbelief as the small attractive blonde shouldered her way past Brian.

'Tell your flunkey to get lost, Tony,' Helen said, backing away from Brian.

Tony waved his hands in a dismissive gesture. 'It's OK, Brian, she's in now, so I'll hear what she has to say. But, it'd better be brief.'

Helen walked over to one of the sofas and sat down. She patted the seat beside her. 'Come and sit down, Tony. I need to talk to you.'

Tony sat.

Helen laughed bitterly. 'All these years and you didn't know I was on your doorstep. Didn't know I was Madge's friend. I was just the neighbourhood drunk, someone who didn't fit into your social circle, someone to be kept at arm's length.' She placed a hand on his knee. 'Would it have made any difference if you'd known I was Helena Lockhart, I wonder?'

'But Madge never said.'

'Madge didn't know. She only knew me as Helen Ferguson and I wasn't going to tell her any different because I didn't want her husband poking about in my life.'

'So why come to me now?' Tony narrowed his eyes.

Helen was still an attractive woman, a mature version of the pretty girl he'd known. A girl he might have married if she hadn't done a vanishing trick. A flicker of regret pulsed through him. Why hadn't he looked for her after she left Dundee? But he hadn't and that was that. Instead, he'd married his childhood sweetheart Madge, hoping she'd provide the respectability he craved.

Her expression hardened. 'Because you've got something of mine and I want her back.'

It was a moment before Tony made the connection, but

when he did he realised that somehow or other she'd found out he had Kara. 'So, you think, for old times' sake, I'll give you back whatever – whoever – it is you think I've got.'

'I don't think, Tony. I know.' Helen's voice was deceptively soft. 'So stop playing games. You've got my daughter and I want her back.'

'And why should I hand her over to you? *If* I've got her, that is . . .' Tony rose from the sofa and poured himself another drink. 'What will you have?'

Her eyes focused on the decanter in his hand and he could almost hear her mental struggle. 'Nothing, thanks.' She looked away.

'You're sure?' he said, returning to the sofa.

'You'd like that, wouldn't you? Solve the problem, get me drunk.' Her voice was harsh with anger.

He laughed, leaning back against the sofa cushions. 'You've had a wasted journey,' he said. 'I can't afford to let off *anyone* who owes me, and Kara owes me. So, if I've got her, which I'm not saying I have, there's no way I'd let her go.'

Helen's cheeks flamed and she jumped up. 'Is that so, Tony,' she hissed. 'Harm her and I'll make sure everyone knows what you've done.'

Tony laughed. 'Why should that matter to me?'

'Because she's your bloody daughter, that's why.'

'My daughter's dead. Some psycho left her in the woods to die.'

'I know, Tony,' Helen's voice softened and she sat down again, 'but Denise wasn't your only child. You have another daughter. Kara.'

'I don't believe you.'

'Why d'you think I left the club when I did? We'd had a row and I was pregnant, that's why. I didn't tell you. I should have, I know. But I didn't want you interfering. I didn't want you telling me to get an abortion, and I didn't want my baby knowing it had a gangster for a father. So I left to make a new life for myself in Manchester – and what a mess I made of that right enough. By the time I'd had second thoughts there was a

Mrs Palmer and I couldn't change things. I was alone and I was desperate, so I cut my losses and married Rafe. Ironic, don't you think? Running away from you and ending up married to another bloody gangster.' Her voice softened. 'He was good to me, mind. He bought a lot of bars in Spain and put them all in my name. I didn't know at the time they were just a front for the weapons and drugs. In the end he got himself killed and I sold up and came home.'

Tony didn't look up.

'Kara didn't want to come back to Scotland. She said Dundee was a cold, miserable place, and she didn't have any friends here. I couldn't tell her you were her father, but remembered Madge from when we were at school together, and it wasn't difficult to get to know her again. I wanted Kara and Denise to be friends. Someday, I thought, I'll tell both of them that they're sisters.' She lapsed into silence. 'And now, it's too late.'

Tony's insides churned. He didn't know what to believe. She could be lying to get Kara off the hook. Helena had always been a good liar. But what if the girl was his daughter? He stiffened. It didn't make any difference one way or the other. Kara knew who Denise's killer was. Kara would have to co-operate with him no matter what.

The door opened.

'Helen! I didn't know you were here.' Madge glanced anxiously at Tony.

'She's just leaving,' Tony said.

Helen smiled at Madge. 'I came to pay my respects,' she said. She stood up and walked to the door before turning. 'Remember, Tony. You can't hurt your own blood.'

'What did she mean about your "blood"?' Madge watched Helen leave.

'Oh, it's nothing,' Tony said. 'I think she'd had a drink or two. She wasn't making much sense.'

'Bill,' Andy strode into the team room, 'there's been an anonymous tip-off that our missing witness has been hiding out with a chum at Clepington Road.' He slapped a yellow post-it note onto Bill's desk. 'The chum's name's Jean Lindsay, a known hooker. Check her out, will you?'

Bill groaned. 'Have a heart, Andy. I've just got back. Haven't even had one sip of this coffee yet.'

'Where've you been anyway? Louise was back hours ago, but she had to go off and see Tony Palmer to prepare him for your little visit tonight.'

Andy laughed. 'I forgot – you weren't here for the briefing.'

Bill sighed with relief. He wasn't losing his marbles after all. 'Thank goodness for that, I was beginning to think I'd missed something. So, what's happening?'

'Several of the missing girls have worked at Teasers. We need to check out whether they've moved on, and if so, where they've moved to. If there's no trace of them alive then we'll have to find relatives and do some DNA checking. If you check the whiteboard you'll get their names. You'll be pairing up with Louise so you'd better leave her a note about where and when to meet up. In the meantime there's Jean Lindsay to check out.'

42

The smell hit Bill as soon as he opened the entry door, something had died here and been left to rot.

He wrinkled his nose in disgust and almost backed out again. It would be just his luck if he found a body when he was on his own.

The lobby was dark and he felt his way along the wall to the foot of the stairs. His foot snagged something lying on the floor.

He bent down, stretched out his arm and probed the object with his fingers.

There was a slight squelching sound and a smell wafted upwards making him gag. But at least it wasn't skin he was feeling.

It was a cold stiff body, covered with clammy fur.

He drew his fingers back. It was a cat, and now his fingers smelt of dead bloody cat.

Wiping his hand down the wall only made the smell seem worse, but he didn't want to wipe his fingers on his jacket or trousers. Holding his hand at arm's length, he climbed the stairs.

'Fuck, what's that smell?' The unkempt girl who opened the door pinched her nose.

'Dead cat,' Bill muttered.

Jean grinned, releasing her fingers from her nose. 'Too bad it's not fresh. The snakes would have loved it.'

Snakes! What the hell had he got himself into?

She looked him up and down. 'You're not touching me while you stink like that. You'd better come in and wash your hands.'

'I'm not a client, love.' Bill couldn't help grinning. She wouldn't be so keen to ask him in when she knew he was a policeman.

'Who the hell are you then?' At least she wasn't closing the door. Not yet anyway.

'I'm the police.' Bill rummaged for his ID card with the hand that didn't smell of dead cat.

'Bloody filth. I might have known, given the stench.' Jean turned her back on him and retreated into the flat. 'You better come in anyway. You'll need to get that gunk off your hand.'

He followed her inside.

'Sink's over there.' She nodded to the window recess. 'What are you doing poking dead cats anyway? Haven't you heard the saying, let sleeping dogs lie? Well the same goes for cats, especially dead ones.'

The water was cold. Bill waited for it to heat up but it didn't. He grabbed a piece of dirty soap from the draining board, rubbed his hands together until he was satisfied he'd washed the stink off and dried them on a grubby towel, which he threw onto the draining board.

'You might hang it up again,' Jean said. 'I like to keep things nice.'

Bill gave her his official police stare, but it didn't have the desired effect.

'Go on then,' Jean said, returning his stare. 'Hang the bloody towel up.'

He picked up the towel and hung it on a nail at the side of the sink.

'Now we've got you cleaned up, maybe you can tell me what you're after.' Jean plopped herself into an armchair and nodded to Bill to take the other one. 'My better half's in the clink, so if you're looking for him you've had it. And I haven't done anything. Not anything you can nick me for. So what are you after?'

Bill swivelled in his chair, aware of a glass tank just inches away; a glass tank containing a comatose python.

A very large python.

The snake moved slightly. Bill looked away. Maybe he'd concentrate better if he couldn't see it.

He cleared his throat. 'I believe a woman named Kara

Ferguson has been staying with you.'

Jean laughed. 'Yeah, so what?'

'We need to interview her urgently,' Bill said.

'Why?'

Bill thought for a moment. He was there to get information, not supply it, and he probably shouldn't. But, what the hell. 'We think she may be a witness in a murder case.' He paused to see what effect this had on Jean.

She laughed. 'Oh, you mean the weirdo who took her to Templeton Woods? She was lucky to get out of that one alive.'

'What d'you know about this punter, Jean? What does he look like? What kind of car did he drive?'

'Don't know,' Jean said. 'I never saw him or his car. Kara just said it was red.'

'Is that it?' Bill exhaled. 'Half of Dundee's got a red car. I've got one.'

'Yeah, that's what I thought. But you can be sure I won't be getting into any red cars. Not unless I know who's driving it.'

Bill spoke softly. 'You'll understand then why we have to speak to her.'

'Yeah, but you'll have to find her first,' Jean smirked.

'Don't be so cheeky.' He was getting pissed off with Jean and her lack of respect. 'Want me to take you down to the station and question you there?'

'Do what you like, love. But I can't tell you what I don't know.'

'You can make a start by telling me when you expect her back.'

'Oh, she's not coming back.'

'You seem very sure.'

'As sure as I can be. She didn't like the snakes, you see. They gave her the willies.'

Bill had almost forgotten the snakes, but now he glanced at the tank, inches from his left elbow. No wonder.

'Well, if she does come back, you can call me on this.' He handed Jean a card with his mobile number printed on it.

'Yeah, OK,' Jean said, placing it on top of a snake tank and offering to show him out.

Louise could still see Tony Palmer's face – anxious, troubled. A bubble of sadness welled inside her and she was desperate to talk to someone, anyone, about something other than murdered girls. But there was no one in the office.

There was nothing Louise would have liked better than to go home and curl up in her chair with the latest Ian Rankin. A pity Bill wasn't more like John Rebus, she thought. But then again, she probably wouldn't be able to tolerate someone who didn't have a sensitive side for more than an evening. But Bill was probably *too* sensitive for his own good, and she still hadn't worked out what was bothering him. Sue had always said Bill was a good guy to have around, lots of fun and plenty of get up and go. Louise hadn't seen any evidence of that side of him. What she had seen was a needy type who couldn't seem to help himself. Someone desperately in need of comfort. Why did she always have to fall for the same type?

Where was he, anyway?

She rummaged in her bag for the packet of tuna sandwiches she'd bought in M&S. The door opened, and a whiff of air, bringing with it the aroma of vinegary chips, wafted through the room.

'That's not fish and chips, is it?' Louise focused hungrily on the paper-wrapped parcel Bill carried.

'How did you guess?' He plonked the parcel on her desk and pulled a chair over. 'I was in the mood for something fried and greasy – just had a run in with one of Kara's pals. Right old slapper she was.'

Louise watched as he unwrapped the brown paper parcel. The fish, covered in golden, crunchy batter, steamed on top of a pile of fat, juicy chips. The smell intensified.

'I'll trade you a tuna sandwich for some of that,' she said wistfully.

Bill looked at her and grinned. 'Nah, not sure I fancy a tuna sandwich right now.'

Louise tore at her sandwich wrapper, eventually peeling it off. 'Fine, I like tuna sandwiches anyway'.

'Just kidding. Help yourself.' Bill pushed the parcel over to her.

'Tell me about Kara's pal.' She tore off a piece of fish with her fingers.

'Jean Lindsay.' Bill popped a chip into his mouth. 'Her pythons were more attractive than she was.'

'Jean Lindsay. Does she live in Clepington Road?'

'Yeah, that's the one. Know her?'

'She's not that bad.' Louise picked up a chip and contemplated it. 'Her boyfriend's in Perth Prison just now so she'll be getting a break.'

'How'd you mean?'

'He takes her money and beats her up into the bargain. She's got two kids in care and she's not going to see them back again while he's still around. Vicious bastard he is.' She bit the chip in half. 'Did she say anything?'

'Not really, just that Kara wasn't coming back on account of the snakes. I wouldn't go back either if I could avoid it.'

Louise scrubbed her greasy fingers with a tissue. 'I feel a bit sorry for her.'

Shaking his head, Bill said, 'Right. You ready to tackle Teasers now?'

Tony pressed his head against the mirrored wall. Below him the music thumped, vibrating the glass against his forehead.

The door opened. 'Brought you a drink, boss,' Marlene said.

'The new girl.' Tony didn't look at her. 'She's not here tonight.'

'No.'

'She's not . . .'

'Nothing a day or two in bed won't cure.' Marlene's voice was flat and uninterested.

'Yeah, well, see she gets a bonus.' Tony sipped his drink.

'I'll see to it.' Marlene headed for the door. 'Need anything else?'

'Yeah, send Phil and Gus up.'

He didn't turn as they entered the room. 'Where've you been, boys?'

'Just hanging around the club, boss.' Phil smoothed a hand over his blond hair. 'Waiting for the go-ahead.'

'That can wait,' Tony said. 'I need her to lead me to the murdering bastard that killed my Denise.' His eyes never moved from the dancers, although he no longer saw them.

The oblong of grey was there again. The door was open, but this time there was no beam of light. Try as hard as she could, Kara couldn't make out whether someone stood there or not.

She squeezed her eyes shut, then opened them again, but it didn't help. Her throat made guttural noises but the words couldn't shape themselves round the gag.

She wanted to scream and shout and scratch at the unknown observer, but all she could do was rock her chair until it collapsed sideways, taking her with it.

Someone giggled, and a shaft of light flickered over her face, lingered on her neck, travelled down her body and back up again.

'Stop arsing around and put the light on.' The man's voice was harsh and unfamiliar.

43

The beat of the music thudded deafeningly in Louise's ears as she and Bill fought their way through the crowd to the end of the bar furthest away from the rowdy mob of thirsty customers.

'It's another one of those student bashes.' The pony-tailed barman didn't take his eyes off them as he continued to polish a glass. 'We've checked them out, though. No one's underage.'

'I don't know why we bother with plain clothes,' Louise muttered to Bill. 'They always seem to know. You'd think we had POLICE stamped on our forehead.'

Bill squeezed her elbow. 'It's like a bad smell that follows you around. You get used to it.'

A young woman with coffee-coloured skin elbowed Bill aside and plonked a handful of glasses on the bar. 'You going to stand there all night, or are you going to help serve that lot down there?' She nodded her head in the direction of a crowd of young lads who were hassling the other two barmaids.

'When I'm finished attending to our friends in blue,' the barman said. He turned his full attention on Bill and Louise. 'You aren't here for nothing, so how can I help you?'

Bill pulled a notebook out of his pocket, opened it at the list of names and laid it on the bar. 'Know any of these girls?'

'Nope,' the barman said, fingering the piece of paper. 'But I don't remember everybody who comes in here.'

'These girls all worked here.'

'Not down here, they didn't, or I'd remember. Try the nightclub. There's lots of girls up there.'

'We're also checking up on the last known movements of Denise Palmer. This appears to be one of the last places she was seen.'

The barman's eyes narrowed. 'Not down here,' he said. 'We weren't good enough for Miss High-and-Mighty. She always went upstairs to the club.'

'You didn't see her on Hogmanay, then?'

'I didn't say that.' The barman leaned over the bar until his face was only inches from Bill's. 'I saw her out the back about eleven, having it off with Phil Beattie. Mr Palmer would go ballistic if he knew.' He picked up another glass and started polishing it. 'Denise liked a bit of rough now and then, but don't tell her dad I said that.'

'Did you see her later?' Bill flicked through the notebook until he came to an empty page.

'Naw, she didn't come back in. Not that I noticed. Mind you, I didn't see Phil come back in either.' He laid the glass down. 'But then, they could have gone upstairs without me seeing them. You want to speak to Marlene. Nothing gets past her.'

'Where can we find Marlene?'

'Upstairs.' He pointed to the door. 'She's always upstairs.'

Kara had been in the dark so long that when the light flicked on it felt like a high-powered spotlight. She scrunched her eyelids shut and turned her face into the floor, squashing her nose and breathing in a layer of dust.

'Pick the bloody chair up and let's see her face,' the hoarse voice demanded.

Rough hands grasped her shoulder, pulling her up. The weight of the chair digging the ropes into her wrists was excruciating. A half scream squeezed through the gag.

'Enough.' It was the harsh voice again. 'There's no need for that. I want her to tell me what she knows first.'

Kara shuddered. First?

The voice came further into the room. 'D'you know who I am?' The man stared into her eyes.

She nodded. There weren't many people on the estate who didn't know Tony Palmer – by reputation if not by sight.

'Then you'll know I don't take to people who cheat me.'

She nodded again but her eyes were defiant.

'Take that bloody gag off her.'

A hand reached from behind her and ripped the gag away. 'Oh shit, that was worse than a bikini wax,' Kara croaked. 'How about untying my hands as well?'

Tony laughed. 'The girl's got spunk.' He leaned down so his eyes were level with hers. 'First things first. You have something I want.'

'Those bastards,' Kara said, nodding towards Phil and Gus, 'know I don't have the money and they know why.' She moistened her parched lips with the tip of her tongue. 'Why don't you go after Kev? It was him who cheated you, not me.'

'The money.' There was no mirth in Tony's smile. 'We'll come to the money later. In the meantime there's something else I want from you.'

Kara jerked back as his eyes bored into hers. 'There's nothing else I've got that you'd be interested in,' she hissed.

'That's where you're wrong.' Tony leaned even closer so that his nose almost touched hers.

Kara resisted the temptation to spit in his face.

'There's someone I want.'

'I've told you. I don't know where Kev is.'

'Fuck Kev.' Tony gripped her shoulders. 'I'll deal with that waste of space later.'

Kara squirmed under the pressure of his fingers digging into her shoulder, but she refused to give him the satisfaction of hearing her yelp.

'I want the bastard who killed my Denise.' His fingers relaxed their grip and he turned away from her. 'And you can help me get him.'

'How?'

'You got away from him. If he sees you again he'll come for you. He'll have to – you can identify him.'

'Oh, no!' Kara's insides churned and she thought she'd be sick. 'I got away from him once. I wouldn't be that lucky a second time.'

'It won't be a question of luck, Kara.' Palmer's voice was silky soft. 'And you don't have any choice in the matter, because if you don't help me . . . well, I don't have any use for you. And you know what that means.'

Kara shuddered. 'Shit either way.'

'Not if we get to the murdering bastard first, Kara. At least doing it my way you have a chance of coming out of this alive.'

'First we'll need to get you cleaned up. Nobody in his right mind would fancy you looking like that.' He wrinkled his nose in disgust and turned to Phil. 'Take her to my office, but use the backstairs and don't let anyone see her.'

Kara swore when Phil grabbed her arm and pulled her from the chair.

'She won't be any use as bait if you mark her, so ease up.' Tony turned to face Kara. 'And you, you would be advised to go quietly. If you do as I ask, you won't find me ungrateful and I'll see no harm comes to you in the meantime.'

'You got to be a member.' The man who stepped in front of Bill and Louise preventing their entry to the nightclub was colossal. If he'd had steel teeth or a white Persian he would have made an admirable Bond villain.

Bill fumbled for his warrant card, but Louise already had hers out. She flashed it under the ape's nose. 'Police business,' she said with a confidence she didn't feel. 'We're here to see Marlene.'

'I'll have to clear it.' He reached for his walkie-talkie.

'Like hell you will.' Bill pushed Louise aside. 'Open the bloody door or I'll see the place is shut down within the hour.'

'Marlene's over at the bar,' the bouncer mumbled as he opened the door.

The bar was easy to spot as the only other lights in the room were the spotlights flickering over the girls as they wound themselves round the silver poles on the raised stage in the middle of the room.

'Interesting.' Louise glanced sideways at Bill whose eyes had been following the gyrations of one of the pole dancers.

'I wonder which one is Marlene,' he said, averting his

gaze.

Louise smiled. 'She's probably *behind* the bar.'

The seating area was in semi-darkness and they had to weave between the tables to get to the bar at the far end of the room. The woman behind it watched their approach with wary eyes. She was attractive with dark honey-blonde hair but was at least a decade older than the dancers.

'You're Marlene?'

'Who wants to know?' She picked up a cloth and started to polish a glass.

Louise was certain she knew who they were and what they wanted.

Bill pulled out his warrant card, smiled and leaned his elbows on the counter. 'We just want to ask you a few questions.'

'I'll get Tony for you.'

'It's not Mr Palmer we want. It's you, Marlene.'

Marlene continued polishing the shiniest glass in the whole club. What was she so anxious about? They hadn't asked her anything yet.

'The police were in here asking questions.' The pony-tailed barman placed a Laphroaig in front of Tony.

'Shit, where are they?'

'I sent them upstairs to Marlene.'

Great timing, Tony thought, just as Phil's taking Kara upstairs. He gulped down the drink. 'I'd better get up there then.' He didn't want Marlene showing them into his office.

Ian was waiting for him at the top of the stairs. 'Sorry, boss, but I had to let them in.'

'That's OK.' Tony patted his arm. Ian, despite his size and ability to use his fists when there was trouble, had a problem with authority figures. It wouldn't have taken much for the police to intimidate him.

'They were looking for Marlene.' He nodded towards the bar at the other end of the room. 'They're talking to her now.'

Tony pushed past the tables and arrived at the bar in time

to hear Bill ask what time Marlene had last seen Denise.

She laid the polishing cloth down. 'It must have been about eleven, maybe a bit before or a bit after. I don't check the clock.'

'Once she left, did she come back in again?'

'She might have, but I didn't see her. She said she was going to hear the bells at the City Square.'

'Was she with anyone?'

Marlene shrugged. 'Not that I know of.'

'It's all right, Marlene. Tell them anything they want to know.' Tony smiled at her.

'But I don't know anything else.'

Bitch is hiding something, Tony thought, but he smiled at Bill and Louise. 'Anybody else you need to see?'

'No, I think that wraps it up.'

'Have you discovered anything of use?'

Louise slid off the stool she'd been sitting on. 'We'll keep you informed if we come up with something.'

'Have a drink before you go.'

'Thanks for the offer but we'd better not.'

Tony watched them leave. 'You know,' he said to Marlene, 'that copper was about to say yes but she got her word in first. I bet he's furious.'

'I think she knows more than she's letting on.'

'She's probably shit scared of Tony.' Bill glanced at his notes before stuffing the notebook into his jacket pocket. 'She didn't mention Phil's rendezvous with Denise.'

'That's right. He must have been the last one to see her alive. D'you think he might be our killer?'

'I'd lay bets he's killed before. Blokes though.'

'How do we tackle him?' Louise didn't know Phil but she'd heard plenty from Sue.

'Not here.' Bill frowned. 'I'll get the lads to bring him in. He won't be so brave in an interview room.'

44

Phil laughed as soon as Tony left the cellar. 'You're all mine now, Kara.' He cut the ropes binding her wrists and ankles. 'So you'd better be nice to me.'

Kara rubbed her legs. She could still feel the cold steel of the knife where it had scraped her skin. Out of the corner of her eyes she watched Phil toy with it and knew he was contemplating using it on her.

'Tony said you weren't to hurt me,' she said, wincing as the blood returned to her legs in a prickly flood.

'Did he? I'd almost forgotten – he has a job for you. But once he's done I'll be putting in my claim.'

From her position on the carpet in Tony's office, Kara watched him talking to a woman who looked vaguely familiar and a man whose face she couldn't see.

The woman looked up and suddenly Kara knew where she'd seen her before. It had been at the welfare. She was the one who had offered to help her. The only one in that office she'd felt she would be able to trust.

For a moment Kara thought the woman could see her. She raised a hand to hammer on the window but Phil grasped it and pulled her to her feet.

'Naughty, naughty,' he said.

Kara pulled her hand out of his grasp and looked despairingly at the window as the man and woman headed towards the exit.

'Damn!' Bill thumped the bonnet of his car.

'What's up?'

'Some wee shite's taken a knife down the side of my car.'

'Maybe it has POLICE written on it as well.' Louise leaned closer to look at the damage. 'It's deep. It'll cost a bit to get repaired.'

Bill scowled. 'The car's not worth it. Time I was thinking of getting a new one anyway.' He opened the door. 'Get in. I'll drop you off beside your car. I'll finish up for both of us.'

'Sure?' Louise was already planning what to do with the rest of the night. First she was going to look for Jean Lindsay. The girl might tell her more than she had told Bill, and with a bit of luck she'd be able to pick up Kara Ferguson before the night was out.

Kara rubbed her wrist. 'Fuck you,' she spat, 'you nearly broke my bloody arm.'

Phil pressed himself against her. 'That's the least of your worries, you wee slag.'

She staggered backwards until she felt the cold leather of an armchair digging into the back of her legs. Phil laughed, placed the flat of his hand over her face and pushed.

'What the fuck's going on?'

Kara hadn't heard Tony come into the room but the tone in his voice made her shudder.

'Bitch tried to bang the window when the police were there.'

'The bloody room's soundproofed, you moron.' Tony turned to Kara. 'You look like shit.'

'You want me to clean her up, boss?' Phil took a step towards her.

'Marlene can do it.'

Kara leaned back in the chair and closed her eyes. They were speaking about her as if she wasn't there. She blinked hard and sat up again. 'I'm quite capable of cleaning myself up, thank you.'

'I'm sure you are, but we'll still get Marlene up to help because you're going to need more than a bit of a wash.' Tony picked up the phone. 'Marlene, get someone to cover the bar for you, we need you up here.' He smiled at Kara for the first time. 'She'll be here in a minute and then we'll get you sorted out.'

The smile warmed his face and the menace vanished from his eyes. Kara was surprised to feel a surge of relief. She fought it. This was one of his games and she wasn't going to fall for it.

He laughed. 'You don't have to worry. I think you'll like Marlene. She has a lot more charm than these two.' He nodded dismissively at Phil and Gus.

A few minutes later Marlene was inspecting Kara. 'Stand up,' she said.

Kara huddled further into the chair.

'I only want to see how tall you are.' Marlene smiled encouragingly at her. 'That's all.'

Reluctantly, Kara stood.

'Turn around for me now.'

Kara turned.

'Where did you get these bruises?' Marlene pulled the edge of Kara's top away from her neck. 'Was it those two?' She turned to Tony. 'You want to keep them under control.'

Kara looked at her in astonishment. She hadn't thought Tony would allow anyone to speak to him like that, but he didn't seem to be troubled by it.

Without waiting for an answer, Marlene continued. 'I can get her cleaned up and looking good but she'll need some clothes. There's nothing here that will fit her. She's a lot smaller than our dancers.'

'You heard Marlene.' Tony glanced at Phil. 'You two are going to have to go to Kara's house and get her some clothes.' He turned to Kara. 'Tell Phil what you want and he'll go get it. Make sure it's something sexy.'

Tony could hear faint sounds of water splashing in the shower. He could imagine her with water running down between her breasts and her red streaked hair plastered to her head. It unsettled him. She'd looked a real mess when he'd brought her up from the cellar but it didn't stop him finding her attractive.

If Helen Fraser was to be believed, he'd no right to be imagining anything of the sort. Surely Kara couldn't be his daughter? And yet, when he looked at her there was something familiar about her.

He'd tried to laugh off Helen's claims. The girl was too small to be his. Denise had been tall, almost as tall as he was. Tears gathered in his eyes. He'd get the bastard who'd left her to die, and for that he needed Kara, daughter or not.

The sound of running water stopped and he turned to look at the bathroom door in the hope that Marlene would bring her out. But the door remained closed.

Part of him wanted to believe Helen. And when he thought of Kara he remembered his mother had been as tiny as she was. Maybe there was something about her eyes that reminded him of his mother. He resolved to look through the old family photos, maybe they would provide some clues to Helen's claims.

Of course there was always DNA testing, but he was hardly going to volunteer for that. As long as there was some doubt he wouldn't have to take any responsibility: Denise would be his only daughter and Madge would never need to know. It would destroy her.

'What d'you think Tony will do to me after I've done what he wants?' Kara wound the towel round her body.

'Provided you do what he wants and don't cross him, Tony's all right. But sometimes he has moods and that's when you have to watch out.' Marlene picked up a hairdryer and brush. 'Now sit down here,' she pointed to a stool in front of the vanity unit, 'and I'll do your hair.'

Marlene wound strands of Kara's hair round the brush. Warm air from the dryer blew gently round Kara's head and she felt her body relaxing. She would have loved to lie down and sleep.

'You're starting to look more presentable.' Marlene stood

back and inspected her. 'Now for a bit of make-up.' She pulled open a drawer in the vanity unit, contemplated the contents, then reached in and selected several items. She opened another drawer and did the same.

'Why does Tony keep make-up in his bathroom?' Kara couldn't believe how many lipsticks, powder compacts, eyeliners and mascaras were in the drawers.

Marlene eyed her speculatively. 'The girls sometimes use the office, if they can't get home after their act. Now sit still so I can get to work.'

Kara had often wondered what it would be like to be pampered by a beautician and under Marlene's expert hands she was getting a taste of it.

'That's it.' Marlene smiled. 'You look completely different.'

'I never knew I could look like this,' Kara said, viewing her new image in the mirror.

'I think it's time to go out and surprise the boss.' Marlene's eyes met Kara's in the mirror. 'And don't worry. He won't do you any harm.'

Tony got out of the armchair when Marlene ushered Kara out of the bathroom. The transformation was better than he'd hoped. Kara stood in front of him, strikingly beautiful. He struggled for breath, then reached out to loosen the fluffy white bathrobe, tempted to see whether her body matched up to the face and hair. His hand hovered over the tie-belt for a moment before he remembered that this girl was not for him. With an exasperated sigh he turned away from her and folded his arms.

'Where the fuck are Phil and Gus?' he said hoarsely. 'They should have been back by now.'

'I'm sure I hear them,' Marlene soothed.

Phil threw a bundle of clothes onto an armchair and walked over to Kara. He fingered the collar of the bathrobe. 'There you go, love. Let's see you put them on.'

'Get your fucking hands off her.' Tony clenched his fists. He ignored Phil's surprised look, turned to Kara and said mildly, 'You can get dressed in the bathroom, and come out when you're ready.'

Kara pulled on the black cashmere polo neck. She wore no bra and it moulded itself to her breasts, accentuating her nipples. She then wriggled into skin-tight PVC trousers.

Tony Palmer was a strange man, she thought, as she slipped her feet into high-heeled shoes. Marlene had warned her about his moods and she'd thought she was seeing one of them when he turned on Phil. But then he'd smiled at her. If she hadn't known better she could have sworn he liked her. But if he liked her he wouldn't be using her as bait.

She emerged from the bathroom and watched their expressions. Tony was the only one who seemed to appreciate her appearance.

He smiled and held out a hand to her. 'If anyone can pull this psycho in, it's you, Kara. Please don't worry, no harm will come to you. And after it's all over we'll have a talk, just you and me.'

Kara nodded nervously.

'Phil! Gus! I want you to take Kara back to where she picked up this bastard. Stay close to her and bring him back to me. And make sure nothing happens to Kara – I mean it.'

He waited until nightfall. Waited until the pubs emptied and the merrymakers had gone. Waited until the streets were quiet. He cruised the dark streets. Watching the street girls. But she was not one of them. Not tonight.

He was patient though. He could wait. She would come. He was sure of it.

45

Tony accompanied them to the car. For the first time he felt a twinge of unease as he looked at Kara's face. The fear on it was plain to see. He could feel her flinch when he touched her arm. 'Don't worry,' he said. 'Phil and Gus have instructions to look after you.'

'Right. Like they looked after me before. If it wasn't for those two I wouldn't be here now.' She shook his hand off. 'But what d'you care? The welfare haven't got your kids. I'm nothing but some cash to you.'

'They didn't tell me you had kids!' Was it possible he had grandchildren?

A tear trickled down her face and she turned away from him. 'I'll never see them again if you make me do this.'

Tony grasped her arm again. 'I said Phil and Gus were going to take good care of you and I meant it,' he rasped. 'When you've done this job for me I'll personally ensure you get your kids home.'

'But how?'

'Just trust me.'

She shook his hand off again and slid into the back seat of the car. 'Anyway, I won't *be* coming back if he finds me,' her voice was breaking. Tony watched until he could no longer see the tail-lights.

There was no response to Louise's knock on the door at the Clepington Road flat, so she reckoned Jean must be working. And if she was, then Louise knew exactly where she would be.

The icy wind chilled her as she left the car park under the Tay Bridge approach road and started to walk towards the warren of streets between the car park and the bus station.

This was the working girls' stamping ground and Jean wouldn't be far away.

Louise found her in Exchange Street. 'How's business?' she asked.

Jean groaned. 'Terrible. I'm only just here and I haven't done nothing yet, so you can't take me in.'

'No, no. I only wanted a word with you.'

'What about?' Jean looked at her suspiciously.

'A friend of yours, Kara Ferguson.'

'I know Kara, but I wouldn't exactly call her a friend.'

'Have you seen her around?'

Jean shrugged. 'Not for a day or two.' She lit a cigarette. 'Why're you looking for her? What's she done?'

'I think she might be in danger and I want to find her before someone else does.'

Jean sucked on her cigarette and looked pensive. 'I wouldn't want anything to happen to her. But it doesn't change nothing. I still haven't seen her.'

Louise fished a card out of her pocket and wrote a number on the back. 'That's my mobile. Call me if you do see her. Even better, ask her to call me.'

Jean's indifference did not convince Louise, but there was nothing else she could do for the time being.

Bill hated doing reports but he had to do something while he waited for the uniforms to bring Phil Beattie in for questioning. Phil wouldn't be so tough in the interview room and Bill was quite looking forward to their session together.

He jabbed the keyboard. Why was it that he always hit the wrong letters? Everyone else seemed to have no problems with their computers but he could swear his was conducting a vendetta against him. He backspaced viciously, deleting an entire paragraph by mistake. Maybe he shouldn't have started the bloody thing at this time of night. His brain wasn't fresh enough, but then it never was.

The door swung open and Andy perched on the end of Bill's desk. 'No sign of Phil at his flat.'

Bill raised an eyebrow. He should have been the one who went with the uniforms to look for Phil, but Andy had come into the office and pulled rank.

'They're going to keep a watch out for his car. We'll get him before the night's over.'

'No point in me hanging about here then,' Bill said, switching off the PC and getting up. 'Give me a buzz if you find him.'

'Drop me off here,' Kara said. They were in the street behind the bus station.

Phil lowered his window. 'You've got the alarm I gave you? Remember to pull the cord out as soon as he approaches you and we'll be there before you can blink.'

Kara patted her pocket. 'It's right here.'

'We can't stay too close,' Phil said, 'or he'll never come near you.'

Kara watched them drive off. She'd never felt so alone in her life. She started to walk towards Trades Lane then changed her mind and turned back. The narrow lanes running between the main streets would be a better bet.

The steeple clock chimed twelve as she turned into Mary Ann Lane, a narrow tunnel-like alley only wide enough for a single car. She was halfway down when a voice came out of the darkness.

'Looking for business, love?'

She jumped, wondering if it was him. She stopped, her hand on the alarm. A man emerged from the shadows and smiled at her. He had a scar running from ear to chin and two missing front teeth.

'Get lost.'

'Don't be like that, love. I know I'm no oil painting but I'll make it worth your while.' He reached out to her.

'Like hell you will,' Kara shouted. She didn't stop running until she reached Dock Street with its late night traffic.

Half an hour later, she was walking up Exchange Street when a voice came out of the darkness. 'Kara!'

Her heart thumped. 'Oh, hi, Jean.'

Jean grasped her arm and pulled her into the shadows. 'Phil and Gus are waiting at the end of the street,' she whispered.

Kara laughed softly. 'I know. It sounds daft but Phil and Gus are keeping an eye on me in case that guy with the red car comes after me. Tony's orders.'

'D'you think he is still after you?'

'I'd put money on it.'

'You're crazy.'

'But he knows who I am now and he's bound to come after me sooner or later. So better now while I've got protection. Look, I don't want to get you involved so it'd be better if you stayed out of the way. You don't want him picking on you.' Kara turned away and started to walk down the street.

Jean watched her go. She had a bad feeling about this. Louise's card still nestled in her pocket and she fingered it, wondering whether she should phone her. But Kara wouldn't thank her for that if she was under Tony Palmer's orders.

The niggle of worry wouldn't go away. Kara could be in serious trouble, and Jean wasn't convinced that Phil and Gus would really have her best interests at heart.

Jean shrugged. Stuck-up bloody tart, who did she think she was anyway? Coming down here and taking business away with her fancy gear and streaked hair. She tried to convince herself that Kara was nothing to her, just an acquaintance whom she didn't even really like. But the worry wouldn't go away.

Reluctantly, she decided to keep an eye on her. After all, it was up to the street girls to watch out for one another. One more pervert off the streets and life would be safer for everyone.

The wind was even icier now, penetrating Kara's sweater and chilling her body. The only other person on the street was one of the working girls, standing in a doorway at the far end.

Behind her, the faint hum of the Merc's engine idling indicated it was parked just round the corner.

She'd had enough. The red estate wasn't going to appear. Phil and Gus would just have to accept it. She turned and marched round the corner to the car. Tapping the window, she said, 'It's obvious he's not coming. Maybe he's seen you. Who knows?'

Phil looked at his watch. 'Give it another half hour then we'll call it a day.'

'It's OK for you sitting in there. I'm out here freezing to death. You might have let me wear a bloody jacket.'

'I'll drive round the block now. If he's watching it'll appear as if you've been propositioning me and had the brush-off.'

'Wanker!' Kara shouted as the car drove off.

She turned back up the street. The other girl was no longer in sight. She was almost at the end of the street when suddenly a hand clamped her mouth and she was pulled into an alleyway.

A familiar voice whispered in her ear. 'We meet again. I knew you'd want to return to the woods, I've prepared a beautiful spot for you. Pity the others aren't there anymore, they would have relished your company. A special girl for my special place.'

Kara froze, her legs and arms didn't feel as if they belonged to her any more. But if she gave into him now she was done for. Desperately she fumbled in her pocket for the alarm but before she could pull the cord it was snatched from her and thrown on the ground.

'What have we here? Oh, what a naughty *Kara* you are.' He swung her off the ground and carried her to the car which was parked further up the alley. She screamed. Her feet flailed, striking nothing but air. 'Now just hold still,' he said, pinning her down in the back seat footwell with one hand and releasing the other to tear a strip of adhesive tape from the roll on the seat.

Kara struggled in the confined space, kicked his shins and reached up with her free hand to rake her nails over his face.

He slapped the tape over her mouth then grabbed both of her wrists which he secured behind her back with something that felt like plastic handcuffs. He did the same with her ankles.

'I don't want to hurt you,' he said. 'If you stay lying down you'll be fine, but if you sit up then I'll have to hit you. It'll be easier for us both if you stay awake.'

He got in the driving seat and started up the engine.

Surely Phil and Gus had heard her scream and would see the car as it emerged onto the main road. But the jolting continued longer than she expected. Lots of Dundee alleyways had more than one exit and he was obviously going in the other direction. It would be a miracle if Phil and Gus spotted them.

He had her. The trees would get the soul they were asking for. She would be saved and purified. A tree spirit rejoicing in her new life. The trees whispered together, their whispers echoing through his brain like a song. Their branches would be waving and rustling. The other tree spirits would be waiting. Waiting to welcome their new companion.

There was too little time. Too little time. He drove faster.

46

Jean slipped out of the doorway. She'd been standing at the entrance to the alley when she heard the car approach from the rear. She had walked these streets for several years and knew that a car in this alleyway was something out of the ordinary. By the time it stopped she was convinced she had to get out of sight and the recessed doorway, deep in the shadows, was the perfect hiding place.

She heard the soft click of the car door closing and sensed a man was nearby. He was too silent to be up to any good and her instincts warned her that this was someone on the hunt. She clamped a hand over her nose and mouth in an effort to quieten her breathing. But suddenly he was standing in front of her. She could see the outline of his back against the greyness of the light filtering into the alley.

Jean held her breath, and just as she was about to explode he moved away with a speed that was frightening.

After that, everything happened so quickly. One moment Kara had been walking past the alley entrance, the next he'd grabbed her and thrown her in the back of his red car. If Jean hadn't been so scared she'd have run after him. But the man's whisper nearly paralysed her with fear, and she didn't want to join Kara in that special place.

She watched the car reverse, then she ran out of the alley and up to the end of the road, hoping to see him emerge from the exit in the next street. But she could only see his tail-lights vanishing in the direction of the bus station.

'Where the fuck's she gone?' Phil surveyed the empty street. 'Drive round the block,' he instructed Gus. 'She must have turned the corner into the next street.' But once they'd gone round the block he realised they'd lost her.

'Fuck! Fuck! Fuck!' he roared.

Gus screeched to a halt and wound down the window. 'What the fuck d'you think you're doing?' he snarled at the girl standing in the middle of the road waving her arms.

'You bastards were supposed to be protecting Kara,' she screamed. 'And now he's got her.'

Phil got out of the car and grabbed her by the shoulders. 'What d'you mean, he's got her?'

'Just what I say – he grabbed her and took off – said he was going to take her to a special place. Bastards,' she screamed. 'Why didn't you stop him?'

'What *special place*?' Phil shook her.

'I don't know, but he said the other girls weren't there anymore.'

Phil pushed Jean aside. 'He's taken her to Templeton Woods,' he roared at Gus. 'Move it.'

Gus shot through a red light, screeched round the corner, sped past the bus station and accelerated towards the roundabout. From the corner of his eye he saw a black taxi speeding towards them. Too late.

The taxi hit the Merc side-on.

Jean heard the crash. She hurried towards the sound and got there at the same time as the police car.

She didn't hang around. The last thing she wanted was a run-in with the police. But how was she going to help Kara now?

Her fingers felt the card in her pocket. Louise had said to phone her if she found Kara. But Louise was a policewoman and she didn't trust the police. Should she? Shouldn't she? She knew there was only one answer. Louise was the only person who could save Kara.

'Stay where you are. I'll be with you in five minutes.' Louise clicked the phone off and ran for the door.

She breathed a sigh of relief when she saw Jean waiting at the corner of Trades Lane because she'd been frightened that the girl would disappear before she got there. Jean's voice had sounded so shocked she hadn't been able to make much sense of the garbled message on the phone.

Louise leaned over and opened the passenger door. Jean got in and slumped in the seat.

'He's got Kara.' Jean's shoulders shook.

Louise put her arm round her. 'Who has?'

'The psycho. It's my fault. I should have stopped him.'

Louise stiffened. Her heart thudded in her chest. Another girl snatched, not just any girl, the only person who could identify the killer.

'It's not your fault.' Her arm tightened round Jean's shoulders. 'You couldn't have done anything.'

'I should have called you when I saw her earlier, but I didn't.'

Louise said, 'Just tell me what you saw. Quickly.'

'Kara said Phil and Gus were looking out for her and they wouldn't let anything happen. But they fucked it up and I heard their car crash up the road.'

'How did the guy get Kara?'

'He grabbed her when she walked past that alley back there.' Jean turned and pointed. 'I was hiding in a doorway and he didn't see me. But I saw him and I heard him.'

'Could you identify him?'

'No, he had his back to me, but I heard what he said to Kara before he threw her in the back of the car.'

'What did he say?' Louise prodded.

'He said he was going to take her to his special place.'

'Is that all?'

'He said it was a pity the other girls weren't there to keep her company.'

Why would he take Kara to the same place now that it was known to the police? Louise shook her head. It didn't make sense. If he'd lost it altogether it wasn't looking good for Kara. He might kill her instead of just leaving her to die.

The urge to drive straight to Templeton Woods was

irresistible but that would be reckless. Despite her reservations about Bill, she'd have to inform headquarters.

'Put me through to CID,' she said, hoping it would be Bill who would pick up. He couldn't be driving Kara to Templeton Woods *and* be in the office.

'DI Michaels.'

'Oh.' She hadn't expected Andy to be there at this time of night. She quickly regained her composure and briefed him about the situation.

'I'll get cars up there right away,' Andy said.

'One more thing, sir,' she hesitated. 'I feel I should be there as well.'

There was a brief silence. 'I'll get one of the cars to pick you up.'

'I don't particularly want to leave my car here, sir. Can't I meet them there?'

'OK, but when you get to the woods, park out of sight and wait for back-up.'

The screech of the fireman's power saw jangled Phil's nerves as he struggled to extricate his mobile from his pocket. Gus wasn't moving and an ambulance was on standby just in front of them. A police car was parked in the middle of the roundabout and one policeman was setting up diversions while the other paced up and down in front of the Merc.

Eventually Phil managed to tease the phone out of his pocket and key in the number.

'Yeah?' Tony's voice was barely audible over the sound of the power saw.

'It's me, boss. We've lost her.' Phil started to shake uncontrollably. 'We almost had him but a fucking taxi crashed into us. I think Gus might be dead.'

'Fuck Gus,' Tony shouted. 'Kara will be dead too because you two bastards have fucked up.'

'But I know where he's taking her.'

'Where?'

'Back to the woods, where he took all the others.'

'What? He'd have to be insane. It doesn't make sense.'

'One of the girls heard him. Said he was taking her to his special place but it was a pity the other girls weren't there.'

The phone went silent and Phil held his breath. He knew his own life wouldn't be worth anything if Kara died.

'Why haven't you gone after him?'

'The Merc's a write-off. A fireman's taking the roof off. There's a couple of policemen here as well.'

'OK,' Tony said. 'Leave it to me. Keep your fucking mouth shut.'

The woods welcomed him. The trees gleamed in the moonlight, their frost-silvered branches waiting for the gift of a new soul. She was light. Easily carried. His heart hammered. The trees whispered. The tune rolling around in his head burst through his lips.

She was trembling when they entered the sacred grove. His special place. He introduced her to her tree. She struggled. But his strength was too much for her and he had no trouble holding her down until she was united with her fate. The tree. Her friend for all time.

47

Midnight had come and gone and the office was as silent as a morgue. The jangle of the phone had woken Andy.

'You've got him,' he said, feeling his heart thump with exhilaration. 'Good work.'

He rang off, then dialled Bill's mobile. It was a moment before he realised that the ringing noise he heard was coming from within the office. He found Bill's mobile on his desk. He was always forgetting it. Andy had no more success with Bill's home number which an automated voice told him was unobtainable.

He rubbed his chest trying to get rid of the heartburn that had been plaguing him all day, then got up to inspect the duty rota. Sue Rogers was on call. She would do.

'Sue,' he said when she answered the phone. 'I need you to come in and interview Phil Beattie. The sooner we get started, the more chance we have of keeping him longer.'

'Be there in five,' Sue said. 'Bill too?'

'Not unless he comes in before you get here,' Andy said. 'He's left his mobile in the office and there's something wrong with his landline.'

Sue laughed. 'He'll have forgotten to pay his bill again.'

Andy took several deep breaths. His heartburn wasn't going away. 'See you when you get here,' he said, 'and if Bill hasn't turned up by that time I'll be doing the interview with you.'

After ringing off he went through to his office. There was a bottle of Gaviscon in his filing cabinet. He took a swig and wandered back to the office.

The phone rang again. It was almost 1 a.m. 'DI Michaels.' He listened while Louise informed him that Kara Ferguson had been abducted and taken to Templeton Woods.

His heart banged in his chest. His breathing became laboured. If what she said was correct then Phil Beattie, who was kicking his heels in a police cell right now, couldn't be the killer.

He responded to Louise in monosyllables, struggling for breath. After she rang off he lifted the phone to arrange the back-up, but only managed to key in the number before a massive crushing pain erupted in his chest.

'Brian, it's time. You know what to do.' Tony laid the phone down. Punching the air with a fist, he shouted, 'We've got him.'

Ever since Tony had been told about Denise's death the nightmares had worsened with each recurring night. Her suffering was now his suffering and he'd been plotting for days. He knew exactly what he was going to do to that bastard and everything was in place.

He phoned Ian. 'Get one of the security guys from downstairs to replace you. I need you for a job now.'

The sports bag was where he'd left it, tucked behind one of the beer barrels in the cellar. He unzipped it and checked the contents: four guns, slingshot and ammo, masking tape, rope, grappling hook, bolt cutter, a yellow polythene sack and four white forensic suits. He took a gun and one of the suits out, there would only be three of them with Phil and Gus out of it.

Payback time.

The car bumped off the road. Kara's eyes widened with terror. Her nostrils flared and her breathing deepened. Visions of dead and putrefying girls flashed through her mind – rotting flesh, maggots squirming under her fingers, cadaverous smiles, the bony arm she'd grasped – visions she'd tried to blot out.

She was wrenched from the back seat and slung over the man's shoulder. She wanted to scream and punch but the gag and handcuffs restricted her. So she swung her feet and kicked him.

He laughed and grasped her legs. 'Not this time, Kara,' he said. 'I knew the first time I saw you on the street that you were meant for my special place. Don't you hear the trees calling?' He stopped to listen.

Kara couldn't see his face but her imagination made up for what she couldn't see. He swung round in a circle, there were trees all around them. They rustled and whispered in the wind.

'Don't you hear them?'

Kara was almost convinced there were voices although she couldn't detect any words.

Branches and twigs tore at her face as he trudged deeper into the wood. At last he stopped and crouched down to separate the bushes before pushing her through into the clearing. Kara gagged on the smell of soil and mould that rose as the leaves were disturbed, and then there was that other foul smell, the one that reminded her of death.

'We're here,' he said. 'My *special* place. Isn't it beautiful?'

Kara moaned.

'Don't be frightened,' he said, stroking her hair. 'Such beautiful hair, and such a beautiful body. But soon your soul will join with the tree. It will be purified and you will be whole again.'

Louise turned into Templeton Road and slowed down. But even then she almost missed seeing the car. It was tucked behind the hedge in a small opening that led into the wood. She kept on driving until, half a mile further along the road, she spotted another opening at the opposite side. Making sure her car couldn't be seen from the road, she pulled in and switched off the engine.

The moon cast a silvery glow over the grass and her footsteps left an imprint as she paced back and forth between the car and the road. Back-up should have been here by now. She looked at her watch for the umpteenth time. It had been a good five minutes since she'd got here. Kara had been picked up nearly twenty minutes ago. She couldn't wait any longer.

Her heart pounded as she walked back to where the estate was parked. It must be his. Why would anyone else be here at this time of night? The wood looked dark and impenetrable. A shiver crept up her spine and she turned away. Her fingers dug into her pocket but her mobile wasn't there.

A rustle in the undergrowth made her jump but it was only a feral cat. It stalked out of the bushes, crossed the road and disappeared. She turned and ran back up the road to where her car was parked. But despite a frantic search she couldn't find her mobile. Commonsense told her that she should wait for back-up to arrive, but she'd never forgive herself if the girl was killed.

This was madness. Silently, she slipped from tree to tree, keeping a careful lookout. She tried to find her bearings in the dark, thinking that if she approached from the rear she would have the advantage.

She had almost reached the clearing when the sound of a car engine echoed through the trees. Moonlight filtered into the clearing, filling it with shapes and shadows. There sat Kara, in front of a tree holding it in a backward embrace. The moonlight gave her pale skin a translucent appearance. Her legs were not bound and her knees were pulled up in front of her to hide her nakedness.

Louise hurried over. 'It's OK, it's OK,' she said soothingly, placing her hand on Kara's shoulder. It was like ice and she could feel the tremor in the girl's body.

Kara's eyes widened, the pupils darted from side to side and she nodded her head in a desperate motion. It was as if the girl was trying to tell her something. Louise reached out to rip the gag off. Kara's nodding increased in intensity and Louise sensed something behind her. The heavy branch caught her on the back of the head and the world went black.

Tony heaved the sports bag into the boot and then slid in beside Brian. Ian took the back seat.

'Templeton Woods,' Tony growled, shuddering at the memory of his daughter's dead face. 'Stupid bastard's gone back there.'

Brian grunted.

'Fuck, where'd you pick up this car?' Tony complained.

'Ninewells car park.' Brian crunched gear noisily. 'Didn't want to pick too flash a model.'

'You might have picked a quieter one.'

They lapsed into silence. The job was now uppermost in Tony's mind. This was the night he would be avenged.

There it was, an estate car tucked into a small opening just off the road.

'Park across his rear. Block him in. Bastard's not going to get away this time.'

Tony got out of the car, opened the boot and unzipped the bag. He handed Ian and Brian a white suit each. 'Put them on. We don't want to leave any traces for forensics.'

The three men struggled into the suits, pulled the hoods over their heads and masks over their faces.

Once they'd put on the latex gloves, Tony handed each man a gun.

'You stay beside the car, Ian, in case he comes back. But stay out of sight, and, remember, I want him *alive*.'

Kara recognised the woman from the case conference, and could only watch in horror as the man secured her hands behind her back with plastic cuffs.

'Silly, silly, Louise,' he said, stroking her unconscious body. 'Why did you have to come here? I never meant to harm you. But now it changes everything and you'll never know how sad that makes me.'

It was at that moment two white-suited figures slipped into the clearing, but he was so busy babbling to Louise that he didn't appear to have noticed. Kara's heart leapt. Phil and Gus must have followed them after all.

One of the white suits held a gun to the back of the man's head. 'Get up,' he shouted. The other man grabbed his wrists, tied them behind his back and then slapped tape over his mouth.

Kara wriggled. They hadn't looked at her but surely now they had him secured they would untie her.

One of them looked over at her as if he could sense what she was thinking. Then he knelt down and placed his fingers on Louise's neck. He nodded. Kara made noises behind her gag but they weren't loud enough for him to hear, so she stretched her leg as far as she could and prodded him with her toes.

He leaned over and removed her gag but made no effort to release her wrists.

'I'm sorry,' he whispered, his voice muffled behind the mask, 'but you're going to have to wait.'

'Please!' Kara said.

He shook his head and stood up. 'We'd better hurry,' he said to his partner.

Pushing the man in front of them, they left the clearing.

'No! Please!' Kara screamed as she watched them go.

A few moments later one of them returned.

They weren't going to leave her to die in this place after all. 'Please,' she pleaded, 'don't leave me here.'

He didn't look at her as he placed a blanket over her.

'Don't leave me!' Kara screamed. 'Come back!' She kept on screaming long after the sound of the car engine had faded into the distance.

The whispers stopped when the lid of the car boot slammed shut. He was confined. He was alone. He couldn't breathe. He could smell fumes.

He started to pray through parched lips, ears straining for the whispers from his special place. He couldn't hear anything but the roar of the engine and the road beneath him.

48

'Come back! Come back!' Kara's scream pierced Tony's brain as he pushed out of the clearing.

'Don't let the fucker get away,' Tony rasped when Brian turned towards him. 'We've no time to cut them free, not until the job's done.'

'It'll be risky coming back here afterwards,' Brian whispered.

'I know, I know.' He'd have to think of some way of getting them out of there once he'd done what he had to do. But for now the job in hand was the most important thing.

Kara's screams followed them all the way back to the car.

Fury boiled up in Tony and he pushed their captive so hard he slammed him into the side of the car.

'Tie his ankles and throw him in here.' Tony opened the boot of the red car. 'Then you two take his car and follow mine. Don't lose me.' He turned on his heel and strode to the car Brian had stolen from the hospital car park.

Arriving at the entrance to Wester Gourdie Walk, Tony pulled into the side of the road. Brian stopped behind him and Ian got out.

Tony rolled the window down. 'There's a bolt cutter in the boot. You'll need it to open the barrier.' He pressed the boot release button. 'You and Brian pull into the driveway and wait while I park his car behind the wall.'

A few moments later Tony climbed into the red car armed with the yellow polythene bag into which he'd put the slingshot and ammo, and the grappling hook. 'OK, now drive up the road until you come to the wildlife centre. Then reverse the car up to the wall to the right of the entrance and park it side-on as close as you can. If we go over the wall there, we'll be hidden.'

Tony was running on pure adrenaline as he got out of the car. He raised the boot lid and smiled grimly at the trussed-up figure inside. 'It's your time,' he whispered.

Brian and Ian dragged the man up onto the roof of the car. Tony followed with the yellow bag.

Brian bent down. 'You first,' he whispered to Ian.

Ian stood on Brian's back and clambered up the wall. Perching on the top he beckoned to Brian to pass the man up to him. Brian and Tony lifted him but couldn't get him to remain upright long enough for Ian to pull him up.

Tony reached into the bag and produced the grappling hook. 'Use this.'

Tony hooked the prongs into the man's bound arms and threw the rope to Ian. The man's head and legs pointed downwards but his arms arced up and away from his body as it swayed on its journey to the top of the wall. Tony thought he heard the crunch of shoulders dislocating.

Once they were all over the wall, Ian picked the man up and slung him over his shoulder. Then the three of them, avoiding the path that ran behind the houses bordering the north side of the zoo, ran silently round.

There was no sign of the pigs, the goats or the donkeys in their enclosures, but the cats were padding about and their eyes gleamed in the darkness. Tony, too engrossed in what he was going to do, took no notice, and after they passed behind the snowy owls cage he led the way through a gate in the wall.

In front of them was a large enclosure protected by a high fence with electric wires on the inside and the top. Tony smiled. He'd never forgotten the time when a boy had broken into the zoo and had his arm torn off by Jeremy, the Sugar Puffs bear. Tony wasn't sure what happened to the boy, but Jeremy had lived to a ripe old age.

But what was going to happen to this psycho bastard wasn't going to be any accident.

They followed the fence as far as the viewing area, a squat round building that backed onto the enclosure.

Tony stopped. 'We need to get him up onto the top of that,' he said, pointing.

Brian looked up. 'Bloody hell, boss, how?'

'Same way we got him over the wall.' Tony strode over to a picnic bench. 'Pull this over,' he said.

Ian heaved the man off his shoulder.

'Careful,' Tony said. 'I want him conscious when he goes in.'

Ian and Brian exchanged glances.

The two men heaved the picnic bench over to the viewing building.

Brian climbed onto the bench. 'It still doesn't get us high enough, boss.'

Tony tossed the grappling hook to him. 'Why the fuck d'you think I brought this? Now less of the chat and get him up there.'

Brian swung the grappling hook until it caught on the edge of the building. Ian heaved the squirming man onto the bench beside Tony and then clambered up.

'OK, pal, I'll go first. You follow.' Brian shinned up the rope.

'You go on up, Ian,' Tony said. 'It's higher than the wall so you'll both need to pull him up.'

Once he was on the roof of the building, Ian detached the hook and lowered it to Tony who quickly attached it to the man's arms.

The man swung violently, battering into the wall of the building as he was hauled up onto the roof.

It was only moments before the rope was lowered for Tony and he joined them on the roof.

'What now, boss?'

'You see that electric fence? He's going over that but you'll have to swing him until he's sure to clear it, because it's alarmed as well as electrified. But we need to get the bears out first.'

'Won't they be hibernating, boss?'

'For fuck's sake. What do you take me for?' Tony eyed Brian. 'It doesn't get cold enough in Scotland for bears to hibernate. They'll be asleep in their den now so we'll have to wake them up first, to make sure that fucker here,' Tony kicked the prostrate body, 'gets to know them.'

Tony reached into the yellow bag and withdrew the slingshot and the package of ammo. 'Hence . . . this.' He handed it to Ian. 'You can do the honours. Keep firing at that low building over there. That's where the bears are. As soon as they appear we'll see to fuckboy here.'

Ian started firing.

'One of the bears is coming out now, boss.' Ian turned to look at Tony. 'And he's not looking too pleased.'

Tony watched the bear emerge from its den. He took the slingshot and ammo away from Ian and laid it on the roof.

'You, my friend,' he said softly to the man lying at his feet, 'are about to meet one of my good friends in there. And I want to hear you scream the way my daughter must have screamed when you left her tied to that fucking tree in the middle of fucking nowhere.'

The man's eyes widened and he wriggled desperately.

'You two, hold him for me while I cut him loose. I want him to be able to run and scream after he goes over the fence.'

'Fuck, he's not making it easy.' Brian said as he wrapped his arm round the man's neck and held him bent down at waist level.

Tony cut through the rope binding the man's legs and wrists. He bent to the man's face until their noses almost touched. 'The next time I wake from nightmares about Denise I'll think of you, dying, and believe me, it will be a pleasure.' Then he ripped off the gag.

'It's time,' Tony shouted. 'Hold his feet tight, Ian. And you grab his arms, Brian. Now start swinging and then heave the fucker over the fence.'

'No! No!' The man screamed, legs flailing and eyes wide with terror.

'Goodbye,' Tony whispered and signalled to his men.

The men swung the man several times and then let go. He sailed over the fence and landed in front of the big brown bear which had been so rudely awakened.

'Make sure that bear's good and angry,' Tony said, handing Ian the slingshot.

Ian took careful aim, shooting the pellets at the bear's head.

The screaming started before they'd picked up all their gear.

49

The whispered 'sorry' had been enough to convince Kara they weren't coming back, and that was when she'd started to scream. She didn't stop screaming until her throat was raw and the sound of the car engines had faded into the distance. Despair flooded through her and she slumped back against the tree.

In front of her the woman lay still. She'd taken a heavy blow to the head and Kara had a horrible feeling she might be dead. Gingerly Kara reached out a foot and poked her. There was no response.

The psycho had replaced the plastic handcuffs with rope when he'd tied Kara to the tree, so maybe the rope would be more flexible. Kara wriggled her back closer to the tree, trying not to dislodge the blanket that was at least stopping her freezing to death. If she manipulated her hands, wriggled her fingers, pulled her thumbs in, maybe she'd be able to loosen the ropes. But no matter how much she struggled she couldn't free her wrists.

She was not going to give up though. Charlene and Billy needed her. And she did not want to die.

In front of her, the woman stirred and moaned.

'Wake up! Wake up!' Kara urged.

The woman's eyelids fluttered. 'What happened?'

'You were whacked on the head. We have to get up now. I need help with these ropes.'

Louise turned her head to look at Kara. 'Oh, that hurts.' Wriggling into a sitting position she said, 'What the hell's he put on my wrists?'

'Some plastic cuffs.'

'How am I going to get them off?'

'You're not tied to a tree. And your ankles aren't tied

either. If you can get up you can untie this rope and we can walk out of here. For fuck's sake, *hurry up.*'

'If I could get my hands in front of me . . .'

'How the fuck are you going to do that?'

'Joanne Lees, remember, that girl who was kidnapped in Australia? She did it. I remember seeing it on TV.'

'Right, try it! And what's your name anyway? I've forgotten. Lisa?'

'Louise.'

Kara watched Louise lower her bound wrists until they were level with the ground, then wriggle her bottom backwards over her hands. 'Keep going,' Kara urged. 'You're sitting on your hands now, just a few inches more and you'll make it.'

Her face contorted with pain, Louise wriggled backwards again but had to stop to draw breath. 'My arms feel as if they're coming out of my shoulders.'

'C'mon, one final push and you'll be there.'

Suddenly Louise's arms were underneath her legs. She pulled her knees up to her chest and angled her feet through her arms. 'I've done it!' She placed her hands on the ground and pushed. 'Maybe I'll be able to stand up now.'

'Try these ropes,' Kara pleaded. 'I'm freezing to death here.'

Louise tottered.

'Fuck, don't pass out on me,' Kara said. 'I need you to untie me. *Come on!*'

Louise staggered a few steps and leaned on the tree.

Kara closed her eyes. When was this bloody woman going to untie her? '*The ropes*,' she said.

Louise bent down and started to pick at the knots.

Kara gritted her teeth and tried to think of something other than the agonising pressure on her wrists. At last the ropes started to loosen.

Kara pulled one hand free and turned her body to help Louise with the other knot. When it had loosened enough she slipped her other hand out of its noose.

'Shit, that was *sore*,' she said, rubbing her wrists. Kara

hauled her clothes on and pulled the blanket around her shoulders. 'Let's get out of this place *now*.'

Tony and the two men ran back the way they'd come but when they passed through the gateway in the wall, Tony turned right instead of left. 'Come on! We'd better shift before he starts attracting attention. This way.' They ran to the emergency exit where Tony snipped the padlock on the first gate, then the second gate, and they emerged onto the golf course.

By the time they reached the car, lights were appearing in the windows of the houses overlooking the zoo.

Minutes later they were driving across the Kingsway.

'Where to, boss?'

'Head for Ninewells. We'll dump the car there and get rid of some of the gear. But pull over somewhere quiet before we get there. We don't want to be stripping off in a hospital car park.'

'I know just the place, boss.'

When the car stopped, Tony opened the boot and transferred the grappling hook, slingshot and ammo into the sports bag. They stripped off the white suits, put them into the yellow polythene sack and tied a knot in the top. Then they took both bags into the car with them.

'This the same car park you took the car from?' Tony asked when they reached the hospital.

'Yeah, it won't have been missed yet because I saw the nurse leave it. She'll be on night shift.'

'Where's ours?'

'Two car parks up.'

'We'll meet you down at the ambulance bay. The yellow bag?'

'Yeah, it'll be incinerated with the contaminated stuff. No problem, I've done it before.'

'Five minutes then and we'll collect you.'

'I'll drive,' Tony said when they reached the car. 'I need you to do the phone call.'

They collected Brian at the ambulance bay on the lower level and headed out of the hospital grounds.

'Have you got the mobile? Untraceable?'

Brian nodded.

'Ian, you phone the police. You've been to Templeton Woods with your bit on the side and you heard screaming. When they ask for your name, just say your wife'll kill you and hang up.'

Tony grinned. He felt guilty about leaving Kara and Louise in the woods but they'd be found soon enough.

50

Sue yawned and stretched. The phone had rudely interrupted a lovely dream although she couldn't quite remember what it was.

That was the worst part of being on call, it interrupted your life.

She threw the duvet off and toppled out of bed. The heating had gone off, so she dressed as fast as she could. The flat was quiet and Louise's bedroom door was open. Sue hesitated in the doorway. Louise should have been home by now.

A mischievous smile tugged at her lips. There was definitely something going on between Louise and Bill, and now they'd both gone AWOL at the same time. It didn't take much brainpower to guess what they were up to.

It was cold outside and moonlight slanted off the frosty road. She started the car's engine, scraped the windscreen and within a few minutes she was pulling up behind Bill's car.

At least he's here, she thought as she banged on the door. When he didn't answer she banged louder.

'OK, OK. I heard you the first time.'

He rubbed his eyes and looked at his watch. 'It's stopped again, what time is it?'

'It's just after two, and you should be at work. Busy, were you?'

Sue tried to peek inside.

'What are you doing here anyway?'

'On my way to the office to do your job,' Sue said. 'Is Louise here with you?'

'No, why would she be?'

'Well she's not at home. I just thought . . .'

'That's odd. I dropped her off at her car just after eleven. Where d'you think she's gone?'

'Hey, she's a big girl. She'll turn up when she's ready.' But Sue couldn't help feeling worried. It wasn't like Louise to just disappear.

'I'm away then,' she said. 'They've got Phil Beattie waiting to be interviewed. You coming?'

'Oh, yes,' Bill said. 'I've been waiting to get my hands on that bastard for a long time.'

A branch whipped Kara's cheek. She rubbed it. 'Damn, these trees go on forever,' she complained. 'You sure this is the right way?'

'Yeah,' Louise said, 'the clearing's quite far from the road. But I'm sure we're heading in the right direction.'

'At least we can see where we're going. Not like the last time.'

'We'd better keep quiet though. In case he returns.'

'Eh, no, he won't,' Kara said quietly. 'There's something I forgot to tell you.'

'What?'

'Well, when you were out for the count, two men in white boilersuits came and took him away.'

Louise leaned on a tree to get her breath back. 'Who?'

'How the hell should I know? They had hoods and mask things on. I thought it was Phil and Gus, but it wasn't.'

'How d'you know?'

'One of them came back with a blanket and said he was sorry. Mind you, the voice was familiar.' Kara shrugged.

'Ssh,' Louise whispered. 'I think I hear something.'

'Maybe it's an animal.'

Kara shivered.

What little confidence she'd found was rapidly evaporating. These woods were terrifying in the dark and anything might be creeping about.

The sound of something pushing through the undergrowth continued. Kara panicked and clung to Louise. 'Maybe those men, whoever they were, have come back to kill *us*. Maybe they're not sorry at all, maybe it wasn't just him that's the weirdo.'

The sounds came nearer and a beam of light hit them. Kara screamed and ran.

Tony poured himself a large Laphroaig as soon as he got back to his office. Then he lifted the phone and buzzed for Marlene to come up.

'That flat next door to you. Who do we have in it at the moment?'

'I don't know his name offhand but I can find out. I think he works at Michelin's. Why d'you want to know?'

'I'm going to make him an offer he can't refuse.' Tony smiled and topped up his glass. 'I want to put a new tenant in.'

'Anyone I know?'

'You'll find out after I've made all the arrangements. But once it's done I'll need you to do the mother hen bit and keep an eye out for her.'

Marlene gave him a steady look. 'Everything worked out all right then?'

'I don't know what you're talking about, Marlene. I've never stirred from this office all night.'

'Right, boss. Will there be anything else?'

'Yes, you can send one of the girls up when they finish.'

'Any particular one?'

'Anyone who'll vouch for me being here all night.'

Bill's head was still fuzzy through lack of sleep and he drove to the office on automatic pilot. He slotted his car in beside Sue's. She must have gone up without waiting for him.

An ambulance was parked in front of the main entrance with its doors open and its engine running.

'Something up?' he asked the driver.

'I'd get out of the way, mate, they're just bringing him out now.'

Bill nodded and stood aside for the paramedics who were pushing a wheeled stretcher through the reception doors. The man lying on it turned his face towards Bill but an oxygen mask concealed his features.

'Don't move,' the paramedic warned, and a moment later they were loading him into the ambulance.

'Isn't it awful?' said Sue as she joined Bill in the doorway.

'Who was that?'

'You don't know?'

'I wouldn't be asking if I knew.' Bill gave her an exasperated look.

'It's Andy. It looks like he had a heart attack.'

'I wondered why he kept nicking my Rennies.'

'He was lucky. If he hadn't been ringing Control when he collapsed he might not have been found, because there was no one else here. When I got here the paramedics were resuscitating him.'

The first few flakes of snow fell as the ambulance, in a blare of sirens, drove off.

'Let's get this interview done. I want Beattie nailed before Tony wangles his release.'

'You sure Phil Beattie's the killer?'

'I'm positive. He's an evil little shit and I'm going to make sure he never walks the streets again.'

A few minutes later Bill stormed out of the interview room. 'Typical! He won't open his mouth until his solicitor gets here and who knows when that'll be.'

'You know this is Scotland and we're not required to wait.'

Bill laughed. 'Yeah, yeah, but he's not budging from "no comment".'

'Ah, there you are,' the duty inspector said. 'I've been looking for you. I sent a couple of cars out to investigate reports of screaming in Camperdown Park about half an hour ago. They've just reported back that there's a body in the bear pit at the wildlife centre. You'll need to take a look. SOCOs are on the way. What a night, we've been run off our feet. What with a domestic in Douglas, another brawl outside Teasers and screaming in Templeton Woods. That's the third report of screaming out there since the bodies were found, so it's probably another hoax. I'll be glad when it's morning.'

A park ranger was waiting for them when Bill and Sue arrived at the wildlife centre. 'This way,' he said and led them to the bears' enclosure.

'Screaming was heard about 2 a.m. so two of us came to check it out. When we got here we had to anaesthetise the bear to get to him, but we were too late. The man's been severely mauled. He was unlucky because the bears usually sleep a lot just now.'

Four policemen were guarding the enclosure. Bill looked through the bars at the body lying at the edge of the water hole.

'You'll see better from the viewing station.' The ranger led Bill and Sue into a semi-circular brick building which had a large window built into the wall facing the enclosure.

'That fence is some height. How on earth did he get in?'

'I haven't got a clue,' the ranger said. 'I always thought it was impossible.'

Sue was peering out the window into the enclosure. 'Don't you have an alarm system?

'The gates and entry doors are all alarmed as well as the electric barrier at the top, but they didn't go off.'

'How do we get to the body then?' Bill wasn't sure he really wanted to know.

'We've locked the bears in. Follow me.'

The park ranger led the way to a low brick building at the rear. Opening a door he led Bill and Sue past the bears' cages. Bill shuddered and closed his eyes but it didn't blot out the sound of the bears moving around. They entered the last cage, which was empty, and emerged through an opening into the enclosure.

'You OK?' Sue asked.

'It's a bit claustrophobic, that's all,' Bill replied. He turned to the ranger, 'Could he have got in this way?'

'I don't see how,' the ranger said. 'There's no evidence of

a break-in and he would have had to pass the bears because the exit they use is the one we've just come through.'

Sue was already striding over the grass to the body. Bill hurried to catch up with her.

'What a mess,' she said.

Strips of torn clothing littered the grass and the body looked like a lump of raw meat. However, apart from the look of horror on his face, the man's head was virtually untouched.

Bill looked at him and was immediately transported back in time to Templeton Woods. Jerry Forbes had been the one who'd been sick in the bushes. The rest of them, Bill included, had jeered at him and called him a wimp. That was his name after that and he went through his schooldays as Jerry the Wimp. In the end he'd become a bit odd and introspective.

Bill would never have considered him suicidal though, nor the kind of guy who would do something like this for kicks.

'D'you think he had a death wish? Came in here to commit suicide?' Bill's stomach churned and he hoped he wasn't going to be sick.

'I could think of easier ways to do it,' Sue said.

The flakes of snow were fatter now and were starting to cover the body. Bill couldn't stop staring at the bloody remnants of the man. 'I know who he is,' he said, swallowing hard. 'Jerry Forbes. He works for the out of hours welfare service.' Overcome with an unexpected sadness, he turned away. 'Let's get out of here and leave it to the SOCOs.'

'Over here!' The man waved the torch, sending its beam dancing through the trees, then shone the torch on himself. The light picked out his uniform. 'You're safe now.'

It was snowing when he led Kara and Louise out of the wood. 'Good job we got here when we did. The temperature's dropping.'

'Under arrest are we?' The officer with the shears grinned cheekily at Louise.

'Don't be such a smart arse, just get these sodding cuffs off me.'

'Can I go home now?' Kara whispered to Louise.

The sergeant snipped Louise's cuffs. 'You'll both need to be interviewed first. I'll show you to an interview room.'

'You'll do no such thing,' Louise said. 'You'll take us up to the CID team room, and I'll get Kara a coffee. She's been through enough tonight.'

51

Sue manoeuvred her car next to Bill's.

'Careful,' Bill said gritting his teeth as the front wheels spun a bit too close. 'I know it's a wreck but it's all I've got.'

Sue seemed deep in thought and didn't give any indication she'd heard him. 'I hope I never see anything like that again,' she said as she got out. She stamped her feet in the snow. 'Come on,' she said. 'Let's have a cup of tea before we interview Beattie.'

The glass doors had just closed behind them when a constable beckoned them over to reception. 'The inspector said to let you know that Constable Walker and Kara Ferguson are waiting for you upstairs. Constable Walker insisted they wait in the team room, sir.'

'Thanks,' Bill said turning to walk away.

'Sir! I believe they were brought back by the officers who were investigating screams at Templeton Woods.'

Bill and Sue ran for the lift.

'Try to find out from Kara what's happened,' he said to Sue before they entered the room, 'and I'll see Louise.'

They were huddled together on chairs beside the coffee machine and Bill didn't know which of the two looked worse. He pulled a chair over beside Louise. 'What happened?'

Kara shuffled closer to Louise. Bill glanced at Sue, 'It's OK. We'll let Louise talk us through it.'

When Louise had finished, Bill sat back and gazed into the distance. Beattie was off the hook. Bill had thought that if Denise was about to tell her father about Phil, then Phil may have tried to stop her. They'd have to let him go.

'Did you see who it was, Louise?' Sue leaned towards her.

'I'm not sure. I only got a glimpse when he hit me. I know it sounds ridiculous but I thought he looked a bit like Jerry

Forbes . . .'

Bill interrupted. 'We've just found Jerry's body in the bear-pit at Camperdown. And I'd say he didn't choose to be there. In fact, I've got a hunch Tony Palmer had something to do with it. If he thought Jerry was involved . . .'

Louise looked shocked and Kara shrank back in her seat.

'The two men in white suits who took this guy away, did you recognise them?'

Kara shook her head. 'No,' she whispered, 'they had masks on.'

Bill wasn't convinced she was telling the truth but he could see he wasn't going to get anything out of her tonight.

Steam rose from the top of the coffee mug that Kara cradled in her hands. She was gradually thawing out. But she didn't like being here; there were too many doors, too many rooms, too many uniforms and too many questions.

'When can I go home?'

'I think we've got all we can for the moment,' Bill said, 'and we don't need to keep you here any longer. But don't go disappearing on us.'

'Why? I thought you were done.'

'Because you're a material witness.'

Kara got up. 'I need to go home now. Will you take me?' she asked Louise.

Louise grasped her hand. 'I don't think that's a good idea, Kara. The flat's a mess, the door's off its hinges and you'd be on your own. Isn't there anywhere else you can go?'

Kara's head spun.

She had to get home. She had to get Charlene and Billy back. She had to get out of Dundee before Palmer came back for her.

'There's nowhere else,' she said, brushing away a tear.

'Don't you have any relatives in Dundee? What about your mum?'

'We don't get on.'

'But there's no way you can go back to the flat tonight.

Won't you at least let me contact your mum? It would only be until your place is sorted out and secure again.'

Kara sighed. Anything to get out of this place.

Louise was surprised at how easy it was to get Kara settled at her mother's. The girl had hardly spoken on the way there, except to ask how her children were and how soon she could see them.

'They've settled down quite well at the foster home,' Louise said. 'But I'm sure they miss you.'

'What if my mother refuses to take me in?'

The door opened as soon as the police car drew up. 'I've been watching for you,' Helen said.

Kara looked at her. 'Is it OK for me to stay?'

'Of course it is. In you come. I am your mother, after all.'

Louise could see Kara bristle at that, but it passed and she slouched in through the front door not too reluctantly. Maybe it would work out, at least for a night or two.

Louise leaned back in the police car. Exhaustion swept over her. Her head was throbbing and all she wanted to do was slide into bed and never get up again.

'I kind of liked Jerry,' she said later when Sue was sitting on the side of her bed. 'I felt sorry for him in a way. He seemed really shy and vulnerable. I never really suspected him even though he was in the room when Kara ran off. I wanted to tell you, or somebody, but I thought it might be Bill. You know, he was there too.'

'What if it had been Bill?'

Louise shuddered. 'I don't know what I would have done.'

'You like him that much?'

'Yes, I do. At least I think I do.'

'Bill's pretty mixed up just now. There's all the hassle with Evie and the divorce, then he was let down by the other girl, Julie.'

'That's the problem. It's probably best that it ends now before it really starts.' Louise slumped back onto the pillows. 'Mum's been pressing for me to go home for a while so I think

I'll take some leave. It'll give me time to think, make sense of things.'

Superintendent Jamieson strode into the office at 9 a.m. sharp. 'Everyone here?' he said, scanning the room. 'Good. Now let's keep this brief. We have statements from Constable Walker and Miss Ferguson, and there seems to be no doubt that the man found in the bear enclosure last night was the Templeton Woods killer. What we have to ascertain now is whether he committed suicide or whether he was *helped* on his way. There seems to be no way he could have got into the bear pit unaided.' He smiled expectantly at the team.

'I have a theory about that, sir,' Bill said.

'Yes?'

'Tony Palmer's daughter was one of the victims and I think Palmer may have something to do with Jerry Forbes's death.'

'Do you have any proof, Detective Sergeant?'

'Palmer hasn't been interviewed yet.'

'Then I suggest you do so.'

Bill didn't like the look in the Super's eyes. Palmer had always said he had friends in high places. 'I'll get onto it today. Oh, and, excuse me, sir, but is there any word about Detective Inspector Michaels? We haven't heard anything since last night.'

'Detective Inspector Michaels had a heart attack and is in intensive care, but his condition has stabilised.'

'Guess who's in the next bed to him?' Sue whispered.

'Who?' Bill said as the Super left the room.

'Gus Daniels.' She laughed. 'I wonder if Tony will be visiting? That should cheer Andy up no end. What d'you think?'

'Probably bring on another heart attack. Poor sod . . . And, eh, how's Louise?'

'Tired and sore. She's seeing the doctor later today and then taking some leave. Going home to her mum for a time. She said she'd catch up with you when she got back.'

52

Kara was still sleeping. Helen tiptoed to the side of the bed and kissed her daughter's forehead. Tears pricked her eyes. It had been so long since Kara had slept in this house. Too long.

In the kitchen she looked at the empty bottles littering the worktop and her body ached for a drink, but instead she gathered them up and opened the back door. Fat flakes of snow were falling and the garden looked like a Christmas card. She tipped the bottles inside the dustbin.

She took her last bottle of malt whisky from below the sink. Just one sip, she thought. She uncorked the bottle, shut her eyes and poured it down the sink.

It was an hour later before Tony came.

'How's Madge bearing up?' Helen asked.

'Not good. The doctor's got her on tranquillizers.'

'I'm sorry to hear that,' she said. Somehow it didn't seem enough, but Helen didn't know what else to say.

A silence hung in the air between them until at last Helen said, 'Take a seat in the lounge, Tony. I'll be back in a minute.'

In the kitchen she grasped the edge of the sink and waited for her heartbeat to slow down. She made a pot of tea, placed it on a tray with two china mugs and returned to the lounge.

'No whisky?' Tony looked at her quizzically.

'No,' she said abruptly. 'And I've no coffee either. You'll have to make do with tea.'

Tony lapsed into silence until after she'd poured.

'So, what is it you want with me?' Helen's voice was brittle. She couldn't let him get under her skin.

'What you said about Kara . . .'

'It's true. She's the image of your mother in her younger days. I'm not lying, Tony, she's your daughter.'

'Have you told *her* that?'

Helen laughed. 'D'you think I'm daft? Of course not.'

'Well, as I said before, I don't know for certain that she's my daughter, but I want to see she's all right. She did me a big favour and I don't forget these things.'

'What do you mean *see she's all right*? D'you mean like you looked after me and all those other girls? I knew you were a bastard, Tony, but I never thought you were as big a bastard as that.'

'That's not what I meant. I want to treat her like a daughter, well, maybe more like a niece, but I wanted your approval first.'

Helen looked at him in disbelief. 'My approval? When was that ever important to you?'

Kara woke with the feeling she'd been kissed but no one was there. The room was familiar. But it wasn't her room or her home anymore and she'd no intention of staying. If she hadn't been so spaced out by what had happened last night, she would never have agreed to come.

She put on a dressing gown and opened the bedroom door. The sound of voices came from the lounge. She padded barefoot downstairs and peered round the door, ready to sneak away if she didn't like what she saw.

She drew back with a sharp breath.

'Kara,' her mother said, 'come in. Tony has a proposition for you.'

'A proposition?' Kara hovered in the doorway.

'Come in. Sit down, Kara.' Tony beckoned her into the room.

'I've just been saying to Helen how much I appreciated the favour you did me. And I'm sorry for any danger that you were subjected to.'

The words 'I'm sorry' brought an image of a white-suited man into her head.

Tony continued. 'My men told me about your Greenfield flat and, frankly, I think you can do better. You won't know it, but I own a lot of property in Dundee and I'd like you to have the flat next door to Marlene. Remember Marlene? You met her last night.'

'I have my own plans,' Kara said firmly. 'As soon as I get my kids back I'm leaving Dundee.'

'Ah, the children. I've already briefed my solicitor to talk to the Director of Social Work and the Reporter to the Children's Hearing. It's just a matter of time. Please don't be too hasty. The offer I'm making is a good one. There would be a job for you, too, and the necessary child care arrangements.'

'A *job*? You mean like one of your dancers?' Kara laughed. 'I don't think so.'

'No, no, you misunderstand. You would be a management trainee under Marlene. It's a real opportunity.'

'Yeah? And what would I have to do for you if I accepted this *opportunity*?'

'Nothing.' Tony shrugged his shoulders and smiled warmly. 'I simply want to repay you for the service you've already done me.'

'What you put me through was a nightmare, and I don't want to think about it ever again. And what about the money Kev owes you?'

'Forget it. That's nothing. This offer is to make amends. You'll never have to do anything you don't want to . . . At least think about it.'

Kara didn't altogether believe him. If she accepted his offer she was scared she'd never be able to just walk away. On the other hand, if he was as grateful as all that why not take him for everything she could? After all, she'd looked after herself up to now and survived. Once she was back on her feet, she could take off, set up a new life for Charlene and Billy. But one thing was for sure, she'd never go back on the streets again – not for Kev, not for Tony Palmer, not for anyone.

Other Books by Chris Longmuir

DUNDEE CRIME SERIES

Night Watcher
Dead Wood
Missing Believed Dead

HISTORICAL SAGAS

A Salt Splashed Cradle

KIRSTY CAMPBELL NOVELS

The Death Game

NON-FICTION

Crime Fiction and the Indie Contribution

CHRIS LONGMUIR

Chris Longmuir was born in Wiltshire but now lives in Angus. Her family moved to Scotland when she was two. After leaving school at fifteen, Chris worked in shops, offices, mills and factories, and was a bus conductor for a spell, before working as a social worker for Angus Council (latterly serving as Assistant Principal Officer for Adoption and Fostering).

Chris is an award winning novelist and has published three novels in her Dundee Crime Series. Night Watcher, the first book in the series, won the Scottish Association of Writers' Pitlochry Award, and the sequel, Dead Wood, won the Dundee International Book Prize, as well as the Pitlochry Award. Missing Believed Dead is the third book in the series.

She has recently published The Death Game, a historical crime novel, which is the first in the Kirsty Campbell Novel series.

Chris also writes historical sagas, short stories and articles which have been published in America and Britain. She confesses to being a bit of a techno-geek, and builds computers in her spare time.

Chris is a member of the Society of Authors, the Crime Writers Association, and the Scottish Association of Writers.

http://www.chrislongmuir.co.uk